Ebook ISBN: 978-1-956335-21-7

Audiobook ISBN: 978-1-956335-37-8

Paperback ISBN: 978-1-956335-28-6

Front cover design by Danielle Fine at Design by Definition.

Swords, desks, gaming system, and sickle drawings by Etheric Tales.

Vampire Hunters of America logo by Stephanie Hirschbrich.

Luma and Elsher maps designed by Fictive Designs.

First published in 2025 by Ringtail Press.

www.melissajacksonbooks.com

 Created with Vellum

MONSTROUS ALLIES

THE
CHARM
COLLECTOR

BOOK 4

MELISSA ERIN JACKSON

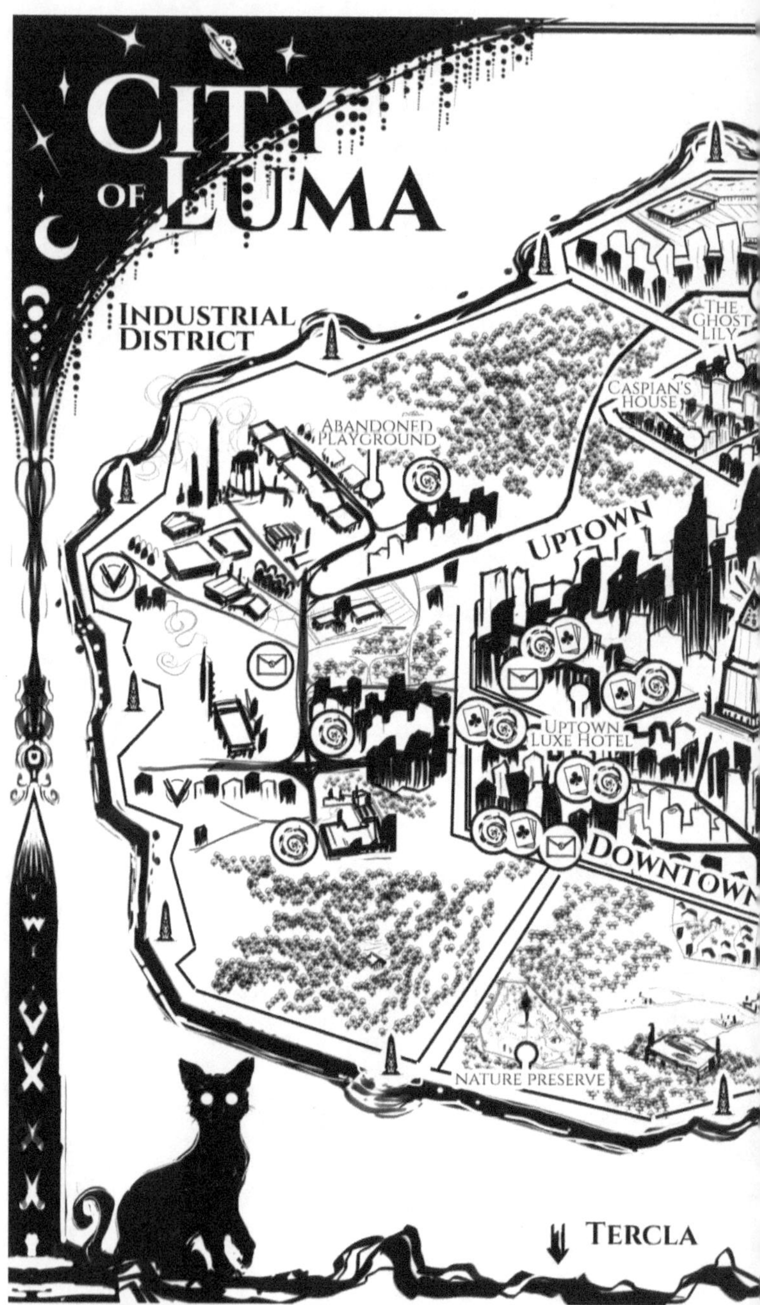

CITY
OF LUMA
INDUSTRIAL DISTRICT
THE GHOST LILY
CASPIAN'S HOUSE
ABANDONED PLAYGROUND
UPTOWN
UPTOWN LUXE HOTEL
DOWNTOWN
NATURE PRESERVE
TERCLA

WAREHOUSE DISTRICT
ARDMORE
KAYDA'S APARTMENT
AL'S BURGERS
DUCK POND
'S APOTHECARY
FELIX'S OFFICE
MONTCLAIRE
VHOA HEADQUARTERS
NECROPOLIS
CALIFORNIA
SACRAMENTO
SAN FRANCISCO
LUMA
LOS ANGELES
SAN DIEGO
VEIL OBELISKS
TELEPAD STATION
CASINO
VISITOR'S CENTER
TELEPOST STATION
SORCERERS' COLLECTIVE HEADQUARTERS

CHAPTER ONE

FELIX

Two Weeks Ago

Bartholomew plopped onto a corner of Felix's desk, right on top of a case file. His beefy arms were crossed over his beefy chest, and the smile he angled down at Felix was so white that Felix saw it in his peripheral vision. The guy was blond and blue-eyed and sort of reminded Felix of the old-school cartoon iteration of He-Man, though Bartholomew's hair wasn't cut into that unfortunate pageboy style. His personality oscillated between derpy golden retriever and class clown.

Felix gusted a sigh and abandoned the report he'd been typing into his computer. He scooted his chair back a few inches and crossed his own arms. Bartholomew had the uncanny knack of being an absolute pain in the ass in the most annoying *and* helpful way simultaneously. He knew Felix hated to be interrupted mid-report, but Felix also knew Bartholomew would only bother him if Bartholomew had worthy news.

"What?" Felix snapped, unable to help it. He'd been working on the report all morning. His bosses needed as much description as possible, and sometimes it was quite tedious to include the details of a bucket's entire contents. Namely, a bucket of teeth—especially when teeth as large as troll molars were mixed in with ones as small as pixie incisors, which were smaller than a grain of rice.

"Yeesh!" Bartholomew said, hands up. "I can come back after you center your chi."

"Out with it, Barth," Felix said, playing his only trump card; Bartholomew hated the nickname. It was bad enough that the last three letters of his name mimicked the sound a kitten made, seeing as Bartholomew was a werecat.

He had the best surname, though, as far as Felix was concerned. But apparently it was hard for a werecat to be taken seriously by the public when introduced as Officer Scratch.

"Got an interesting call on the tip line this morning," Bartholomew said.

Felix sighed when Bartholomew didn't elaborate. "And?"

"The five-year anniversary of Naomi West's death is coming up in a few days, and her mother is making a trip out to Luma to unveil a new headstone. She said she's got some intel on who might have killed her daughter."

Felix's brows shot toward his hairline, his irritation melting away. "Is this *new* intel, or is the looming anniversary loosening her tongue?"

Bartholomew shrugged his big shoulders, visibly straining his too-tight uniform. "She said she wants to talk to someone in person. I told her I'd pass along her contact info to the next available officer."

Bartholomew reached finger and thumb into the breast pocket of his shirt and pulled out a folded slip of paper. As he stood— knocking over a cup of pens that clattered to the tile floor like hail —he held the paper out to Felix. Felix resisted the urge to point out that knocking shit off surfaces solely for the enjoyment of hearing said items hit the floor was a very catlike thing to do.

"Here you go, Next Available Officer," Bartholomew said. "She gets here Wednesday."

Bartholomew headed off, stepping over the pile of dropped pens and waving a hand in parting without looking back.

Shaking his head at his friend, Felix unfolded the slip of paper. All that was written was the name of a hotel in uptown, a cell number, and "Denise West."

Felix wasn't technically a member of Luma's police force, but while bounties issued by the sorcerers were his top priority, when it came to cases involving humans, the defining lines of his job blurred. Cases and information were shared freely between the various branches and subbranches of law enforcement who worked in the Tower. Towers across the globe shared resources as well, a practice made essential after the first time a perp used the telepad system to teleport across state lines in a blink.

Some cases—mostly the ones that hit the werecats' desks— were locked behind confidentiality and security clearance walls. But everything else was fair game.

Most days Felix appreciated the lack of bureaucratic hoops he had to jump through to get information, but he also knew that was largely because the Collective cared less about human cases. He imagined one of his early human predecessors scheduling a meeting with a sorcerer, knees knocking, as he got up the courage to ask for more transparency between the Tower's departments. Once the sorcerer realized the quaking bounty hunter merely wanted more help solving human cases efficiently, the sorcerer in question probably waved a dismissive hand. *"Oh, this is a mundane concern? Sure. Whatever you need to clear your plate. Are we done here?"*

When Naomi had first gone missing, and then her body found on the shore of Luma Creek that ran through the southern end of the Industrial District, Felix had assumed it was just a terrible thing that had happened to one of Harlow's coworkers from the bar. But the deeper Felix got into his research about the Bliss trade, and how the supposed cartel in Luma might have been behind Nelson Fletcher's death, the more he realized the two things were related.

Felix's first warning had been getting beaten so badly he'd fallen unconscious in a bathroom at work. When he'd awoken with a killer headache, a couple of broken ribs, and blood in his mouth, the assailants had told him to back off. He hadn't listened.

The next day, Naomi went missing.

Felix had kept nosing around, unaware just how deep Naomi had gotten. The day her body was found—a week after she'd gone missing—Felix was cornered in the parking lot of the apartment complex he'd lived in with Harlow. The same pair of guys who'd jumped him in the bathroom were back, and this time they'd been armed with stacks of photos instead of a pair of crowbars. They'd told Felix point-blank that Naomi's death was a message and that he either needed to drop the investigation or work for them instead—if he chose anything else, Harlow would wind up dead next.

The goons had peppered Felix with questions about Camila and whether she and Harlow were still in contact. The ambush had at least tipped Felix off to the certainty that Camila was alive, even if he had no idea where she was or how to get in contact with her.

They'd tossed the photos at Felix's feet before stalking off.

Naomi, they'd said, had been a spy sent by their bosses' enemy. The goons had never deigned to tell Felix who those bosses were. Felix's best guess was that the thugs were the actual spies, likely paid by someone in the Collective—someone who had a vested interest in keeping the dirty details of the Bliss trade a secret. Anyone who got too close to that secret got threatened, recruited, or dumped beside Luma Creek like trash.

Felix knew now that, beyond the usual reasons a cartel would keep the details of their business hush-hush, Bliss runners were also protecting the drug's ingredient list, seeing as the secret sauce was vampire venom.

The photographs they'd tossed on the bathroom floor were of Harlow leaving home, going in to work, and talking and laughing with Naomi. There'd also been a few of Naomi's dead body lying next to a newspaper on a dirty warehouse floor—the date marking her death as two days *before* authorities found her in the Indie.

The message had been clear: If Felix didn't either sell his soul to the goons' bosses or stop poking around, Harlow would be dead. Felix had no idea why they hadn't killed him, too, but he supposed the torture of paranoia was worse than death.

In hindsight, he wished he'd given up everything, grabbed Harlow, and fled Luma. She would have gone with him. He knew that now. They could have gone searching for Camila. They could have tried to outrun the Bliss cartel, who'd targeted them both.

But he'd been so damn scared, he'd chosen the quickest, cleanest option. He knew if he left, Harlow would immediately be safe. He hadn't wanted to force her into a life on the run just because he'd been a dog with a bone and couldn't leave well enough alone—and then she'd ended up on the run anyway.

And on the run with someone else, at that.

His jaw ticked at the mere thought of Caspian Blackthorn. Felix knew little about the guy; not many people did. All Felix knew was that Harlow felt safer with Caspian than she did with him.

Felix wasn't entirely sure where Harlow even was right now. He checked in on her periodically, but she ignored him more than she answered.

Tensions were high in Luma lately on the best of days. Adding worries about Harlow would only make things more stressful. He hoped for her sake—and for his own sanity—that her latest adventure kept her far away from the city for a while.

WHEN FELIX WENT ON HIS LUNCH BREAK A FEW HOURS LATER, HE waved off an invitation from Bartholomew and their usual group of colleagues and left the Collective Tower by himself. He had a private office on the southern edge of Montclaire—putting him close to both downtown and the Necropolis. It was a risky location, given how close it was to Harlow's old place, but no one had ever accused him of being smart where she was concerned.

After grabbing lunch to go from a burger place a few blocks from his office, he found he didn't want to sit in that one-windowed room alone. So instead he set off down the sidewalk with no real destination in mind. Grease-dotted bag in hand, his mushroom-and-Swiss burger tucked safely inside, he blew out a deep breath and hit call on the number he'd typed into his phone ten minutes ago.

"Hello?" a woman answered cautiously after the second ring.

"Hello, Ms. West?" he asked. "This is Felix Turner. I'm a ... consultant with Luma PD. I'm very familiar with your daughter's case. I understand you'll be in the city soon? I'm sorry your return isn't for a happier reason."

"Thank you," she said tightly. "And thank you for returning my call so quickly."

"Not a problem. Are you traveling between hubs or from the outside?"

"I'll be traveling from Maine's hub," she said.

That would be at least two jumps; it was too far to teleport in one go without significant risk to life and limb.

"Needed to get as far away from California as I could," she added.

Felix knew Naomi had been half fae, but he didn't know if it had been her mother or father who'd been a faun. He'd find out soon enough, he supposed. "I wish you safe travels. I'll make time for you whenever you're available. And I can meet you wherever you wish; you don't need to come into a station. I just wanted to touch base with you and make sure you had my number."

"I appreciate it," Denise said. "The new headstone is going to be unveiled on Friday. It would be nice to get our chat out of the way when I first arrive so I can use the rest of my time in Luma to focus on the ceremony."

"Sounds good to me," Felix said, making a mental note that he only had two days to get fully reacquainted with the nitty-gritty details of Naomi's case.

"I'll be in touch soon, Mr. Turner."

Call over, he wandered down the curving sidewalks of a quiet residential neighborhood. He stopped abruptly at the base of an unlabeled archway made of rusting metal marking the start of an asphalt path flanked by wooden walls. Curiosity pulled him beneath the archway. He idly hoped the pull was of the mundane variety and that he wasn't being lured to his demise by wood nymphs.

It turned out that the wooden walls lining the asphalt path were made by the back fences of several homes. He could make out little snatches of yards beyond the periodic gaps between boards. The curving path eventually dumped him into a small, peaceful park that didn't boast much more than a handful of benches, a duck pond, and a swing set. He sat on a bench overlooking the pond. Three teal ducks lazily paddled about, occasionally tipping headfirst into the water. He'd never seen ducks with feathers that hue, and he pulled up Forage on his phone to do a quick search. They were cyan ducks—a species that had materialized after the Glitch, when ducklike birds from the fae realm bred with mundane mallards. It appeared that two of the ducks were male, while the one with more subdued coloring was the female.

He pulled his burger from the bag, hoping it was at least still lukewarm. He took a bite as he watched the ducks' bobbing tails as the birds searched for their own lunches. Unseen songbirds twittered in the trees. The occasional dragonfly or butterfly winged past.

Some of the tension left his shoulders.

A shadow passed across his lap, and he looked up sharply, wondering how long he'd been zoned out. He held his burger in both hands in his lap; he'd only eaten half of it.

A Latina woman around his age stood there. She was pretty in a decidedly human way. There was a visceral sense of relief at the realization that she was a mundane; it leveled the playing field.

Despite her beauty, she looked worn out—almost pale. He didn't think she was sick so much as she probably needed a really good nap. Her black hair was pulled up in a ponytail. Using a hand like a visor against the sun, she said, "You're in my favorite seat."

Felix glanced around the deserted park, eyeing each of the empty benches. He glanced down at the one he sat on, then grabbed the greasy bag that still held the tray of french fries and placed it on his other side. He motioned toward the open spot. "You're free to join me, but I'm not moving." He jutted his chin toward the pond, where all three ducks had their feathered rumps pointed into the air. "The view's too good."

The woman nodded once and sat beside him. She had a bagged lunch with, her too, but hers had come from a sandwich shop. As she took out her food, she said, "Not sure if you noticed, but there are two males and one female. Mundane ducks only mate for a season, but cyans mate for life. I've been coming here long enough to know that there used to be two pairs here most afternoons. One day, one of the males arrived alone. Been alone ever since, but he still shows up with the other two."

Felix eyed the ducks again, suddenly feeling incredibly sad that one of them was a widower, going through the motions even though his partner was gone. After a long beat, he turned his attention to the woman. "How long have you been coming that you know the sordid details about these ducks' lives?"

The woman had freed her turkey sandwich from its white waxy paper, but she'd made no move to grab it. She gripped either side of the wrapper as if unfastening the single strip of masking tape holding it closed had sapped her of what energy she had left.

"At least six months," she said, gaze fixed on the paddling birds. "I needed a place that was far from my office. Helps clear my head. It's *usually* deserted here ..." The sideways look she shot him was more playful than irritated.

"I needed to clear mine, too," he said. "It's a good spot for that."

They fell into companionable silence as they ate.

After she'd polished off her sandwich and cracked open a small bag of chips, he asked, "So what is it you do that you need to escape to relative isolation?" He turned to drape an arm over the back of the bench and gave her a deliberately over-the-top scan. She was dressed casually in jeans and a plain T-shirt, wasn't dolled up with makeup or jewelry, and wore sensible shoes. There was a quiet confidence paired with a cautious reserve that was oddly familiar. "I'm guessing PI. A *mundane* PI."

She chuckled. "The general idea is right, but the details are decidedly not."

His brow furrowed at that. She clearly didn't want to elaborate about the nature of her job, but she didn't seem hard-pressed to flee, either. Plus, she'd *chosen* to approach him. She either really thought he'd pack up and go so she could have her favorite bench to herself, or some part of her had wanted the company.

"Okay ..." he said slowly, thinking. "So is this a case of a job that sucks your soul dry, or do you like the job but hate your boss or coworkers? Is Janice from Accounting being an unreasonable monster again?"

The woman snorted. "Neither, really. I love the job, but it's exhausting. And I'm technically the boss, so I guess now, on top of everything else, I should be worried that my team hates *me*. Thanks for that."

"Ah," Felix said, nodding, unfazed by her sarcasm. "*You're* the monster. Got it."

She grinned. It was a very nice smile. "What about you? You avoiding the job or Janice from Accounting?"

"I'm not sure if I'm offended that you didn't think I could be a monstrous boss, too," he said.

She cocked her head, staring up at the gently waving canopy of the mulberry tree above them as she contemplated something. When she finally looked at him, she had a brow cocked. "I'm guessing you're in public service. Social work?"

It was *his* brows that hiked now. "What makes you think that?"

She shrugged. "You're good at striking up conversations with total strangers. You picked up on the fact that light teasing would amuse and not offend me. And you're also good at knowing when to read the room, so to speak, and pivot the conversation to keep the other person chatting even if you hit a topic they don't want to talk about." She nodded once, as if satisfied with her own assessment. "Social work. Possibly with troubled teens."

Felix employed an expression that he hoped telegraphed quiet awe. "That's incredibly perceptive."

She beamed at him, and he found himself unable to keep his own smile in check.

"Unfortunately, you're *super* wrong," he said.

Her pretty grin disappeared. "Wait, really?"

He'd finished his food, but he grabbed a fresh napkin to give his fingers another quick wipe before he pulled the slim case of business cards out of his pocket. He hesitated for only a moment.

Other than her interest in the love stories of ducks, he knew nothing about her. Not even her name. So he didn't know why he cared that she might avoid her favorite park indefinitely after he told her what he did for a living. She'd been reluctant to talk about her work, too, but Felix figured that was because she was worried hers was too strange or dull.

He held out one of his cards.

She eyed him curiously for a beat before taking the card and reading it. "Huh. I guess a bounty hunter isn't *that* far off from a social worker. I imagine you need conversational skills to keep the bad guys from bolting." She wrinkled her nose. She had a cute nose, too. "I'm kind of glad I didn't tell you about my job first."

Felix offered her a purposefully dramatic wince. "Oh no. Are you the head of an accounting firm? It's not that you're Janice from Accounting, but that you eat lowly Janices for lunch?"

"Were you audited as a child and you've never recovered? I'm sensing some deep-seated finance-related trauma here."

Felix laughed. "I'm really bad at math, and I'm very intimidated by a woman who knows her way around a spreadsheet."

She was about to say something else when her cell rang. The proverbial wind went out of her sails, returning her to her previous exhausted state. "Time to get back to those spreadsheets, I guess."

Felix watched as she packed up her trash, her phone continuing to ring in the small purse she had draped over the side of the bench. She hadn't even looked at the phone to see who was calling, just hopped to her feet almost immediately. He supposed it could be a person-specific ringtone, but it sounded generic enough. Maybe she'd just needed an excuse to leave. The call, after all, could have been from a telemarketer.

He wondered if perhaps a controlling partner was calling her, wondering where she'd disappeared to for all of half an hour. Perhaps she didn't have a job at all but had ventured out on her own to experience a few minutes of freedom and had lost track of time. Felix quickly scanned her arms, her neck, her face. There were no bruises, but that didn't mean there weren't any hidden under her clothes.

He wasn't sure if his experience with so many domestic abuse cases had made him overly perceptive or overly suspicious.

She slung her purse across her body, the small bag resting against her hip. The phone stopped ringing, only to resume again a moment later. She surprised him by saying, "I'll be back tomorrow around the same time if you'd like to eat lunch adjacent to me again. Assuming, of course, that you aren't chasing down criminals."

He tried to come up with a witty reply, but he really wasn't sure if he should be worried about her or not. "What's your name?" was all he managed to get out.

She tucked her wadded-up trash under her arm and hastily rummaged around in the front-zippered pocket of her purse. The flap was embroidered with nesting vertical zigzagging lines of orange, red, and blue. Producing a business card of her own, she thrust it at him and then darted toward the fence-lined path with surprising speed. "Maybe I'll see you tomorrow, Felix!" she called over her shoulder.

Her cell phone stopped ringing, but that was because she'd finally answered it.

By the time he focused on the card in his hands, she was gone. And when he saw what was on the card, he figured she'd fled because of his potential reaction more than needing to attend to whoever had been blowing up her phone.

The Vampire Hunters of America
"Protecting you from what goes bump in the night."
Marisol Ortiz: Luma Chapter Point of Contact

He spluttered a laugh. And here Felix had been sure Marisol had a boring, normal job and that she would be scared off by *his* profession.

She wasn't a monster; she *hunted* them. If Felix didn't know

Camila and Nelson had met through VHoA, he would have regretfully tossed Marisol's card in the trash along with his burger wrapper and called it a day, discounting her as a conspiracy-obsessed loon. In his defense, Luma's outreach team for VHoA was … a lot. They were usually posted up downtown, their necks slathered in red paint, while they screamed at passersby about the end of days, thrusting pamphlets about their cause into people's faces.

Marisol had *seemed* sane.

He figured he'd drop by the park again the following day, if only so she wouldn't be self-conscious about her career choice. Besides he, too, was now invested in the emotional recovery of the widowed cyan duck.

Felix arrived at the park earlier than planned the next day, just to make sure he didn't miss Marisol and ghost her accidentally.

She was already sitting on their bench when he got there.

He grinned like a damn fool.

CHAPTER TWO

FELIX

A Week and a Half Ago

F elix sat at a back table in the restaurant of the Uptown Luxe
Hotel, nursing a tumbler of seltzer water. He hated the stuff;
it tasted like the sound of TV static. But at first blush, it could pass
as a clear alcohol, and while he wasn't *technically* on the job, he

needed a clear head, and he didn't want to jeopardize that with something stronger.

He couldn't get Marisol Ortiz out of his head. They'd had lunch together three days in a row now. He wasn't sure if it was time to ask her out on a proper date. He was fairly certain she was interested, but maybe she just didn't like eating lunch alone.

He was almost positive he was overthinking it.

"Mr. Turner?"

Felix glanced up from his barely touched glass of liquid sadness. The sight of the woman standing beside the table stole his breath for a moment. She looked so much like Naomi, he believed for half a second that she hadn't, in fact, been murdered and that she'd merely been on the run until now.

But a breath later, he clocked the differences. Denise's hair was jet black, rather than Naomi's light brown. They had the same dark-brown eyes, but while Denise looked closer to thirty than her more likely fifty, there were faint wrinkles around her eyes and mouth that hadn't graced Naomi's young face. Denise was probably closer to five foot five, whereas Naomi had been five foot eight or so, like Harlow.

She was dressed in a simple but elegant white silk blouse and dark-washed designer jeans, and delicate pearl earrings rested in her earlobes. A large leather handbag hung from her shoulder, the front adorned with nothing but the golden logo of a designer Felix didn't recognize. Denise's nails were lacquered in red, and a mother of a diamond ring glinted on her right hand.

Felix cataloged all of this in a few moments, then deftly stood, hand outstretched. "It's nice to formally meet you, Ms. West."

She shook his hand. "You can call me Denise. And thank you again for meeting with me."

"No problem," Felix said, gesturing to the chair opposite his. "Would you like anything to drink? Beer, wine ..."

They took their seats.

Denise waved a dismissive hand at his offer, her ring winking under the fluorescent lights. "I'm okay. I'm, uh, a recovering alcoholic."

Felix winced internally but kept it from reaching his face. "Iced tea, soft drink, water?"

She smiled tightly. "Iced tea sounds great."

"I'll be right back." He got to his feet again, then navigated through the maze of tables and chairs that separated their table from the bar on the other side of the room.

The restaurant was nearly dead at this hour, and while the Uptown Luxe Hotel was swanky, the restaurant's staff was rather lax in their customer service until well after noon. The well-to-do apparently slept in.

The bartender behind the counter was focused squarely on his phone, chuckling softly to himself as he presumably watched a video. He glanced up the moment Felix approached the bar, though, and plucked one of his earbuds free. "Decide you need something with more punch?" the guy asked.

Perhaps he, too, thought seltzer water was an affront to humanity.

"Unfortunately not. Can I get an iced tea?"

Within seconds of handing over a chilled glass of tepid-looking tea, the bartender had already slipped his earbud back into place and was chuckling at whatever was onscreen.

Denise startled slightly when Felix deposited her glass in front of her. She recovered quickly and angled a soft smile up at him. "Thank you." She grabbed the glass and dragged it toward her but didn't take a sip, merely gazed into it as if future-revealing tea leaves rested at its base.

Her giant purse hung from the back of her chair. The corners of a few papers poked from its mouth.

"How many jumps is it from Maine to here?" Felix asked, figuring a softball question might break the ice a bit. Or at least crack it.

"Oh, umm ..." Denise said, glancing up. "It takes three, but I went for four, simply for safety. Turned it into an hour-and-a-half journey instead of forty-five minutes, but I made the mistake last week of reading an article about a guy who tried to make the jump in two and well, they still haven't found his torso."

Felix winced. He wondered if it had been the oversight of a telepad attendant who allowed someone to make such an unsafe trip. Maybe the traveler had paid the attendant to look the other way. Telepad travel had such an extensive digital footprint, though, it was unlikely the attendant's blunder—whether through greed or negligence—wouldn't be investigated. Felix didn't think being in a hurry to get from point A to point B would ever be so dire that one should risk misplacing vital body parts.

They managed a bit more small talk—consisting almost entirely of Maine's weather versus California's—before Denise finally broached the subject she'd clearly been trying to avoid, despite it being the reason for their meeting. "I've been doing a lot of armchair detective work since Naomi was found. I've collected newspaper articles and blog posts and printed out podcast transcriptions. I've taken tons of notes."

Felix kept his expression neutral, silently encouraging her to continue, though his gaze did flick to her oversized purse again. He assumed it was full of her research notes.

"I didn't actually find out that she'd been … I didn't find out about her murder until almost six months after her death," Denise said, color rising in her cheeks as her gaze returned to the contents of her glass. "I was living in the Nevadan hub at the time. My ex-husband and I had a rough marriage, and it only got worse when Charlie went missing."

"Charlie was your son? Was he older or younger than Naomi?" Felix asked, though he already knew the answer. When Felix had started researching Naomi after her death, details about her past and her family had been muddy at best. Police and news reports contradicted each other about whether Naomi had had a brother at all. It had taken a lot of digging for Felix to find solid answers—but by the time he'd landed on the truth, he'd been locked into a Soul NDA and couldn't tell Harlow what he'd found out about her friend.

"Younger by a year," Denise said.

Felix hadn't found out about Charlie until *after* Naomi's death. He wasn't even sure Harlow knew about him. "How long had he been missing before Naomi disappeared?"

Denise stared at him for a long beat. "You've done your research, too."

He nodded. "I researched the circumstances of Naomi's death quite a bit." He hesitated for a beat, not sure if he should share his personal connection to Naomi. But then he remembered that his bosses cared little about cases like hers and that he wasn't locked into secrecy since he'd done all this research on his own time. *Fuck it.* "Naomi happened to be a close friend of my ex-girlfriend."

Denise's tear-filled eyes instantly snapped up to Felix's. "Really? You knew her?"

"I did. She came over to our apartment for several game and dinner nights. She and my ex were waitresses at the same bar."

Denise's lips flattened into a thin line. "I'm surprised a cop would be comfortable with his girlfriend working at the Ghost Lily. Unless she wasn't human, I guess. Stranger things have happened—I married a faun, after all." She chuckled darkly to herself.

Felix's brows smashed together. "Uhh, they worked together at the Blind Mongoose, not the Ghost Lily."

Denise shook her head. "Naomi worked at more than one bar, then. I *know* she worked at the Ghost Lily—I asked around there myself, showing her picture to the staff."

That definitely hadn't come up in Felix's research. But it wasn't a surprise. The Ghost Lily seemed to run by its own rules —an entity unto itself. Despite Harlow and her friends figuring out that Bliss was being trafficked into the bar while drugged-up fae girls were being smuggled out, the place was still in business to this day.

The official word out of the Collective was that all the allegations about the owner's and staff's criminal behavior were "under investigation." The investigation wasn't being conducted by humans like him, so he had no idea if the so-called investigation was actually happening. Felix's guess was that the owner of the hellhole was either a Collective sorcerer or in a sorcerer's pocket.

The staff of the place had gone through a major overhaul in the last few weeks, but Felix would bet good money that that was less about taking out the trash and more about firing anyone who *wasn't* corrupt—making the Ghost Lily even more dangerous for the vulnerable young fae who got lured in.

Oliver Randal—the caracal shifter who Harlow's sword had killed, thereby resulting in Harlow going on the lam—had been one of the scumbags who'd operated out of the Ghost Lily. Randal had made promises to aspiring young actresses and models about getting them gigs, only to toss them aside once he'd gotten them to sleep with him. The prettiest of the fae were drugged with Bliss and trafficked out of Luma and into the hands of hybrid vampires on the other side of the veil.

Felix couldn't say he was sorry that Randal was dead, even though the circumstances of his death had turned Harlow's life upside down.

"Did you hear about that shifter, Oliver Randal, who was killed here a couple months ago?" Denise asked now, as if she'd heard Felix's thoughts. She chuckled to herself again. "Of course you'd have heard about it. You're a cop. Sorry. Well, I talked to that guy before he was killed."

"Oh?" Felix asked, trying not to telegraph his intrigue.

"Yeah. A, uh, … friend of the family showed me the article in the *Luma City Times* about Naomi six months after my baby girl was already gone. That friend had been trying to help me get sober for a long time, and it was seeing that article—especially six months *after* my daughter was gone—that made me get my crap together. I got sober, went to meetings, and cut myself off from my piece-of-shit husband once and for all.

"I moved out of the hub system for a while. The temptation of alcohol is bad enough—but fae alcohol?" She shook her head. "Once I got better, I started looking into what happened to Naomi. The article only mentioned that she had been a waitress at a popular Luma bar—so that's where I started. I came to Luma a few times and visited damn near every bar in the city. My poking around finally led me to the Ghost Lily and Oliver Randal. After talking to a few of the girls who worked there—though most of them were too scared to tell me anything—I decided I'd talk to Randal myself. I was convinced *he* was the one who'd killed Naomi, and I wanted to confront him face-to-face. I needed to know why he did it."

Felix gusted a sigh, fighting the urge to tell her that it was incredibly dangerous for civilians to confront people like Oliver Randal and poke around places like the Ghost Lily, especially as a human armed with nothing but grief-fueled determination. But it wouldn't do any good—Randal was already dead, and Denise likely had known the dangers and had actively chosen to ignore her common sense.

Denise said, "I knew soon after talking to him that he wasn't her killer. He didn't do any of the dirty work himself."

"Was he actually forthcoming with information?" Felix asked, dubious.

Several of Felix's female coworkers—all mundane with the exception of one ocelot shifter—had tried to go undercover at the bar over the last few years in an attempt to get close to the leaders of the trafficking ring. No one had gotten past the guards manning the entrance to the private rooms on the second floor. That hadn't been surprising, either; the traffickers were only interested in fae, and Felix's colleagues all agreed that recruiting young, untrained civilians for the task was entirely too risky.

It had taken Welsh's exceptional glamouring skills to get anyone—namely Welsh himself and Harlow—beyond the black curtain.

"A bit," Denise finally said. "The girls I talked to mentioned more than once that Oliver Randal only paid attention to the most beautiful of fae, and everyone else was practically invisible—people not worth his time. Being human, I figured that would work against me, regardless of how attractive he found me. Not to mention I was probably too old." Her lip curled minutely. "One of the girls suggested I get into contact with a guy named Mr. Brown. He's apparently good at getting people new identities—as in not just new IDs and such, but a whole new face if the customer is able to afford it."

Felix's brows hiked. He knew from Harlow that Mr. Brown was one of Zander Welsh's aliases. Thing was, Welsh was notorious for refusing to work with humans.

"It took a lot of hoop-jumping and a two-week waiting list to actually get an appointment with Mr. Brown. I met him in the back room of a hole-in-the-wall burger joint, of all places. He took one look at me and told me he couldn't help me—nearly slammed the door of his dingy office in my face," Denise said. "I told him I was there because of my half-faun daughter who had been murdered. That at least got him to let me into his office. In the end, he said he felt for me but couldn't sell me one of his glamour tonics. He said human constitutions were too weak, and he didn't want to waste one on someone who likely wouldn't survive the transformation, no matter how temporary."

That all sounded like Welsh all right.

"I eventually convinced him to sell me a few glamoured accessories—a wig, a nose ring that gave me an instant rhinoplasty, and a pair of earrings that elongated the tops of my ears so I looked like an elf. The cost almost cleaned out my savings, but I bought them anyway." Denise pursed her lips. "The disguise was good enough that the bouncers at the door let me in for free. The way they leered at me almost made me blow my cover, I was so mad. The idea that any one of them could have looked at Naomi that way made my skin crawl. Not to mention how terrified the waitresses I talked to had been."

Felix's hold on his glass of seltzer water tightened. If he could get away with it, he'd stalk out of here right this instant and burn that damn bar down to its foundation.

Denise said, "I sat at the bar and asked the bartender if Oliver Randal was there. I said I was looking for a job. The bartender looked like he was debating telling me to run and never look back, but he just sighed and said he'd make a call for me. Within ten minutes, Randal slid onto the stool next to me."

Felix wanted to ask a million questions but willed himself to stay his tongue. He had no idea how many people Denise had told this story to, but he had to guess it hadn't been many. It sounded like she'd likely burned a lot of bridges on her road to sobriety; she probably didn't have many people left she could confide in. He regarded the diamond ring on her finger and her overall posh attire. How much did her new husband know about her checkered past?

"The worst part about Randal was that, within ten seconds of being in his presence, I instantly knew how women—especially young ones—had gotten pulled into his orbit. He was Hollywood-star gorgeous, was charming as hell despite clearly being a little drunk and possibly high, and was attentive in a way that made you feel like you were the only person in the universe. Plus he had dimples when he smiled. *Dimples.*" She shook her head again. "I'm honestly embarrassed that my first impression of him made me think he couldn't possibly be Naomi's killer simply because he was so ... so ..."

"Fae?" Felix finished for her.

"Yes," Denise said, offering him a grateful smile. "Anyway, I pretended initially that I was looking for a modeling gig, claiming I knew about his line of work through my daughter who had come to him for the same reason. I showed him a picture of Naomi on my phone, hoping to get a reaction out of him. I didn't get one. He *did* tell me, though, that I could possibly get a job as an item model for an auction if I 'lost a few pounds,'" she said, making air quotes. "He also suggested he could expedite getting me a job if I, uh, *serviced* him first."

Felix's nose wrinkled. "Classy."

"Yeah. That's when I left. On my walk back to the house I was renting, I had a feeling I was being trailed. I ducked into an alley, and a few seconds later an absolutely massive grizzly bear rounded the corner."

"Oh shit."

"I tried to run, but if running from a mundane bear is stupid, running from a shifter is *monumentally* stupid. He knocked me to the ground almost immediately, shifted into a human, and … beat the ever-loving shit out of me," Denise said in a flat, detached way. Felix figured removing emotion from the recounting was the easiest way for her to get the words out. Even still, her eyes rimmed with silver as she spoke, though the tears never fell. "Most of the glamouring accessories were either torn off or ripped off during the beating, so he saw what I actually looked like. When I was nearly unconscious, he told me never to bother Oliver Randal or step foot inside the Ghost Lily again, or he'd kill me just like they'd killed Naomi."

Felix was having his own flashback of being accosted. He wondered if one of the goons who had beaten him had been the same guy who had threatened Denise.

"I honestly should have left Luma then, but after a few days, when I'd mostly recovered, I started loitering near the Ghost Lily, trying to talk to the waitresses as they walked home after their shifts. Most of them wouldn't talk to me, but I finally got the name Tatton out of one of them. She said I needed to stop asking questions because Tatton was crazy. A day later, I got back from running errands and someone had broken into the rental where I was staying. The house was trashed, smelled of urine, and the words 'nosy bitch' were painted on the wall of the living room in red paint. The paint was still wet. *That* was when I finally left Luma—I was gone within twenty minutes of finding the message. Today is the first time I've been back in four years or so."

Felix gusted a sigh, thinking it was miraculous Denise was still alive. Then again, he could say the same about himself. "You don't worry this Tatton person is going to know you've returned to Luma?"

Denise shrugged one slender shoulder. "I moved to the hub in Maine two years ago. I've been keeping up on the news in Luma as much as I can, just in case something about Naomi—or even Charlie—materializes. It wasn't the news that Oliver Randal was killed that affected me the most in recent months. It was the stories from all those fae teens that really lit a fire under me. Those poor kids were trafficked and drugged—same as Naomi and Charlie—and they somehow found the courage to talk about it afterward. If they could be that brave, then I want to try, too."

Felix mulled that all over for a moment. "Have you found any evidence suggesting Charlie is still alive?"

Denise's eyes welled with unshed tears again. "No. The odds are virtually nonexistent that he survived. He was gone for almost eight months before Naomi was kidnapped as well. And I know that her trying so hard to find him is what ultimately led to her death. I know all of this is incredibly dangerous. But ..." Her shoulders rounded. "I didn't do right by my kids. It's the greatest regret of my life. If I can somehow spare other parents from the pain of losing their kids to these monsters—even if it kills *me* in the process—then I want to do everything I possibly can."

Felix heaved a sigh.

Guess this was yet another case to add to his endless stack. It wasn't an official job through the Collective, so he'd be working on his own time—as if he had much of that these days.

But it wasn't as if he'd tell Denise he couldn't help her track down Naomi's killer. He'd gotten in too deep on this case in particular, and even when it had grown cold, it had never gone away. Not really. Naomi's ghost had always been there in the back of his mind, silently waiting for him to solve the mystery of who had discarded her lifeless body like a heap of garbage.

And just behind Naomi's patient specter was Nelson's. Even though Nelson had been Harlow's father, he'd meant a lot to Felix. His death had been a sucker punch.

To solve one murder would lead Felix to the solution of the other. He knew that in his bones.

"I'm not even sure what I'm asking you for," Denise finally said. "I just have all these little pieces, and I don't know how to put them together. Naomi's killer is still out there. I want to help stop him before he hurts anyone else. The guilt that my inaction probably caused the death of others eats me up every day. It's much harder to cope with when I'm sober." She punctuated that with a sharp, bitter little laugh.

Pushing aside his untouched glass of seltzer water, he said, "Give me what you've got, and I'll get started right away."

Twin tears did fall from Denise's eyes then. She hastily swiped them away as she pulled her designer bag onto her lap, smiling softly to herself. She had been worried Felix would tell her he couldn't help her, he realized. Taking two stuffed folders out of the bag, she deposited them on the table with muted thuds.

Denise really *had* done her homework.

Seltzer water definitely wasn't going to cut it. He'd need coffee —a *lot* of coffee.

But the promise of new information rekindled the dormant embers of his hope.

Holding tight to the bulging folders, Felix walked Denise to a nearby telepad station. Denise's next destination was on the other end of the hub to see the updated headstone prior to the ceremony. Apparently friends and family, what few there were, were going to start arriving that evening.

As he bade goodbye to Denise, he promised to keep her abreast of his progress. The woman just looked relieved that her research was literally in someone else's hands now.

He walked a couple of blocks to a coffee shop run by a nature witch. He ordered the largest coffee they had and sprang for a double shot of a Level 2 clarity of mind tincture. He was going to need all the extra help he could get.

CHAPTER THREE

HARLOW

Caspian stirred next to me. We still had an hour before we had to meet Sorceress Rhiannon at the Collective Tower, so I'd been stalling on waking him. He'd looked so wrecked the last few days, I figured he should grab whatever rest he could.

He grunted and muttered something under his breath before turning onto his side and flopping an arm over my stomach. My brows hiked. He murmured sleepily, tucking his hand underneath me and scooting closer. I froze. His warm breath ghosted across my ear.

A breath later, Caspian snorted awake and, in one fluid motion, propped himself up on an elbow. He stared down at me, bewildered, his eyes a little bloodshot. I wasn't sure if that was from the alcohol or because he was still in a sleep deficit.

His brown, slightly curly hair wasn't that long, but it still stuck up sharply on one side. He squinted one eye closed; maybe the effort of keeping them open at the same time was too difficult. He smacked his lips, as if parched. "Hi."

His arm was still wrapped around me, his warm hand splayed underneath me on my back.

"Hi," I said, trying not to laugh. "Did you sleep so hard you're now unsure what century you're in?"

"I'm not even sure what planet I'm on." That was when he realized where his arm was. "Oh!" he said and hastily yanked it free before tucking it close to his own side, though he still loomed over me, propped up on his elbow. "I, uh … sorry."

Color rose high in his cheeks.

It took all my powers of self-control to resist the urge to smooth down the tuft of wild hair on the side of his head. He somehow looked better *and* worse than he had when I'd found him creeping down the hallway like a cat burglar.

He asked, "Did *you* sleep okay? I was probably snoring like a freight train."

"If you were, I didn't hear it. Slept like the dead." I chewed on my bottom lip. "Guess you're my white-noise machine, too."

"Glad to hear it." He rubbed the heel of a palm against an eye. "Guess it's good to know there's an alternative to Welsh's sleeping drafts, since I'm without my supplier for the foreseeable future."

My gut twisted. I hadn't checked my phone to see if there were any updates from Vaughn. I wasn't sure if seeing a *lack* of texts from the vampire would somehow make me feel even worse.

It had been less than twenty-four hours since Vaughn had carted an unconscious Welsh away. I could still see the ghostly image of a man superimposed on top of Welsh's form. Vaughn had recognized him—a vampire named Teo. It sounded like Teo had once been part of the Vampire Council with Roch, or at least closely associated. Until he went to the dark side and went hybrid, anyway.

Teo apparently was able to communicate with Welsh through shadows. I didn't know if that was a result of Welsh's blood poisoning after being bitten, but anecdotal evidence suggested it was. Things had gotten dire as hell if it currently felt like Welsh was safe in Tercla, surrounded by pures—pures Welsh had a history with. I still didn't know the full story there.

When Vaughn had shown up with Caspian and me at the Airbnb, Welsh had been so furious he'd practically been vibrating.

Gesturing at Vaughn with a whole-body thrust of his arms, Welsh had asked, *"Of all the people in all the Goddess-damned world you could have contacted, Harlow, why did it have to be* him?"

I hoped Welsh would forgive me. I'd wanted to help him any way I could and had been unknowingly enthralled by Vaughn to force the meeting between him and Welsh.

I willed away the memory and refocused on Caspian next to me.

As his sleep fog lifted, I decided he looked miles better than he had a few hours ago—sounded better, too—but he was nowhere close to being at peak form. It was too bad we couldn't buy ourselves another day to recoup. If *I* was this exhausted and heartsick over what had happened to Welsh, I could only imagine how Caspian felt. He needed to be on top of his game if we had any hope of figuring out how to help Welsh. He couldn't slide back into insomnia, staying up till all hours poring over his tomes.

"Maybe we need some sort of system," I said. "If either of us is having trouble sleeping, there's an open invitation to take advantage of their personal human white-noise machine."

My mind then pulled up an image of handsome Samar for some reason. He'd said he wanted to take me out for a beer once I got settled back in Luma. The whole "open invitation" thing with Caspian could get disrupted if something developed between me and Samar.

Bringing a guy back here would be weird as hell. Samar had already questioned whether Caspian was my stuffy attendant or my boyfriend. How odd would he find it if he discovered I *lived* with Caspian? Granted, the living situation was because my place had gone up in flames, and Caspian was helping me out while we were both on the lam.

But Samar would probably be more focused on the "me living with a guy who'd he suspected I was dating" part.

Luckily for Samar, I was absolutely *not* Caspian's type. A nerdy sorceress with a love of dusty books crammed with rune theory I was not.

"If I end up abusing the system, you have permission to cut me off," Caspian said, refocusing my muddled, sleep-addled thoughts.

I scanned his face. He was more lucid now, at least. His eyes still looked so bloodshot they made my own itch in sympathy.

"Not sure if I should feel flattered that you're already planning to abuse this open invitation or worried that you think you'll need to," I said.

His gaze flicked down to my mouth for a brief moment before drifting up to my eyes again. It took him a long, calculating moment to finally say, "Might be a little of both."

My cheeks heated.

Wait, why was *I* blushing?

Caspian coughed awkwardly and broke eye contact, fussing idly with a loose thread on the edge of the pillowcase below my head. "It'll, uh, make me clean my bedroom, if nothing else."

"We talking a filthy-bachelor-pad situation or a mad-librarian kind of deal? I picture half of your bed piled with notes, books, and wadded-up sheets of paper more than stacks of empty pizza boxes, if I'm honest."

He stared at me for a beat. "Am I that predictable?"

I wrinkled my nose. "Kinda."

He considered that. "And is that a good thing or a bad thing?"

"Hmm. Depends on the situation, I guess. Being reliable isn't exactly a negative trait."

"But it can be … boring?"

My brows pinched. He didn't sound particularly perturbed,

merely curious, but the very slight edge to the question made me wonder for the first time if all my joking about him being a bland bookish-professor type had gotten under his skin. Especially in light of what he'd told me about Marcus and how sorcerers who attended the academy were beaten down year after year, the ones who remained having lost their hardened edges. If he was a less spontaneous, more predictable person now, it was because the Collective's training program had made him that way.

"Being reliable isn't boring," I finally said. "It's incredibly comforting."

"Comforting," he repeated slowly, as if testing the word out for the first time.

I really wasn't sure what was going on right now.

"Question," he said.

I arched my brows.

"Would you be more or less concerned if half of my bed wasn't covered in the spoils of a librarian's wet dream but, say, stuffed animals?"

I blinked at him. "How many stuffed animals are we talking about? And is it one kind of animal or is it a menagerie?"

Caspian cocked his head and surveyed me as if I were a unique insect trapped under glass. "Would it being more than one type make a difference?"

"Uh, yeah," I said. "If someone likes stuffed animals in general, they're constantly on the hunt for ones that catch their eye. If they're, I don't know, only interested in hippos, that's a whole other obsession. If I walked in there and a sea of different animals was looking at me, I'd be feeling one thing. But if I strolled in there and a herd of two hundred hippos were staring back, I'd be extra unsettled. Why are you so obsessed with hippos specifically? It's like Ronan the siren's love of chickens. Why chickens? There's a story there. And it's probably weird."

"A bloat."

"Uhh, what?"

"A group of hippos is called a bloat."

I resisted the urge to comment on the Caspianism and instead said, "See? Reliably informative."

He squinted at me. "Oh, don't give me that diplomatic bullshit. Welsh isn't here to point out my many foibles, so now you'll have to pull double duty."

Barking a laugh, I said, "Fine. So out of *everything* I said, you were most hung up on the correct word for a *group* of hippos? Why did you even ask about stuffed animals?" My eyes widened. "Oh no. Is your room *actually* full of stuffed animals? Did I guess hippo correctly, and that's why you're so testy about the right term?"

I started to roll to get out of bed to check for myself, but his arm landed next to my side, caging me in. I flopped onto my back again.

When he'd apparently convinced himself I wasn't going to go sprinting into his room, he removed his arm but stayed lying beside me, head propped on one fist. "I found a bowl of cereal under my bed last night that was so old, the milk had turned to something like cement."

I winced.

"Welsh cleaned up after the werecats trashed the place, but he's told me more than once that he's not a housekeeper. He'd obviously found the cereal bowl, as he'd left a Post-it note on it that said, 'You're disgusting.'"

I snorted a laugh, then immediately choked back a sob. "He's so awful."

Caspian sighed. "I miss him, too."

"So ... your room is a combination of bachelor pad and mad librarian?"

His nose wrinkled. "The bowl of cement milk is still there."

"Cas!"

"I was under emotional duress!"

"You probably couldn't sleep last night because it smells like rotting food in there." I bit my lip. "You're always so ... reliably put together. I have to see how bad it is. Please let me see it."

"Harlow. Don't. It's not fit for company."

"Couldn't you pay the pixies extra to help do light house-keeping?"

Caspian grimaced. "I tried. After a few months, Julip quit."

My whole body went rigid with the all-consuming need to see how disgusting his bedroom was. I didn't know why I needed such a thing at that moment, but I needed it like I needed air.

An arm slammed into place on my other side again.

When I was flat on my back again, Caspian's nose was only a couple of inches from mine. *"Please,"* I begged. "I was actually hoping earlier that you were a secret hoarder, but somehow this is better."

"We've been through a lot together, and yet your desperation to see my disaster of a bedroom is somehow one of your stranger reactions."

I managed to shrug while still lying down. "I like learning new things about you."

My face flushed hotter than a thousand suns. Why the hell had I said *that*? I mean, it was true, but it suddenly felt like too inti-mate a thing to say when his face was so close to mine.

"That so?"

I bit down on my bottom lip.

His gaze flicked to my mouth again.

Wait.

Wait, wait.

What was happening? Was he still intoxicated? Was I?

"Harlow?"

The door to my room flew open.

Caspian and I both flinched so hard, we managed to thunk our foreheads together. It sounded like the crash of two bowling balls. Caspian groaned and flopped onto his back.

"Oh my Goddess, sorry!" came my mom's voice from the doorway.

Wincing, I glanced over to find her standing there with her

hands clamped over her eyes. "In my defense, the door was unlocked!"

"It was also *closed*! What if I was in here doing naked yoga?" I sat up and swung my feet to the floor.

Mom dropped her hand to properly level a look of bewilderment my way. "Are we talking *actual* naked yoga, or is that a euphemism? I haven't had naked yoga in so long, I might no longer be hip to the lingo."

I propped my elbows on my knees and buried my face in my hands. "Someone kill me."

"What's this about naked yoga?"

I groaned as Soren joined my mom in the doorway.

Mom said, "I'm still unclear. I may have walked in on the *start* of naked yoga."

Uncovering my *very* warm face, I said, "What are you two even doing up here? Your rooms are downstairs!"

"I assume they were in the mezzanine library," Caspian said, skirting his side of the bed and walking to the door. He turned to walk backward, placed his palms together, and bowed gently toward me. "Naked namaste."

I chucked a pillow at him. Soren cackled uproariously.

"Sorry, Low," Mom said, but she was doing a terrible job of not grinning. "I might still be a little drunk. I just wanted to make sure you were awake. We need to leave in half an hour."

"Got it. I just need to take a shower." I quickly added, "If *any* of you make a comment about working up a sweat during naked yoga, I'm leaving Luma to join the circus!"

All three of them snickered like teenagers, then left the room. I'd just reached the door to close it when Caspian reappeared in the doorway.

He stared at me for a long beat before saying, "Thanks for letting me crash with you, by the way. I can't tell you how much better I feel. Other than the goose egg."

I instinctively rubbed the sore spot on my own forehead. "Open invitation still stands."

His soft smile was a little shy, and color tinged his cheeks as he said, "I'll let you get to that shower."

Then he was gone.

Blowing out a breath that puffed out my cheeks, I shut the door—*and* locked it.

I hoped the already chaotic—and frankly confusing—morning wasn't an omen for what awaited us at the Tower.

As Soren drove us to the heart of Luma Proper, Geraldine Stone's words echoed in my head once more: *"All I know is that you can't trust what the Collective says. Don't turn yourself in, all right? You run, and you don't look back. If you go into a precinct, you won't come back out. I'm sure of it."*

And what of walking into the Collective's headquarters? I wanted to ask her. *What then?*

Caspian placed his hand on the seat between us, palm up. I glanced down at it, then up at him. I couldn't read the expression on his face. Something had shifted between us, but I still wasn't sure what. I didn't know if it was the experience of losing Welsh to the pures, or Caspian opening up to me about Marcus, or whatever the hell had happened this morning in my bed. Maybe all three.

Maybe he just needed a friend because he was as worried as I was about what awaited us at the Tower. It wasn't as if interacting with Collective sorcerers gave him the warm fuzzies, either.

I clasped his hand with mine, and he gave it a comforting squeeze. We stayed that way for the entire drive to Luma Proper.

I figured we'd have to park at Luma Central Station and then hoof it to the Tower, but I'd forgotten that not only did Collective sorcerers never deign to wander the streets among the unwashed masses on their way to and from work, but one of the Collective's former minions was riding shotgun.

My sword was stuffed into the pocket of the seat in front of me, while Tim—my sword's recently awakened, pretentious twin—was wedged into the other. I'd asked Tim if he wanted to stay at Caspian's house, but he'd bellowed *UNACCEPTABLE!* in my head without further explanation. Caspian planned to place a camouflaging spell on both swords so Tim, especially, could come with us and stay hidden until we decided to let Rhiannon know I now had two of them. Caspian seemed sure that Rhiannon would be more interested in how he and Ronan Doherty had awoken the sword than she would be in pilfering both swords for herself.

I remained skeptical.

Mom was convinced that the sample of the feral attractant tucked into the front pouch of my backpack would be of such high value to the Collective that they'd hardly bat an eye at an additional sentient sword.

I was skeptical about that, too.

Not only was I skeptical, I doubted that all our infractions would be forgiven simply because Mom had direct access to an elder vampire on the Vampire Council.

Not that I had any idea what the Council did.

My problem with all of this was that, before the discovery that Vincent Roch had "perfected" the attractant, Mom's only bargaining chip had been sharing with the Collective her extensive knowledge of vampires.

Why did sharing such information need to happen in person?

Caspian's concerns had become my own. I'd been so desperate to return to Luma that when Sorceress Rhiannon had offered a path back with a clean slate, I'd agreed after requesting only a few stipulations.

Now I worried Rhiannon had accepted my terms because this little meeting was less about antagonistic forces casting aside differences for a mutual cause and more about the Collective luring us back to Luma by lining our individual traps with enticing gifts tailor-made for each of us.

But now we had no choice. The trap had been sprung, and if we didn't show up for our appointment, Sorceress Rhiannon would send the cats after us. Cats who were already pissed at Caspian and me—mostly me—and were even madder now that our disappearing act to Lake Nacimiento had resulted in the cats getting torn new ones for letting us slip past them.

The secrets about how to get into the Collective Tower were locked behind a Soul NDA, so Mom and Soren eventually had to switch places. Mom had tried to tell Soren which turns to take, but the words got trapped in her throat. One of the NDA's apparent loopholes was that Mom could *show* us one of the Tower's many hidden entrances. It wasn't that useful of a loophole—just because someone knew the location of a door, that knowledge didn't matter much without a key.

Mom drove into an uptown neighborhood and stopped at a guard shack in front of a gated townhouse community. She didn't roll down her window. The guard who shuffled out of the shack was rail thin and couldn't have been a day under eighty. He sported a bushy gray mustache, which he wiped with a napkin as he approached the SUV. Though he was older, he was spry. I had no doubt he was a werecat.

His put-upon expression said he didn't appreciate having his lunch break interrupted. That, or he was used to identifying "residents" on sight and didn't have to leave his shack often.

He stood outside the tinted window, fists on his hips. His mustache wiggled like an agitated caterpillar as his mouth bunched up in irritation. Finally, he rapped three times on the window in quick succession.

Mom chuckled to herself and then hit the button to lower the window. As soon as Mom's face was fully in view, the crotchety expression on the man's face vanished.

"Camila!" he said, hand to his chest. "As I live and breathe! Didn't think I'd ever see you again." His mustache drooped. "I was real sorry to hear about Nelson, hon. He was a good man. One of the nicest people I've ever met. I know it's years too late, but I've been upset all this time that I never got a chance to say that to your face."

My throat tightened.

Caspian squeezed my hand.

"Thanks, Artie," Mom said, her voice catching.

In the space above the center console, I tracked Soren's hand as it reached toward my mom's shoulder. His hand hovered a few inches away, then his fingers curled into a fist and his hand retreated. Mom didn't notice.

To Artie, Mom said, "Clearly you haven't heard the news that my exile status has been lifted."

Artie's bushy eyebrows arched. "No one told me you'd been exiled in the first place, but there were rumors. The bounty mirror said you went AWOL. I never believed it." His next comment was muttered under his breath, but it sounded a lot like *"Those bastards."*

I decided I liked Artie, if only because he didn't know the details of what had caused Mom's exile yet was on her side by default.

"Well, now they've let me back in. Can you call ahead for me? I'm guessing my old password won't work anymore."

Artie tapped the side of his nose twice, pointed at my mom, and then jogged back into his kiosk. I peered out the passenger-side window as we waited. All the townhouses were chocolate brown, tan, or beige, with black accents. They stood in three-story blocks. All the windows that faced the "welcome" gate had their curtains or blinds drawn. It reminded me of Tercla, in a way. But while Tercla's front-facing residential buildings had housed dozing vampires who preferred the dark, these homes were filled with people sworn to secrecy. Hells, most of these places could be empty. They could be nothing more than props, like set pieces in a play, meant to keep outsiders from asking too many questions.

Artie got the necessary approval and hit a button to unlock the rolling gate. He and Mom waved to each other as she drove through. Artie's smile was both wistful and sad, reminding me all over again that Mom had lived a life I knew little about, even while we'd been in the same city.

A five-minute drive through the quiet streets of the townhouse complex brought the massive Tower ever closer. It stood so much taller than the surrounding buildings, it was almost laughable. The top ten floors or so seemed to grow steadily smaller as they inched toward the mast at the building's peak. The mast—reminiscent of a radio tower—and a good portion of the exterior walls of the upper floors were covered in intricate runes. The veil magic that poured from the mast was what did the heaviest lifting to keep Luma hidden. Losing the Tower would mean Luma would be laid bare for all to see.

The Tower, despite being flashy due to its height, wasn't flashy in design. It was made of limestone and glass, looking more like a generic corporate skyscraper from New York City than the head-quarters for werecats, sorcerers, and their human bounty hunters. It was not only the heart of the hub's veil magic, but the heart of Luma's government.

I resisted the urge to pull my sweaty hand out of Caspian's so I could wipe it on my pants. I really had no idea what to expect when we got in there.

Mom trusted Sorceress Rhiannon. I trusted Mom. That had to be enough.

When we finally reached one of the entrances at the Tower's massive base, made up of thick, tinted glass, Mom pulled up to yet another guard shack. It barred our entrance to the under-ground parking garage. The woman who stepped out was so obviously a werecat, my sixth sense pinged an alarm.

I pegged her as mid-forties. Her stockier build made me wonder if she was something like a bobcat in feline form. Her freckled nose was crooked, like it had been broken one too many times. "Park on Floor C," she said as she approached Mom's window and handed her a black plastic card that looked like a hotel room key. "This will get you past Floor 10. They're expecting you."

Instead of walking away, the woman craned her neck to look past Mom at me. While her expression was mostly neutral, the look said I better start praying to the Goddess if she and I ever ran into each other in a dark alley.

Without a word, she retreated to the guard shack. A moment later, the gate before us started to rattle open.

Mom whirled in her seat to look at me. "What the hell was *that* about?"

"What was what about?" Soren asked.

Though Caspian still held my hand, his grip hadn't changed to imply he'd read anything into the silent interaction, either.

I said, "Regardless of what the Collective is telling them, at least some of the guards think I'm guilty. The sword *did* kill four of them."

My sword pulled itself out of its seat pocket to tap its hilt on the seat cushion a few inches from mine and Caspian's hands. The sound was muted. Its blade flashed red in annoyance.

Though I couldn't see the pissed-off guard anymore, I still felt like I was being watched. "O'Neill watched his partner get murdered in my apartment. He thinks I can command the sword. He's not going to care what his bosses say. Shit, he doesn't even care what *I* say. There's gotta be a brotherhood among guards like there is with mundane police—maybe even more so because of the whole pack thing. I took down several of their own. I'm on a werecat shit list."

Mom pursed her lips. She silently told me she was not pleased with any of this.

I pointed a finger toward the sword hovering by my head, hoping the gesture clearly conveyed, I *wasn't the one who murdered them.*

The sword's blade glowed a chipper shade of blue.

Mom and I both rolled our eyes.

Gusting a sigh, Mom said, "I suppose I understand your reluctance even more, Caspian."

He squeezed my hand, but it almost seemed instinctive. "I do hope what knowledge I acquired about norvinic pairings and boranig chains is enough to prove Harlow isn't a puppet master of the cutlass. Surely they can't blame her for the actions of an autonomous entity."

"A lecture on chains even *you* think are boring isn't filling me with too much confidence, kid," Soren muttered from the front.

It said a lot about Caspian's anxiety level that he didn't even attempt to correct Soren.

Mom sat properly in her seat again, offered the guard a wave, and then drove through the now-open gate. The tires rolled over smooth concrete down the slight slope into the dark parking garage, like a tasty morsel sliding down the gullet of an awaiting monster.

CHAPTER FOUR

HARLOW

The elevator wall had buttons for floors A through E and the lobby. Mom might have a card that granted her access to higher levels, but this elevator wouldn't take us there.

The doors slid open to reveal a sleek, modern lobby. Mom and Soren stepped out first. Caspian started after them but stopped when he realized I hadn't moved. Though he'd let my hand go when my mom pulled the SUV into a parking spot on Floor C, he'd stuck by my side as we made the short walk to the elevator that brought us up through the bowels of the Collective's Tower and to the lobby that stretched out before me now. I resisted the urge to reach my hand out and silently ask him to take it again. My sixth-sense danger alarms were blaring with all the force of foghorns.

Caspian had thrown a camouflage spell over both swords before we'd even gotten out of the SUV. I could sense them hovering on either side of me now, even if I couldn't see them. There was no off-kilter hum to give my sword's location away. Either it wasn't as nervous here as it had been in Tercla, or being semi-invisible had given it a boost of confidence.

Tim, as usual, was eerily silent.

"Harlow?" Caspian asked, hand held out not to take mine, but to retrigger the doors' sensor so they trundled back open.

My backpack, though not filled with much, felt heavy on my shoulders. Mom figured the feral attractant was safest with me since I had stabby bodyguards. She'd given me the car keys to hold, too, as her only other personal effects were her wallet and phone. She'd left the wallet in the glovebox.

Keeping as little flotsam on your person as possible was a bounty hunter thing—probably a vampire hunter thing, too—and I figured old habits die hard.

I swallowed, blew out a slow breath, and forced my legs to move. *Get your shit together, Harlow. You were invited. They want Mom alive. We have information they need.*

I walked to the beat of my own mantra. *This isn't a trap, this isn't a trap, this isn't a trap …*

The lobby had rows of benches lining one wall. Only two people were sitting there, making the emptiness of the seating area seem even more stark. The ceiling stretching far above dwarfed them even further.

A civilian woman sat across from an officer who held a small piece of paper that I guessed was a photograph. Though the woman had tears streaming down her face, she was the one leading the conversation. She gestured wildly as she spoke, periodically jabbing a finger toward the photograph. They were too far away for me to make out what they were saying.

The six of us stopped in the space between the bench seats and a giant circular reception desk standing in the middle of the cavernous lobby. The dozen men and women behind the desk answered and redirected a seemingly endless string of phone calls. No matter which of the three entrances one took into this lobby, someone at that round desk would see them coming. While they deftly answered calls, at least two of them were always peering up to scan the area. Once we were spotted, several kept their gaze fixed on our little group.

Beyond the desk was a wall of shiny steel interrupted in only two places by open doorways. A burly draken guard stood watch at the mouth of each. I guessed banks of elevators awaited behind them.

"Maybe you should do the talking, Camila," Soren suggested when none of us moved.

Mom frowned. She'd been strutting around confidently enough, but it was clear she didn't love being here any more than I did.

Standing straighter and pulling back her shoulders, Mom broke from our group and headed for the desk. Two more receptionists glanced up. One guy's mouth dropped open, while the other dropped his phone, which smacked the desk's surface, making a couple of his coworkers flinch. Mom kept moving while we stayed rooted in place. Soon all twelve of the receptionists had abandoned their tasks and were on their feet, peering at us as if we were an exhibit at a zoo. If only they knew two cloaked swords were here, too—then they'd *really* be freaking out.

The continuous ringing of the unanswered phones sounded in the background.

I wasn't sure if I was comforted or unnerved that the attention wasn't all on my mom—a woman exiled for any number of purported crimes who had then been reinstated by the Collective.

Just as many of the receptionists eyed me and Caspian warily. Further proof, as Caspian suspected, that a company-wide memo hadn't gone out prior to our arrival. Even if Sorceress Rhiannon's colleagues had agreed to alter the veil's magic to let Mom back in and to clear our names—at least on paper—for our various crimes, they'd done little, if anything, to change public opinion about us.

Mom placed her hands on the raised counter of the desk. A pair of ladies took a cautious step back. Felix had told me that a good number of Mom's former colleagues thought my parents had wound up on the wrong side of the Bliss trade and that a deal had gone wrong with their supplier. They assumed Dad was killed in the crossfire and that Mom fled in fear of her transgressions affecting me.

Total bullshit.

In reality, a pack of ferals had shown up at the perfect time to ambush my parents and their team. It could have been a really horrible coincidence that the ferals had arrived when they had, since vamps and Bliss were inexorably linked. Or someone in the Collective was working with a hybrid and had called in a favor, and said hybrid had sent its attack dogs after my parents.

Either way, my dad was dead, my mom had been exiled, and I'd been left to pick up the pieces.

If anyone had a right to gawk right now, it was me. These people in their matching black polo shirts were the ones working for a corrupt organization—I at least had scruples.

I clenched my jaw as one woman stared me down, then leaned in to whisper to the lady next to her. If Mom had been slapped with labels like "deserter" and "turncoat," what labels had they given me? "Cop killer"?

A cop killer who knew more of the Collective's secrets than most because I'd been a bounty hunter in training until the day my dad was killed. They likely thought I was the pissed-off daughter of drug-running parents who held a grudge against police of all stripes in Luma. A pissed-off drop-out who teamed up with Caspian Blackthorn, who was a drop-out in his own right.

Caspian had been on the precipice of graduating when he'd fled the sorcery academy in the wake of his best friend's tragic death—a death Caspian blamed the sorcerers for. Caspian, like me, knew more secrets than most about the Collective because he'd been a Collective sorcerer in training.

With my rage and his access to dangerous illegal weapons, we'd apparently set out to tear down the government that had wronged us.

It all made for a great story.

He and I were painted as the villains—like Bonnie and Clyde. Problem was, *the Collective* was the villain ... with full control of all the paintbrushes.

I clenched my jaw even tighter.

Though I couldn't see the swords, I could still sense them nearby. My sword had a tendency to feed off my emotions, and I currently wanted to punch someone. I silently willed my sword to stay hidden. The sight of it was sure to be the final straw, sending the angry observers over that circular desk to try something stupid. Then we'd be on the run all over again, trying not to slip in the blood my sword spilled across the shiny tiles as we made our escape.

I tried to refocus. Mom was waving the black card in a receptionist's face, explaining that we'd been granted special clearance. The draken guards didn't need enhanced hearing to listen in; sound carried easily here. Their attention was angled Mom's way, but neither one moved or said a word.

I knew muscling our way past them to get to the elevators wasn't an option. My run-in with the draken goons at Haskins's shop was proof enough of that. If it hadn't been for Igor and Pratt being scared shitless of my diabolical sword, I wouldn't have made it out of the warehouse without being assaulted and/or in a body bag.

"Ma'am. *Ma'am*, you're not listening. I said I need to call ahead and make sure they're receiving walk-ins. It's company policy," the woman said, her voice increasing in both pitch and condescension with each subsequent sentence. "Ma'am. Please have a seat."

"Enough with the ma'am shit, *Darlene*," Mom snapped. "You act as if I haven't known you for years."

One of Darlene's eyes twitched.

A few of the receptionists broke off at once to attend to the phones, whose incessant ringing had ratcheted up the tension even more. While keeping her eyes fixed on Mom, Darlene picked up the receiver of an old-school phone and pressed it to her ear.

Soren angled himself toward my ear. "I'm not sure if I'm more worried about your sword or your mom going nuclear."

A faint hum sounded above me. That hum could have meant anything, so I ignored it, lest I encourage the thing by accident. At least I knew the semi-invisible menace hadn't zipped off on its own to wreak havoc.

AWAITING INSTRUCTIONS, Tim said in my head. He almost sounded … excited. Ugh. If this thing was fueled by blood lust too, things could go sideways very quickly.

My sixth sense pinged anew, and I stood ramrod straight, head cocked.

"What?" Caspian asked, but a moment later, he either heard or felt it, too. "Oh …"

Soren glanced from me to Caspian and back again. "Oh? What do you mean by *oh*?"

I physically felt it then. I had a brief flash of memory of my apartment complex being raided and the destruction that had come afterward. There was a faint rumbling beneath my feet.

Werecats, and a lot of them, were on their way.

Caspian deftly moved in front of me, as if he intended to use himself as a meat shield. His hands and arms were already in motion, constructing a rune array. Soren cursed and stumbled back a step to stand beside me. I still didn't know much about runes or how to read them, but I could recognize Caspian's wind spell on sight. This was something else. Perhaps this one would conjure fire—the same array he'd wanted to use to nuke Sweeney … and possibly the entire Washingtonian motel we'd been holed up in.

By the time the glowing, translucent disc of magic was projected in front of Caspian like a shield, six werecats had barreled past one of the draken guards and charged into the lobby. A blink later, and my little group had half a dozen snarling cats squaring off against it. They formed a V, with the lead cat directly in front of Caspian.

I instantly recognized the cat: a giant orange-and-black tiger with a scar running across his left eye. It was a wound my sword had inflicted during the scuffle in my apartment what felt like centuries ago. The tiger's fur vibrated, like ripples across a pond. The vibration wasn't from purring, though, I knew that much.

There was a mere six feet separating my group from the cats. In my peripheral vision, I could see Mom had gone stock still. My sword was humming so loudly above me, I figured it was only a matter of time before its quaking rage knocked its camouflage glamour free.

AWAITING INSTRUCTIONS. AWAITING INSTRUCTIONS. AWAITING INSTRUCTIONS, Tim the sword said on a slow, creepy loop, like a homicidal AI system.

While I had no doubt Caspian could loose his array and fry the pack of werecats before they could reach us in one powerful bound, I knew the act would exhaust him. He wouldn't be able to get another array up and ready by the time the next wave of cats showed up. They could already be on their way. Not to mention that if the tiger died in the encounter, it would instantly make the guy a martyr, ensuring all his feline cronies would be even more desperate to take me out.

Five long seconds ticked by before the lead werecat seamlessly morphed from cat to man.

"Nice of you to stop by *my* place this time," the tiger, O'Neill, said to me.

I'd once dubbed him Good Cop. Any hint of his cordial attitude from our first interaction was gone. His milky-white eye only made him look ten times more pissed off.

"The Collective has business with your mother, not you, Harlow," O'Neill said. "Why don't you and I air our grievances outside?"

I didn't like to think of myself as a coward, but I'd be lying if I said I didn't angle closer to Caspian. "Pass!"

I felt a brief wash of heat from above, and I groaned internally. Seconds later, my sword, fully visible, had its razor-sharp tip pointed toward O'Neill's chest. It hovered above Caspian's head, but the distance between itself and O'Neill wouldn't matter if my sword decided to go in for the kill.

AWAITING. INSTRUCTIONS, Tim said with a hint of frustration.

O'Neill's snarl was all feline. "I knew you were here somewhere, sword. I figured once your master was threatened, you'd show yourself. Always ready to do her bidding, eh?"

The blade blazed red. I figured it was more offended by the "master" comment than anything else. I wondered if O'Neill would be more or less horrified by the reality that the sword was running its own show, only listening to me out of what I assumed was respect.

I opened my mouth to voice some version of "Hey, what are you doing antagonizing the murder sword, stupid?" to O'Neill when Caspian angled his head toward me and whispered, "Attacks are prohibited on Collective grounds. If someone starts a fight, anyone else is allowed to finish it. Spilling blood could bring the wrath of every bounty hunter, werecat, and sorcerer down on said someone's head."

So O'Neill *wanted* the sword to strike first. Goading it into action might risk his own life, but it would mean the entire werecat squad who held a grudge against me and my sword could come after us.

"Stand down, sword," I snapped. "He's not worth it."

The blade began to cool.

"You *are* her little bitch," O'Neill told the sword, chuckling.

O'Neill's goons, still in cat form, laughed. It was some unsettling combination of hissing and growling.

A flash of red.

"*Sword*," I said from behind Caspian.

AWAITING MISSION PROTOCOLS!

You stand down, too, Tim!

REGRETTABLE.

My sword's blade didn't cool. In fact, it only grew brighter. O'Neill grinned. Muscles bunched and rippled under the sleek fur of the pumas and panthers waiting behind him. Caspian's rune array pulsed a brilliant gold, as if he'd just injected it with a shot of caffeine. Mom took a few slow steps toward us. Soren adjusted his posture beside me, getting into a wider stance and holding up his fists as if he planned to punch his way out of this mess.

The tension was stoked further as more of the cats shifted into human form. Some turned toward my mom, calling her out for crimes she hadn't committed. My sword fed off our energy, issuing that odd hum again. I kept yelling at it to stop, to not give in—which was made even more difficult by my needing to mentally scream at Tim to cool his proverbial jets, too—but O'Neill wouldn't let up.

We needed to get out of here.

O'Neill stopped his tirade abruptly and turned to the woman nearest him. She'd been a puma when she first arrived, and now she was a tan-skinned woman with her jet-black hair pulled into a severe ponytail. She was only five foot five at most, but she was ripped. Her glare told me she was desperate for an excuse to tear my face off. Worse still, the more I stared at her, the more familiar she became. Knowing my luck, this was Harrison's—aka Bad Cop's—younger sister, hell-bent on revenge.

"Come what may?" O'Neill asked.

The woman nodded, then jerked her head side to side to crack her neck. I would have laughed at the theatrics if I wasn't so sure she was planning to disembowel me. "Come what may," she agreed.

O'Neill swung his mismatched gaze back toward us, peering at me over Caspian's shoulder. He grinned. His canines elongated before my eyes. "Fuck the rules."

Several things happened at once: O'Neill shifted into a tiger and lunged at us; my sword, redder than a cherry, harpooned down toward O'Neill; and Caspian flung his rune array. I slammed my eyes closed and geared myself up to accept death's sweet embrace.

I *tried* to close my eyes, anyway. They got stuck at half-mast. In fact, everything around me had frozen. Caspian's rune circle had broken apart, like a smashed ceramic dish—thousands of tiny pieces scattering. O'Neill had managed to launch through it as it broke, his gleaming canines mere inches from Caspian's jugular. My sword's tip hovered an inch from O'Neill's neck. Mom was in mid-sprint, stuck with her arms pumping and one foot off the floor. I couldn't turn my head to see Soren. I had no idea if Tim still wore his camouflage.

I was able to move my eyeballs in my skull, though, and willed them to the right. A woman strode toward us, sidestepping frozen humans, draken, and werecats as if they were props in a maze.

Everything about the woman was unremarkable, save for her self-assuredness. She couldn't have been taller than five feet. She didn't stroll into the lobby with a cape flapping behind her or every step punctuated by the click of her stiletto heels. In fact, there was a persistent slight squeak as the rubber soles of her tennis shoes made contact with the polished tile floor.

Her red hair was more of a rusty brown, and it hung limply around her shoulders. It was kept out of her face by a plastic headband that would probably look better on a prepubescent girl. Her mustard-colored top was a bit too big for her thin frame, and I guessed the waist of her washed-out jeans sat well above her belly button. She looked like a mousy librarian who'd needed to fish today's clothes out of her hamper. And yet she'd cast a spell on the lobby that froze two dozen people and two sentient swords in their tracks.

Her voice, unlike her appearance, was crisp and commanding. "For the new arrivals, don't be too alarmed about the state you're in. Time isn't *completely* stopped; your bodies are all still moving, just so slowly, you can't tell. I, however, can move about my frozen playground at whatever speed I wish. This particular spell doesn't affect the speed of your thoughts; I wanted you all to be aware of what's going on. If I wanted to flit about frozen time without you knowing—well, you wouldn't know, would you?"

Creepy.

She turned her focus on the tiger. "This little crusade of yours has gotten out of hand, O'Neill. You and your lackeys attacked first. You're all suspended without pay for a month and will be enrolled in anger management and community service programs, effective immediately. Failure to attend every session will result in termination."

I wondered if she meant termination of his job or something more permanent.

The woman had made her way to O'Neill's side and had her head cocked curiously beside his outstretched maw. "Enough innocent civilians have had their lives upended by your actions. One would have thought multiple internal affairs investigations would have been enough to encourage you to course-correct. Clearly, we misjudged you." Her dull green eyes assessed the frozen cat. "If you can't control yourself in your workplace where such actions are strictly prohibited, I must admit I worry all these allegations against you are true. You really have gone rogue, haven't you?"

I wondered why she was just suspending the guy and not outright firing him. If anything, piling on additional rules would only make him act more rashly when he didn't have a job to occupy his time.

I felt terrible that my sword had killed O'Neill's partner in its attempt to keep us both safe, and I didn't blame the guy in the slightest for hating the ground I walked on, but something else must have happened between then and now. He'd gone from Good Cop to Unhinged Cop in a matter of months.

I supposed, though, that he and Bad Cop could have been a couple. Perhaps my sword had gutted the love of his life.

This was why my sword and I needed ground rules on homicide! Killing people willy-nilly tended to have consequences.

NOT IF ALL WITNESSES ARE ELIMINATED.

I internally flinched at the voice in my head, wondering just how many of my thoughts Tim could listen in on at any given time, especially when I wasn't even touching the damn thing. *Not now, Tim!*

The woman said, "If any of you fail to meet your requirements for the programs, your Soul NDA will be torn free, and you'll be required to undergo a memory leaching. This will be followed by permanent exile from the entire hub system."

I winced. That was my answer: She wasn't firing him and his minions because she was giving them the option to rehabilitate themselves—as the alternative was miles worse.

Sorceress Rhiannon had told me that Felix *could* get a procedure to remove his Soul NDA, but the process was "unpleasant," assuming the person survived in the first place. I wondered how far back one's memory was "leached." Then, in O'Neill's case, he'd be booted into the mundane world—a mundane world he probably knew nothing about. It would be like dropping off an amnesiac teenager in a foreign country and calling out "Good luck!" before peeling away.

Death was probably better.

She turned toward Caspian then, her arms tucked behind her back. She scrutinized the frozen shards of his rune array as if they were part of an art installation.

She tsked. "It's a shame you didn't finish your studies, Blackthorn. Your work is exceptional. But you're clearly still as brash now as you were then. Just like your aeorci who keeps harassing my courier birds." A small smile graced her otherwise bland face.

I figured then that this woman was Sorceress Rhiannon herself. There *had* been something familiar about her voice, but the flat tone she'd used on the phone with us was not the confident one she employed now.

Suddenly, the woman started an incantation, her arms and

hands flitting about with effortless grace. In a matter of a minute, she'd moved the array out of O'Neill's path and stitched it back together. The array hung there in its full, golden glory for only a moment before it collapsed in on itself and winked out.

In quick succession, she conjured up rune arrays of her own, then launched the first one at O'Neill. I recognized them instantly. Wind spells—Caspian's element of choice. She flung them like a magician flicking playing cards.

They traveled slowly through frozen time, giving her the chance to get the arrays in position before she got out of the way and then turned time back on. Our squared-off group was launched backward as if a bomb had been detonated between Caspian and O'Neill. Caspian, Soren, the swords, and I were knocked toward the row of bench seats, while Mom and the were-cats were tossed toward the reception desk.

It wasn't lost on me that the gust that slammed into my own chest was more of a hard shove that resulted in me landing ass-first on a cushy bench seat, while O'Neill's thick feline skull cracked loudly on the side of the massive desk. He'd traveled a good twenty feet, while I'd gone less than five.

I hastily swung my backpack off one shoulder and plopped it in my lap. I tentatively eased open the front pouch. Vaughn had warned us that spilled attractant "smells like pungent garbage inside in a floral-scented trash bag that's been left out to bake in the heart of summer." Since I wasn't currently gagging on the stench, that was a significant clue that the vials of feral attractant had survived the encounter, but I needed to be sure.

I heaved a relieved sigh when I *didn't* see liquid seeping out of the carrying case Roch had given us.

Mom started to run over to check on us, but when she saw what I was doing, she came up short. "Safe?"

"Safe," I said.

Mom's expression hardened and she rounded on the sorceress. "Rhiannon—*a word?*"

She didn't wait for Rhiannon to reply; she grabbed the

sorceress by the elbow and hauled her away from the group at large. I didn't think Mom should be doing anything to piss the lady off, but Rhiannon allowed the manhandling with little fuss.

A pained groan pulled my attention down and toward the wall of tinted windows that served as a backdrop to the seating area. Caspian had managed not to brain himself on any of the metal legs of the benches, but he hadn't been gifted with as soft a landing as I had. He groaned again as he pushed himself to his feet. The air spell had caused him to belly-flop onto the tile. He was lucky he hadn't cracked his chin on the floor and bitten off his tongue.

I scanned the immediate area, searching for the swords. A few bench seats down, my sword was stuck in one of the cushions. A gash in the leather preceded its location, like a flying saucer that had just crash-landed on earth. The sword could have easily pulled itself free, but instead it went molten and melted its way out. My nose wrinkled at the stench of burned leather and plastic.

I quickly scanned the area for Tim.

"Camouflage is back up on him," Caspian said softly. "He's more compliant, so the chances of him breaking the glamour are slimmer. I figure there's no point shielding the cutlass now."

My sword blazed red in my periphery, offended yet again.

Soren lay flat on his back between bench seats. His chest and shoulders quaked, a hand over his mouth. I was pretty sure he was silently cackling. I had no idea why. Maybe the guy had finally snapped.

I wondered where the civilian and the cop who had been chatting in the lobby had disappeared to. They'd probably done the smart thing and fled the moment the hotheaded werecats charged in.

My gaze snagged on the cats in question, who were still woozily trying to stand up. A few shifted back into their human forms, checking for bruises and broken bones. The puma was still out cold from the look of it.

I turned on the bench seat to glance behind me to where Mom

and Rhiannon spoke. Well, Mom spoke—*whisper-yelled*—while Rhiannon listened quietly, arms crossed. Rhiannon appeared nonplussed by my mom's tirade. Possibly bored. That little, mousy, librarian-looking woman was making my sixth sense go haywire.

I'd heard Caspian be lauded as uniquely talented by at least two sorcerers now—people who didn't offer compliments often, backhanded or otherwise. I'd seen him use his magic enough to know firsthand that, while the magic unleashed from his arrays was powerful, it wasn't quick.

Even to a magic-less human like me, it was clear how much more skilled Rhiannon was. She was quick, she had exceptional control over her magic, and despite freezing us all for what had to be a minimum of ten minutes, she barely looked winded.

Were all the ruling sorcerers this powerful? I was no fan of the Collective, but it was also no wonder sorcerers above all other fae had risen to the top of the food chain. I hadn't even known time manipulation was a thing.

By the time Mom had stalked away from Rhiannon, who watched impassively as she left, O'Neill had regained his bearings. Still in cat form, he trained his one good eye on me. From across the lobby, he bared his canines and hissed. Getting hissed at by a house cat could be alarming and sometimes comical. Getting hissed at by an eight-hundred-pound tiger was not recommended.

"Your first class begins in a few hours, guards!" Rhiannon called. "I suggest you get cleaned up. Business casual is required. It shows you're taking this seriously."

A round of grumbles—both human and feline—rose from the cluster of werecats, but none of them protested. The puma, back in her yoked-out human body, started a slow shuffle toward the elevators with the aid of a guy who kept his arm wrapped around her waist. The whole group filed out—save for O'Neill.

My sword floated over to hover by my shoulder. It was the

sword's way of letting me know it was there if I needed it. To O'Neill, it probably looked like a threat.

"Now, O'Neill!" Rhiannon snapped.

With a final, silent promise to kill me horrifically at a later date, O'Neill turned and loped away, his long, striped tail flicking behind him like a whip.

"The cats are going to be a problem later, aren't they?" Caspian asked as he plopped down next to me. A bruise had begun to bloom on his cheek. Maybe his skull had made contact with the floor after all.

My sword answered for me, dropping to tap once on the tile.

CHAPTER FIVE

FELIX

One Week Ago

Felix stared across the table at his newest informant. She hadn't stopped talking in nearly twenty minutes. He'd talked to her enough times by now to know interrupting her was a fool's errand. He honestly didn't even know what she was talking about. He'd listen for a bit, zone out, then zone back in, only to find the topic had shifted so abruptly he couldn't have interrupted with anything other than "huh?" even if he'd actually wanted the answer. Which he didn't. He wasn't stupid enough to admit he hadn't been listening, as he'd only get an earful about how "no one respected her," so it "was no surprise he didn't, either."

He zoned back in now and found her crouched behind her soup bowl, arms and hands mimicking holding a rifle. Or maybe it was a machine gun. She popped up and positioned her "gun" on the lip of her bowl before offering a series of *rat-tat-rat* sound effects. She ducked incoming fire, screamed "You'll never catch me, coppers!" and ducked out of sight again.

Felix slapped himself in the forehead. "Aster! What in the *world* does this have to do with the disappearance of your friend's daughter?"

Aster's tiny face reappeared. Her "bowl" was actually a shot glass filled with several spoonfuls of the house stew. Felix thought the stuff tasted like watered-down motor oil—and that was probably an insult to motor oil—but Aster seemed to like this place. Whether that was because it had a menu that catered to pixies or because she actually liked the taste of the horrible food, he couldn't say.

Though the shot glass was indeed a very small receptacle for soup, the thing still looked big enough to serve as a hot tub for Aster. She rested an elbow on the lip of the shot glass and peered in for a moment before plucking out a pea. She took a bite out of it as he might an apple. She wiped her forearm across her mouth.

"Normally I'd razz you for not listening to me like usual," Aster said. "But my friend's kid ain't missing."

Felix glowered. "Why the hell am I here then?"

She stuffed the rest of the pea in her mouth and talked with her mouth full. "I knew you'd show if I gave you some sob story. Then I just had to distract you for a while."

Felix's heart rate ticked up. He didn't think Aster was the type to sell him out for money—or whatever it was pixies valued.

There *was* a certain type of acorn they were rumored to covet so badly, they'd knife their own mother for them. She *was* a pixie though, and they were nothing if not opportunistic, so he couldn't say she *wouldn't* purposely ruin his day—month, *year*—if a tempting-enough scheme presented itself.

He was so busy glaring at the pixie, who was chewing her way down a single noodle that was seemingly longer than she was tall, that he didn't realize someone had approached their table until a guy slid into the booth behind Aster's spot on the table.

To be fair, the diner they were in was loud and bustling, and the newly arrived man had been as silent as a cat. He was a good-looking white guy with a head of tousled curly hair Felix assumed required more time and gel than he'd ever have the patience for. Not to mention genetics guaranteed "tousled locks" wasn't even a possibility for him. When Felix grew his hair out, he ended up with a fro, and, unfortunately, his line of work made long hair a liability. A few years ago, he'd had half a head of hair burned right off his scalp thanks to a teenage fire elemental who'd had a bounty on his head for repeat arson attempts. A colleague had doused Felix with the only thing he had with him—cold coffee. Felix had kept his hair closely shaved ever since.

As a mundane who lived in a place like Luma and worked for sorcerers, and whose colleagues could shift from human to giant cat, Felix had gotten used to interacting with the magic-touched. He knew he wasn't a bad-looking guy, but it was easy to feel subpar when in the presence of otherworldly attractive fae. The guy in front of him was one of those. The kind Felix's female colleagues would be struck dumb over as this fae walked by, words trailing off mid-sentence. Felix knew that, in a lot of cases, it was the magic wafting off fae like pheromones that caused the reaction. But it still had taken a while for the constant sting of rejection to fade when fae were around.

The day a bounty had been called in for an incubus—who'd been running an illegal brothel, like an utter cliché—had left most of the human men on the force feeling like slobs.

As for Felix, he'd stopped feeling jealous of the too-pretty ones a while back. Now he was just leery. The too-pretty ones were trouble. The too-pretty ones filled countless locked, magic-suppressing cells in the Tower, often hauled in by werecats because, in addition to being too attractive for anyone's good, the beautiful fae were also too magically powerful for human bounty hunters like him to handle.

Being a human in Luma—in any hub—was an all-around humbling, if not debilitating, experience.

Felix sat back against the booth seat, arms crossed as he took in the perfect curl lying against the guy's pale forehead, the dimple in one cheek as he smiled warmly at Felix, and the folded hands on the table. Each of his thumbs sported a plain gold ring. The trench coat was odd, though. It wasn't sweltering outside, but it certainly wasn't cool, either. Even more alarming than the too-pretty face and the weird attire was the fact that something about him was familiar. It made no sense whatsoever that his ... aura or soul or countenance or *whatever* ... seemed familiar, even though his face didn't, but this was Luma, and Felix knew to trust his gut.

Aster had wandered to the middle of the table, and with her head tipped all the way back, she looked from Felix to the mystery man and back again. She propped her fists on her hips. "You two boys going to say something or just stare at each other all day? I gotta start testing out that new buttercream recipe, Welshy, so if my work here is done ..."

The guy's overly friendly smile slipped off his too-pretty face as he angled his now-annoyed gaze at Aster. "What did I tell you about the nicknames?"

Aster zipped into the air to be at eye level with him. "Since when do I care about you and your dumb requests?"

"Since the day I threatened to rip your wings off."

Aster blew a raspberry at that and dismissively waved a tiny hand. "You're not as awful as you want everyone to think, Welshy."

"Welshy" slipped a hand onto his coat and patted an inside pocket—an inside pocket that crinkled in response.

Aster's wings stopped fluttering for half a second, causing her to plummet an inch toward the table before they resumed their frantic beating. "Is that the cinnamon icing recipe? Did you figure it out?" She did a one-eighty to face Felix. "My recipe was too spicy. Not hot-spicy but spice-spicy. Cinnamon goes a long way, especially for pixies."

Felix didn't have the first clue what she was going on about, but that was par for the course with Aster. It was like she was hopped up on caffeine 24/7.

She whirled back to "Welshy," who Felix had just realized must be the one and only Zander Welsh. He knew *of* the witch but had never met him. Welsh and Caspian were a big part of the reason Harlow hadn't been caught by the Collective in the weeks after she'd stolen the dragon sword and was rumored to have gone on a murderous rampage. The rational part of Felix was grateful Welsh had kept Harlow safe. Irrationally, his long-dormant jealousies were stirring to life. His chances of reconciling with Harlow were slim to none anyway, but with friends like this guy, Felix knew he didn't stand a cold chance in *any* of the hells.

And if Felix were honest with himself, he wasn't sure he wanted to reconcile with Harlow. Not romantically, anyway. He knew they'd both moved on in that regard, but she'd always be important to him, even if he wasn't sure what shape he wanted his relationship with her to take.

Felix zoned back into the conversation to find Welsh's composure had dissolved, and he was now whispering at Aster about disrespect, a finger jabbing toward her little face, while she was apparently so angry, her furiously beating wings pulsed red.

"What am I doing here, *Zander*?" Felix asked loudly enough to startle them both out of their argument.

"Ah!" Aster said cheerfully, wings back to their usual translucence, as she turned to smile at him. "Finally figured out who he is, eh?" She dropped to the table so she could root around in her no doubt cold stew, and plucked out a hunk of what Felix assumed was meat, but given its lumpy texture and unsettling color, he wasn't sure. She ripped off a piece with her teeth. "Sorry about lying to you, but Welshy forced me into it." After ripping off another piece, and with her mouth full of stringy mystery meat, she added, "He twisted my arm."

"Uh-huh," Felix said flatly, eyeing her incredibly tiny limbs for a moment before shifting his attention to Welsh, an eyebrow raised in question.

"Are you still investigating Bliss-related cases in your free time?"

Felix blinked, temporarily dumbfounded. "Uhh … yeah. How do you—"

Welsh waved a dismissive hand. "Not important. Are you also still investigating how Bliss is getting trafficked into hubs?"

Felix struggled to understand why Welsh would set up a meeting to discuss this. Did Harlow have something to do with it?

After a few long, silent seconds, Welsh snapped his fingers in front of Felix's face, shocking him out of his confusion. He resisted the urge to slap the hand away. "You awake, kid? I asked you a question."

"*Kid*?" Felix asked, knowing that was the least important question he could have asked, but this guy was sort of an ass. "You can't be much older than I am."

"Sure about that?"

For the span of three seconds, Welsh's too-pretty face shifted to that of a heavily wrinkled man in his nineties, at a minimum. The whites of his eyes held faint signs of jaundice, while one iris was clouded over with a cataract.

That face, Felix knew.

Felix blinked and the person staring back at him was youthful again.

Felix had seen the old guy countless times over the years. In the grocery store near his parents' place, complaining to a worker about how all the apples were bruised or about the spilled juice in aisle two being a hazard. Shuffling down the sidewalk on his morning walk on the handful of mornings Felix had to go in to work before seven. Waiting at a bus stop, where the old man chatted amiably with fellow passengers. The guy was so old—ancient, really—that Felix recognized him every time he saw him. He'd even made bets with his parents about how ancient Old George, a fixture in their neighborhood, truly was. If Felix had learned that Old George had been 110 at the time of the Glitch, and some magical anomaly had turned him immortal, but the catch was that he was going to be 110 forever, Felix wouldn't have been surprised. Felix's dad called Felix on a weekly basis to inform him that Old George's obituary still hadn't made an appearance in the pages of the *Luma Times*, thereby keeping the man's age a secret for at least another day.

How could Welsh *also* be Old George? Was Old George one of his many personas, like a person's collection of winter coats, or the real him? Felix wondered if that familiarity he'd sensed earlier was due to sensing Old George beneath the surface or if it was because Felix had seen, talked to, and interacted with Welsh unknowingly dozens of times before this while he wore countless other faces. How many other people in Luma were like Welsh, able to change their entire appearance on a whim? Felix knew he could trust his gut, but apparently he couldn't trust his eyes.

A small, mischievous smile graced Welsh's too-pretty face, as if he knew Felix was suffering from an existential crisis and found it delightful.

Felix cleared his throat, then glanced around the bustling diner. Cooks and waiters shouted orders and table numbers, a phone on the wall rang every few minutes, and the din of customers' voices was loud enough to almost drown out the constant sizzle of baskets of fries, onion rings, and breaded meats being dunked into popping vats of oil.

No one was paying Felix and his companions any mind. Which was saying a lot when one such a companion was a pixie. Aster had managed to purloin the straw from Felix's drink, had snipped a section off the end through unknown means, and was now guzzling the oil-slick broth out of her shot glass of stew as if it were a milkshake.

Normally, Felix liked meeting informants or clients here *because* it was so noisy, but it was currently proving to be more of a distraction than usual. He tried to remember what Welsh had asked him.

Then, all at once, the boisterous din of the place died down to a muted warble. It was as if they sat beneath an overturned glass.

"Sound-dampening spell," Welsh said, gesturing to one of the rings on his thumbs. Welsh was a witch, but even he needed talismans to utilize certain magics he wasn't otherwise able to wield. "No one can hear us. Will that make you less twitchy? You're worse than a long-tailed cat in a room full of rocking chairs."

Aster spluttered a laugh. "You *must* be older than dirt if you trot out nonsense like that." She snickered, muttering, "*Room full of rocking chairs ...*" to herself.

"Yes, I'm still investigating Bliss," Felix finally said, unwilling to admit that the dampened noise had helped considerably.

Welsh rested his forearms on the lip of the table and leaned forward a fraction. "Have the vamps been showing an interest in fae that goes beyond aesthetics? It's been established that the vamps want beautiful fae to use them as a lure for the humans the vamps want to catch. But are vamps targeting fae for any other reason?"

Felix resisted the urge to ask why Welsh was asking Felix, of all people, about this. Felix was nothing more than a low-tier mundane bounty hunter with an unhealthy obsession. And why had Welsh gone through all the trouble to use Aster as a liaison instead of just coming to him directly?

Yet, as defensive as Felix felt about Welsh's connection to Harlow, *and* about being ambushed, he was honestly glad someone wanted to talk about this at all. His colleagues—both the human ones and the werecats—were more concerned with their current workloads. They didn't have time for conspiracy theories.

Frankly, Felix didn't, either. But that's what caffeine and late nights were for.

Much of this particular theory required sleuthing and research that fell outside his assigned cases, meaning a good chunk of it should also fall outside his Soul NDA. But he wouldn't know that until his tongue locked up and his brain fritzed out on him. He thought of it like a wrong answer given during a game show. *Enhh! Try again.*

Felix said, "Across the board, elfin teens are trafficked the most. For a long time, we assumed the preference reflected what mundanes showed the most affinity for—that trial and error with different fae types had led the vamps to use the kind of fae that worked best as a lure.

"We know now that elves in particular were chosen because of the Shades. They fed them the lie that Lachlan Shade was their elfin savior, and he was coming back to offer a path home to fae in general and elves in particular. Shade needed kids he could manipulate easily, and I guess he figured they'd be most likely to listen to their own kind."

Welsh nodded. "Did Harlow tell you about her run-in with Domino the orc?"

Felix sighed. Harlow *hadn't* told him, but his VHoA contact in Washington, Fiona—who Felix had gotten Harlow into contact with in the first place—had filled Felix in. "I heard about it secondhand, but I'm sure I only got a small portion of the story."

"Well, one of Domino's minions was an elf, and she'd crafted a localized veil to shield them from Harlow and Cas until they were ready to attack," Welsh said, rightly guessing Felix hadn't heard *that* part. "That would suggest elves can not only tear holes in veils—they can *create* veils. Now, maybe the elf had a powerful talisman." He gestured to one of his rings again. "But it's a worrying development, regardless—either elves wield veil magic as easily as sorcerers do, or there's someone giving a very specific power to people who probably shouldn't have it. It's not up to me to decide who *should* have that power, but I'd rather not live in a world where any rando with a grudge can buy an item capable of destroying the secrecy of the hub system."

Felix frowned. Welsh had a point.

"I figure this all means elves are being selected for multiple reasons," Welsh said. "Their beauty for trafficking and their magical stores so Lachlan could siphon enough juice to power the portal back here, but also because of their specific magical ability—in this case, veil magic. I'm wondering if, when it comes to the second and third reasons, the Shades are elitist and are only selecting elves, or if specific magical abilities of other fae also interest them. I include hybrid vampires as members of the Shades, by the way." He idly scratched at his neck.

There was something suddenly a bit off with the guy, but Felix couldn't put his finger on what. Welsh didn't seem nervous exactly, but he wasn't totally composed, either. It almost seemed as if this line of questioning held a personal component for Welsh, rather than him just seeking information.

"There have been a few anecdotal stories about disappeared fae who we believe were originally trafficked and were later found dead. The deaths were ... unusual, all things considered, and were suspected to have been at the hands of hybrids," Felix said slowly, searching Welsh's once again stoic expression for any sign that Felix's words triggered a reaction. "For whatever reason, it's mostly been witches, usually elementals. They all suffered from what looked like infected vamp bites. The victim's skin is almost translucent, regardless of race, and their veins were black. Death by blood poisoning sounds like a horrible way to go."

"How many cases?" Welsh asked.

Felix shrugged. "I've got web alerts set up for any number of keywords related to Bliss, death by vampire, infections, kidnapping, disappearances, stuff like that. I've got a buddy in VHoA checking for me, too. I'm sure I've missed some, but my best guess is fifteen. That's nationwide, though. It's a big enough number to make it sound like the start of a pattern but not big enough to look like an epidemic or anything. Most of the cases cropped up in the last year."

Welsh stared into the middle distance for a few long seconds, mulling that over.

Felix was almost positive the guy was asking for personal reasons. But was it for himself or someone else?

"Is there any evidence that those fifteen individuals had been targeted in any way—say, for their unique abilities—or were the poor bastards just in the wrong place at the wrong time?" Welsh asked.

Felix's gaze flicked to Welsh's neck, where the witch had been scratching. Had he been bitten?

"It's an interesting question," Felix said, recalling offhand that the circumstances of the deaths varied quite a bit. It wasn't as if they'd all been found in squalid vamp nests. A couple of them had been found in their own beds, black blood leaking from every orifice. "I can look into it for you. I have access to most of the vamp cases."

Welsh nodded tightly. "I have something to offer you in exchange."

Felix's brows hiked.

"Do you know who Marisol Ortiz is?"

Felix honestly wasn't sure if the guy was trolling him. Felix had eaten lunch with Marisol every day at "their spot" for nearly a week. He'd finally gotten up the courage to kiss her two nights ago, though he hadn't talked to her since then. He wasn't sure why.

Casually, Felix said, "Sure. The de facto leader of Luma's VHoA chapter."

"I work ... *unofficially* for her," Welsh said, somehow making "unofficially" sound ominous as hells—like he was her hired hitman. "My day job, for lack of a better term, is to make people disappear."

Oh shit, what if he actually is *a hitman?*

"Disappear on paper," Welsh clarified. "New identity, get

them out of the hub and set up somewhere else, that kind of thing. People come to me a lot about missing kids, mostly wanting to know if I helped their rugrat skip town. That's how I got clued in to the missing fae problem in the first place. I started looking into it because I wasn't sure if someone was encroaching on my territory, so to speak.

"Before I ever met Harlow, I started to wonder if fae teens were being trafficked out of the city. The Ghost Lily hadn't been on my radar, but a bar on the edge of the Necropolis—the Golden Muskrat—was. I didn't suspect the owners of the bar specifically, just that they didn't know, or care, about the shady shit that happens there. They don't card minors. It's as good a place as any to meet with someone underage because no one will cause a fuss as long as you buy something.

"A couple of years ago, I was there scoping the place out and locked onto a middle-aged sweaty guy with a terrible comb-over. He was acting squirrelly as hells. Fidgety. Constantly dabbing his sopping forehead with a napkin. He couldn't have looked more nervous if he tried.

"After about ten minutes, a very young, very pretty fae girl awkwardly approached his table. They talked for all of thirty seconds. She never sat down. They left together. Now, anything could have been going on there—"

"But it was weird enough that you followed them anyway," Felix interrupted.

Welsh nodded. "He opened the passenger door for her, and when he closed it, he pulled a travel talisman out of his pocket and slapped it to her door. I trailed them to one of the designated exits in the Indie—one of the roads for transport vehicles. That alone was suspicious enough, but before the car passed out of the veil, a pair of ferals ran *in*. I damn near shit a brick. That was the first time I'd ever seen a feral. I didn't even know what they were.

"The ferals jumped on Sweaty's car, then off, then pranced around it—like dogs excited that their owner just got home. They might have been *acting* like harmless pets, but they still looked like something that had crawled out of the underworld. They ran back out through the veil, and the car followed. I might have kept trailing Sweaty had it not been for the ferals. Fear overrode curiosity for once."

"Was the sweaty guy a mundane?" Felix asked.

"Yep," Welsh said. "I'm also fairly certain the girl was elfin. Harder to tell for sure when they're teens, but I'd bet money on it."

"No wonder he was sweating bullets. What defense does a mundane errand boy have against ferals?" Felix asked.

"I told Caspian about the ferals—though I think I initially called them 'demonic zombies.' Caspian is always up for solving a scientific mystery, so we eventually came up with a plan to try to capture one of the ferals to figure out what they were. We set up arrays that would, in theory, work like a rabbit trap. The rabbits kept tripping said traps without getting caught, though. While I was out there one night trying to catch one—I think Caspian was hosting one of his insufferable auctions—I met Marisol. She'd been on patrol duty along the veil. I learned more from her in one night about the feral problem than I ever could have on my own."

While all this was interesting enough, Felix had no idea what direction this conversation was headed now. Aster was apparently so bored by Welsh's tale, it had put her to sleep. That, or she was in a food coma. She lay flat on her back, limbs thrown wide, and she snored with her mouth wide open. The sound reminded him of the faint buzzing of a vibrating phone buried deep at the bottom of a bag.

"I ... got a call last night from someone who wants help getting out of Luma," Welsh said in a measured tone that instantly made Felix's brows smash together. "I met with her early this morning. She's a rehabbed hybrid."

When Welsh didn't say more, Felix cocked his head, resisting the urge to ask "*And?*" Felix knew rehabbed hybrids existed. They might be rare, but seeing a person covered in runes and with wall-to-wall black eyes was a hard sight to miss.

"She'd gone feral." In that same measured tone, Welsh said, "She went *completely* feral before she was brought back."

Felix blinked at him several times, waiting for the punchline.

It didn't come.

"Ferals *can't* be rehabbed," Felix said, wondering if perhaps Welsh was even nuttier than Aster. "Sometimes you can catch them on the *brink* of turning, but feral is feral. It's like … I don't know—rabies. There's no treatment. It's not reversible."

Welsh smiled. "Interesting example. A very small number of people have survived rabies, even if nine point nine times out of ten it's fatal. She's got full-black eyes and necrosis of the extremities, and she walks with a significant curve to her spine. Her voice is rough—like she had a pack-an-hour smoking habit. Or someone took a scouring pad to her vocal cords. But she's as lucid as you and me."

"Are you saying she survived turning feral or that someone cured her?" Felix asked.

Welsh sat back in the booth and drummed his well-manicured fingers on the table. Aster didn't stir.

"Here's where you come in," Welsh finally said after an excruciatingly long—perhaps five seconds—pause. "The thing Harlow … I won't say *understandably* because she does very little that makes sense … the thing she most *notably* focuses on when she wallows about the demise of your relationship is the fact that you left her high and dry. You broke her heart when it had already been shattered, blah, blah. What *I* focus on is that you got hold of a theory like a dog with a bone, and you didn't let go. Not when you got the shit kicked out of you by street thugs. Not when Naomi West wound up dead. Not even when you lost the woman who very well could have been the love of your life. You kept at it. Some would call that kind of drive self-destructive. I think it's tenacity."

Felix's jaw was so tight his teeth ached. It was a peculiar thing to be so thoroughly insulted and praised at the same time. Welsh wasn't even framing it as a backhanded compliment. He wasn't being passive-aggressive. He clearly meant every word. Felix couldn't decide if he wanted to clock the guy in his perfect jaw or storm out the door.

"You also don't shy away from a theory if it skews heavily in the conspiracy direction," Welsh continued, either unaware of or unconcerned with Felix's scowl. "And I've got a doozy for you."

Felix's head instinctively cocked to one side, like a dog reacting to a curious sound.

"This feral, Laurel, claims she was a member of a rehab clinic here in Luma," Welsh said. "A clinic that's in the tower *your* bosses operate in."

The Collective's Tower stretched over twenty stories above ground, and at least ten below, but he suspected it went lower. There were rumors galore about secret passages, doorways, and even entire floors. The sorcerers were big believers in keeping their employees on a need-to-know basis. And unless it was about a specific case, bounty hunters didn't need to know much. The most fantastical rumors were the ones about feral testing facilities somewhere below ground, beyond the parking levels.

Belowground floors were labeled by letters in descending order. There was a gym on Floor F that the cats mostly used, but hunters could use it too, if they were brave enough. Felix had only been in there a handful of times and had never gained access lower than that. The buttons on the panel of the elevator made it clear there were levels he didn't have clearance to see, not to mention rune arrays that needed to be activated in addition to using a key card he didn't have.

He couldn't fathom how ferals, of all things, could be transported down there. None of the hunters—at least not the ones he knew well—had ever seen anything to suggest a secret facility full of dangerous monsters lurked far below their cubicles. Someone would have said something. Office gossip ran rampant, regardless of the industry.

Felix was also on a first-name basis with several maintenance workers and members of the cleaning staff. Those people saw more than most. But none of them had ever mentioned anything, either.

Hunters worked at all hours, so even bundling unconscious feral test subjects into the elevators in the dead of night would likely get noticed by someone eventually. Felix had very few werecats on his trustworthy list, but either those colleagues were excellent at keeping secrets, or they were just as clueless as Felix was.

"So, what, she was given some kind of treatment, deemed cured, and then set loose in the general population again?" Felix had seen his fair share of rehabbed hybrids. The runes covering large swaths of their bodily real estate worked like a suppressant—burying their vampiric urges so far down they were difficult to unearth. But even long-buried corpses could rise to the surface, given the right conditions; it wasn't a foolproof solution.

When he'd first heard about them, he'd assumed that he'd end up on countless bounty runs to capture members of a population rife with repeat offenders. But from his experience, rehabbed hybrids stayed on the straight and narrow. He figured they'd been through hell and back—probably more than once—to end up on the right side of sanity, that they did everything they could to stay there. Life couldn't be easy for them—their eyes never went back to normal, and the runes coating their skin forever labeled them as "other," even among fae not native to this realm. For some reason, a large number of their admittedly small population in Luma ended up as cab drivers or delivery workers.

"Runes were used in her treatment, but they weren't the cornerstone of it, like they usually are. They're more for maintenance or maybe a second line of defense," Welsh said, reminding Felix that he'd asked Welsh a question before his mind had spun off on a tangent. "She was given a very invasive gene therapy treatment. Obviously there'd been no consent, as ferals don't have enough cognitive power left to do much thinking at all, let alone have the ability to hold a pen to sign on the dotted line on of a document they can presumably no longer read. Most don't survive the treatment. Yet not only did Laurel survive, she's slowly getting her memories back." He paused, seemingly for dramatic effect. "And before her addiction won and she was lost to the high, she'd been a Bliss runner for a vampire in the mundane world."

Felix's mouth dropped open as if the hinges on his jaw had just given up the ghost. He snapped his mouth shut with a sharp clack of teeth. "No shit?"

"No shit," Welsh said. "She's been in a kind of parole system since she was let out of the treatment center about a year ago. She has to report to a Collective-appointed doctor every few months to make sure the therapy is still working and to touch up her tattooed runes if needed. She says the necrosis is starting to recede. She'll likely always have a hunched spine. Sounds like she got lucky: Few of the healed ferals in her program ever regained the ability to walk upright.

"Part of her parole stipulations is that, if she proves to be a threat to fae in particular, her assigned doctor has express permission to essentially flip a kill switch buried in her genetic code that can be activated via one of those runes on her body. Laurel doesn't know if that's merely a threat to keep her in line, but it's not really a thing a person wants to test, is it? She figures there has to be some truth to it, as she's purposefully violated her less-fatal rules—like breaking curfew—numerous times just to see if someone is watching her. No one seems to be. Her appointed doctor is currently out of town for a week, so she came to me, hoping I had information about where she can go once her parole's up. Since I'm good at getting people new lives some-where else, she figured I must have some insider info on the best places for rehabbed ferals. Places where her past etched all over her body won't immediately make people run away screaming or call the authorities."

Felix blinked at him. There was so much to unpack here, he didn't know where to start. "For the sake of argument, let's say all of this is totally accurate. Did they give her an end date to her parole? Did they really tell her that if she's a good little feral they'll deactivate the kill switch, and she can just go on her merry way?"

Welsh canted his head. "Her doctor said this time next year she'll be free to go. Now my trust issues are even worse than Harlow's, especially when the Collective is involved, so I call bullshit. But you … *you* work for them. You have a healthy relationship with reality. But you're also willing to give wild conspiracy theories the benefit of the doubt. So I ask you: Are they going to let Laurel go in a year?"

There was no way for Felix to know that. The Collective sorcerers might technically be his bosses, but he didn't know any of them that well. He didn't even know the exact number of them that resided in Luma. Sorceress Rhiannon was the only sorcerer he trusted *almost* implicitly, but she would have no reason to even *hint* at a secret feral rehabilitation program to him. This was all way, *way* above his pay grade.

Rumors existed for a reason, though. A nugget of truth, no matter how tiny, usually lived at the heart of them. Felix had heard countless rumors about the sorcerers, born mostly out of how little everyone knew about them. Lack of details and a shroud of mystery resulted in fanciful tales. And yet, one constant remained: They were practical to a fault. If they did anything, it was to gain something tangible for their efforts. Acting altruistically—which one did, in Felix's opinion, in large part to make oneself feel good—wouldn't be enough. Good feelings and a sense of self-worth would be wasted effort.

This all cycled through Felix's head in a matter of seconds. "No. They aren't going to let her go. It'll either be the *illusion* of freedom, but they'll still keep her on a long leash, or they'll hit that kill switch in a year or two or ten after they've collected the data they need. They put too much time and effort into her just to let her go. She's serving some purpose."

Welsh nodded once, as if he'd been expecting this answer. "I'm not making her any promises. I'll do what I can to help her, assuming it's even possible. But in the meantime … I don't run a charity, either. She's got insider information on the Bliss trade that could be invaluable to you and your investigations."

Felix arched his brow. "And what if I can't find any useful information about the fifteen dead witches? Would that still be considered a fair exchange in your eyes? I figure there's no turning this offer down, and that Laurel agreed to talk to me, since you somehow already knew this kind of shit is right up my alley."

"I don't know what Harlow was talking about. You're not even *half* as dumb as you look."

Felix leveled a flat stare at him.

Welsh shrugged. "Time will tell if your efforts are deemed sufficient. If not, we'll just say you'll owe me an unspecified favor sometime in the future."

"Years from now, are you going to show up on my doorstep demanding my first born?"

"What could I *possibly* want with a mundane child? I'd rather get a vinegar enema," Welsh said, his too-pretty face scrunching in distaste. "Do we have a deal or not?"

Felix didn't hesitate. "Yeah."

"Excellent." Welsh slammed a palm on the table. "Rise and shine, pixie!"

Aster sat bolt upright, like a tiny, leaf-bedecked Frankenstein's monster. A single piece of grated carrot had been inexplicably draped across her eyes like a sleep mask. It fell into her lap. "Whaa?"

Welsh reached into his trench coat again and pulled free a folded piece of paper. A quick incantation and the activation of his second ring resulted in the paper shrinking to a miniature square that lay in the middle of his palm.

Aster shrieked in delight. She launched into the air and plucked it from Welsh's hand a breath later. "This is really it? You truly figured it out?"

"If you're doubting my abilities, I can take it back," Welsh said, reaching for her.

She clutched the paper to her chest and glared fiercely at him. There were a few pieces of chewed-up noodle in her hair. "Me and the girls would ruin your life if you took this from me."

"The same girls who laugh at you when you say you're starting your own business?" Welsh asked.

Aster sniffed. "Where they fail at emotional support, they excel at elaborate sabotage."

"That I believe," Welsh said. "The sizing spell on that will wear off in a few hours, so just make sure it's not inside your house when it returns to full size."

"The roof's still not fully patched from last time," Aster said mournfully. "Maybe I'll transcribe it into my notebook and then eat it so no one can steal the recipe! Thanks again, Welshy!"

Felix tried to imagine what could happen to her body if the paper swelled to full size in her tiny stomach. Would she explode in a burst of blood-soaked confetti?

She was gone in a streak of blue before Welsh could reply.

Aster's exit popped the bubble of the sound-dampening spell, and the bustling cacophony of the diner rushed back in with all the force of crashing cymbals.

As if reading his thoughts, Welsh said, "Don't worry. Her stomach acid will probably dissolve the paper and prevent her from dying horribly."

Felix noted the word "probably."

Welsh fluidly slid out of the booth and gave his trench coat a few adjusting tugs. He reached into another one of his inside pockets, then pushed a slip of paper across the table. "That's Laurel's number. She's expecting your call."

A question that had been niggling at Felix finally forced its way out of his mouth. "What's the urgency? Why does Laurel want to get out now when she's got at least a year before her parole's up?"

Welsh shrugged. "No idea. Don't care. That's the kind of thing you can ask her when you call. I deal in logistics, not feelings." He took a couple of steps back. "Goddess speed on the research. I hope for your sake the search proves fruitful. If not, I promise the mysterious favor will be *much* worse."

Felix watched him stride out, sure that sooner rather than later he was going to regret making a deal with a fae.

CHAPTER SIX

FELIX

One Week Ago

It took a couple of days for Laurel to agree to meet with Felix. She'd said it had to do with the schedule she had with her parole doctor, but Felix was only seventy-five percent sure on that. Welsh had said the woman's voice was "rough." He'd undersold her condition. There were chunks of their phone conversations that Felix had found so indecipherable he hadn't even bothered to ask her to repeat herself. He hoped it was better in person.

At Laurel's request, they met in a makeshift park in the Industrial District. The same one, it turned out, where he'd last physically seen Harlow. They'd met here after Harlow had gotten her hands on Bliss—the real thing, too, and not one of the watered-down tabs law enforcement often found during raids. Somehow she and her new criminal pals had infiltrated the Ghost Lily and smuggled two tabs out in one night—a feat his colleagues hadn't come anywhere close to accomplishing.

This place was much worse in the middle of the afternoon. And even though no kids played here, Felix still felt like a creeper sitting in the park alone.

Trucks rumbled by at a steady pace in the lot across from the playground, hauling goods into or out of the area. A factory nearby that made the raw materials for synthetic fae essence—a magical form of neon—belched great plumes of bluish smoke that blended almost seamlessly with the color of the sky. Smelled a little like sulfur, though. Between that and the cloying stench of cat piss wafting out of the playground's bed of wood chips, Felix was starting to feel like he could *taste* the air. It made his stomach roil.

He often turned his phone off when he was going to meet potentially jumpy clients. Even the buzz of a phone on silent could set off a client if they were anxious. So he just sat there on the bench, doing nothing other than looking like a potential deviant.

Laurel had five minutes before he was out of here.

She showed up in four, casting an unexpected shadow over Felix as he stared down at the softly ticking minute hand on his wristwatch.

He glanced up sharply, thanking his years on the job for ensuring he kept his expression neutral when he took in Laurel's hunched appearance. Her entire person was a war of contrasts; for every feature that screamed feral, another would firmly classify her as human. Wall-to-wall black eyes. A full head of silky red hair that brushed her uneven shoulders. A fair-skinned complexion that bore a subtle pink hue at her cheeks, a smattering of freckles over her button nose, and black veins that inched up her neck like the rotting roots of a dying tree. She was dressed in business casual, making Felix wonder if she'd asked to meet him on her lunch break. The only thing off about her attire was that one of her black tennis shoes had a thicker sole than the other, clearly to compensate for her legs not being the same length. She walked without a cane, though, so her treatment had granted her enough stability that she'd been able to shuffle out of the rehab facility on her own two feet.

If Felix hadn't been told that Laurel was a rehabbed feral, he wouldn't have come close to labeling her as such. She looked off in some decidedly foreign way, but the accessories and accommodations for her disability would have made him assume she suffered from a supernatural sickness. Which, in a way, was true.

He'd been wondering how a rehabbed feral would be able to move about in the world—either in a hub or in a mundane city— and not fall prey to judgment, harassment, or fear. But even a pair of sunglasses added to her ensemble would have cut her issues in half.

"Are you Felix Turner?"

He mentally winced. The voice was a definite problem. It wasn't only that it was a deep, raspy voice that didn't fit the mostly put-together woman, but it sounded painful. Felix's own throat itched in sympathy. He resisted the urge to cough.

He remembered his manners then and got to his feet, hand outstretched. "Yes, sorry. A lot on my mind recently. Thanks for meeting with me, Laurel."

She shook his hand; the back of hers was striped with veins as black as pitch. Her fingernails were neatly manicured and painted pink, despite—or in spite of—her fingers from tip to second knuckle being stained black, as if coated in ash. He wondered if she ever considered wearing gloves.

"No problem," she said. "Hopefully I can be helpful. My memory comes back a little more every day."

Felix let her hand go and gestured toward the bench. She sat with her clasped hands between her knees. When he took a seat beside her, he was mindful to keep a good two feet between them so as to not crowd her space.

He couldn't tell if she was shy, reserved, nervous, or just quiet. He didn't get the feeling that she wanted to bolt, as he often did when meeting with domestic violence victims. But he knew, in those circumstances, the mere fact that he was a man could be enough to make them uncomfortable. Laurel didn't glance over her shoulder frequently, or check the time, or fidget. There was something preternaturally still about her, which ran counter to the constant, frenetic movement he associated with ferals.

He started off by telling her a little more about himself, his interest in Bliss-related cases, and reminded her she could opt out of answering anything that made her uncomfortable. She remained completely still for the entirety of Felix's monologue, keeping her hands between her knees and her gaze focused on the toes of her uneven shoes. When he finally stopped speaking, she let out a single croaked, "Okay."

Felix had deep misgivings about being recommended to talk to this broken woman, but his curiosity about what those wall-to-wall black eyes had seen spurred him forward.

"Did you always live in the mundane world?" he asked after several long seconds, realizing that once it came time to truly ask her questions, he wasn't sure where to start.

She spoke haltingly at first, keeping her attention on the ground, but she eventually sat back against the bench seat and even glanced his way a few times. She told him of a life lived first in Walla Walla, Washington, with her mother and little brother. Her mother's family line, unbeknownst to her father, carried the genetic marker for vampirism, though her mother wasn't a vampire herself. Vampirism manifested in Laurel when she was ten. Her father eventually found her fangs-deep in the neck of a stray cat. Her father, horrified that his wife had never disclosed this genetic anomaly, abandoned the family soon after, taking Laurel's non-manifesting brother with him.

Laurel's mother had never warned her children about vampirism running in the family, hoping they'd be spared the life her own mother and sister had endured. Laurel's aunt, a vampire herself who sold venom to a local Bliss dealer, invited Laurel and her mother to stay with her in Fresno, California, until they figured out how to cope with Laurel's condition.

Darius, the vampire who ran Bliss and purchased venom from Laurel's aunt, was intrigued by young Laurel, as born-vampires were relatively rare, and he'd yet to meet one so young. He convinced Laurel to start selling her own venom as a way for him to test if hers was more or less potent than that of other vampires, as well as a means for Laurel to make her own money. As she entered her teenage years, Laurel began to push back on her mother's insistence that Laurel hide her vampirism and blend into human society.

Laurel was seventeen the first time she tried fresh human blood from the wrist of a willing donor instead of out of a refrigerated blood bag. By nineteen, she'd tried fresh fae blood from a less-willing faun donor who'd been strung up in a back room of an underground club.

Felix had done well in keeping his reactions off his face until then. Laurel instantly clammed up at the sight of his grimace, her pressed-together palms squeezed between her knees again rather than a hand resting atop either thigh.

"Sorry," Felix said, giving his head a light shake. "It's less a judgment about your choices and more sympathy for that faun who'd ended up in a bad, probably fatal, situation. I often see these fae kids after they've been drained—mentally and physically." He awkwardly cleared his throat. "I've never heard a story like this from a hybrid's perspective. And definitely not from a feral. Please continue."

It took Laurel a long minute to resume speaking, and when

she did so, she'd slipped back into the halting cadence she'd mostly lost before Felix had inadvertently interrupted her. "It's not that I didn't have any sympathy for the faun."

Felix debated about fumbling through another apology, but kept his trap shut.

"It was like …" Laurel said in her deep, scratchy voice. "It was like I'd been on a diet my whole life without knowing other food existed. Imagine only eating, I don't know, celery for years. No significant flavor. Not particularly filling. No enticing scent. Then one day you smell coffee for the first time. Or sizzling bacon. Or baking bread. That's what it was like walking into that room with the bleeding faun boy. The smell of his blood—which was dripping out of his wrists and splattering on the floor, while older blood coated the walls and ceiling—was like smelling baking bread for the first time. Suddenly I was more ravenous than I'd ever been because I'd never eaten *anything* that satisfied my hunger. But I didn't know that until I walked into that room. I was horrified by what I saw for all of … five seconds? … and then the smell overrode everything else. I was doomed from the second Darius led me inside."

Felix thought Laurel's mother had done her a great disservice by not talking to her daughter about any of this. Shielding her family from it all had doomed every member in different ways. He wondered if Laurel's family knew what had become of her.

Laurel told him that her mother saw the swirling black in the whites of Laurel's eyes that night and instantly knew her daughter had picked up the same addiction as her own mother— an addiction that had turned the woman feral. No one knew where Laurel's grandmother had ended up after the addiction finally overtook her. No one knew if she was alive or dead. Laurel had grown up believing her grandmother had overdosed on a mundane street drug when Laurel was a baby.

After months of trying to get Laurel into a rehab program, her mother abandoned her the same way her father and brother had.

"I don't know if I blame my mom for giving up on me," Laurel said. "I was furious and hurt as a teen when she left, of course, but I *was* a lost cause. There was no turning back. If I hadn't been forced into that rehab program, I'd be dead. The life expectancy for ferals isn't long."

Darius had taken Laurel under his wing in the wake of her mother's abandonment, teaching her how to control her cravings. He'd paid her to not only supply venom for his Bliss production, but also to be a driver who picked up trafficked fae teens from airports, bus stops, and train stations. If she promised Darius not to ask how the teens were selected and then delivered them to him without divulging to the teens what fate awaited them, Darius supplied her with as much free fae blood as she could stomach.

"A lot of my time between then and now is fuzzy," Laurel said. "Some of it is just a black hole in my memory. One day, a couple of years ago, I woke up in a sterile room that smelled like burnt lemons. The bright lights hurt my eyes. My bones felt like they were on fire. I tried to scream, but making sound come out of my mouth hurt worse than my bones did, so I just writhed and cried a lot. Writhing was hard, too, because I was strapped to a cot."

Felix was unable to hide his wince again, but Laurel didn't seem to take offense, since the sympathy was aimed at her this time. "And this rehab clinic was in the Collective's Tower?"

"Welsh said you'd be most skeptical about that part," Laurel said, the corner of her mouth ticking up half a fraction—the first time she'd come anywhere close to a smile. "There are buildings all over Luma that are fronts for other things."

Felix nodded, thinking of the townhomes that dotted the neighborhood surrounding the Tower and the homes that stood outside the main entrances of Luma, occupied by draken, witches, and werecats who served as an additional line of defense should mundanes ever try to storm the hidden city.

Laurel said, "There's a tunnel system under Luma. Some of the fake buildings hide nothing more than an elevator that'll take you belowground. Tunnels lead to other tunnels, and those lead to the elevator and testing facilities under the Tower."

At least that explained why none of his colleagues had ever seen a hint of ferals being smuggled in and out.

"My house is one of those fronts," Laurel said. "That's part of how they keep track of me and keep me where they want me. There's a set schedule for planned drop-ins, but every once in a while there's an emergency. Or someone is spotted on the way to their original drop-off location, and they need a new one in a pinch. I'm on call most days, just in case. I'm not under house arrest, but it's close. So if someone comes to my house needing access to the tunnel system, and I'm not there ..."

She pulled back the cuff of her long-sleeved shirt and revealed an arm covered in tattooed runes. One in particular, drawn over her wrist above prominent black veins, was a series of intricate runes encircled by a thick, dark ring. It made him think of a button—but he supposed in this case it was a switch.

After a few moments, she covered it up again. She coughed awkwardly. It sounded like it hurt. "I've been out of the program for almost a year. Even though I trust my doctor when he says they'll let me go eventually, this array makes me worry they can call me back anytime they want. Or use it to drop me to my knees out of nowhere and make it look like a heart attack. I need to know if this"—she tapped at the fabric of her sleeve over the rune—"is actually a kill switch, or if it's like when people get a tattoo of a Chinese character thinking it says 'mother' but it really says 'I like apples' because the person getting the tattoo doesn't know the language."

Felix barked a laugh. A real, full smile graced Laurel's face for a brief moment. Somehow the sight of it made Felix want to help her even more. This woman had been through something he couldn't even quantify, and yet she'd managed to hold on to not only hope, but a shred of her sense of humor. He *liked* helping people. The more help they needed, the more invested he became. This was why his caseload was always too large. Why he ate microwaved burritos for dinner most nights and subsisted on coffee and little sleep.

He supposed if he was constantly trying to solve everyone's problems, he could ignore his own.

"Can I take a few pictures of the runes?" he finally asked. "I can't guarantee my contacts are going to better equipped than Welsh's—"

She pulled her sleeve back again and all but thrust her wrist in his face. "I appreciate you trying, no matter the outcome. And no matter what happens, I'll tell you any time one of my memories resurface about my time with Darius. The more my memories come back, the worse I feel about how many teens I brought him. I was so lost to the addiction, it was like I wasn't fully in control of myself. Now that I have that control back, I feel like even more of a monster than when I was feral. Most days I feel like I don't deserve to be here at all."

Felix sighed. She was hitting every damn sympathy button he had. He really shouldn't be taking on more cases when he was already running around town in his free time tracking down leads about Naomi West. Denise had already come and gone, the memorial ceremony over, but she checked in every day, asking if he'd made any progress.

Ignoring his growling stomach that clearly sensed he'd be skipping lunch yet again, he pulled his phone out of his pocket. He wished he trusted Sorceress Rhiannon enough to show *her* the pictures. But there was always the chance that she was the one spearheading the program and that the mere existence of these photos on his phone could mean Laurel's theoretical kill switch would get flipped. Who knew what would happen to *him* if his bosses thought he knew too much. His list of sorcerer allies was even shorter than his list of werecat ones, but he'd do what he could.

He turned his phone back on to take the pictures, then made sure it was on silent. He was in the middle of thanking her for her time and assuring her that he'd get back in contact as soon as he had any information when she cut him off.

Laurel wrung her blackened hands. "There's, uh, one more thing."

His stomach flipped.

"I … uh … I don't need to get out of Luma just because I need more freedom," she said. "Life here isn't so bad, all things considered. But, uh …"

Felix felt some small bit of satisfaction that his gut had been right: There was a level of urgency here that felt off. Every person —every *species*—deserved freedom and quality of life. But if Laurel had been told she had a year before her version of house arrest was up—why was she so desperate to get out now? Especially when she lived in a city where her kind could live a relatively peaceful existence.

Laurel heaved out a quick, sharp breath, like a curse. "I'm pregnant."

Felix gaped at her, unable *and* unwilling to keep the emotion off his face this time.

He supposed he could chalk it up to the wonders of the human body and leave it at that. But Laurel technically wasn't human. In order to go feral, one had to be a vampire first. Vampirism, by Laurel's own admission, ran in her family. While her vampirism had been inherited, going feral had been a choice. That choice had altered her body so thoroughly—not to mention the therapy the Collective's doctors put her through—that she was changed down to the genetic level. There was no telling what resided in her uterus. Assuming it could be carried to term at all.

Felix understood in that moment that Laurel wasn't worried the Collective would flip the kill switch in a year. The wealth of data that could be gleaned from a healthy child born to a vampire who'd been brought back from being feral would be too valuable for the Collective to give up. She wanted out of Luma before her parole doctor discovered her condition, *and* she wanted some sense of how safe her child would be once they were gone. Perhaps she suspected there were tracker runes on her body.

Trackers made more sense to him than a kill switch. They'd want to monitor her over time, to see how a rehabbed feral aged. Killing her off when they'd sunk so many resources into her would only be a last-ditch effort to save their secrets.

An absolute flood of questions crashed through his mind. He finally settled on one. "Is the father … uhh …"

"He's human. He doesn't know about the baby yet. We're limited in how much we can see each other lately because of his job. I haven't been fighting him too hard on that this last couple of weeks. We met at MOA—Magical Opioid Anonymous. He's been clean for three years now. He'd gotten hooked on black diamond."

Felix's brows hiked. The name "black diamond" was a misnomer that had thrown off law enforcement for years. The pills looked like small, misshapen gray pebbles—petrified raisins. When they'd first hit the black market, they were cut with almost pure faun hoof. Fauns shed the lining of their hooves like deer shed their antlers, and the stuff was used in various common medicines.

Faun youth donated their hoof lining for extra cash the way some humans donated their plasma. In low doses when used as an additive, it worked like a painkiller. In high doses—like in black diamond—it numbed pain to the point of nonexistence. Problem was, when it wore off, the pain came back tenfold.

It wasn't long before demand outpaced supply, and manufacturers started lacing black diamond with kevara scales, which offered the same properties as faun hoof but with five times the potency. Kevara were an invasive aardvark-like fae species that had ravaged crops in the months after the Glitch. They'd adapted over time and now were akin to squirrels in some places, mostly living in harmony with native fauna.

They were driven to near extinction at the height of the black diamond crisis, though. The kevara-scale-laced pills, in addition to temporarily eliminating pain, granted users enhanced senses.

Suddenly having heightened sight, smell, or hearing might sound great in theory, but going from mundane hearing to hearing so attuned that one could hear everything from a plane overhead to the flutter of a butterfly's wings could lead to insanity in a matter of hours. Some users inflicted self-harm in attempts to escape the onslaught. Others suffered fatal aneurysms. No two mundanes had the same reaction to black diamond, but the results were often catastrophic. If a user survived the drug, especially after multiple uses, they often came away physically changed.

"Kevara have a strong sense of smell," Laurel said, lightly wringing her hands. "They were like truffle pigs in the fae world. There was a root similar to ginseng that grew five feet underground, and kevara could be trained to seek it out and dig it up. A super-sensitive sense of a smell is a common side effect users pick up. Bob has to wear nose plugs most of the time. It killed a lot of his nerve endings too, so his sense of touch is almost nonexistent."

Color flushed Laurel's cheeks then. Felix opted not to ask for details.

"We bonded over surviving our addictions *and* the fact that we were changed down to the molecular level and are still standing." Laurel placed a hand on her stomach. "I want to do right by this baby. I want her to know who I am, who her father is, and who she could be. Right from the start." She paused. "I can't give her that if she's here, or if they take her from me to run tests on her, or if they get to Bob. We need to escape before the doctors find out."

"How far along are you?"

"Sixteen weeks. When I go in for my mandated appointments, they mostly check the runes to make sure they're holding, and they test my reactions to fae blood exposure. I wear baggy clothes, and any weight I've put on just makes me look healthier, since I was skin and bones when I entered the program. They care less about our well-being, because if we're regressing, we need to be put down like a lame horse anyway. But they do full physicals every six months or so. I have maybe two months before my doctor finds out."

Felix blew out a breath that puffed out his cheeks. "Have you seen a … you know, OB/GYN since you found out? How do you know … I mean the chances … it's just that—"

"She's alive," Laurel said with more conviction than anything else she'd told him.

Felix figured that whether she "just knew" the baby was okay, or if she'd had medical confirmation of this from a doctor whose identity she didn't want to give up didn't matter. He was either going to help her or he wasn't.

"Did you not tell Welsh this part because you worried he wouldn't help you?" Felix asked. "Especially since Bob is human?"

Laurel's eyes welled with tears. "Maybe. Welsh is a good guy, deep down, I think. It seems like he doesn't want anyone to know that, though. He makes sure you never forget that this is a business deal. And he charges … a lot. He said you investigate Bliss cases on your own time. You haven't mentioned money even once."

Because Felix was an overworked sucker.

He said, "Welsh really should know about this." After a long pause, he said, "Bob needs to know even more than Welsh does."

Laurel let out a shuddering breath. "I know."

"I'll do everything I can to help you—*all* of you—leave Luma safely."

Twin tracks of tears slid down Laurel's face. "Thank you. Whether or not you're able to help us, it means the world to me that you'll still try, even after hearing my story."

After they said their goodbyes and Felix had watched her limp out of sight, he checked his phone, which had buzzed several times in his pocket after he'd turned it back on. He hoped nothing significant had happened in the last hour. Maybe he could convince Marisol to meet him at their park for lunch.

A red "16" sat in the corner of the phone icon on his home screen—which was actually a lower number than he'd been expecting. His email inbox number ticked up by three in real time. He had forty-three texts.

He checked those first, quickly scanning for both Harlow and Marisol's names. Nothing from Harlow. The lack of texts from Marisol disappointed him more than he cared to admit.

With no immediate fires to put out, he decided to head to his private office. He had at least three lower-level sorcery-academy-dropout contacts he could show Laurel's runes to. The person who could probably help him the most was Caspian Blackthorn, but it wasn't as if he had that dude's number.

Felix sat there for a few more minutes, growing a little light-headed from the mingling scents of ammonia and sulfur, before his resolve gave out.

He pulled up his text threads.

Felix
Hey

Marisol
Hi. Wow, you actually messaged me first for once.

Had he always waited for her to make first contact? Probably.

Felix
I have a bunch of excuses but none of them are any good.

Marisol
So you're not avoiding me?

Felix
Definitely not. Can I make it up to you?

Marisol
I'm listening

Felix
Dinner tonight? We're both bad at taking a break from work, right? Tell you what—I'll leave my phone in my car. You'll have my full attention.

Marisol
You *are* serious

Felix
I'll even wear a tie

Marisol
Sold. (I'm not leaving my phone behind, but I'll leave it on silent and keep it in my purse.)

Felix
I'll take it

Marisol
I should be out of here by 5. I'll check in with you in a bit.

Felix
Sounds good. Looking forward to it!

Spirits lifted, Felix got to his feet and headed for his car. He had a lot of work to do before his date with Marisol. He had several emails to answer, rogue sorcerers to track down, and, most importantly, he needed to buy a tie.

CHAPTER SEVEN

HARLOW

While Mom, Soren, Caspian, the swords, and I loitered in the lobby, Sorceress Rhiannon laid into the group of receptionists for not sending us up immediately. Most of them kept their heads bowed as they took the verbal lashing, but a couple openly glared at us. I wondered what effect this open hostility was having on Felix. Were they all treating him like crap for having a history with me?

When we were finally ushered forward by Rhiannon herself, I pointedly ignored the stares from the dozen workers and a surly draken guard as we made our way to an elevator. I thought not flipping them off was *very* mature of me.

We piled into the elevator, and I heaved a sigh of relief when the door slid closed without incident. Soothing jazz music heavy on the saxophone wafted out of the speakers as we gently rocketed up to the twenty-first floor. I realized after a moment that the elevator car was made of glass. My stomach didn't know how it felt about seeing the chrome elevator shaft rushing by.

I eyed tiny Rhiannon standing with her back to us, searching for any sign that she knew there were two swords in here and not just the original one. Tim excelled at being unsettlingly quiet and still, at least.

I still had no idea what this meeting would entail, other than it being a small gathering with sorcerers Rhiannon trusted most. A second, larger gathering of sorcerers was due to happen later in the day—but I knew even less about that one.

The feral attractant Mom had gotten from elder vampire Vincent Roch seemed to be the star of the show. Sure, the stuff sounded like it could help level the playing field when it came to the battle against hybrids and their feral minions, but I didn't know why this clandestine meeting needed to happen first.

Perhaps it was tied to the apparent faction war going on among the sorcerers, but I couldn't see how.

What I *did* know was that I was finally going to meet at least two other Collective sorcerers. I was initially a little surprised that the draken guards hadn't stuffed themselves into the elevator with us. Wouldn't it be like the President not being escorted by the Secret Service? But after seeing that Rhiannon could literally freeze time, I supposed the diminutive sorceress didn't need a guard.

Perhaps it was *us* who needed extra protection. We were heading into their territory, after all. And it wasn't like we had many sympathizers here. If we ran into trouble, no one in the building except maybe Felix would offer aid—unless it was to toss our lifeless bodies down a trash chute.

I wasn't sure "lifeless" was even a requirement in that scenario.

"I do apologize for O'Neill's less-than-warm welcome," Rhiannon said, snapping me out of my dark thoughts. She still faced the doors with her hands folded in front of her. "You were given a black card to avoid any of that. Tensions *are* running high, though. That tension is, ironically, exactly why we need you here."

No one replied.

My sword was slowly floating around the top of the elevator doing who knew what. It periodically tapped its blade on the glass, followed by short hums as if it were talking out loud to itself. Maybe it didn't love being trapped in a hurtling box of glass, either.

Tim was behind my left shoulder. I could feel it floating there. It also occasionally said AWAITING INSTRUCTIONS in my head. It was … unsettling.

"Who else are we meeting with?" Mom asked.

Rhiannon took a moment to reply. "Avery and Macrae."

Mom sighed. "Macrae hates me …"

Caspian said, "He hates me, too, if it's any consolation."

"It's not," Mom said.

Soren nudged me with his elbow. "Isn't it fun not knowing what the hell is going on?"

Rhiannon glanced back at that. She gave Soren an assessing scan from toes to platinum-blond head. "I'd keep the commentary to yourself, Mr. Larsen. You're here as a favor to Camila. She assures me you have even more boots-on-the-ground experience when it comes to dealing with ferals than she does. But if you give me a reason to throw you out on your ear, I will take it. And it won't take much."

Once Rhiannon's back was turned toward us again, Soren angled his comically widened eyes my way and thumbed toward the tiny sorceress. He offered a dramatic frown, as if silently asking *What crawled up* her *ass and died?*

I tucked my lips between my teeth to keep from laughing. If I hadn't seen him lop heads off ferals with my own eyes more than once, I'd wonder how he'd managed to get involved in all this. He and Mom were on opposite ends of the spectrum when it came to vamp hunters. Either you let the job harden you like it had Mom, or you didn't take *anything* too seriously, like Soren. Neither option seemed particularly healthy.

SHALL I NEUTRALIZE THE TINY ONE? Tim asked.

"Absolutely not," I hissed, realizing a moment later that I'd just replied verbally to a question no one else had heard.

My sword dropped to the floor with frightening speed. *Tap.*

"Don't encourage him!" I whispered sharply.

Rhiannon turned on her sensible shoes to eye me and then my sword in turn. She narrowed her eyes minutely, then her gaze flicked to my left for a brief moment before she turned to face forward again.

I winced. Did she just freeze time and find Tim hiding behind me? Would she be pissed that we hadn't told her there was more than one sword?

I refused to feel guilty about trying to keep an ace up my sleeve when I was so completely out of my depth.

When the glass death trap finally eased into place on the top floor, my eyes nearly bugged out of my head. I turned in a slow circle, able to take in the entirety of the floor without leaving the elevator car. I glanced down, grateful the floor beneath my scuffed boots wasn't made of glass as well.

"Here we are," Rhiannon said unnecessarily and with too much false cheer.

Mom grabbed Rhiannon by the elbow. "They *are* expecting us, aren't they?"

Rhiannon gently pulled her arm free. "In a way," she said vaguely, then stepped out of the elevator.

Mom cursed.

The cautious way Mom stepped out of the elevator told me she hadn't been up here before. Plus, the space was a lot to take in. It was like a study, a library, and a laboratory all smashed into one. We were clearly at the top of the Collective's Tower; the way the ceiling beams funneled upward gave the room an onion-dome shape. The room was bigger than I would have expected, and I wondered if magic was in effect here, giving the area more square feet than mundane physics would allow.

Directly across from the elevator's doors was a seating area dotted with red leather couches and love seats. Thick, elegant rugs patterned in black-and-white geometric shapes were topped by ottomans and coffee tables. The couches were occupied by two men. They were both older, perhaps in their sixties or seventies. One sat with his legs crossed and held a pair of glasses in one hand by the temple tip as he spoke. An open book sat perched on his knee, spine up. He was apparently so consumed by his own monologue that he hadn't heard the elevator's arrival.

The other man sat diagonally across from him with his chin on his fist. He'd been listening to the first man drone on, but he'd perked up when he spotted the group of us pour out of the elevator. His gaze landed on Mom first and stayed there. I wasn't sure if he was more surprised that we were apparently an hour early or that my mom stood in his sanctuary.

Beyond the seating area, a wooden, spiral staircase twisted up several feet to a walkway that hugged half the wall. Sunlight from the abundant oval-shaped windows cast shafts of yellow across the towering bookshelves, desks, and couches that populated the landing.

The homey, comfortable atmosphere clashed horribly with my expectations. I'd imagined something more like the lobby—modern, rigid, monotone, and crisply professional.

The man who had spotted us stood, seemingly pleased to have an excuse to abandon his conversation. He wore several shades of brown, including a thick cardigan that belonged on someone's sweet old grandpa. I wondered if he had caramels or peppermints stuffed in those oversized pockets. The other man broke off his rambling, turning his bleary gaze our way as if waking from a trance.

"The rumors are true then," the guy in the cardigan said. "I didn't believe our own Camila Fletcher would actually return, invitation or no."

When Mom didn't reply, I glanced over to find her arms crossed and her jaw tight. Her hands were squeezed into fists. "Banishment usually makes it hard for someone to swing by and say hi," Mom finally said.

Cardigan Guy smiled wide. His teeth were so bright white and uniform, I wondered if they were veneers. "Feisty as ever," he said, as if Mom were a mischievous puppy. In a tone dripping with condescension, he asked Rhiannon, "And what precautions, if any, have you taken to ensure these ... *guests* won't go blabbing about this meeting to whomever they choose? These certainly aren't the time, place, or circumstances we agreed on. Those traveling here for the meeting will be displeased that you've circumvented the plan. You've stepped on quite enough toes lately. I'm starting to think you enjoy being in hot water."

Rhiannon didn't appear the least bit flustered. "In exchange for them providing us with information we desperately need, I promised them their freedom. That means their *entire* freedom. None will be signing Soul NDAs, other than the one Camila already has in place. If we're trusting them enough to allow them back into Luma, we have to trust them fully. Forcing their loyalty will result in more hostility than already exists."

Both men clearly found this quite detestable. As far as I knew, the stipulation that we were required to sign Soul NDAs in order to have this meeting had never come up. Perhaps that had been part of the argument Mom and Rhiannon had had in the lobby after O'Neill pulled his little stunt. Perhaps Rhiannon had never considered making us sign one. As much as the tiny lady scared the bejesus out of me, she was definitely growing on me.

I just didn't know how badly her "circumventing the plan" was going to piss off her fellow sorcerers. Though the hot water comment suggested that ship had already sailed.

Cardigan Guy held out his arms. "Well then, guests! Come, have a seat. We apparently have much to discuss."

Caspian and I shared a "what the shit is going on?" look before we perched ourselves on the edge of the couch already occupied by the other man. The book was still propped on his knee, but the glasses were on his face now. He sat with his arms crossed and assessed the group at large. His bushy salt-and-pepper eyebrows were in desperate need of a trimming. They jammed together on his wrinkled forehead, looking like a recently electrocuted fuzzy centipede.

Cardigan Guy took a seat across from me, his gaze settling in the general direction of my waist. "I presume your murderous cutlass is with you? Has Blackthorn figured out a way to shield it from view?"

He said this without actually acknowledging Caspian's existence.

It took me a second to realize the guy must have thought I kept the sword strapped to my person at all times. I actually had no idea where it was. It and Tim had taken off as soon as the elevator doors opened. "It's floating around here somewhere."

Both men looked scandalized, like I'd just exposed one of my bare ankles to them while out of wedlock.

The second man quickly snatched the book off his knee and slid it onto the coffee table. He scanned the ceiling, head jerking left and right as if he expected my sword to rocket toward him like a torpedo at any moment.

And, knowing the sword, that wasn't an invalid worry. Tim at least asked first.

Permission granted?

I flinched hard. "No!" I hissed.

I didn't even know what Tim was asking permission *for*.

The group at large stared at me as if I'd lost my mind.

Awkwardly clearing my throat, I said, "Guess you didn't get the memo that the sword does what it wants." I tried channeling my mom's "I might be a mere human, but I'm not scared of sorcerers" energy while also actively ignoring how hard my heart thumped. "That's why that whole smear campaign that made everyone think I'm a cold-blooded murder was so annoying, by the way. *I* didn't do the stabbing. If you're going to turn an entire city against a lady, you should at least be operating with accurate information."

Mom offered me a discreet approving nod. Soren stood beside my mom, chewing on the inside of his cheek. I was half convinced he was going to bolt at any second.

Cardigan Guy studied me as if I were an intriguing insect pinned to a board.

A distant clock softly ticked away the seconds.

Rhiannon cleared her throat, making Cardigan Guy lose our staring contest. I let out a little shuddering breath as he looked away.

Since arriving in Luma, I'd been doing my level best to ignore the myriad reasons I hated the Collective. There were bigger problems to contend with right now than my personal ones. But looking at these two old men sitting in their comfortable tower made those reasons bubble to the surface. My life, my family's lives, and the lives of my friends had been turned upside down over and over and over by the ruling sorcerers.

I wanted to help thwart whatever nefarious plan Lachlan Shade was cooking up. I wanted to help the swords figure out how to deal with their sentience so they could exist freely without fear they'd end up in the hands of people like Haskins, Domino, or Likho. I wanted to help stop the seemingly endless tide of feral vampires that threatened populations both inside hubs and out.

Teaming up with the Collective could help with all of that. An enemy of my enemy is my friend or whatever.

I'd be the first to admit that I'd gotten a bit ... reckless in the last six years. Being reckless in a place like Luma when you're human means ignoring the fact that quite a few species who shared your zip code had a long list of creative ways for you to meet your end. But reckless or not, I wasn't stupid or naive.

These sorcerers either knew exactly what had happened to my dad or they'd turned a blind eye to it. No other options existed. My parents had stuck their noses into places the sorcerers took offense to, and they'd completely fucked them over. The sorcerers had done it again to me mere months ago. They did it to Caspian. And Kayda. Welsh's entire very lucrative business was built on helping people escape the hub system and get out from under the Collective's thumb. Now he was in hiding with fucking pures because we trusted *them* to keep Welsh safe far more than we did the Collective.

It was somehow scarier that the sorcerers possessed power that went far beyond their magic. Their resources meant that if I— if any one of us—rubbed them the wrong way, we could be snuffed out.

Cardigan Guy pulled a white-and-red peppermint out of his pocket. His gaze flicked to me as he popped the candy into his mouth. His small, warm smile sent a chill down my back.

Though everyone else had taken a seat by now, Rhiannon remained standing at the entrance of the seating area like a teacher before a classroom. She went around the room giving introductions. Cardigan Guy was Avery, and the grumpy, bespectacled one was Macrae.

She turned to Mom. "Camila, please bring us up to date on what you've seen on the ground as far as vampire activity is concerned, both in recent months as well as during your consulting work in other states. Soren, you may add anything you deem worthy of our attention."

The two older men leaned forward in their seats. The peppermint occasionally clacked against Avery's teeth.

As I listened to Mom and Soren tag team on their experiences with ferals and hybrids, I couldn't help but wonder all over again why such a conversation needed to happen in person. This could have been covered in a phone call. Even an email. And surely their patrolling werecats knew the basics about vamps.

Rhiannon deftly guided Mom toward the topic of Vincent

Roch, and I knew then that the feral discussion had served a purpose after all. Both men had looked utterly fascinated by Mom and Soren's vampire TED talk. It kind of pissed me off that these two were so out of touch with what us peons had to deal with on a daily basis that they were clueless about how bad the feral problem had actually gotten.

And if these two were on Rhiannon's short list of colleagues she trusted, how disconnected from reality were the rest of them?

It was clear that Rhiannon had wanted Avery and Macrae to hear how knowledgeable Mom and Soren were on the subject so that, by the time Roch and his attractant entered the discussion, they were primed to listen.

Mom understandably left out the part about her torrid love affair with Roch. First, it was irrelevant and none of their business. Second, the details would give stuffy Sorcerer Macrae the vapors.

When Mom and Soren were done, Rhiannon turned to me. "Harlow, it's my understanding that you're currently in possession of the feral attractant?"

I looked at my mom for confirmation. She nodded tightly. Carefully, I extracted the carrying case from the front pouch of my backpack. Whenever I had to handle the case, I inadvertently treated it as if it were a bomb about to detonate. It was like doing everyday tasks with splayed fingers after painting my nails, worried I'd scuff polish that had been dry for over an hour.

It didn't take much for the memory of the ferals in Roch's lab to surface. The attractant had turned them into single-minded killing machines when, only minutes before, the three had peacefully cohabited their cell. I'd eat my boot if the Collective didn't have a similar feral zoo somewhere in this tower. The thought that spilling any of this stuff could send those bloodthirsty monsters skittering down hallways, up stairwells, and crashing through doors toward me was the stuff of nightmares.

As much as I'd be glad to not have the attractant in my possession, I didn't love the idea of handing it over to Collective sorcerers. There was a small comfort in knowing Mom had her own smaller carrying case with a backup vial currently stashed in the glove box of the SUV. Caspian was sure Welsh had a connection or two we could contact who could tell us even more about what was in the stuff than Roch had.

The oval, hard-shelled carrying case was lined with dark, thick foam. Inside, three vials of the nearly clear attractant were nestled into their partitions. I handed the case to Rhiannon.

As Mom told the sorcerers what the attractant did, Rhiannon joined Avery and Macrae. They each plucked a vial from the case, holding the little glass bottles between finger and thumb as sunlight made the swirling tendrils of silver sparkle. "A small amount is enough to make them come running. We saw a demonstration with our own eyes. The results were … terrifying."

"And your vampire says more of this can be manufactured?" Avery asked, carefully depositing the vial back into the carrying case that lay open on a nearby coffee table. He wiped off his fingers on his cardigan, nose wrinkling.

"In exchange for offering more protection and veil fortification for Tercla, yes," Mom said.

Macrae scoffed. "We can hardly spare more. We're stretched thin here as it is."

Mom stalked toward the sorcerers. Caspian, Soren, and I had to scoot back on the cushion to avoid a collision of knees. Unceremoniously, she snatched the vial out of Macrae's hand and then scooped up the carrying case. She strode back toward us, then stood at the front of the seating area as Rhiannon had earlier. "Then the one in Rhiannon's hand is the only one you'll get. Maybe your scientists will be able to recreate it, but it'll take you a while. The stuff is potent. If a drop gets on someone's clothes, if a scientist doesn't wash their hands properly enough, and they find themselves in the wrong place at the wrong time …" She shrugged. "*My* vampire is fighting the same fight you are. They want the feral problem taken care of. You can either accept his help and have something else in your toolbox to fight these things, or you can continue to keep your heads up your own asses and wait for Luma to get overrun like Mulgrew did."

"I'd ask how you know about Mulgrew already," Macrae said, eyeing Soren with disapproval, "but I have my guesses."

Mom said, "I get that asking for help from vampires *against* vampires is counterintuitive, but the feral problem gets worse by the day. Now Lachlan Shade is on the loose on top of that. You need all the help you can get, even if that help comes with fangs."

Macrae's lip curled.

Rhiannon asked Mom to tell them all she knew about Lachlan, and I filled in with what I'd learned from Kayda, repeating a lot of the same things I'd told Roch. Again, this seemed like information they should have already had. Their own werecats had shown up in the aftermath of Lachlan's escape. They'd been the ones who'd had to collect the bodies of all those dead elf teens. The sorcerers had no doubt saddled their human bounty hunters with the mundane task of informing those sixteen elf families that their teenagers had been killed.

Factions were forming between sorcerers, though. I'd always thought of the Collective as being a single entity, in a way. So much of how they operated was shrouded in secrecy, it was almost easier to think of them as sharing a hive mind. One brain with many bodies. They all thought the same. They all wanted the same things.

Clearly that wasn't true. It was a government body made up of individuals. Tasks and decisions were probably divvied up. It would be impossible, I supposed, for every member of the Collective to know everything that was happening in Luma at all times, especially if the priorities of one faction were diametrically opposed to that of another.

It had fallen quiet for a moment after I finished speaking. I'd like to think the sorcerers were giving the dead elf teens a moment of respectful silence. But seeing as Macrae was glancing between me, Caspian, and Soren as if he were moments from ralphing on his own shoes, I figured he was trying to decide what he should and shouldn't divulge next.

Sighing dramatically, Macrae fixed his gaze on me. "A year ago, a sunken pirate ship was found off the coast of Washington. Some unscrupulous types got ahold of most of the cargo before the Collective could seize it. Those goods have wound up on auction blocks across the country. There have been reports in three separate states now of weapons that have come to life. So far, only one has been successfully captured and deconstructed. It—"

My sword was by my side in an instant, the blade cherry red. I sucked in a gasp. Where in the hell had the thing come from? Perhaps it hadn't wandered as far as I'd thought.

Stand down, Tim, I said mentally, just in case it was getting any ideas.

Though Macrae's eyes practically bugged out of his head behind his glasses, he didn't otherwise react. "We believe we've isolated the rune sequence that granted the weapon sentience. We would like to hire you once again, Caspian, to work with us to craft weapons we can send into battle on our behalf."

He'd been addressing Caspian, yet he still only looked at me, as if he refused to grant Caspian the privilege of eye contact. Either Macrae was one of Caspian's former professors who felt personally slighted by Caspian's dramatic exit from the academy, or the guy was petty as shit. My bet was on the latter.

My sword's blade cooled, flipped itself so it hovered horizontally, and then jabbed its hilt into Caspian's chest. Caspian grunted, but I didn't think the sword had used much force. The sword darted away to hover vertically above the nearest coffee table and tapped twice on the wood. Its blade went molten, and then it tapped on the table twice more.

Oblivious, Macrae added, "With the attractant in play, we can perhaps rely more heavily on range-based fighting, which will save more lives."

Caspian ignored him and instead focused on my upset sword.

"What if this could help turn the tide, cutlass? There has to be a way to grant the weapons a kind of autonomy without it—"

Tap-tap.

Caspian looked at me, but I could only shrug. I didn't know the solution here. I knew my sword hated to be used as a mere tool, but I hadn't been able to get Domino's words out of my head for days. The fact that I agreed with a mob boss wasn't something I was particularly proud of.

"Weapons like that sword can be taken apart and used to make others," Domino had said. *"Fighting the ferals would be a hell of a lot easier if weapons could be sent into the battle on their own. A feral can't tear out an opponent's throat if it doesn't have one."*

"This is fascinating, I will admit," Avery said.

I shot him a glare. He was unfazed, especially since he only had eyes for Macrae.

"Is it possible Felix has been telling the truth?" Avery asked. "He said he saw the weapon in action and claimed it had acted independently." He glanced my way for a moment. "Felix Turner *is* your ex-boyfriend, correct?"

I pursed my lips. He knew damn well he was. Did he want me to be distressed that Felix had talked to them about me? Did he want me to second-guess telling Felix anything because it would eventually get back to his bosses? Was he just being an ass?

Permission to neutralize the rude one?

I hesitated.

Mission accept—

No!

Disappointing.

Avery stared at me for a few long beats. His tone was off-putting when he next spoke, but I couldn't put my finger on why each word made me uncomfortable—like there was an itch between my shoulder blades that I couldn't reach.

"It's a shame how everything turned out. Seems that in the wake of your parents' ... extracurricular interests, your reaction to the events drove Mr. Turner away from you—and straight toward us." The peppermint knocked against Avery's teeth as he idly moved it around in his mouth. He pointed a finger and wagged it between Caspian and me. "This pairing *does* make more sense. Like calling to like."

My sword hovered in the inverted position above the coffee table, but I knew somehow that it faced Avery. Its blade slowly grew redder. The entire weapon quaked.

Awaiting instructions, awaiting instructions, awaiting instructions ...

A small, sweet smile graced Avery's face. *Click, click* went the peppermint.

That latent anger I'd been squashing started to break free of its confines. How dare this pampered old man speak to me like this? He was passive-aggressive, condescending, and smug.

There was no way that giving either sword permission to lop off the guy's head would go well for me.

I wouldn't do well in prison. Antarctica was cold.

Click, click.

I clenched my teeth. I dug my nails into my palms.

But it would probably be worth it.

Caspian's face suddenly took up most of my vision and I flinched, scooting back a couple of inches on the couch cushion. "Whatever he's saying to you, only you can hear it."

Brow creased, I peered around him to eye my sword. Normally when it was pissed off, its blade went from steel gray to cherry red in a matter of moments. It was currently still slowly heating. It sensed *my* anger and was incensed on my behalf, but it hadn't actually heard Avery.

And despite the mental connection I shared with Tim, the second sword hadn't heard Avery, either. Tim was still asking for instructions on a loop in its monotone, bloodthirsty AI voice.

I shifted so Caspian and I were face-to-face again. "Telepathy?" I whispered.

"Yes, but it's more than that. He can't control or read your thoughts so much as place them in your mind. He can make you *think* you're sad, or happy, or angry. Little subliminal thoughts running around in the back of your mind, gnawing away like termites, that you don't realize are there until it's too late. With enough time and a well-planned strategy, he could drive a person mad," Caspian said, still keeping his voice low. "It's the kind of power that's great for passing secret messages when communication lines are compromised. It's also the kind of power used to break someone's mind in half."

I frowned.

"It's harder for him to do it to other sorcerers," Caspian said, idly chewing on his bottom lip for a moment as his eyes glazed over with memory. "He was often the professor who worked with human students to help train them on how to ward off mental attacks." The look he punctuated the sentence with told me Avery's training methods were sketchy at best.

I wondered if Caspian's friend Marcus had been one of the unfortunate human students who'd had to contend with Avery.

Macrae sighed dramatically. I knew it was him without looking, as even his breaths managed to sound grouchy. "Please save the canoodling for your personal time, Blackthorn."

Arching his eyebrows at me, Caspian silently asked if I was no longer seconds from allowing the swords to commit murder. I nodded.

Caspian took up a normal seated position beside me again. "Crafting weapons from scratch is doable, but it's time-consuming. I could maybe forge one every three days, but—"

Avery held up a hand. "When you deserted your job with us, we hired others to finish the work you started. Between that and collecting illegal weapons from smugglers, black-market auctioneers, and foolhardy mundanes, our armory is well stocked. What we need is someone to complete the runework. There are very few with the skill set for such a task, which says a lot about how dire this situation has become, given that we're willing to throw our hat into the ring with someone so ... flighty."

I hazarded a glance at Caspian, whose expression had

completely shuttered, giving him a mask of calm indifference. Which meant he was *pissed*.

I wasn't sure which one was worse—Avery or Macrae. Macrae had a constant pinched expression, so it wasn't a stretch that he had a sour disposition. Avery, though, still looked like someone's sweet grandpa. He was the kind of guy who would smile warmly in your face before casually knifing you in the kidney, all while whispering sweet, malicious thoughts in your mind that convinced you that you were grateful.

I wasn't sure how he was any better than Yannick the pervy vampire.

So far, it seemed that the elite sorcerers on high each possessed some type of specialized magic. I didn't want to know what kind of awful skill Macrae possessed.

Was that the missing piece from Caspian's schooling? Maybe he'd never chosen a specialization since he'd dropped out before he completed his final exam.

"And if I refuse?" Caspian asked.

My sword's blade flipped from a dull red to a nearly neon blue. It tapped once on the table.

"We've got a list of your infractions a mile long," Macrae said. "Your folder is brimming with witness accounts, paper trails leading to your auction houses, and even a handful of suspicious deaths that can be tied back to your previously crafted weapons. One phone call will land that folder on the desks of our best detectives, along with the promise of a substantial bonus should one of them bring you in.

"Friends and family of the mundanes killed by your weapons would miraculously learn your name. By then, once your arrest is backed up by evidence and honest work by our hardworking gumshoes, it would be up to the courts to decide what to do with you, not us. It would be a runaway train so far off the rails, we'd be unable to right it again."

I clenched my teeth. So they *had* been keeping tabs on Caspian all this time.

The day I'd had my first real conversation with the guys, we'd discussed Caspian's previous gig with the Collective making weapons for them. He'd said, *"We parted ways with the promise that we'd keep each other's secrets and leave each other alone—both of us knowing that their ability to destroy me far outweighed my chances of destroying them. I knew it was too easy, though ... the way they let me go without a fuss."*

"They wanted to end things on good terms," Welsh had said. *"Keep the door open in case they needed your services again."*

The door, I guessed, had just been kicked off its hinges.

Avery clicked his peppermint. "A Soul NDA would have prevented that folder from even existing, as the work you did directly for us would have been protected. But you refused to sign one. It would be unethical of us to allow a wanted fugitive back into Luma's fold without consequences. What kind of example would that set for everyone else?"

My sword began to glow like an ember in my periphery again. Tim's request for instructions repeated on a loop in my head. One of my eyelids started to twitch.

"If you were to assist us in creating weaponry that could very well turn the tide in this war brewing with the ferals and their masters," Avery said. "I believe we'd be hard-pressed to find anyone who would disagree that such an act would absolve you of past sins."

Click, click.

In addition to malicious empathic skills, Avery also possessed the ability to make succumbing to blackmail sound heroic.

My sword was now some odd shade of purple. It, too, was conflicted.

"Fine," Caspian said through gritted teeth.

Avery nodded. "Excellent."

Rhiannon spoke up for the first time in a while, apparently having felt no compulsion to rescue us from Avery and Macrae's harassment despite her supposedly being on our side. "Camila,

Soren, and I will meet with the parties necessary to discuss the best ways to utilize the attractant."

Avery turned to me. This time he wagged his finger between me and my sword. "Macrae and I will escort you and Blackthorn downstairs to the armory. We need to figure out how you woke up your cutlass." *Click, click.* "But first, I've arranged a tête-à-tête with an old friend of yours."

CHAPTER EIGHT

HARLOW

We huddled near the elevator in relative silence while we waited for the trio of sorcerers to finish their hushed powwow in a corner of the seating area. I readjusted the straps of my backpack on my shoulders. It felt so light now that the case with the attractant was no longer inside. The only things in the front pouch now were the keys to the SUV. I'd stuffed the main part of the bag with a toiletry tote, a change of underwear, and a small first-aid kit, just so there would be more in it than the attractant. I'd also wanted a bigger bag with me than a purse in case I needed to stash a sentient weapon or two. Not that either one of them would fit easily. Nor did they want to be contained.

Mom and Soren were having their own hushed conversation. It was mostly Soren trying to pull Mom back from the abyss. She had gone into one of her broody moods where she stared angrily into the middle distance.

My sword was still mad at us. If either Caspian or I tried to talk to it, it would invert itself so its hilt was pointed toward the ceiling before shaking itself at us. I wasn't sure if that was the equivalent of a finger wag, a stuck-out tongue, or getting mooned, but either way, it wasn't happy. Occasionally the blade would glow a sickly shade of yellow that I took to mean, *You disgust me* or *You should be ashamed of yourselves.*

Welsh had once offered the sword an alliance should it ever tire of me. Perhaps it was considering taking him up on it now—even *with* Welsh being stuck in Tercla.

At least Tim had finally shut up. I had a raging headache.

Even after the sorcerers concluded their little chat, though, and the group at large split off into two factions, my sword stuck by my side.

When the elevator silently glided into place and opened, I took a step forward, only to have Sorcerer Avery shoot out an arm to block my path.

"You all go first," Avery said, gesturing at the others with his chin.

Mom turned around, her gaze flitting between me, Avery, and his outstretched arm. My sword softly vibrated near my shoulder.

Avery cut my mom off before she could speak. Tone dripping with sarcasm, he said, "If I harm a hair on her head, you'll make me rue the day I was born, etcetera, etcetera. She'll be fine. Blackthorn will be fine. The cutlass will retaliate should anyone try anything untoward."

My sword dropped to the cement floor and tapped once.

They will bathe in a sea of blood, Tim added silently in my head.

I wasn't sure if I should feel flattered that the psychotic sword was beginning to like me. *Glad to know you find me worthy now.*

Negative.

Rude.

Jaw clenched, Mom glanced at me, brow arched. I nodded once.

She huffed a breath out of her nose, then got into the elevator with an already-waiting Rhiannon and Soren, who held the door open with one large, splayed hand.

The elevator dropped out of sight a few seconds later, leaving the large rectangular cube empty. Through the glass, I spotted a pair of people I assumed were sorcerers loitering by a bookshelf on the other side of the room. They were in their thirties, female, and were clearly talking about us. They were too far away for me to even hear the hum of their whispered conversation. I wondered if they were people Caspian knew from his academy days.

Sorcerer Macrae grumbled to himself as he ambled toward a metal rectangular box sitting atop a pole, like a signaling device found at a crosswalk. There was only one button on the panel—a red circle marked with a down arrow. Macrae slammed it with his fist. He folded his arms high on his chest, making him look like a little kid who'd just been scolded. He glowered at the empty elevator box. I was semi-tempted to ask who'd crapped in his oatmeal this morning but decided I didn't care.

I glanced over at Caspian to find his expression calm as he stared into space—the kind of expression you'd expect on a guy waiting for an elevator. Which meant his brain was working overtime.

Wanting to give him time to process, I reluctantly turned to the only person left: Sorcerer Avery. He fussed with the wrapper of another peppermint. I tried to come up with a neutral topic to ensure a few minutes of asinine small talk.

"So ..." I said casually. "Why'd the Collective publicly frame me for Oliver Randal's murder?"

Avery flinched, his peppermint shooting out of the slippery cellophane wrapper. The hard candy ricocheted off the glass wall of the elevator compartment, hit the floor, then rolled until it hit the toe of Avery's loafer and flopped onto its side. He frowned down at it.

Macrae stood with an elbow resting atop the elevator call button. His beady little eyes peered out at me from between his bushy monobrow and the top of his bifocals.

Tearing his forlorn gaze away from his downed peppermint, Avery offered me a polite smile. "The cutlass *did* cut Oliver Randal down, did it not?"

My sword dropped to the floor, tapping once.

Avery asked, "And it was projecting your likeness when it did so?"

Tap.

"One tap means yes, and two means no," I explained.

Macrae stared at me blankly. "We quite figured that out, thanks."

"So, Miss Fletcher," Avery said, redirecting my focus away from the vivid mental image I'd conjured of me with my hands around Macrae's neck and his little eyes popping out of his skull like grapes. "How were we to know it hadn't *actually* been you who killed him? Several witnesses placed you at the scene."

I glanced at the sword. "Did anyone see you when you killed Randal?"

Tap-tap.

"Are you sure?"

Tap ... tap.

Maybe.

From what I'd heard, Oliver Randal was even more elitist about fae being superior to humans than Welsh was—so I was curious as to how on earth the sword had lured the guy outside. But when the sword donned my likeness, there *was* something decidedly unsetting—even otherworldly—about it. My hair whipped in the wind. My expression said if you looked at me the wrong way I'd gut you like a fish. Either Randal had been scared of me or attracted to my threat of violence. I wondered what would have happened had one of the security guards—Wallace or Travis—seen "me" threatening Randal in the bar. They would have grabbed for me, only to have their meaty hands slip through my form. My sword had risked so much that night. I still didn't know why the desire to kill the guy had outweighed the risks. Maybe I was trying too hard to assign human-like motivations to something that was decidedly *not* human. My sword had only been "awake" for a day before it had zipped off on its own to commit homicide. Perhaps it had been in a kind of irrational frenzy that first day, unable to focus on anything but its instinct for revenge.

But somehow that didn't seem accurate.

Eyeing my sword, I asked, "You lured him toward the back of the parking lot, right? Where it was dark?"

Tap.

"Did you leave the crime scene still looking like me?"

Tap-tap.

No. So it must have taken to the sky after completing the deed. I asked as much.

Tap.

I arched a brow at Avery. "It can't guarantee no one saw it after it killed Randal, but it didn't go strutting down the street looking like me after the guy was dead."

Macrae and Avery shared a long, silent look. Though, given what Caspian had told me about Avery's magical specialty, it might not have been that silent.

Recalling what Leon had told Welsh and me in that private room in the Ghost Lily, I said, "The sword killed Randal. That part isn't up for debate. It killed him with one quick stab to the gut. The thing is, the sword killed him at the Ghost Lily. After the body was discovered, an employee of that hellhole was instructed to take Randal to a second location. *That* was when witnesses had seen 'me,' not after the initial murder. Someone—a sorcerer— glamoured himself to look like me at this second location and made *sure* people saw me. *That's* where the frame job happened. I want to know why. I'm guessing there aren't that many rogue academy-trained sorcerers running around doing your bidding."

"While that *is* true," Macrae said slowly, eyeing Caspian on my other side, "there are more of them than you'd think."

Of all the things I'd just said, Macrae was honestly only focused on the rogue sorcerer part?

The elevator arrived with a whoosh and a muted ding. Everyone quietly piled inside. I stood facing the back of the elevator car for a moment, staring at the pair of ladies who continued to outright watch us. They both looked pissed. Any member of our little group could be the subject of their ire. My sword hovered by my shoulder as if it watched them, too. The best I could tell, Tim hovered directly above me.

Caspian sidled up on my other side.

One of the ladies offered us a mocking salute.

"Friends of yours?" I asked.

Caspian shook his head. "I was going to ask you the same thing."

With a friendly wave, I turned my back on them just as Avery slid a card into a slot in the wall panel. Once he'd hit the button for Floor F, he yanked the card free and dropped it back into his cardigan pocket. The armory, apparently, was below the ground floor.

"For what it's worth," Avery said out of nowhere, "I, too, would like to know the reason for the frame job."

The fact that he was as clueless as me was not remotely comforting.

Neither was the fact that I still didn't know which "old friend" of mine Avery wanted me to talk to. What was this person doing in the armory? Mathias's worried little face popped into my head. I thought of the golden goblin-made crossbow bolt I'd procured for him and how he'd reverently run the fletching made of phoenix feathers across the pads of his small gray fingers. Did the Collective have a file full of my clients' names and every charmed item I'd ever sold them, just like they had a dossier of Caspian's plethora of illegal exploits?

Grayson Ipram was my second guess. The water elemental had been a client for a long time, and he'd even tried to purchase my sword. Those teenage boys at the park had witnessed my sword's attempt to flay Grayson as well as the way Grayson, at my behest, had tried to drown us so he could get away. Maybe the boys had ratted us out. Kayda had mentioned a couple of times that she hadn't heard much from the elemental witch since the night Lachlan climbed out of the portal. What if he was MIA because he'd been in Collective custody?

The elevator ride was silent. Macrae's eyes were a bit glazed, and I wondered if he was listening to a mental soliloquy from Avery.

It irked me that the sorcerers had been baffled by my and my sword's version of the Randal Oliver murder story. It wasn't possible that they'd *truly* believed everything they'd claimed in that newscast, was it? Had they turned the city against me not because they were being duplicitous, but because they honestly believed I was a dangerous mundane driven mad by the magic coursing through the illegal dragon sword?

I'd always used the word "they" to label the people who had turned me into a fugitive over a crime I hadn't committed, but I didn't even know how many people "they" encompassed. It could include Avery and Macrae. It might not. The details that had gone into the newscast that showed all of Luma that I'd turned into an unhinged loon from a post-apocalyptic movie could have been decided by the entirety of the organization. Or each word and phrase could have been selected by majority vote or a unanimous vote, or it could have been handled by a select few. Or it could have been a single sorcerer behind it all, one fueled by a personal grudge.

Just like with any other governing body, this one was filled with good apples and bad. Some downright rotten.

Rhiannon had specifically arranged for this meeting not only to happen earlier than planned, but she'd also made sure we had a private audience with Avery and Macrae. She trusted these two more than whoever was on the master guest list for the larger meeting.

I wasn't going to have a sudden change of heart and suggest we braid each other's hair and have a pillow fight or anything, but I'd try to at least entertain the idea of giving Avery and Macrae the benefit of the doubt.

Then an image of my father flashed in my mind.

My father was killed because someone—or several someones—in the Collective had wanted to shut my parents up. Rhiannon, Avery, and Macrae may not have had a hand in that, but it had been one of their colleagues.

It might not be fair to abhor an entire organization, blaming every individual associated with it, but it was a hell of a lot simpler. They were bad. Everyone else was not. End of story.

I gusted a sigh.

The elevator doors slid open to reveal a narrow horizontal hallway. On the smooth cement floor, bright white paint announced that to the right were the women's locker rooms and to the left were the men's. Directly across from the elevator were two glass doors that led into a room that looked more like a gym than an armory.

Once again, when I tried to move forward, Avery's arm shot out to block me.

"Miss Fletcher and I have an appointment on Floor H," Avery said when Caspian realized I wasn't beside him. "Sorcerer Macrae will escort you to the armory, Mr. Blackthorn. We will meet with you once she's done."

Caspian, his jaw tight, studied my face, searching for any sign that I wasn't okay with this. As much as I hated that our little group was being systematically broken into pieces, I gave myself another pep talk. Mom trusted Rhiannon. Rhiannon trusted Avery and Macrae. We had to trust that they were on our side—at least temporarily.

I nodded tightly.

If the sorcerers tried to take my swords from me, though, there would be trouble.

"Come along now, Mr. Blackthorn," Macrae said, already walking away.

Caspian sent me one last pained look before turning to follow Macrae. According to Caspian, Macrae hated him.

Absolutely no one was having a good time right now.

I took a couple of steps back and watched as Avery pulled his key card from his cardigan pocket again and then slipped it into the wall panel of the elevator. He also activated a rune array on the wall—a step I'd missed last time as my attention had been elsewhere. Avery hit the button for Floor H. The first five lettered floors were parking levels. Who knew what was on the lower levels or how far into the ground the Tower went.

I really hoped my theory about a feral zoo had been wrong. Just like in outer space, if some horrible fate befell me down here, no one could hear me scream.

As the doors closed, my sword started up its discordant hum. That wasn't a good sign.

"What on earth is the matter with your weapon?" Avery asked, casting a disdainful look upward, where the sword hovered near the top of the elevator car, its blade an odd shade of yellow.

"It gets motion sick," I said.

Avery's peppermint clicked against his teeth as he regarded me. "Your use of humor as a means of deflection is childish at best. You're as mouthy as your mother, but at least she has a useful skill set that makes her insubordination tolerable."

I had no idea if he was using his ability on me again or if he was being an asshole out loud. His unchecked power had clearly gone to his head. That, or his malicious empathic ability had eroded whatever natural empathy he'd once had for people. Though I supposed he could hate mundanes as much as Welsh pretended to. Either way, I wasn't thrilled to be stuck with the guy.

The doors slid open.

My first impression of the space before me was that it looked like the hallway of a jail or asylum. Ten feet from the elevator stood a towering slab of smooth cement that stretched far in either direction. The massive wall was broken in only three places by long hallways hewn out of the cement. Between the wall and the elevator was a swath of open space—like a lobby someone had forgotten to decorate. The center hallway yawned directly ahead of me and was lined with metal doors. Each door had a slot in the middle, and above that was a single small window lined with bars. I had yet to step foot out of the elevator, suddenly worried that the "old friend" Avery wanted to introduce me to was a jail cell. I'd eluded capture for months, after all. According to Caspian, as well as Derrick Andover the werecat, a reward had been reissued for my arrest despite our new arrangement with Rhiannon.

When the elevator doors began to close again, Avery turned, offered me a look of exasperation, and held out a hand to retrigger the doors' sensor. They slid back open.

"The more I interact with you, Miss Fletcher, the more I'm sure Felix *had* been right about you and the cutlass. Your bravado dries up at the first hint of danger," Avery said. "You're either an exceptional actress—which I *sincerely* doubt—or you've got an uncanny knack for being in the wrong place at the wrong time."

I crossed my arms. Getting casually insulted every time the guy opened his mouth was getting old quick. "It's called self-preservation. You and your cronies have been making my life hell for months now. I have no idea where you're taking me or who you're keeping down here. If you want me to be *more tolerable*, I suggest you start giving me details."

"Maybe I like surprises." When I didn't budge, Avery gusted a sigh out of his nose, sending a long white nose hair wiggling like a worm sticking out of a hole. "I promise that none of these cells are meant for you."

I pursed my lips.

Mom trusts Rhiannon. Rhiannon trusts Avery and Macrae, I reminded myself.

Awaiting instructions on Operation Peppermint, Tim chimed in. *Neutralize: yes or no?*

I snorted a laugh. Operation Peppermint? Did Tim have a sense of humor?

Humor is an inefficient use of time.

I frowned. *Do not neutralize Agent Peppermint.*

Understood.

I stepped out of the elevator, ignoring the way Avery eyed me curiously. This wasn't the first time I'd seemingly reacted to something only I could hear. If it wasn't until today that he'd begun to believe I wasn't a criminal mastermind, it likely meant he hadn't fully let go of his assumptions just yet. Which meant there was a possibility he still thought the magic in my dragon sword had turned me mad.

I glanced to the far left and right, eyeing the hallways on either side of the central one. "What kind of prisoners do you keep down here?"

The lack of guards of any kind was a slight comfort. If the folks in here were nonviolent offenders, maybe hulking draken guards weren't needed to patrol the halls. Though I supposed if the prisoners were never let out, guards weren't needed anyway.

It was eerily quiet here, save for the hum of my sword high above me and the soft buzz of electricity. Either these prisoners were very quiet, or those heavy steel doors suppressed sound.

Avery headed for the rightmost hallway without a word. I scrambled to keep up with him. "This is where we keep mundanes, lesser fae, and those with weak magic," he said. "Enemies of the hub. Petty thieves. Offenders who have the possibility of being reintegrated into society should they cooperate."

I followed him down the hallway. The windows in the doors were six feet from the floor, allowing me to see snatches of the beige-colored walls in each room but not much else. The walls of the hallway were made of unadorned cement, the metallic green doors providing the only color. The material reminded me a bit of the weather-worn bronze of Roch's statues that dotted Tercla.

My chest squeezed at the thought of Welsh. It hadn't even been a full twenty-four hours since Vaughn had whisked my unconscious friend away, but it felt like a lifetime.

As I passed the fourth set of doors, I spotted a blue-skinned creature grasping the sill of a window to my right, her dragonfly-like wings fluttering behind her. She hissed like a ticked-off cat when we made eye contact, her canines elongating before my eyes. She pounded her tiny fists on the glass, snarling. Her short black hair burst into blue flames.

More upsetting than her instant rage was that I couldn't hear her. I didn't know what she'd done—or was accused of doing—to get thrown in here, so maybe she was as dangerous as her short temper implied. But perhaps she was furious simply because she was losing her marbles.

Avery eventually stopped a few doors down, standing before a cell that looked no different than the others. The only adornment was the small black plaque above the door that had 18-A etched in white. All the rooms down this hall so far had an A after the number.

None of the doors had knobs, keyholes, or card slots.

Avery stepped to the door and placed his hand in the middle of the green-hued metal. Much like with the doors of Caspian's home, the act of touching the door caused a rune array to appear. The array was made of three nested circles, lighting up a bright blue as if he'd just shone a black light over symbols that had been written in fluorescent ink. Something deep inside the metal door groaned and clicked. The massive door gave a hiss and then popped ajar. I braced myself, half expecting a pissed-off winged demon to come flying out and attack me.

Avery pulled the door open with a slight groan, then casually ambled inside. Cautiously, I crept in after him. Once I'd crossed the threshold, the door closed behind me, the mechanism inside giving another great groan and click before the magic powering it settled. The hairs on my arms stood on end, though the crackle of magic I'd felt when he unlocked the door had faded.

I cast a quick look around the space, a little confused to find it looked like a tiny one-bedroom studio apartment more than a cell. It wasn't cozy or inviting by any stretch, but not as bleak as I'd been expecting, either. Nothing adorned the plain walls—all painted beige. A small table with one chair stood near the door.

The bed was twin-size, rather than a cot or bunk bed, and a sturdy trunk sat at the foot of it, presumably for holding clothes and other personal belongings. In one corner sat a one-drawer nightstand with a TV atop it. The screen was currently dark. A door in the back right of the room stood—which I assumed led to a private bathroom—stood slightly ajar. There didn't appear to be a refrigerator or cooking surface anywhere in the room, but the empty cafeteria-like tray on the table implied meals were delivered at least once a day.

I didn't immediately see the occupant of the room and wondered if it was a lesser fae with camouflaging ability. I racked my brain, cycling through my mental Rolodex of clients, trying to recall if someone fitting that description could be in here.

The creak of a faucet turning off sounded from the direction of the bathroom.

"Ugh, I hate that damn spell," came a male voice. "It's not like I have any magic or even significant strength to take out a draken or a sorcerer visitor. It's very inconvenient getting frozen while I'm covered in soap."

Baffled, I turned toward Avery, searching for an explanation for his "surprise."

Several agonizingly long seconds later, a man wearing nothing but a towel around his waist walked into the room. His flip-flops smacked loudly as he walked.

My sword, which was somewhere above me, unleashed a short, high-pitched buzz, reminiscent of a startled shriek.

My mouth dropped open. *"Haskins?"*

Haskins's gaze was focused upward. "I fucking *knew* it was you who raided my place!" He jabbed a finger toward my sword while leveling his beady little eyes on me. "That's *my* sword."

The sword in question shriek-buzzed again and hurtled toward Haskins like a damn rocket.

"Sword, no!" I said, assuming my command was too late even before the words left my mouth.

Haskins yelped, lost hold of his towel as his hands flew up to protect his face, and tumbled backward into the bathroom. Luckily, he'd fallen out of the way at the last possible moment; his considerable bulk hit the floor a breath before the sword thunked loudly into the wall. I heard it trying to yank itself free.

Without thinking, I bolted past Avery and into the bathroom. The tiny space only had a toilet, sink, and shower/tub combination. The sword had pierced the flimsy shower curtain, thereby tearing it from its rings, and was now stuck in the wall. Haskins flailed around on the cement like an overturned turtle. A *naked* overturned turtle.

"Oh my Goddess!" I yelped, clapping a hand over my eyes.

The sound of the sword attempting to pull itself out of the wall once more reminded me that I had more pressing issues than seeing far more of Haskins than I ever needed to see in my lifetime. I jumped into the still-wet bathtub, almost slipped, then lurched forward. I grabbed the hilt just as my sword pulled itself free.

"No murder!" I said, trying to aim the blade upward despite it wanting to harpoon downward—namely into Haskins's chest. It felt like trying to wrangle a firehose turned to full blast—made all the harder by the surface under my feet being slippery as shit. "Sword, stop it! The guy is a weasel, but we have to find out why we're here first!"

"*I'm* the weasel, when *you're* the one who robbed *me*?" Haskins shouted indignantly from the floor. All I could see of him was flailing limbs as he tried to get off his significant backside while in a very tight space. "How is that *I* was arrested? I'm the victim!"

"You ..." I said, then yelped when my sword wrenched me to the side with such force I almost slipped and face-planted into the porcelain tub. "You only had—sword! Stop it! You only had those things because you bought them at an illegal auction, Haskins. Not exactly a victimless crime, dude!"

Haskins grabbed hold of the tub's lip and glared up at me. "You don't even know how to control it! No wonder people are dying left and right around you. Idiot girl didn't even steal the alloy-powder-infused glove!"

My sword stilled so suddenly, I finally *did* slip then. The sword shooting out of my hold and straight toward the ceiling resulted in me pitching backward and landing square on my ass. The hard-shelled case of the first-aid kit in my backpack slammed into my spine. I gasped a wheezing, pained breath. The last soapy remnants of Haskins's shower soaked into my jeans.

Miraculously, I didn't brain myself on the tub, though. Something hard and unforgiving had prevented that, and it was stretched across my shoulder blades now, propping me up. I faced the far wall of the bathroom now.

My new position gave me a clear view of my sword, which was spinning wildly near the ceiling, issuing shrieking buzzes every few seconds. Clearly, it was trying to convince itself to listen to me instead of its instincts—which were telling it to gut Haskins.

Neutralize Agent Weasel?

That was when I realized it was Tim who was behind me; he'd come to my aid to ensure I didn't end up with a concussion or worse.

"You have *two* of them?" Haskins asked, incredulous. He clambered to his feet and I got an eyeful of his junk—again.

"Haskins! Towel!"

A shift of movement in my periphery made me crane my neck toward the doorway. Avery stood there, gaze flickering between me, Haskins, my lunatic sword, and Tim. Avery angrily clicked a peppermint around in his mouth.

"Has the second one been with you the whole time?" Avery asked, his expression implying he was considering throwing my lying ass in a cell after all.

I offered him a toothy grimace. "Surprise!"

CHAPTER NINE

HARLOW

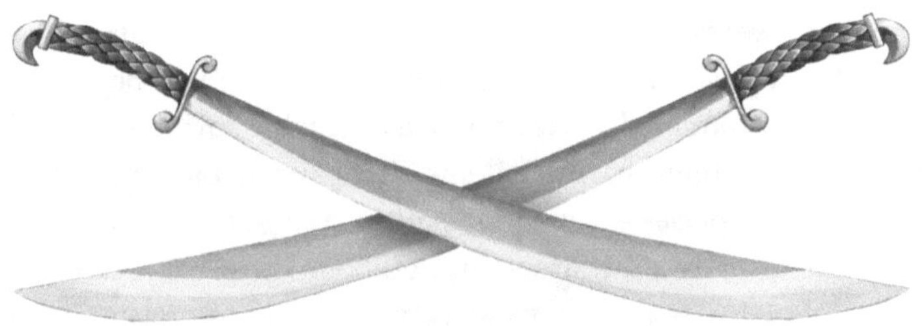

It took a solid twenty minutes for me to calm my sword down enough that I was—mostly—confident that it wouldn't kill Haskins. Avery watched the spectacle from his spot by the door, looking some combination of bored and disgusted. Thankfully, by then Haskins was no longer naked. Though he'd had to get back in the shower at one point when he'd realized he still had shampoo in his hair.

With both swords hovering near the ceiling, I took a seat in Haskins's one chair, dropping my slightly damp backpack on the table. Haskins plopped unceremoniously onto the end of the bed. Avery remained leaning against the door.

When several awkward seconds ticked by in silence, I swiveled toward Avery. Brow arched, I asked, "What exactly did you expect from this impromptu visitation? I know *of* Haskins, but it's not like we were buddies."

Avery's lips puckered in distaste as his gaze flicked between me and Haskins. "The rumor that you were his scorned lover who ratted him out to the authorities so you could get ahold of his stash is inaccurate, then?"

At the same time that I said, "Ew!" Haskins said, "She could only be so lucky."

I turned in the chair and leveled a flat stare at Haskins. "If I remember correctly, the last time we talked, you were flirting with me *pretty* hard. I was one coy smile away from getting you to give up every detail I wanted, right down to your Social Security number."

"You were practically in my lap, sweet cheeks." Haskins swept a hank of sweaty hair out of his face. How the man's hair and skin looked that greasy twenty minutes after a shower was beyond me. I'd always wondered if Haskins was actually half fae, given his knack for finding charmed items. If he were part anuran—an amphibious species—it would explain the sweaty skin, round body, abnormally short arms, and bulbous eyes. "You can blame the alcohol for why you were coming on to me faster than a freight train. Or maybe," he said, leaning in my direction with his elbows on his knees, "the alcohol lowered your inhibitions and allowed you to finally give in to the sexual tension between us that's so potent you can practically see it shimmering in the air."

I had recoiled more with each word until I was practically pressed against the wall behind me. "What, like a mirage only you can see?"

He swiped a pale tongue along his bottom lip. "You one of those chicks who gets a lady boner for guys behind bars? That why you brought her here, hoss?" he asked, finally looking at Avery instead of me. "Arranging a conjugal visit for me is nice and all, but not even she's enough to turn me into a snitch."

I cast a bewildered glance up at Avery who looked as disgusted as I felt.

The sorcerer offered me a pained smile. "I'll be the first to apologize. Your morals might be questionable, but I can see now that it's impossible that you were so taken with this loathsome creature that you threw your life away simply because he kicked you to the curb."

"You can insult me with your fancy words all you want, hoss, but I'm not going to crack. I'm not gonna roll over on my friends —no more than you already *forced* me to, anyway," Haskins said, his jaw tight. "You ripped everything out of my brain already. You said yourself that another dose would turn me into a slobbering idiot. So your only choices are to kill me, give me a sentence term I can earn out, or let me go." He angrily poked the side of his head. "There's nothing left in here for you to take."

They *had* truth-serumed him, then. Goddess only knew what secrets had been pulled out of him. I didn't know the guy well— just that he was reckless in a way that made potential clients nervous. Haskins was too pushy, too aggressive. Given how illegal charm collecting and dealing was, clients valued runners who were discreet. Haskins was not discreet. It was his ability to practically sniff out the locations of charmed goods that kept him in business, not his personality. Even still, not many were eager to work with him.

"Did you really find and sell a griffin egg?" I'd always wanted to know if that rumor was true or if it was a bullshit story he'd started himself.

Haskins grinned. "Two."

"No shit? Intact?"

"Yep," Haskins said. "Last I heard, one of them hatched."

I whistled. "Were they tunneled or stationed?"

Haskins stared at me for a beat. "One of each."

My brows hiked. "Were the sales sticky?"

"Ulma stuck the tunnel, but the crack got stationed in the can."

"Safer out there," I said, nodding.

The slow smile that stretched across Haskins's wide face wasn't lecherous this time. He was just happy that he and I spoke a language that Avery didn't. I'd worried my fluency in the code had grown a little rusty over the last few months, but it had come back to me easily enough.

There was a real possibility that Avery would use his mind powers on one of us to force us to decode the messages, but for at least this shared moment, we'd gotten one up on the sorcerer.

Haskins had just told me that one griffin egg had been found in Luma while the other had been smuggled in. The one that hatched had ended up with a buyer in Canada, while the other was still in the city.

Avery cleared his throat. "My offer still stands, Mr. Haskins. If you can give me any information that results in either the apprehension of a criminal who raided the *Element of Surprise* or the location of one of the more—how do you say—problematic weapons that were aboard, you will be free to go. You already informed us that the auction in which you acquired the cutlass now hovering above us was composed almost entirely of items found on that exhumed ship."

My sword issued another sharp buzz of fury.

"You already knew Haskins was the one who purchased you, sword," I said, without even bothering to glance up. "Save your righteous indignation for *new* information."

"You know, hoss, you constantly reminding me of the all shit I told you against my will doesn't help your cause as much as you think it does," Haskins said, his tone deadly serious.

Ohh, Haskins hated Avery *way* more than I did. He *loathed* the sorcerer—and I didn't think it was just because of the whole "being jailed indefinitely" thing. Maybe it was Avery himself who had truth-serumed Haskins. Maybe Avery had used his malicious empathy on Haskins one time too many. Whatever the reason, it was clear Avery and Haskins were at an impasse. It wasn't because Haskins had scruples—because he absolutely did not—it was because sorcerers in general and/or Avery in particular had infiltrated the one place most individuals had exclusive access to: their own minds.

From my recent experience with Yannick the pervy vampire, and even Vaughn's more subtle use of his enthrall power, I knew that having your mind overtaken and controlled by someone else was *beyond* a violation. I didn't like Haskins one bit, but in his shoes, I think I'd risk my own freedom just to spite the mind-invading jackhole, too.

Haskins refocused on me, his tone still no-nonsense. "Is it true you're in contact with the ghost? Seems hard to believe, since he's spooked by mundanes."

Though "the ghost" wasn't a code name I'd heard that often, Welsh immediately popped into my head. He was known all over Luma under any number of names, and he used multiple faces. I only knew about the Mr. Brown, Bosworth Hemmingsley, and Dawn the draken personas—two of which I knew about only through Kayda. Plus the sore-encrusted zombie lord and the elderly female goblin personas. A few knew his real name, but that list was fairly short.

"Yes," I said, deciding not to mention that Welsh was currently suffering from blood poison while being cared for by pure vampires.

"Can you arrange a meeting for me when I get out of here?" Haskins asked. "Gonna have to start from scratch."

Avery scoffed. "Not sure it's wise to be freely discussing rejoining the criminal underbelly the moment you gain your freedom."

Haskins wasn't talking about restarting his black-market enterprise, though. He wanted to get out of Luma altogether—which was probably one of the better ideas the guy had ever had.

"I can't guarantee she can get you what you need—starting with her isn't cheap—but I can promise she'll at least talk to you." I swiveled in my seat to smile sweetly at Avery. "The ghost likes to keep her identity a secret since she makes her millions by getting ex-cons hooked into MLMs. Given Haskins's exceptional sales ability—I heard he once sold the boiling laryngeal gland of a manticore to a kid who thought it was a harmless whoopee cushion—he'll become the ghost's power leg in no time."

A gusted sigh out of Avery's nose sent that too-long nose hair flapping once more. "I truly can't tell if you two are communicating via Miscreant Code again."

Haskins worked his jaw as he glared daggers at Avery. "Your truth serum is only as good as the questions you ask. If your questions suck, you're less likely to get the information you want. Now … I can't give you the exact names of most of the players because I don't know them. We use code names, aliases, etcetera, for exactly this reason, hoss. I can't give you answers if I don't have them. Code names change all the time, too, so what intel I have could be obsolete by now."

Avery moved closer to Haskins, as if the promise of information had a magnetic pull. The toe of his loafer pressed up against the trunk at the foot of the bed.

Haskins eyed me warily. "You promise you'll get me in contact with the ghost?"

"Promise," I said, uncomfortable with the level of sympathy I currently harbored for the guy.

Haskins nodded once, as if having a mental argument with himself. "When news started coming in that there were goods from the ship coming into Luma, it was referred to as 'the wonder.' The runners put up flyers advertising a traveling circus as a way to recruit attendees. The Wonder Twins were the main draw."

I remembered that circus. I'd *gone* to that circus with Kayda.

The downtown street performers, Enrique and Carlo, popped into my head. Enrique was a fire elemental, and Carlo was human. The pair often used Enrique's magic to help showcase Carlo's impressive, though mundane, acrobatic skills.

The Wonder Twins had been snake shifters who were also contortionists. They had the ability to partially shift, expertly turning parts of their bodies reptilian and back again at an alarming speed, giving the impression their bones were made of rubber.

I'd loved it. It had made Kayda vaguely ill.

"The circus was a front for moving the goods—they were smuggled into Luma in the circus trucks and caravans," Haskins said a bit smugly. "And before you go banning every traveling circus that comes through town, hoss, they never smuggle the big stuff in the same way twice."

Avery's jaw worked so much, I was a little surprised I couldn't hear his teeth grinding together.

"If you wanted to be a buyer at the auction, you had to go to the circus on the second night, go to the ticket stand, and tell the cashier you wanted to go to Clown Alley. In return, you got a regular red admission ticket as well as an identical one in green. For the sellers, you had to use the code 'mud show' on the third night, and then you got a blue ticket with a phone number on the back. Call the number, say you're looking for a good cherry pie, and you got further instructions. I wasn't selling at that one, so I don't know anything beyond that."

This all reminded me of the hoops Caspian and I'd had to jump through to get into Domino's auction.

"On the back of the green ticket was an address written in invisible ink that you had to reveal with heat. The heat also burned the ticket to ash after a minute or two. The message was a location in the Necropolis. The building where it was held was already abandoned before the auction was even set up there, so we didn't have a specific address. Can't tell you what it was before, either—no one told me, and I didn't ask." Haskins smiled softly in response to Avery's irritated sigh. "I spent most of the night seated next to a lady named Cricket. She was quite the dame —fire-red skin, black hair down to her ass, horns long enough to get a good grip on, you know what I mean?"

"Gross," I said.

"Uncouth barbarian," muttered Avery.

Unfazed, Haskins said, "Cricket won the bidding on a sledge-hammer that gave me the same feeling as those two," he said, pointing toward the ceiling. "Can sense that weird buzzy magic from across the room. That cutlass was next up, and Cricket said she wasn't interested in it, even though it's very obviously a superior weapon."

I glanced up solely because I knew that, even if the sword detested Haskins, its blade would still glow blue at the compliment.

I wasn't wrong.

Shaking my head to myself, I returned my attention to Haskins.

"Get this, hoss," Haskins said, resting his elbows on his knees again. "Cricket said she wasn't buying the hammer for herself but for a client. Said this client has been offering top dollar for years to anyone able to find this specific item. Cricket made two hundred G's on that find."

Avery's fists were clenched by his sides, though I wasn't sure if he was trying to control his excitement or his desire to pop Haskins in the mouth for calling him "hoss" too many times. "Who was her client?"

"Didn't get a name, but Cricket said she was a *pure* on the East Coast somewhere."

My brows rose, remembering something Roch had told me about Lihko. *"He proposed a great number of intriguing uses for weapons like your sword. They weren't the kind of thing that appeals to pure vampires on principle—we value the old ways. We like to stalk our meals ourselves. Using a magic-fueled weapon to do it would cheapen the whole experience."*

Pures weren't a monolith, yadda yadda, but two hundred thousand dollars to obtain a specific sentient weapon when pures typically didn't care for weapons at all was … curious. I figured the pure wasn't one from Tercla, so I was already out of ideas about who this client of Cricket's could be. It gave me an excuse to contact Vaughn, at least.

"Your mother's connection to pures may prove useful once

again," Avery said, his expression telegraphing that he still wasn't sure if *my* value ran much deeper than a puddle.

"That enough, hoss?" Haskins asked.

"I would have preferred a more definitive lead or name, but the revelation about the circus used as a means to get charmed goods into the city is more helpful than you realize," Avery said, his unfocused gaze aimed somewhere over Haskins's head. "I'll begin the appropriate paperwork."

"And how long will *that* take?" Haskins asked, exasperated.

Without a word, Avery turned on his heel and, in two quick strides, placed his hand on the door. I sprang to my feet and snatched my backpack off the table, startled by Avery's abruptness. The ring of nested rune arrays revealed themselves from smallest circle to largest, like the ever-widening ripples produced by a rock dropped into a still pond.

Haskins cursed a blue streak so filthy, I turned to him, bracing myself, as I assumed he would be barreling toward us like an enraged bull. But the toadlike man was still seated where he'd been moments before, though his right arm was held up now at a ninety-degree angle, elbow pointed at the wall. A tattoo, the ink dark and fresh, marred his fleshy bicep. It was a rune array housed in a circle with a thick, outlined edge. I got the strangest impression that he'd lifted his arm not to show me his guns, but to showcase the tattoo. The spell that unlocked the door also froze the occupant, and Haskins had taken the only action he could.

Haskins had to know, though, that I had no idea what the array said or what the magic within did. If I wasn't sure Avery would stop me, I would have taken a picture of it to show Caspian.

The oddest thing was that Haskins wasn't moving save for his eyes and mouth. As a pulse of magic swept over me, like a light buzz of static electricity, Haskins's gaze very deliberately angled toward his tattooed bicep several times. He could still talk, but he clearly didn't want Avery to overhear.

Stranger still, my sword shot down from the ceiling and

placed itself in Haskins's upraised hand, even though Haskins couldn't close his fingers around the hilt. A breath later, it shot toward the ceiling again.

The door issued a muted hiss as it popped open. Since my back had been facing the door, I had no idea what Avery had witnessed. Hopefully Haskins's and my sword's antics had been shielded.

"Off to our next destination, Miss Fletcher," Avery said. "If you've somehow decided you'd like a conjugal visit after all, we'll need to reschedule."

My face involuntarily screwed up in disgust.

"You're not hairy enough for me anyway," Haskins said, still frozen in place. "Get me in contact with your ghost, yeah? Might not matter, given my path, though." Another deliberate flick of his gaze toward his arm.

"Paths can be changed," I said, strapping my backpack on, using it as a way to stall my departure.

"Might be too ingrained."

Shit.

Haskins's lips pursed. "Stay off my path. A single detour makes you a snout. Eye the dip. Not a kite, but not exactly my choice in a lightning storm, either, you know?"

I nodded once. "Thanks. I'll do what I can."

Turning, I faced Avery, who waited by the open door, keeping it propped open with his foot. As he reached into one of his cardigan pockets to pull out another of his infernal peppermints, Margaret Fengast of all people came to mind. Her official job had been as a seamstress while she kept a secret forge in the basement of her shop. She'd stitched runes into her clothes that granted the garment magical enhancements, such as bottomless pockets.

Haskins had just warned me that a dose of truth serum not only forced the victim to spew their secrets, but it branded them with a rune array that potentially doubled as a tracking device.

In charm-collecting circles, there was always a worry that any new person we encountered could be a spy for the Collective—a snout—who was trying to sniff out the identity of collectors, the names of buyers, or the location of goods, like a pig rooting out truffles. As a form of professional courtesy, if one thought another collector was under threat of being found out, they were told, "There's a snout in your path." Meaning you were being tracked by a Collective narc.

Haskins trusted Avery as much as one could in his position. He believed the paperwork for his release would get filed; it was just a matter of how long it would take. Avery, in his mind, wasn't a kite—a scam artist—but that didn't matter much if the tracking array on Haskins's arm meant the Collective could find him whenever they wanted, potentially forcing Haskins to divulge even more secrets about his colleagues against his will. Hence him wanting out of Luma.

Most worrying for me was Haskins's warning to "eye the dip." Watch his pockets.

Avery had truth serum on him, and one dose would be enough to give the Collective access to my movements. Caspian and I had gotten a small taste of that when we'd been branded by tracking runes, thanks to Sorcerer Albert Sweeney. Sweeney's tracking runes were the only way Domino the orc mob boss would allow us to leave the auction house with the treasure chest *and* my sword—which the orc had wanted for himself. Domino had tracked us to Shane and Alice Winchell's home, bringing his troll and elf minions with him.

They'd almost killed us.

I'd rather never be magically tagged again, thanks.

When it came to tracking legitimate criminals—especially the worst of the worst who were sent to the Antarctic hub—an argument could be made that, in those cases, an invasion of privacy was imperative for safety reasons. If one of them staged a prison break, it was in everyone's best interests to get them caught quickly and stuffed behind magic-infused bars again.

But to tag the folks who Avery himself said were so low level they were fit to be cast back into society? Tracking them—tracking *me*—to turn us into bait to catch the bigger fish? That was a rights violation if I ever heard one.

And Avery currently had the serum in one of his damn pockets.

Tim?

*A*WAITING INSTRUCTIONS.

Operation Peppermint is as follows: If Agent Peppermint attempts to inject me or forces me to consume anything he produces from his pockets, you are to knock said item from his hands.

*U*NDERSTOOD.

With that, and with my swords flanking me, I stepped back out into the hallway with Avery, the scent of peppermint thick in my nose.

CHAPTER TEN

KAYDA

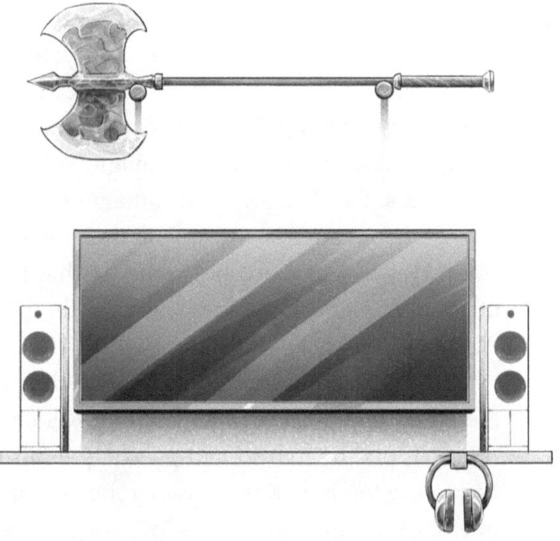

Kayda's too-large frame was wedged into one of the uncomfortable desk chairs in front of a computer in the VHoA Necropolis headquarters. She needed to remind Marisol for the millionth time to place an order from the elephantine fae office catalog. Kayda's legs were going to lose circulation one of these days.

She wrinkled her nose and rubbed at the spot between her eyes. If she was this cranky, it was a sure-fire sign that she needed to be in bed curled up beside Henri instead of sitting in front of this damn screen. Sleep continued to elude her; she and sleep had been on shaky ground since the night Lachlan Shade escaped exile. That had been strike one.

Strike two had come when she'd watched the videos of Mulgrew's veil breach. She could still hear the panicked screams of strangers if she thought about the breach for too long.

The third strike had come from learning that Welsh had not only been bitten by a hybrid, but that the bite had become infected. Now her grouchy friend was suffering from blood poisoning. Kayda still didn't understand the extent of what being a shadow vampire meant, but it sounded like the victim ended up as a vampire who needed blood not to survive, but to stave off insanity. Sufferers of the blood poison also could wield an unholy, even more potent, version of their inherent magic.

As an added bonus, the shadows that came with the transition served as a way for the victim's sire to spy on their creation.

Learning that Welsh was now holed up with the pures in Tercla—one of the few safe places for Welsh on the planet—did little to quiet Kayda's anxiety.

The final strike had come when Kayda and the San Diego chapter of VHoA had been *this close* to rescuing Kessler—a nyad who had been kidnapped by hybrid vamps—only to discover that she and the team were too late. Kessler was gone, and in his place had been a message in the form of a pile of severed hybrid vampire heads. One such head had a domino shoved into each eye socket.

Kayda was convinced orcs must have been behind the massacre and kidnapping, and that the tiles were a connection to Domino, the orc mob boss Harlow had had an indirect hand in killing.

One of Kayda's newest concerns—one she hadn't told anyone, not even Harlow—was that someone within VHoA was passing info from the forum to outside sources. Someone, perhaps, who had aided in Kessler being kidnapped. What were the odds that orcs would have known where to find Kessler in the first place, as sequestered as he'd been in a hybrid vamp nest in a rural area surrounded by the dying trees of an apple orchard? Orcs weren't exactly known as calculated strategists. They relied on brute strength—which they had in spades. And, clearly, the orcs hadn't been in league with the hybrids in the nest, seeing as the orcs had slaughtered the lot of them.

Kayda had gotten frustrated with Marisol on numerous occasions for sharing too much on the organization-wide forum. But VHoA was a close-knit group; the organization was Marisol's life. She felt safe—as most members did—sharing everything. They believed being as informed as possible saved lives.

But what if someone—or several someones—was exploiting that? And, Goddess forbid, what if there were Shades lurking within VHoA's ranks?

Despite all this, tonight Kayda's thoughts kept straying to last night's patrol. It had been uneventful—*again*. Which made the Mulgrew breach even more troubling. No other breaches had occurred in the weeks since, nor had anyone been able to figure out why Mulgrew had been hit.

Had there been something in Mulgrew specifically that the Shades wanted, or was this yet another distraction? Did Lachlan want VHoA focused in one direction while he quietly enacted another part of his plan somewhere else?

Kayda was still pondering this twenty minutes later when the door to the War Room burst open. Kayda was on her feet so fast, she toppled her chair *and* accidentally elbowed the poor sod sitting next to her in the face.

When the person heaving at the door turned out to be a VHoA member who had run over from the other unit on the property— and not a shadow monster sent to tear their limbs from their bodies—Kayda felt kind of bad about her reaction. She clapped Cathy on the shoulder and gave her a little jostle. "Sorry about that."

Cathy had both hands cupped over her nose, and she audibly winced at Kayda's aggressive apology. When blood started to trickle between Cathy's fingers, she offered Kayda a death glare before excusing herself to scurry into the bathroom.

Marisol shot Kayda an exasperated look over the bank of computers.

The guy still heaving in the doorway loudly cleared his throat. "Uh … Mari?" He waved what looked like a cordless phone. "It's Joe Taylor."

Marisol pushed back her chair and walked over, hand out. "From Kensey or Elsher?"

"Elsher," the guy said.

Marisol laughed. "Really? I said Elsher as a joke …."

The guy didn't look remotely amused. Kayda could hear his heart thundering like a jackhammer. He swallowed hard. "It … uhh … it might be another breach."

"That can't be right …" Marisol grabbed the phone and pressed it to her ear. "Hey, Joe. Long time, no talk. Nguyen said there was a breach, but I must have misheard—" Her head jerked back. "Whoa, whoa. Joe, slow down."

Everyone was out of their chairs now, eyes trained on Marisol. Kayda was sure they all hoped Marisol would put the phone on speaker, but when it was clear she wasn't going to, Kayda adjusted the dials on her hearing. Closing her eyes helped her further home in on Joe Taylor's voice. Kayda had never heard his name come up before, and she had even less of an idea about where Elsher was.

Joe's voice was muffled. Either he was whispering, or he had a hand cupped around his mouth as he spoke. Kayda pictured him crammed under a desk. "An hour ago, one of our aeorci reported that a fleet of SUVs was coming up the access road. At least a hundred ferals were running ahead of and alongside the cars."

Kayda racked her brain trying to recall what an aeorci was. Then it clicked. Harlow had told her they were sort of like draken but of the avian variety. Caspian's eagle—or was it a falcon? Harlow could never remember—was an aeorci. Rory was a magic-touched bird with a human-like consciousness. Apparently Rory and Caspian could communicate telepathically.

"Did the ferals get in?" Marisol asked.

"Not yet, but they're close," Joe said. "The Collective sorcerers here have been refortifying the runes on the obelisks to strengthen the veil, but that won't do shit against the ferals. Besides, there are only three Collective sorcerers here. There are also a few witches, but combat magic isn't their bag. The VHoA contingent is me and two others. No one else—and I mean *no one*—is prepared for this. The nearest VHoA chapter is well over twenty-five hours away by car. The chancellor put in calls to other hubs for werecat reinforcements by telepad, but it's been an hour. I heard her make the calls myself. Each one sounded more desperate than the last. No one's coming to help us. It's a multi-jump trip, but that wouldn't slow them down this much. Something's not right."

"That sounds like the start of a *conspiracy*, Joe ..." Marisol said, somehow sounding more intrigued by *that* than by the threat Joe currently faced.

Kayda met Quaid's eye. The guy was annoying and a little weird, but they'd bonded—kind of—over their obsession with finding Kessler. Now they were further bonded over failing him.

They also shared a mutual concern about Marisol's love of conspiracy theories. Kayda wondered if there was a way to restrict Marisol's access to certain sections of the forum.

It was silent on both ends of the line for several long seconds before Joe spoke again.

"We're as off the grid as you can get here. The only reason I'm able to call you now is because there are a couple of spots in the town center that get okay-ish reception. The rest of the place is a dead zone. Hardly anyone cares about that here. It's a research hub full of scientists. They're constantly studying and talking about rune construction. I don't know what in the hells they're even talking about most of the time when I overhear conversations.

"Not many people in the hub system know about this place, and you basically have to be an Einstein to land a job here. And even after that, you have to get security clearance from the Collective in order to accept the job. I'm here as a glorified rent-a-cop, and even *I* needed to get extensive clearance.

"So how in the *fuck* did a convoy of hybrids and their ferals make it here, let alone know where here *is*? If a band of lunatics were barreling toward the gates of Area 51, a lot of folks with guns would be waiting to take them out. The chancellor issued a warning call—*several* calls. Where's our backup?"

Marisol asked, "Are the outgoing calls getting blocked somehow? Maybe the system is down?"

"Or the calls were intercepted. Someone doesn't want anyone to know we're in trouble out here," Joe said. "Say what you want about the Collective, but they wouldn't go through so much trouble to keep this place under wraps just to let their best and brightest get their throats torn out by ferals."

"Why's he calling *you* about this?" Kayda asked, realizing a moment later that she'd said that out loud. Her eyes popped open, and she found half a dozen gazes angled her way. The room had been deathly silent, save for Marisol's half of the conversation, before Kayda spoke.

Even as Marisol offered Kayda an exasperated look for eavesdropping, she repeated Kayda's question to Joe. She also belatedly put the phone on speaker so everyone could hear his answer. All eight of them huddled around Marisol and the outstretched phone.

"I've been keeping up with the chatter on the forums, and it sounds like you've got an in with a werecat or two, right?" Joe asked.

"Right ..." Marisol said slowly.

"I trust your judgment over the judgment of anyone here at

this point. You and me go way back, Mari. If you've got an up-and-up werecat you can get in contact with, we need them. We needed them an hour ago. I've got a real bad feeling. If a hundred ferals are given the okay to raid this place, every last one of us is fucked. And if someone in Elsher is working with them? Then we're *super* fucked."

"Shit," Marisol said. "Okay. I'll call Jasmine right now. Keep us updated, okay? Text me. Call me. If you can, post some of what you just told me in the forums. I'll put out a call on the message boards that we need trustworthy werecats to get to Elsher as soon as possible."

Several of the VHoA members in the War Room darted to their computers and started clacking away on keyboards. Two others pulled out cell phones and called contacts.

Joe sucked in a shaky breath. "Thank you, Mari. And … if I don't survive this—"

"Don't," Marisol said, cutting him off.

"If I don't survive this, you tell your parents that meeting them changed my life for the better, okay? Tell them I owe them everything."

Kayda had no idea what Joe was talking about, but the stricken expression on Marisol's face said she did.

"I will," Marisol said. "But you'll be fine, Joe. Okay? We're on it."

"All right," Joe said, but he sounded resigned.

When Marisol hung up, she just stared into space. Kayda grabbed hold of Marisol's elbows and gave the woman a light shake. "Don't shut down on us, Mari. What do you need me to do? You need to call Jasmine."

The glazed look in Marisol's eyes dissolved. "Can you watch the message boards and forums for any news about Elsher specifically? Especially if it's something from Joe. It won't be very exciting work, but we need to know the moment something changes. Everyone else, we need werecats. We need to get reliable people into Elsher before the ferals cross the veil."

Kayda *hated* when Marisol assigned her desk duty. She wanted to be *doing* something other than sitting in these damn circulation-destroying chairs. "What about us? Joe says he needs help *now*. We can be in a telepad to Elsher in five minutes flat."

Marisol shook her head. "You heard Joe … you need clearance to hitch a ride there. A werecat is our best bet. They'd have clout with the Collective, and only a Collective sorcerer can issue clearance to get into that place. We're at the bottom of the chain."

Kayda was quiet for a beat. "You think this is Shade?"

Marisol sighed. "Probably. Which means he either already knew about Elsher, or someone's been feeding him information about it."

"What do they do there that Shade would care about raiding it?" Kayda asked.

"No idea," Marisol said, shrugging. "Joe's been there a few years and has never told me what they're researching there. I don't think he's locked into a Soul NDA, but whatever he *is* locked into makes sure he keeps his mouth shut."

Kayda nodded once, then headed for her computer, her teeth clenched.

"Hey, Jasmine," Marisol said, stepping out of the War Room with her phone pressed to her ear. "We have … a situation …" She closed the door behind her, making it difficult for Kayda to eavesdrop.

Instead, Kayda toggled back and forth between the forum and the various message boards, waiting for an update from Elsher. Her leg bounced constantly under her desk.

Ten minutes passed before a message from JoeTaylor2 finally popped up on the VHoA-wide forum. Kayda's leg bounced harder.

The message was only eight words long: The sirens have started. Goddess help us all.

ELSHER
LAB8
RENATA'S LAB
LABORATORIES
TESTING SECTOR 1
TESTING SECTOR 2
ELSHER'S LOOP
TELEPAD
TELEPAD
ELSHER'S LOOP
RESIDENTIAL SECTOR
TELEPAD WAREHOUSE
TELEPAD
EARTH WITCH HOUSE
GROUNDWATER WELL
CO-OP GARDEN
WATER WITCH HOUSE

CHAPTER ELEVEN

RENATA

The blaring wail of the town-wide sirens made Renata's pen tip jitter across the page. These sirens weren't quite as intense as the air-raid ones, but they were close. Her head snapped up and she met the equally saucer-wide gaze of Dalton across from her. They'd both been hard at work on a dystilian loop they could—*hopefully*—use to keep the quarter-jump portal open for longer than ten seconds. It would also be ideal if the portal didn't turn into a vacuum and suck everything around it into itself. But that task had been assigned to Paola and Baker.

Renata glanced over at the pair now, who looked no less bewildered. The town-wide sirens were tested once a month—which had happened just last week. She knew the mundane world had oft-tested emergency sirens and warning alerts, too. Everyone, she guessed, knew what the public broadcast system alert sounded like, but no one ever expected to hear it in action.

Her little hub of Elsher was a notorious dead zone as far as cell phone signals went. They were well and truly off the grid here. A fact her parents were none too pleased about, despite Renata being only a few telepad rides away. She'd never really liked cell phones, but she wished she had one now.

Renata flinched as a voice piped into the lab from the intercom embedded in a wall. "This is not a test. I repeat: This is not a test. The town's veils have been breached. Barricade the doors. If you possess defensive magic, gear it up now, and prepare for a fight. Goddess be with you."

Renata blinked, her pen still poised above her notepad.

What?

Breached?

How? *Why?*

Hardly anyone outside of portal-study circles even knew Elsher existed. Hells, she'd been working here for a year, and not even *she* knew the extent of what was researched here. Their lab wasn't the most important one in the hub, but they were no slouches. The paper she and Dalton planned to submit to the Sorcerer's Symposium would launch their careers, she was sure of it. Even the mega-famous, much-respected Joan-freaking-Calder thought their discovery was extraordinary. Granted, no one outside of the portal studies community would have any idea who Joan Calder was, but to Renata, she was as A-list as one could get.

Renata was still a little embarrassed that her "professional" email to her idol had turned into a gushing fan letter, as if Renata were a teenybopper and Calder was the lead singer of a boy band. Dalton had assured her it was a good email. But she'd caught his slight wince when he started reading the already-sent message.

Renata eyed the single purple-black flower that sat in the delicate white vase on her workstation. In moonlight, the petals took on an iridescent sheen, like the feathers of a starling or the carapace of a beetle. A little smile tugged at her lips as it always did when she looked at the flower.

Calder hadn't been scared off by Renata's ridiculous email. It had been two-thirds gushing and one-third about her and Dalton's proposed theory. Calder had replied, thanked Renata for her kind words, and called their work "ingenious." Calder had politely asked several questions over the course of a few emails, clearly humoring her starstruck fan. It was incredible that the kindness of one person could instill confidence in a stranger hundreds of miles away.

Ingenious! She'd called them ingenious.

Even still, no one else knew about the paper. People made mind-blowing discoveries here every week.

The sirens renewed their wailing cry, startling Renata out of her thoughts. Right. A breach. She shook her head, trying to clear it. Nothing about this made any sense. Her mind was glitching.

Paola moved first. She jumped from her stool so quickly, it clattered to the floor. The crash snapped Dalton and Baker out of their fear-induced stupors. Unlike Renata and Dalton, who were relatively fresh out of sorcery academy, Paola had worked in Portal Relations for three years after she graduated from an academy in Italy. She'd bounced all over the world researching portals. Somehow, she'd ended up in this research hub in the middle of nowhere in Canada's Yukon territory.

Being in an area removed from people meant the science-loving sorcerers here could experiment with unpredictable magic —namely, portals. *Most* of the theories that populated Frederica Kensey's writings were based around unpredictable magic, and

Kensey herself had established this place, naming it after her beloved husband.

It was crazy to Renata that, while the rest of the magic-touched world believed Kensey had lost her mind and then slipped into obscurity, she'd actually been here, researching portals out of the limelight. The science had always meant more to Kensey than notoriety.

Paola was shouting orders Renata was only now tuning in to. "Portal research notes and books into Safe A. Runework research into Safe B. Just like we practiced." Dalton and Baker were scrambling now—stuffing loose notes into binders and slamming books closed. "Goddess, Renata! Get out of your head. Move!"

Renata scrambled to her feet. She pulled notebooks from drawers and piled runework tomes in her arms, waddling under the weight of it all to a safe in the corner that had once been hidden beneath removable tiles. She stuffed her haul into it, then hustled out of the way so Dalton could stow another pile of research.

There hadn't been any more announcements over the intercom system, and while the wail of the sirens hadn't let up in the background, she didn't hear anything else that told her what was happening beyond the walls of their research lab.

Renata made two more trips to the safes before her work area was cleared away. Save for her beloved flower … and the lone notebook she couldn't bear to part with. The notes for her co-authored paper with Dalton were written on those pages. Notes for a paper that could change the way people looked at portal creation. If their theories were right, it could change everything.

Her notes might be safest in their magicked hiding place, but what if this was the last time she ever stood in this lab?

Shooting a glance to her right, she found Paola busy with getting the safes hidden again. The woman's arms whipped about in a frenzy, casting a rune array so complex, it would have taken Renata herself at least twice as long. While Paola was distracted, Renata grabbed her notebook and flipped to a random page, just to be sure this was her *important* notebook, and not the notebook she scribbled recipes in that she never had time to try. This was what she got for buying identical notebooks in bulk.

We postulate that, by distilling a whimal chain before restructuring it with dystilian loops and frybol underpinnings, we can then begin to—

Satisfied that she had the right one, she stuffed it in the waistband of her pants, the notebook's cool cover flush against her warm back. As she pulled her shirt taut, her wide eyes met Dalton's. He'd seen the whole thing. Her face heated.

They'd been friends for most of their lives. They'd met at summer camp when they were twelve. After five summers of friendship, they'd applied to the same sorcery academies, both getting into Kensey. They'd studied together, geeked out over portal theory so much that it was hard to maintain other friendships, and helped keep each other sane when the grueling study load had almost broken their spirits. They hadn't planned to end up in Elsher together, but Renata had been delighted—*more* than delighted—to learn he'd landed a position here, too. The hiring process for Elsher was kept as secret as everything else. Seeing a familiar face had calmed the homesick part of her when she'd realized just how removed she'd be from her family and friends.

She gently shook her head at him now. Dalton hesitated for only a moment, then nodded. He wanted to publish just as badly as she did.

Renata, Dalton, and Baker set about casting rune arrays on the doors of the lab. They used the same types of spells that Paola employed—filling in the seams of the doors' outlines. Or, in Paola's case, the seams around the removable tiles. Anyone looking hard enough might notice that the lines of grout in two corners of the room weren't *actually* grout. But should the thieves spot the slight anomaly and pull the tiles free, they'd then have to get past the wards on the safes.

As Renata poured more magic into her rune array for concealment, she prayed to the Goddess that the intruders wouldn't find her and her colleagues. None of them, except maybe Paola, were fighters. Hopefully the intruders were the type who took live hostages, not the kind who killed all potential witnesses.

She still couldn't fathom who would want to raid Elsher. It wasn't as if there were rival Portal Relations groups or warring scientists. The pressure to publish was ever present, sure, but not to this extent. Sorcerers from all over the world lived and worked here. They were all bound by the same quest for knowledge—to find a way to open stable portals. To communicate with people in other realms. To, possibly, one day reopen the gateway between the earthen and fae realms that had been inaccessible since the Glitch.

Elsher, as far as she knew, was no closer to unlocking the mystery of why the portals to the fae realm had been stuck closed for a century. So why was this happening now?

Unease prickled the back of Renata's neck like cold fingertips ghosting across her skin. Someone was watching her. Without thinking, she spun toward the windows, breaking her concentration so thoroughly that she lost hold of her array. It broke apart in the air like golden dandelion fluff on the wind. Paola had just joined her in casting magic on one door while the men cast on the other. Renata heard Paola admonishing her for breaking her array, but Renata was unable to look away from the windows.

There were only three in the rectangular building, and they were all on the same wall. They were positioned opposite the pair of doors that opened into the hallway shared by all the offices in Lab 9, where she was now. The windows boasted the breathtaking view of Lab 8's backside, where it sat empty on a cracked-asphalt surface. Wild grasses grew around the bungalow, the weeds swaying gently in the breeze. She sensed no other movement outside, and yet she took a few steps toward the windows, sure something had triggered her senses.

Elsher had a mostly rectangular design, with the town center standing in the, well, center. The labs made up the research sector at the north end of the hub and were arranged in two rows—four in front, nearest the town center, with five more behind them. Lab 9 was in the back row, and the building's closest neighbor, Lab 8, had been closed for at least a year. If intruders were searching for people or valuables, they'd most likely be found in the residential sector in the south. Lab 9 wouldn't be anyone's top priority.

Yet Renata's gaze was inexplicably drawn to the windows again—specifically the middle one. She cocked her head. The sound of her colleagues calling out spells was a drone of noise in the background, mixing with the ever-present wail of the sirens.

A head popped up on the other side of the glass, and Renata froze, grabbing hold of a table's edge to steady herself. The face peering back at her, only visible from the nose up, looked both human and not. The person might have once had shoulder-length black hair, but what strands dotted the smooth scalp now grew in stringy patches. Maybe it wasn't growing at all, and this was what was left because the rest had fallen out. It used to be a man, she thought. Maybe a middle-aged one.

The human-like thing suddenly cocked its head. It was such a quick, unnatural movement, Renata gasped. The wrongness of it was so off-putting, she couldn't get out a word to her colleagues that the danger they faced might be not human *or* use the doors to gain entrance. Some part of her worried that, while she'd been tucked away in the middle of the Yukon, her nose buried in research tomes, the world had been invaded by zombies. Perhaps the entire population of Earth had been ravaged by the undead, and places like Elsher were all that remained.

The creature's eyes were wall-to-wall black.

It tipped its head back and … howled? A breath later, another face appeared—this one was in the leftmost window. That creature stared at Renata for only a breath before it forcibly slammed its forehead into the glass.

Renata yelped.

The thing did it again.

The glass cracked—a fissure of spiderwebbing cracks skittering across the surface like bolts of lightning.

"We've got a problem!" she yelled, unable to tear her gaze from the pair of beasts who were now both slamming their skulls into the glass with no regard to their own wellbeing.

Dalton lost hold of his array at the sound of her call. She heard him asking her over and over what was wrong. It had only taken him a few seconds before he'd seen the monsters, too. He'd run back to the others, telling them to drop their arrays.

Paola came up beside Renata now. Baker took up a spot on Dalton's other side.

"Shit, shit, *shit*," Paola muttered to herself. "Those are ferals."

"As in *vampires*?" Baker asked, his voice shrill.

"Yes," Paola said. "*Cazzo!* Change of plans. These things are fast. If they get in, we're screwed. We have to take down the concealment spells we just put up. Leave that to me. In the meantime, grab anything you can use as a weapon."

Voice still an octave too high, Baker asked, "What if they're in the hallway, too?"

"Then we're fucked," Paola said. "But I'd rather take my chances out there than be trapped in here."

Renata swallowed.

She was not cut out for this. She'd never been in a fight in her life—her scuffles with her younger sister notwithstanding. Renata was not a violent person. She was the type to huddle in the fetal position when scared. What good would she be against something that frightened the experienced, well-traveled Paola Russo this badly?

The leftmost window was seconds from shattering altogether. Trickles of blackish blood ran into the feral's eyes from its self-inflicted head wounds. Renata didn't know how she could tell it was looking at her when its eyes were nothing but lifeless black pools, but she could. It stared at her as it slammed its head into the glass over and over and over.

I'm coming for you, its unblinking gaze seemed to say. *I'm coming for you, and there's nothing you can do to save yourself.*

"Go!" Paola yelled.

They scattered, scouring the room for anything they could use to defend themselves. Baker and Dalton each grabbed a metal stool. Renata ran in frantic circles until she inexplicably settled on an industrial broom. It was propped up against a low bookshelf that had once been lined with books. Books that were now stuffed into warded safes buried beneath the floor.

Crack!

Renata, Baker, and Dalton spun toward the sound. The feral had finally broken the glass and was crawling through the shattered window like a swamp creature creeping out of a well. The jagged glass sliced up its shoulders and arms on the way in, but it didn't seem to notice.

Baker was muttering a stream of curses or prayers behind Renata, she wasn't sure which.

Paola was the only one who had run for the nearest door, her shouts of an unlocking spell managing to penetrate the panicked, nonsensical ramblings of Renata's mind.

The feral fell unceremoniously to the floor, splattering black blood everywhere. The blood didn't bubble and hiss where it touched wood and plaster, as acid would, and that fact comforted Renata somehow.

The two men huddled close to Renata, flanking her, while also forming a wall between the feral and Paola. The more seasoned sorcerer worked hard to undo the magic they'd layered on the door only minutes before. Renata gripped the broom handle in two hands, the wide brush held out like a shield. The men on either side of her held their stools by the seats, ready to jam the metal legs into chests and throats to keep the monsters at bay until Paola could get the door open.

If Renata were in a B-rated horror flick, she'd say something pithy and terrible to the feral, like *Don't come any closer or I'll sweep the floor with you!* She cackled to herself, causing Dalton to swivel a sharp look her way.

Great. She was starting to lose it.

The feral stood on all fours. Its fingers and toes had gone black, as if the skin had rotted and died from frostbite. Tendrils of black snaked from its hands and feet, traveling up forearms and calves. Even if it *weren't* a zombie, there was still something unsettlingly "walking corpse" about it. It just stood there for a moment, reminding Renata of a big cat or wolf, but in stretched-too-tight human skin. Raggedy clothing that might have once been a T-shirt and jeans hung off the feral like the tattered remains of a ghost ship's sail. Baker's muttering started up again. She could confirm now that he was praying.

In the same moment that Paola shouted, "Got it!" and wrenched the door open, the feral lunged. Renata's brain misfired as the thing leaped clear across the room at them, blackened hands spread wide like claws.

Baker screamed, dropped his weapon, and bolted out the open door.

The crash of the stool snapped Renata out of her fog.

She didn't think, just reacted. She thrust up with all her might and managed to slam the wide brush of the broom into the feral's chest at the last possible moment. The force of the hit knocked the feral off course, sending it onto a nearby desk. It also knocked Renata onto her backside. She heard the thud of the feral hitting the floor a second after she did, guessing it had slid across the smooth metal surface of the workspace before careening off it.

Spots swam in her vision.

Paola hooked her hands under Renata's arms and hoisted her up so fast, Renata hardly had time to register the pain in her tailbone. By the time she was on her feet again, another feral had crawled in through the broken glass.

"Decapitation is the only sure way to kill them!" Paola

shouted. "We can't outrun them, so don't even try. Find a way to sever the spinal column, and it's game over."

Dalton met the new feral with a wild swing of his stool, doing nothing more than stunning the beast. "Are we going to turn into one of them if it bites us?" he asked, his voice wild with a level of fear she'd never heard in her friend before.

"Chances are slim, since we're all magic-touched, but don't let them do it," Paola said, casting a rune array at the feral that had pegged her as his target. "It'll still hurt like hells."

Renata thanked the Goddess that Paola had stayed instead of fleeing the way Baker had. Renata hoped Baker was okay, but she wasn't sure she'd ever forgive him for running.

She thrust the wide end of her broom into the chest of the feral that kept swiping at Dalton. The hit knocked the thing back a step, but now it was furious with *her*. Renata darted forward long enough to kick the fallen stool abandoned by Baker, sending it crashing into the feral's legs. It went down hard but was back up in a second.

Renata and her colleagues weren't doing anything other than wearing themselves out. The feral wasn't remotely deterred by Renata and Dalton's feeble attempts to keep it away.

Sever the spinal column, huh?

Renata glanced down at her broom. Thinking quickly, she flipped it around. The feral lunged. Renata jabbed the thick, rounded end of the handle into the feral's sternum. The monster came up short and gave a gasping choke. Its breath rattled on the way out. Had Renata managed to break a rib?

Didn't matter.

Renata yanked the broom back and jabbed it forward again, this time aiming for the feral's throat. Surprisingly, the handle punched a hole right through the feral's neck as if it were made of paper. Did these things have weak spines? The life in its limbs went out in an instant. Its deadweight body tipped toward Renata, gravity pushing the broom's handle farther into the hole. Black blood oozed down the wood like tar.

The reverberating clang of metal hitting flesh yanked Renata out of her horror and she hastily let the feral-kebab go. The broom and dead feral hit the floor with a meaty thunk. She didn't have time to pull the weapon free.

Dalton was warding off yet another feral, while Paola threw tiny pulses of fire at the one Renata had knocked to the floor earlier. Without enough time to properly cast arrays, all Paola could manage were ping-pong-sized fireballs. The fact that she could cast them this quickly, regardless of their size, proved all her training with Dalton had paid off. The small fireballs were keeping the feral distracted, but it was able to dodge most of them. Paola would deplete her magical stores sooner than the feral would tire.

A feral had Dalton backed against a table now. The metal legs of the stool were pressed into the feral's torso, but the stool's legs were twisted and bent, shortening the distance Dalton could maintain between himself and the monster. One good swipe from the feral, and Dalton's throat could be torn open.

A horrible chittering sound reverberated from outside—like a monster truck–sized squirrel high on meth. The two ferals in the room repeated the sound. The brief distraction allowed Paola to cast a fireball the size of a tennis ball this time, and it hit the feral directly in the face. His few strands of straggly hair went up in smoke, filling the room with an acrid stench. The feral was enraged now, and though it looked as if the skin around one eye had melted, it lunged at Paola nevertheless. A wind spell knocked it back a few inches, but the monster kept coming. Dalton cried out as his feral clawed him across an arm, splattering several drops of bright red blood on the floor.

Renata eyed the open door, knowing she could bolt the same way Baker had. There was no way they were going to survive this.

Instead, she ran for the nearest table and started chucking everything she could at the feral squaring off against Dalton. Mugs, pencil holders, staplers. She missed it more than she hit it, but eventually a ceramic mug clocked the feral in the dead center of its forehead, and it stumbled back. Dalton reacted, swinging the stool like a baseball bat. The jagged end of one of the mangled legs tore a slice in the feral's shoulder. Black blood ran down its arm. The feral roared and charged toward Dalton again.

Another mug hit it, but in the back of head this time—and it had been heaved with the power of a pitcher throwing a fastball. She silently thanked Paola. The feral went down but Renata knew it wouldn't stay that way for long.

Renata ran to the body of the feral still shish-kebbabed on the broom handle. She placed a foot on the dead feral's chest and yanked the handle free. The feral nearest Dalton was back on its feet. Renata managed to swing the broom in a wide arc and clocked it in the side of the head with the brush end before it could attack Dalton. The feral stumbled back a step, then charged for Renata. Flipping the broom around, Renata stabbed the handle into the throat of this one, too. And just like before, the handle punctured what felt like paper-thin skin. The handle shot out the other side, severing the spinal column. Lights out.

This time, Renata pulled the handle free right away, giving the dead feral a kick to the chest to alter the body's fall. The feral toppled backward onto the floor.

"You all right?" Dalton called out.

Renata started to reply, but realized he wasn't talking to her. She turned, finding Paola with one hand propped on a desktop, and the other against her side.

"Are you hurt?" Renata asked.

Though she was breathing hard, Paola took her hand off her side to wave away Renata's concern. No visible wounds marred the woman's side. Perhaps she'd only been recovering from a stitch. Casting her gaze downward, Renata noted that the first feral that had tumbled into the room now lay on the floor behind Paola. Renata could only see part of the feral's head—the rest of its body hidden behind a desk. The completely charred face told Renata the thing was dead. Its features were unidentifiable. The scent of cooked flesh mingled with that of burnt hair. She looked away.

Renata was slick with sweat, and her heart beat too fast. The notebook she'd stuffed into her waistband was still there, pressed flush against her back. She hoped the sweat coating her skin wouldn't damage her notes somehow. "What do we do now?"

No other ferals crawled in through the windows. Renata couldn't hear any chittering.

It registered then that the sirens had stopped. It felt eerily silent in the room now that the sirens had quieted and the ferals had been dispatched. Dalton breathed a bit too heavily, but that was a welcome sound—he was still alive *to* breathe.

"We have to see what state the rest of this place is in," Paola said. "We're on the far end of everything out here. Maybe the ones we just killed were the stragglers or the ones who ran off looking for easier prey. We have to see if anyone needs help."

Renata was glad someone else was making decisions. She readjusted her hold on the broom's handle, giving it a cursory assessment. It was holding up okay so far, but she had to guess the wood would splinter on her eventually.

Paola stepped over the charred corpse of the feral behind her and disappeared from view as she opened the cabinet of a credenza pressed against the wall. She emerged a moment later with a fire extinguisher. "Really wish I'd remembered earlier that this thing was in there."

Safety regulations normally required that fire extinguishers be placed somewhere easily accessible. But for whatever reason, any time in the last few months that they'd opened a pair of interspatial portals in this room, it would suck the fire extinguisher right off the wall and into one of the portals, no matter the distance. The extinguisher would then hurtle out of the secondary portal with all the speed of a locomotive. When a flying extinguisher had knocked out a new colleague and left him with a significant concussion, they'd had to figure something else out.

If it was in the cabinet, it remained stationary.

Paola gestured toward the door with a tilt of her head.

The trio fled the room.

Out in the hallway, it was quiet. Most of the doors opening into it were closed. They stood just outside the doorway, waiting for some sign that another feral lurked nearby. When ten seconds ticked by without any signs of the monsters, then twenty, the trio trotted down the hallway toward the main door. If they made it outside, they'd have to run across a long walkway to reach Lab 4. The town center lay just beyond that—the town center where the majority of the population was congregated at any given time.

Where the most carnage had probably taken place.

The trio only made it halfway down the hallway when Renata spotted something on the wall. "One second," she called.

She slammed the broom's handle into the glass cover, which shattered easily.

Paola let out a string of curses and then jogged toward the exit, muttering angrily that she needed to make sure no one—feral or otherwise—had heard the crash.

Renata knocked several pieces of glass free, and then pulled out her prize. She held the small ax out to Dalton. The words on the glass had instructed her to break in case of emergency. If this wasn't an emergency, she wasn't sure what was. She didn't touch the white fire hose hanging like a coiled snake.

Dalton took the ax tentatively, then tested the weight in his hand. He stared at her for a long beat. "You've surprised me today."

She nodded, her face flushing. If she thought about it too hard, the sound of the broom's handle punching through the feral's neck replayed in her head, making her stomach churn. But the thought of the feral harming Dalton any more than it already had had pushed her to act. She didn't like what she'd done to keep them alive, but she didn't regret it, either. "I've surprised myself."

"I think I like it." The expression he wore was even more foreign than the fear she'd heard in his voice earlier. "If we make it out of here alive, we're going on the date I've been too scared to ask you on."

Heat flooded her cheeks. "Deal."

With that, they headed for the door Paola stood in front of, hand on the handle.

Renata hoped death didn't wait for them on the other side.

CHAPTER TWELVE

RENATA

Paola crept outside first. When she *wasn't* ripped to shreds, she motioned for Renata and Dalton to follow. Giving her broom handle a fortifying squeeze, Renata stepped out of the semi-safety of her research wing and into the bright sunshine baking the cement path that would lead them to Lab 4.

The door quietly clicked shut behind Dalton.

The trio gripped their weapons tightly and waited. Renata strained to pick up sounds from the monsters. Though she doubted the silenced sirens meant that the danger had passed, she was thankful they weren't wailing in the background. If they *had* still been going, it would have been ten times harder to hear the beasts coming. She wondered if that was the reason the sirens had been shut off. That horrible chittering sound the ferals made, presumably their version of communication, would haunt Renata's nightmares forever. Assuming she lived through the day and was able to experience the luxury of sleep again, that is.

"Let's go," Paola said, and she trotted forward, her head on a swivel.

The wide concrete building straight ahead was even larger than the one they'd just left. Renata thought it might be safer to go *around* Lab 4 and through Testing Sector 1, but she knew Paola wanted to check for survivors.

Paola was much braver than Renata.

Sighing, Renata trailed after her. Dalton's footsteps sounded a few seconds later.

The landscaping around the buildings in the research sector left a lot to be desired. The paths between buildings were maintained well enough, but the weeds in some places were as tall as her knees.

The layout of Elsher, she knew, had changed a lot over the years. The research sector was the one that had seen the most change—several of the buildings slipping into disrepair as the focus of study in the hub shifted every decade or so. A couple of the freestanding units roasting in the sun had largely become storage units. Had the ferals tried ransacking those places, too, or had they beelined for buildings they'd sensed people in?

Though it was a pleasant seventy-five degrees, a chill raced across Renata's arms. They were deep into the summer months, so there was nearly twenty-four hours of sunlight. She'd heard that the first magic-wielding scientists—led by Kensey herself—who had set up shop in Elsher had attempted rune arrays that would create an artificial nighttime here, giving those living in the hub some semblance of normal. The magical expenditure proved to be too much, though, and everyone eventually invested in blackout curtains instead.

Somehow the ferals running around in broad daylight made all this even more disconcerting. Weren't vampires supposed to only roam the streets at night?

Conflicting lore aside, Renata knew that whatever had happened to twist and mutate the ferals into something more horrible than "normal" vampires had slotted the creatures into a different box entirely.

Her gaze swung to the left, where one of Elsher's two designated outdoor testing areas stood. Testing Sector 1 was all scarred and barren earth, dotted periodically by training dummies, massive chunks of stone, and freestanding wooden signs. All the objects standing vigil in the wide, flat field were charred and battered.

Rune arrays that controlled the elements were best done outside and performed on inanimate targets. Traveling via portal, even short distances, was often best performed outside, too. Partly because portals were unpredictable, and getting flung around in open space was better than getting flung into furniture. And partly because portal travel made many people nauseous. Losing your lunch was *definitely* better done outside.

Renata saw no movement in the direction of the testing sector, either.

Lab 4, unlike her own lab, was a two-story building, housing twice as many research offices. She hoped Paola didn't want to check every one, as if the trio were members of an elite military team, shouting "Clear!" once they found a room to be free of ferals. She figured teams like that had better weapons than an industrial broom and a fire extinguisher. Dalton's small ax was pretty formidable, at least. It didn't mean Dalton knew how to wield the thing properly, but Renata tried not to think about that. She also tried not to think about the fact that they'd gotten lucky so far and that their luck was bound to run out sooner rather than later.

She gave her head a light shake. She tended to get doom and gloom when she was anxious.

When they were a few feet from the door, Paola slowed. She got a better grip on the fire extinguisher, then offered Renata a "gird your loins, because this is happening whether you want it to or not" nod. In seconds, Paola had opened the door and slipped inside the main hallway of Lab 4.

Whimpering to herself, Renata followed.

The trio stood huddled just inside the entrance, their weapons held at the ready. Scientists weren't exactly a rowdy lot, but Renata could instantly tell the building was too quiet. At least five doors opened into this section of hallway. All the doors stood open. A door in the middle of the linoleum-tiled floor had been detached from its hinges. It flopped over inside the room, resting on whatever was pressed against the wall in front of the door-jamb, creating a triangular opening into the office. That was her friend Megan's lab. Renata was torn between wanting to check if Megan had escaped and wanting to run back to her own familiar workspace, as compromised as it was. If a feral came scuttling under the fallen door, Renata was fairly certain her bravery would flee the same way Baker had.

It wasn't until that moment that she realized she'd left her beloved flower behind. The vase had probably toppled off the desk, shattering on the floor. Had those beautiful purple-black petals been crushed under someone's heel? She wasn't sure if she wanted to scream or cry.

After fifteen seconds went by without a sound, they word-lessly crept forward. Renata walked up the center of the hallway slowly, the broom's head held out in front of her. To her left, Dalton peeked into open doors and did a cursory check for move-ment, while Paola did the same on the right. Renata wasn't sure how she'd become the group's scout.

After a minute of walking, the main hallway curved slightly.

Renata held her breath as she cautiously rounded the bend ahead of the others, sure there'd be a feral ready to spring toward her, necrotic fingers outstretched like claws. But the new stretch of corridor slowly spreading out before her was just as quiet as the rest.

Quiet, but not empty.

Renata stopped abruptly, her broom's head hitting the floor with a muted thwack as one of her hands flew up to cover her mouth. Dalton and Paola peppered her with questions, hurrying to her. When they fell into place on either side of her, though, their questions trailed off.

Bodies were strewn across the floor in the building's lobby. Slash marks raked across faces, torsos, and limbs. Entrails, blood, and what Renata could only assume were bits of brain coated the floor and dotted the walls. It looked as if half a dozen people had been torn apart by wild animals that had then feasted until they were glutted. Just beyond the carnage, the glass doors that led outside were covered in smeared, red handprints.

Renata swallowed down bile.

The bodies were a good hundred feet away. If any hungry ferals were still in the building, maybe Renata and her colleagues could turn tail and run back the way they'd come before the ferals reached them. But as Renata recalled how fast the monsters had moved in her lab—the way they'd launched clear across the room in one bound—she knew that no amount of distance would save them.

"Keep moving forward," Paola whispered, readjusting her hold on her fire extinguisher. "If any of us runs into trouble, start calling things out. Give as much information as you can so the other two can help fight."

Dalton added, "Or figure out a way to escape without dying."

Paola nodded. "That, too."

Resuming her two-handed hold on the broom's handle, Renata moved forward with the others. Even from a distance, it was obvious these people were all exceedingly dead. The metallic tang of blood was overwhelming. Renata tried to breathe out of her mouth instead of her nose, but she felt like she could *taste* the blood. Her stomach was already churning, and the low, constant hum of buzzing flies made it worse. How soon after death did it take blowflies to arrive? Ten minutes? Twenty? Her sister would know. Her sister was obsessed with crime shows.

Renata's throat tightened at the thought that she may never see her sister again.

She willed herself to focus on the fly-swarmed bodies, silently asking the scene to give her a clue about what to do next. As she swatted away a fly, she supposed the time of death didn't matter. The monsters could still be inside the building somewhere. Or they might circle back at any moment to finish their meal.

A reception desk sat off to the right. A body lay across the shiny wood, the man's feet hanging off the front. One of his shoes was missing, his white sock soaked with blood.

Renata wondered if the bodies were clustered by the entrance because these people had been trying to escape and were ambushed here, or if the ferals had dragged their kills to one area so they could feast as a group. Her gut told her it was the former —that they'd been mere inches from getting out when they'd been attacked.

With her broom held at the ready, she stood a few feet from the pile of bodies, their thick, congealing blood more of a sickly black than the bright red blood that had welled from Dalton's fresh cut. She stared down, her face contorted, as a puddle of molasses-like blood oozed away from the torn-apart torso of a woman she didn't recognize. The sticky mess crept toward her own tennis shoes.

Dalton and Paola had peeled off to check rooms on either side of the entrance.

Renata looked away from the river of blood and toward the blood-splattered front doors. It would take a few minutes to reach the town center from here. There hadn't been any movement beyond the doors yet. All Renata could see was grass on both sides of the curving cement road that led to town, a smattering of trees, and the tops and sides of a few buildings in the distance. Even though one of the testing sectors was nearby, the landscapers tried to keep the grassy areas around the town center and the front of Labs 1 through 4 looking presentable. Once one reached the other five labs, and the further reaches of the testing area, the scenery got a little … bleak.

Despite the smeared blood on the doors and a very dark stain on the small cement porch beyond them, the view from Renata's current vantage point was peaceful. Serene, even.

A fly buzzed loudly by her head, and she flailed as if she'd been cattle prodded. The head of her broom dropped and hit the mangled body of the woman lying sprawled in front of her. She winced, quickly lifting the broom. The bristles came away with blood dotting their tips. A misshapen glob of something wiggled like jelly on the corner of the broom's head before plopping back to the floor.

Okay, maybe serene was the wrong word.

Dalton and Paola returned a few moments later, both looking a bit pale, but otherwise okay. Renata didn't ask for any details, assuming Dalton in particular had found something gruesome, given the sweat dotting his brow.

Heaving out a breath, Paola jutted her chin at the doors. "Be ready. We might have to run."

Renata wanted to ask "Yes, but in which direction?" but kept the question to herself.

A shameful, not insubstantial part of her was relieved that Paola had apparently decided to leave the second floor unexplored.

Skirting around the horrifying mess congealing on the floor, the trio headed for the exit. Paola eased one of the doors open, the sweep of fresh air carrying away the smell of blood that Renata was sure had embedded itself into her clothes and hair. She could only imagine how rank it would get once the bodies started to decompose. Her throat tightened again and she pushed away the urge to slump to the floor and cry.

"Keep your eyes and ears peeled," Paola said, then crept out the door.

Out on the small, stained porch, Renata immediately heard the distant sounds she'd expected from the start: people screaming, monsters snarling, objects crashing. She swung her wide gaze to the side and met Dalton's equally bewildered expression. His attempt at a reassuring smile was tight.

They all flinched when a resounding explosion tore through the air. The ground beneath Renata's feet quaked for a moment, then settled just as quickly. A plume of black smoke rose in the far distance a moment later. Had that come from the residential sector? From Testing Sector 2?

Paola took up a slow jog.

Sighing in defeat, Renata followed.

She couldn't help but feel like a hapless deer bounding out into an open field when there were hunters nearby.

The town center was roughly circular, with a paved road ringing it. Residents had dubbed the road "Elsher's Loop." Straight ahead were the backsides of the two most popular restaurants in the hub. Housed in the left side of the building was a buffet-style place that was open twenty-four hours. There was an "international" section that featured foods not from other countries, but from the fae realm. The foods weren't exactly the same, obviously, since this realm didn't have the same ingredients as the fae realm, but they were cooked in a way reminiscent of those styles. The draken tinka fish bowls were Renata's favorite. On the right was the hub's only ice cream parlor.

As she jogged up the paved path with her two colleagues, Cuisine from Across the Realms looming ahead, she thought about the fact that many of the people who worked in the town center weren't scientists—many weren't even sorcerers. There were people here who had been drawn to the hub for work. People who wanted to live in a small town had found comfort in Elsher's slower, off-the-grid vibe. Since scientists lived in Elsher for years, they often fell in love, married, and raised families here. Children attended the K-12 school. Teenagers worked in the shops to save up money to attend college or move to other hubs. Hells, some of those who called Elsher home were in-the-know mundanes who were paid handsomely to do landscaping, construction, and maintenance. How had all those people fared in the wake of the veil breach?

Two telepads were located in the town center. An additional one was in the residential sector, and a large vehicle telepad was situated in the southwest corner of the hub, in Testing Sector 2. Renata hoped the telepads had been put to good use as soon as it had become clear Elsher had been compromised.

The sounds of battle and distress only grew louder the closer they got, but the trio kept moving forward anyway. Forward was the direction of any hope of escape. Forward meant telepads. Forward meant access to the LAN connection in the chancellor's office—the LAN connection Chancellor Thorpe must have used to inform other hubs that the research center had been overrun by ferals.

Help was on the way. It had to be. Renata couldn't accept the alternative.

She and her colleagues darted across Elsher's Loop and huddled against the back of the buffet restaurant. In the northeast corner of the town center, where they were now, sat an elaborate flower bed ringed by a low brick wall. It was lined by Elsher's Loop on two sides, so anyone traversing the road to make deliveries or who was out for a stroll would pass the installation. Though it was only a few months old, it was a popular addition to the town center, partly because it was such a riot of color compared to the barren landscape of Testing Sector 1 on the other side of Elsher's Loop. Renata loved the installation and had spent many a lunch break with Dalton sitting on that brick wall. They'd talked about their research. They'd talked about nothing at all. They'd eaten their lunches, soaked up the sunshine after hours of being holed up in their office, and enjoyed each other's company.

Bright-green ferns grew among vibrant yellow, red, and orange flowers. Tucked between the clusters of flowers, roses bloomed large and full from gorgeous teal-blue ceramic pots. One such pot now had a torn-apart man draped over it, his lifeless limbs splayed wide, and his dead eyes staring, shocked, at the cloudless blue sky. A crow pecked at the man's ruined chest.

The shouts of alarmed residents and the snarling of monsters hadn't let up. Renata looked down at the broom she still held so firmly, her knuckles white and her palms sweaty. She didn't know what Paola expected them to *do*. There was a war zone beyond the wall of her favorite restaurant—beyond the flower bed installation now coated in the blood of some poor bastard who had been cut down by wild animals wearing human skin. And all she had to defend herself with was a Goddess-damned broom, for fuck's sake!

The sound of muttered words seeped into her mind, staving off her mental collapse for a while longer. It was Dalton who was casting this time, though, not Paola.

"He'll cast a shield array for us, and we'll stand behind that while we round the corner to get an idea of what we're dealing with. We need to get to a telepad. It's the fastest way out of here. If we can get out, maybe we can bring help back with us," Paola whispered to Renata, sounding frustratingly calm. "If we survive this, we need to strongly suggest to Chancellor Thorpe that she figure out a walkie-talkie system of communication or something. We're flying blind. There could be fifty of those things running around. We could be the only ones left alive. There's no way for us to know. Being off the grid is all well and good until you need the grid to keep from getting your entrails pulled out of your body like a mundane magician pulling an endless string of hand-kerchiefs out of his fucking sleeve."

Renata grinned at her.

"What?"

She shrugged. "Just glad you're losing your ever-loving shit, too."

Paola barked a laugh.

A moment later, Dalton thrust his hands out, a glowing rune array hovering in front of him. Renata noted that he'd wedged his ax between his belt and waistband to hold it in place. Instead of a hovering, vertically facing circle, like most shield arrays, this one spread out in a dome—almost like a translucent umbrella.

With his fingers cocked at unnatural angles and his arms stretched out before him, Dalton angled the umbrella toward the corner of the restaurant. Paola and Renata quickly took up positions just behind his shoulders.

Dalton said, "This array has been lasting for a good ten minutes lately, but I don't know how long it would hold up against a direct hit from a feral."

Renata and Paola were very familiar with this array. Renata knew that he'd perfected it as a kid growing up in a household of older boys who liked to torment him.

Paola had gotten in quite a bit of fireball practice against Dalton and his shield over the last six months in particular. Dalton would erect his shield and Paola would hurl fireballs at him. They'd bounce, the array lobbing them back at her like the most dangerous game of tennis ever. It not only trained Paola to dodge flying objects faster, but she'd pushed herself to cast the spell faster and faster, trying to get as many thrown at Dalton as possible before the shield spell eventually fritzed or Dalton was spent. Dalton had to continuously reinforce the spell while it was under the constant barrage of fire.

Renata had practiced with him, too, though her preferred element was water. She wasn't as fast as Paola, and when under pressure, Renata's magic often refused to cooperate. But when they were alone in the open fields of the testing sector, Renata could cast just as fast as Paola. If Renata was truly relaxed, she could freeze globules of water and hurl fist-sized chunks of ice.

Even so, creating arrays—even with constant training—was

relatively slow. Dalton needed at least a full minute of uninter-rupted casting to form the shield in the first place.

As if reading her panicked thoughts, Dalton muttered, "I really hope we don't die," before stepping out of their hiding place.

CHAPTER THIRTEEN

KAYDA

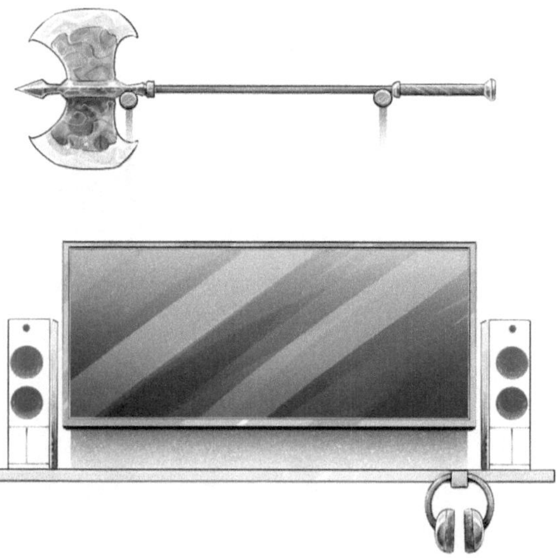

Within twenty minutes of Joe Taylor's desperate call from Elsher, the War Room had eight werecats prowling around in it. They were thankfully all in their human forms at the moment, but they were still stressing Kayda out. The cats got like this just before a patrol, too—amped up and ready for a fight. It wasn't unlike the vibe in the bowels of the arenas she used to cage fight in. Her hands opened and closed into fists by her sides as Marisol caught the cats up on everything.

Most of the cats had been vouched for by Jasmine—otherwise known as Officer Magnan—who almost everyone at VHoA had grown to like quite a bit. The werecat was gorgeous—both as a human and in her sleek black panther form—and Kayda had a feeling it was *that* fact that had eventually won over a few of the older, grumpier guys on Marisol's team. Jasmine didn't seem to have any problem turning on her girlish charm when she felt it necessary.

After Marisol caught the cats up on the events of the last hour, ending with the warning sirens going off in Elsher because the ferals had likely breached the veil in droves, Jasmine took over.

"I got approval from Sorceress Rhiannon to lead a team into Elsher," Jasmine said, her light and airy voice warring with the anxious tension in the room. "I'm happy to have any of you join me. I've fought alongside all of you and would welcome the opportunity to do so again. Marisol's crew knows how to deal with the ferals even better than the guards do."

A few of the cats scoffed, but a murderous glare from Jasmine shut them up.

"I asked you here personally," she said, pointedly making eye contact with each of the skeptical shifters. "You're either on board with this *entire* plan or you're not on board at all. And in that case, you can kindly get the fuck out. We don't have time for egos or petty bullshit. There are two thousand people in Elsher who need help. I don't want to worry that you won't have each other's backs because someone's fragile feelings are hurt. Are you in or out?"

She got firm "I'm ins" from the three dissenters.

Yeah, Kayda definitely liked her—even if she *was* a cat.

Jasmine continued, "We have to make two telepad jumps. One from here to the hub outside Vancouver, and then from there to Elsher. It's too far to do it in one jump."

In addition to getting clearance to travel to Elsher, Jasmine had also gotten her paws on something very few people had access to: a map of the research hub. Eight werecats and ten VHoA members stood huddled around the paper map Jasmine had spread out on a recently cleared-off table. Kayda noted that, despite being in the good graces of Sorceress Rhiannon, Jasmine clearly had no idea what kind of experiments happened in those nine laboratories that made up the northern end of the hub.

Jasmine was in the middle of laying out her plan of attack when a curse from the bank of computers startled her. As a group, they turned toward Ben—one of the triplets. He and a new recruit were the only ones keeping an eye on the forums and message boards. The other two members of the trio were presumably at home asleep after their night shift. Ben had managed to re-injure himself during the training session outside the abandoned zoo a couple of weeks ago, and, as Marisol had promised, re-injury meant desk duty.

"What is it, Ben?" Marisol asked, breaking away from the group.

His eyes were wide as he swung his attention away from the screen. "There are three normal-size telepads in Elsher and one large vehicle one. Whoever invaded the place just blew up the large one."

Jasmine swore.

A cornerstone of the grand plan had been to utilize larger telepads so the group could barrel into Elsher with at least three SUVs packed to the gills with gear. Now they could only take what they could carry, and it would have to be snugly packed onto their bodies so they didn't lose anything in transit.

The new recruit piped up from behind her computer screen. Kayda could only see the top half of the young lady's face. "Someone just confirmed Lachlan is in Elsher. Elf. Missing half his left arm. It's Shade, several elves, and at least five hybrids. Ferals are running wild."

Jasmine swore again.

"Everyone pack what you can," Marisol said. "We'll take the telepads in Montclaire. We'll figure shit out as we go. Ben, live-text me updates. You too, Ingrid. Ben, give her my personal number."

Jasmine said, "We'll head out first, since we can get there faster. All your names are in the telepad system with special permission to get into Elsher. Sorceress Rhiannon is in contact with Chancellor Thorpe—the leader of Elsher—and we've been assured she's fortified the telepad east of the town center. Thorpe can craft a temporary veil over the telepad so we can get in safely. Thorpe put out several calls for aid that went unanswered, so we're currently all she's got.

"There are two elemental witch contacts in the residential sector who have the sole telepad station in that area protected as well. We want you all to use that one. Another of the Collective sorcerers is working with the witches to shield the station from detection. We don't know how much information Lachlan has on Elsher and its layout. It's been a well-kept secret until now—or so we thought. Last I heard, the residential sector hasn't been hit the same way as the town center. I honestly don't know what that means, only that there might be a method to the slaughter. Communication is spotty at best. We might not know something has changed until we get there. Guess it's good we like to improvise."

"Do you also like suicide missions?" someone muttered, but this was only met with a smattering of nervous chuckles.

Wordlessly, Marisol opened the door to the War Room, then the door to outside. From out of sight, she called, "Clear!"

Almost simultaneously, the werecats shifted from human to cat. Two black panthers, three pumas, a tiger, a cheetah, and a snow leopard now crowded the room. The VHoA members stepped back, several with their backs pressed against a wall. With a roar, the black panther nearest the door took off for the exit. The other seven bounded out after her, the floor quaking. Somehow, all eight massive beasts made their way out of the house in a matter of seconds. Claw marks and a faint layer of cat fur decorated the wooden floor. Someone sneezed.

Silence descended on the room. Marisol slowly walked back into the War Room.

"Are cats or VHoA from anywhere else coming to help?" Kayda asked, her voice seeming to echo in the quiet room.

Marisol stared out the open door. "I sure as hells hope so."

CHAPTER FOURTEEN

HARLOW

The trip from Floor H back up to F happened in silence, though I kept a wary eye on the back of Sorcerer Avery's head the whole time. The fact that he hadn't asked me anything about Tim was stressing me out. Wasn't my supposed skill in communicating with the sentient weapons the whole reason I'd been included in this meeting of the minds at the Tower?

Once we stopped on the now familiar Floor F, the swords and I followed Avery across the hallway and through the pair of glass doors Caspian and Macrae had headed through earlier.

The space had been designed with the same discerning eye for detail and grandeur as the parking garage levels—unblemished concrete from floor to ceiling, the latter being held up by the occasional blocky pillar. The area we strolled through first was dotted with thick black training mats—some even lining sections of the wall and ceiling—training dummies, punching bags, and racks of weights.

Another set of glass doors—these ones foggy—opened into an area stuffed to the brim with exercise equipment: treadmills, full-body machines, bench presses, racks of medicine balls, bosu balls, kettlebells. And a veritable shit load of werecats. While the previous area had been deserted and deathly quiet, the room on the other side of the foggy glass was cacophonous, humid, and pungent. If the sheer speed at which people sprinted on the tread-mills hadn't been enough to give them away as cats in their human form, the musky scent—like wet fur—would have. Sweat immediately started to pool at my lower back, made all the worse by my backpack.

I briefly wondered if Avery had led me in here to let the cats shred me to pieces. I didn't see any sign that Caspian had met his bloody end, though.

Hardly any of the cats even broke stride—which was saying a lot, since I was being trailed by two floating swords. The tension in the room was as cloying as the stinking, humid air, though. The sound of fifty-plus men and women working out was practically thunderous. My sword hovered so close to my shoulder, the side of its hilt pressed against my arm. Still, no one called out a threat-ening remark or attempted to approach us. I suspected that was because I was being personally escorted by one of their bosses. Plus Caspian and Macrae had made this walk of awkward not that long ago.

Did the cats' good behavior speak to their respect for Avery or their fear of him?

The next set of doors were solid metal, the rivets lining the edges as wide as quarters. A pin pad was embedded in the wall, as well as a slot for a key card. Beside that was a dark screen.

A burly guy a few feet from the doors jumped rope like he was trying to break a world record. *Thwack, thwack, thwack.* The rope hit the floor with such sharp precision, it made my eye twitch.

When I glanced over, he glared so fiercely, I had no doubt he wished he could use the rope to strangle me. *Thwack, thwack, thwack.*

O'Neill's allies were more numerous than the small group we'd run into in the lobby. If these cats had to choose right this moment to follow Sorceress Rhiannon or the opposing faction, I wondered how many of them would cross to my side of the line.

There had to be other paths into the armory. Parading Caspian and me through a sea of amped-up werecats had to be a power play on the sorcerers' part. My sword's low hum, which sounded a lot like a growl, said it wasn't terribly pleased to be here, either. Though perhaps it was more upset about what lay beyond the doors, knowing at least one of its brethren was being held captive. Tim offered no commentary.

Once Avery had jumped through the various hoops necessary to get the heavy metal doors' locks to disengage, Avery grabbed a handle and heaved, clearly struggling with the weight.

I leaned toward my sword, pitching my voice low. "No matter what we see in there, you can't fly off the handle—uh ... hilt—okay? Keep a level head. Blade. Whatever." I sighed. "Just ... don't stab anyone until we talk about it first."

The blade flashed a happy, agreeable blue, but it was still growling. The mixed message wasn't comforting.

Same goes for you, Tim.

It didn't reply, which was even less comforting.

I followed the sorcerer into the room. Motion-activated lights overhead flicked on. By the time the heavy metal doors shut behind us with a decisive thud and the locks re-engaged, my mouth had dropped open.

It was immediately clear that the armory was *huge*. It was broken into rectangular sections, as if concrete blocks had been lined up in a column. A wide chunk had been carved out of those concrete blocks, creating a straight walkway. Two or three sections separated us from a lit-up area farther down. I couldn't hear a peep from the gym on the other side of the doors, but a faint murmur of voices drifted down the hallway toward us. I figured that was where Caspian had ended up. There wasn't much visible in that section from this distance, but I could make out part of a large industrial table. A large swath of the armory between me and Caspian was lost to darkness, as there was no one in those sections to trigger the lights. It felt like we were separated by an uncrossable abyss.

My attention didn't stray far from our little nook of the armory for long. The collection on either side of me put Haskins's basement and Domino's lair to shame. Sections were made up of three walls on either side of the center walkway. Each eight-foot-tall wall was covered top to bottom in the kind of weaponry that kept my rent paid and electricity on.

To my right were walls covered solely in daggers—stiletto, hunting, quillon, seax, karambit, and several of my favorites ... the wavy-bladed kris. They weren't arranged by type, but magic level. Even though the daggers that lined the top of the wall were a good two to three feet above my head, I could feel and see the magic wafting off them like a hovering mist. I instinctively took several steps away from the weapons at large, positioning myself in the dead center of the aisle.

My sword flitted around the lit-up area, touching its blade tip to weapon after weapon as if it hoped to wake them from their slumber. Tim remained behind me, hovering like a silent, stoic bodyguard. I turned 180 degrees toward the area opposite the daggers. Here were small axes. While activated dragon scales graced several hafts, none were as completely coated in scales as my sword or Tim's hilts. On these, single scales were treated as a focal piece—their iridescent sheen a bright spot of eye-catching ornamentation. But I knew even one scale could elevate a normal hatchet to something twice as deadly.

Avery stood patiently nearby, hands clasped behind his back, as I gawped at the sheer volume of charmed weapons. And this was only a very small portion of the armory.

Eventually the sorcerer headed for the lit-up area in the

distance. Lights clicked on in the next section, illuminating walls of hammers and spears. The next was populated with maces, flails, and whips. My head was spinning—both from the depth of the collection and the faint buzz of magic, as if I was walking through the physical manifestation of TV static. The amount of cash I could make on the black market or in auctions off this stuff would be enough to set me up for life.

ABHORRENT, Tim muttered in my head.

I opted not to get into a mental argument with him.

COWARD.

The voices of the others grew louder as we passed into the next section, full of crossbows on one side and short swords on the other. The casual, lighthearted chatter from the others implied they didn't know we were here. At least Caspian seemed to be having a better time than I had been with Haskins.

I shouldn't have been surprised that this section of the armory was lined with tools of the bladesmithing trade—a lot of which I'd seen in Margaret Fengast's old forge: ball-peen hammers, pliers, chisels, tongs, small saws, files. I felt the shift in temperature as we passed into the next section before I spotted the reason for it. Several open flames dotted the giant industrial table. They looked like miniature coal forges, but they were clearly magical in nature, given how each flame sat in the middle of a ring of runes etched onto the table. Nothing like a brazier held the flames in place; they crackled merrily an inch above the table, their intensity never wavering.

Small containers of familiar items littered the table as well— items I knew were magical in origin, not something picked up from a local craft store. Feathers, horns, powders in various colors, and, of course, dragon scales.

Books of runes lay open or were propped up on small stands.

Seated around the table were half a dozen people diligently working on various stages of weapon creation. While the forging of the weapons themselves seemed to be complete, people were adding ornamentation and runes to hafts, hilts, and blades.

Caspian sat beside a redheaded woman around our age. She was dressed plainly, as all the sorcerers around the table were. Her skin was blemish free and dotted with dull freckles. Her auburn hair was plaited into two braids that hung over her shoulders. One hand rested gently on Caspian's forearm as he gave a soliloquy on Goddess knew what. The woman was clearly enraptured with every word Caspian uttered.

He noticed our arrival a few moments before the others did. "Harlow!" he said, springing to his feet and sounding as guilty as a kid caught with his hand in the cookie jar. The woman's hand fell away from his arm.

Chatter among the rest of the group trailed off.

Color rose high in Caspian's cheeks, and I cocked a brow.

He hurried away from the now confused-looking redhead and sidled up next to me. "You okay?"

"Are *you*?"

He awkwardly cleared his throat. The tips of his ears went redder than a tomato. "Yes, well," he muttered.

"It seems like you've won over your team already," I said.

"I, uh, already knew some of them from my time at the academy." His desperately uncomfortable tone made me glance up at him. His expression implied he wished for the floor to open up and swallow him whole. "The, uh, redheaded young woman is Meredith. My, how do you say, ex."

I let out an involuntary gasp that interrupted whatever Avery had been blathering about to the group. I had no idea where Macrae had wandered off to. "*That's* her?" I whispered as softly as I could.

"Yes."

"She's very pretty."

His face somehow went redder.

"How are you feeling about the whole thing? Do you want me to flirt with you to make her jealous or go sock her in the jaw?"

"Neither. Please. I know Macrae arranged this solely to mess with me. Can you *please* not make this any more awkward than it already is?" he asked me, pained.

I grinned up at him. "No promises."

He huffed a laugh. "You're impossible." His gaze lingered on my smile for entirely too long. Blushing furiously, I looked away, finding the redhead's gaze flickering between me and Caspian.

Even if we had time, I didn't want to get tangled up in messy ex drama. All I knew about her—other than the fact that they'd had a booty-call situationship—was that when Caspian had fled the academy after Marcus had died, Meredith had seemingly stopped all communication with him. I didn't know if she'd decided that him dropping out of the academy was as shameful as his parents and professors thought it was. Maybe she'd turned her back on him, breaking his heart on top of the grief he'd already felt over the death of his friend.

Your bubbling fury suggests it would behoove me to slaughter her, Tim intoned grimly. *Is she an old enemy you've not seen since your time upon the battlefield?*

I flinched. *I'm not bubbling!*

*A coward **and** a liar.*

Were you forged from the remnants of a bloody medieval broadsword or something? Did your bladesmith watch too many war movies when crafting you? You are dramatic as hell, dude.

There was a long pause. *Is that a yes or a no on the slaying?*

No!

The rest of the group looked a bit shell-shocked. I couldn't imagine that my interrupting Avery warranted such a reaction, but then I realized most of them were focused on something slightly to my right. Tim, no doubt.

My sword's location was currently unknown.

"Did Sorcerer Macrae inform your new apprentices of the plan we have in place for them, Mr. Blackthorn?" Avery asked.

Caspian said, "He did. He excused himself to use the facilities a few minutes ago, but he should return shortly."

"Good, good," Avery said, then turned toward the apprentices. "Caspian is not only one of the best students to ever grace the halls of Luma's academy, he's also familiar with the fabled sentient weapons of yore. He's here to lend us—to lend *you*—his expertise. Until further notice, being his apprentice is your sole priority. Your other projects are to be completed on your own time once Mr. Blackthorn has dismissed you for the day."

I scanned the faces of the people ringing the table. They were all impassive, like little sorcerer robots, but a few clenched their jaws or tightened their grips on the tools they'd been holding when my arrival disrupted their work. I wondered if they took offense to being forced to answer to Caspian, if they were frustrated by the repeated information, or if it was Avery they took umbrage with.

Avery cast a glance behind me, upward, then to the left and right. "Harlow, where is that infernal sword of yours? The original, murder-happy one. I expected more oohing and ahhing, but the thing isn't even here."

I resisted the urge to point out that Tim was just as murder-happy; he was just more polite about it. No, not polite. Formal.

"I know even less about this second one," Avery said, eyeing Tim warily. "It *does* seem better behaved. Miss Fletcher, can you give the group a demonstration of what a sentient sword is capable of?"

Tim, would you like to introduce yourself to the group?

Negative.

You could show them how agile you are.

No answer.

I turned around to face the floating sword. It hovered in the inverted position and the curve of the blade was level with my nose. Fists on hips, I said, *If you don't want to perform aerial stunts, you could heat yourself up and show them your runes. These people would fuss over your runes as if you were a damn celebrity. If you think Caspian is nerdy about your runes? Hoo boy. You'll basically have a fan club.*

I'd rather be used as a butter knife.

A breath later, the iridescent glow of his scales went dark, and he dropped to the cement like a stone, clattering loudly.

I yelped. *You're so dramatic!*

The stupid thing had gone into power-down mode again. Groaning, I picked up the useless sword and squeezed the slightly warm hilt—hard. No reaction.

"Stabby?" I called out, wondering if it might want a more formal name, like Tim. It was odd thinking of Stabby as anything other than "my sword," though. "Can you come over here? There are some people who'd like to meet you. They think you'd be *much* more interesting than *Tim.*"

I turned in a slow circle, listening for any sign of my sword. I tried not to make eye contact with any of the sorcerers around the table, or Avery, as every last one of them was looking at me as if I'd lost my damn mind. And maybe I had.

I *especially* didn't look at Meredith. For … reasons.

Reasons I didn't want to think about right now, thank you very much.

Caspian offered me nothing at all save for a small, smug smile that I assumed meant this was payback for feeding into his embarrassment over Meredith's presence.

Several beats of awkward silence passed. The only sound was the occasional creak of a chair as one of the newly appointed apprentices adjusted their position and the constant whoosh of the ever-burning flames on the table. My cheeks warmed.

Distantly, I heard a reply. *Tap-tap.*

I turned on my heel. There were four sections between here and the doors we'd come through. With the second sword in hand, I marched away from the group and into the wide aisle. The area nearest to this one—where the short swords, machetes, katanas, scimitars, sabres, and cutlasses were—was lit up, so I figured my sword was flitting about in there, still desperately attempting to ignite a connection between itself and its fellows.

The section of the armory nearest the entry suddenly lit up, and I figured Macrae was on his trek back from the bathroom.

"Stabby! Now!"

Tap-tap. Pause. *Tap-tap.* Pause. *TAP-TAP.*

"You're giving Tim a run for his money in the dramatic department!" I shouted, shaking the sleeping sword above my head as if I were heading into battle. One would think Tim would appreciate the display, but he remained quiet. "This is happening whether you want it to or not! You might as well help oversee it."

Tap … tap.

"Besides, if I manage to wake up another one, don't you want to be there? You'll be the first familiar face … uhh … blade they'll see."

"What's going on?" someone muttered behind me.

"Is this the Harlow? The fugitive? I thought she killed several were-cats because the sword drove her insane, and she now believes she's a long-lost dragon princess."

I was amazed that whacko rumor still had legs.

"She definitely seems … unstable."

"Stabby. You're embarrassing me!"

Quick as a snake, my sword was in my face, buzzing angrily. It zipped around me in several dizzying circles, stopped directly in front of me again, then hummed something reminiscent of a lullaby played on a broken xylophone. It was creepy as shit. It dropped to the floor and tapped its hilt on the cement ten times in a row. It slowly rose to hover a foot away from my face but did so with its hilt pointed to the ceiling. It was the opposite of its usual inverted "I'm on your side till the end!" position.

Frowning, I asked, "Are you done?"

My sword flipped itself around, its blade glowing red for five long seconds before instantly cooling. It hummed once in a quick short burst.

"Honestly," I said. "Sometimes you have to do stuff you don't like. It's part of being a member of society. I promise to consult you as much as I can, though, okay?"

Tap.

"I promise as well, cutlass," Caspian said.

The blade glowed blue for a moment.

It seemed appeased for now. I wasn't under any illusion that my sword had seen the error of its ways or agreed with me. I guessed it had finally accepted that its method of communicating with the other weapons—the method it'd used with the ax back on the Winchells' farm—wouldn't work here.

"As you can see," Avery said, addressing the apprentices once my swords and I had rejoined the group, "the cutlass is unlike anything we've encountered before. We have yet to perfect the rune construction needed to grant sentience, but we believe that, by studying this particular cutlass, we can recreate something similar."

My sword vibrated by my shoulder but managed not to pitch another fit.

Macrae approached the group just in time to add, "The sword is a bit too … wild for our tastes. Your assignment at hand is to help Mr. Blackthorn complete his task but with restrictions. We need weapons *without* a personality. Weaponry experiencing existential crises isn't conducive to our needs."

Tap.

I wasn't sure which part of that my sword agreed with and decided not to bother asking.

Macrae noticed the sword grasped in my hand and his lip curled. "There are *two* of them? Since when are there two?"

Avery ignored him. "Macrae will stay here while Miss Fletcher and I go meet a friend of the sword's."

"You have another sentient weapon here?" I asked, my heart jackhammering. I didn't think I could handle a *third* one. According to Shane Winchell, there were five total.

The sword zipped over to Avery, startling him into taking several stumbling steps backward. A swirl of magic wafted off my sword like a fog. Caspian and I sighed. Why was the fool sword doing this now? If it suddenly decided that the solution to its problem was to murder one or two high sorcerers, we were in deep shit. But once the body had been formed—its back facing me

—all it did was jab the pointer finger of its free hand toward its chest several times.

"Yes, sword, you can join us," Avery said once he'd figured out what the sword wanted, speaking to the weapon as if it were a child. "In fact, I insist on it."

My sword's blade flashed blue, but my sixth sense pinged.

Macrae's ever-present grouchy demeanor dissolved in an instant. He crept toward the figure still holding the sword. Though I couldn't see her face, I knew the blue shirt she wore was torn across the stomach, her jeans were ripped, and she wore my face. The curls wafted about her head in an unseen wind.

A couple of Caspian's new apprentices stumbled out of their seats. They looked from me to the figure, to me, and back. They muttered among themselves about what in dragon lore would account for the sword's ability to do this. I glanced up at Caspian, wondering if he wished he could be on *that* side of the dividing line my sword had inadvertently drawn. The sorcerers on one side, and me and Caspian—the cast-outs, the dropouts—on the other. He glanced down at me and smiled. One of his rare, genuine smiles.

It was Avery who broke away from the group of awestruck sorcerers first. He peered at me over my apocalyptic self's shoulder. "You spoke the truth," he said, though he sounded vaguely disappointed.

I didn't think "duh" was a particularly helpful response, so I kept it to myself. Maybe he harbored some level of guilt over the realization that they'd turned me into a fugitive over an assumption.

My sword, unlike Tim, apparently enjoyed being fawned over, because my likeness began offering various poses for them to admire. She gave them fierce battle stances, rigid military poses, and at one point, my likeness tossed the sword into the air— which then did a wildly complicated series of flips and twirls, while offering a light show of colors winking off its blade—before catching it deftly in one hand. Several of the apprentices clapped politely, but given their little smiles and wide eyes, I figured this was like a crowd going wild when their home team scored a goal.

"All right, sword," I said. "Enough preening."

My likeness whirled around to face me. She flapped her arms, pointed at the people behind her, fluffed her curls on one side with a flat palm, and then planted her fists on her hips, the glowing red sword jutting out to the side and nearly impaling a confused young woman watching the spectacle. I honestly had no idea what the sword was trying to convey now, other than that it was irritated.

I stared it down.

My likeness eventually sighed as if she bore the weight of the world on her shoulders, and then the image dissipated, like ink in water.

Avery stared at me, but it felt as if he were looking through me rather than *at* me. Given the way his eyes slightly darted around in his skull, and the way Macrae gazed into space, I figured the two sorcerers were having another of their one-sided mental conversations. This was further evidenced by Macrae nodding periodically.

I leaned toward Caspian. "I'm scared to know the answer, but what is Macrae's special magic power?"

"That's a complicated question."

"Complicated because it's *actually* complicated, or complicated because sorcerers are long-winded?"

The mental gymnastics going on behind Caspian's eyes made me think it was a combination of the two. "Think of it more like a honed specialty. Just like people have hobbies based on their preferences, sorcerers, during their schooling, begin to gravitate toward certain types of magic."

"Like you and air spells," I said.

"Right. People who major in science don't study *all* of science. They niche down to biology or geology or astronomy. And then those niches have niches. One can focus on elemental magic in general or one element in particular. Throwing around gusts of air is one thing, while manipulating the air in someone's lungs is quite another. And causing a tornado is another still."

I shot him a look that I hoped conveyed *you're dangerously close to getting off track.*

"Anyway," he said, reining himself in, "Macrae gravitated toward what is essentially healing magic. He tried countless times in my last year to convince me to join his course. His niches are disciplines like welding and mending, as well as the same time-magics Rhiannon specializes in. He's been rumored to possess the ability to heal everything from minor wounds to broken bones. With his training in time magic, he could potentially reverse the aging of cells and prolong life. He's still working on that, the last I heard. The implications are huge. The discipline could lead to cures for diseases like Alzheimer's or cancer.

"Unfortunately, not only would it have tacked on a minimum of eight more years of study, but the heavy experimentation needed often results in wear and tear on the sorcerer. And like any branch of study, especially the niched-down ones, any slip-up in rune construction can result in horrific consequences. An array went wrong with his last apprentice a few years ago. She aged forty years in a matter of minutes, and the cancer lying dormant in her body grew exponentially. She was dead a month later."

"*Damn*," I muttered, horrified that drawing a rune incorrectly could result in something that catastrophic.

I remembered then that it had been a mistake in rune construction that had granted my sword sentience. One mistake had given an inanimate object something akin to a soul.

Macrae stood just outside the group at large, staring off into space. Thinking of his lost apprentice, I supposed Macrae had good reason to be grouchy. Apprentices were probably hard for the guy to come by as it was, even though his chosen speciality held the possibility for so much good.

With every list of positives that came from a magical discipline, there was always an equal list of ways that power could be used for nefarious purposes. If Macrae could potentially heal cells, he could kill them, too. Did the biological processes that happened within hybrids and ferals intrigue Macrae? I thought of the necrosis that turned a feral's extremities black and how their blood turned to something thick and putrid, like old motor oil. Could someone like Macrae reverse that?

Would he want to?

"Come, Harlow," Avery finally said, snapping me out of my thoughts. He turned and strode toward the next section of the armory. From what I could see, that section was the last one, as another intimidating steel door lay just beyond it. There *was* a second entrance into the armory after all; the old geezers had made us walk through the werecat gym solely to scare us and incense the cats.

"Goddess speed," Caspian muttered to me, then gave my arm a squeeze before approaching the table where his new charges had slowly reclaimed their seats. They still watched my sword with a mixture of apprehension and awe. All save for Meredith. Despite wearing an unflattering gray T-shirt, no makeup, and no jewelry, there was something striking about her. Perhaps it was how vibrantly green her eyes were in an otherwise pale face. Her focus was entirely on Caspian.

I moved past the table after Avery, my sword trailing after me. Macrae watched us go.

Instead of stopping in the final section of the armory—this one lined with broad swords on one side and shields on the other—Avery led us to the metal door. I hazarded a glance over my shoulder, but Caspian was no longer visible from here, tucked as he was into the alcove of his section.

This door was different from the one we'd entered through. It was a single door that, once Avery had gone through the necessary rigmarole to get it open via keypads and access cards, didn't swing open but rather trundled into the ceiling.

"Right this way," Avery said before heading toward the right side of the room.

There were no other doors.

Weapons didn't line the walls here. In fact, the walls were all blank, calling even more attention to the only two pieces of furniture in the narrow room. On each side of the room was a large, ebony-colored stand, each at least eight feet long. My morbid brain conjured up images of daises for sarcophagi. Six wide drawers arranged in two columns sat below the black marble tops, silver handles gleaming under the fluorescent lights. What was most striking, though, was the three-foot-tall rectangular glass case that sat perfectly atop one stand. A velvet pillow in a size befitting a horse lay inside the box. And lying on that, looking diminutive in all that space, was a sickle. I didn't sense movement from inside the box, but I crept forward cautiously all the same. My sword slowly flew around the box, periodically tapping at the glass as if testing its integrity.

Avery stood several feet away, arms behind his back as he regarded us. If he was alarmed or put off by my sword's poking and prodding, he kept his comments to himself.

As I slowly circled around to the other side, I found a door in the middle of the box, complete with a latch. The door was wide enough that I could easily fit both arms through, but I wouldn't have been able to crawl inside. I reached for the latch, only to pull my hand away before my fingertips touched metal.

"Don't hold back on my account."

I shot a death glare at Avery. Macrae might enjoy having mental conversations with the guy, but I didn't. Talking to Tim that way was bad enough. I gave the sword in my hand another violent shake. No response.

Avery didn't offer one, either.

I blew out a slow breath, then unlatched the door, my curiosity outweighing everything else. As I peered into the open door, I noted that the glass—or maybe it was reinforced plastic—was an inch or two thick. Scratch marks and deep gouges marred the inside of the enclosure.

My sixth sense started pinging again.

What had Macrae said earlier?

"There have been reports in three separate states now of weapons that have come to life. So far, only one has been successfully captured and deconstructed." Yet Avery had said, *"We need to figure out how you woke up your sword."*

I chewed on my bottom lip.

Mere minutes ago, Avery had told the sword, *"Yes, sword, you can join us ... In fact, I insist on it."*

I peered at Avery through the thick glass, his figure a bit distorted. He still stood just inside the doorway, hands in the pockets of his khakis, the picture of casual.

Returning my focus to the box, I tentatively reached a hand into the enclosure—not to grab the handle of the sickle, but to follow a hunch. I pinched some of the black fabric of the pillow and lifted. As I suspected, it came away from the marble surface easily. Below it lay a thick layer of silvery powder.

I didn't know what Avery was playing at, but something didn't sit well with me.

My sword was on the other side of the box now, closer to Avery and the door out. It had been acting like its usual curious self this whole time, but suddenly it froze as if struck by a thought.

"Sword ..." I said slowly.

The blade went from cool steel to cherry red in an instant. It shot up over the top of the box and zipped in my direction. I stumbled back a few steps, more out of confusion than fear. I realized what was happening a second too late. Before I could get a word out, the sword harpooned through the open door of the box. The heat of its blade snuffed out, and it crashed into the opposite wall of the enclosure, hitting the pillow with a muted thud—like a bird crashing into a window.

Unlike Tim, who had powered down on purpose, my sword had just been involuntarily knocked out by alloy powder.

My stomach lurched. Not thinking, I deposited Tim on top of the box, then I shoved my arm into the enclosure, needing to get on tiptoe to even get my fingers to brush the edge of the sword's hilt. There were no other doors on the box, and the glass itself was welded to the marble tabletop.

Groaning in frustration, I pulled my arm out and rounded the massive stand to ask Avery what the hell was going on. But my demands died on my lips. Avery was gone. Metal rubbed against metal, and I jerked my face upward. The door had begun its quick descent out of the ceiling. He was locking us in here? I bolted for the exit, but the door slammed into place just before I could reach it. I slapped a palm against the metal.

"Avery! What the hell?" I pounded my fist against the door, but it didn't even issue a muted rattle.

If the door was as thick as the ones that separated the armory from the gym, then the sound of my voice wouldn't carry. I hurriedly pulled out my cell phone, intending to text Caspian to get me out of here, but of course there was no reception. I shoved my phone back into my pocket. There wasn't anything of use in my backpack. Maybe I could use the nail file in my toiletry bag to chisel my way out of here. I unslung my bag and tossed it on the floor.

I pressed my back to the door as I eyed the enclosure that now housed my sword and the sickle. The other enclosure in here was set up exactly the same way, but it was empty.

Your help would be appreciated, Tim!

Nothing.

The question now was whether the sorcerers had actually woken up the sickle on their own but had implied otherwise. Had they stuffed the thing into the box to quell its murderous tendencies, or was the thick layer of alloy powder more of a precaution? It still wouldn't explain the scratches and gouges I'd seen *inside* the box.

If the sickle had been in the box by itself, I would have just parked my ass on the floor with my sword and waited Avery out. But my sword had been rendered inert. I couldn't abandon it in there.

I recalled the way my sword had abruptly flown into the box.

It wasn't as if it hadn't operated under its own agenda dozens of times, but I had a sneaking suspicion that Avery's mind-magic could be used to manipulate the sword much the same way as Roch's enthrall. Avery had forced my sword to fly into the magic-nullifying box because he knew I'd do whatever I could to get it out.

Arms crossed, I made my way to the still-open door of the enclosure. If I grabbed hold of the sickle, I could use it to fish my sword out.

Just to be sure, I checked all six drawers, hoping to find an alternative tool, but they were empty. So were all six on the other marble-topped stand.

The longer I stared at the scratches inside the box, the more I was sure the sickle's consciousness was already online, even if it was currently incapacitated. The stupid sorcerers hoped my sword and/or I could corral the sickle into compliance based solely on the relationship my sword and I had. Perhaps Avery hadn't asked any questions about Tim simply because my connection to the second sword only proved that I had the ability to form relationships with these weapons—relationships I couldn't explain, nor had they been accomplished through anything other than dumb luck. And Tim didn't even cooperate half the time because I was unworthy!

Now I was locked in a room with one that was possibly even more unstable.

Fantastic.

CHAPTER FIFTEEN

RENATA

Renata's heart galloped in her chest as she, Paola, and Dalton rounded the corner of Cuisine Across the Realms. If she couldn't get her breathing under control, she was sure to pass out before they ever reached the battle. Dalton's umbrella shield glowed brightly. Though she knew it would provide excellent protection—at least for a while—the fact that it was translucent was doing little to calm her anxiety about getting torn apart by a monster from her nightmares.

Renata tried not to think about getting ambushed from behind. Perhaps it would be a mercy not to see it coming, though.

As they inched toward the front of the restaurant, another explosion rattled the air. She flinched so badly, the handle of her broom thwacked Paola in the calf. The woman glared at her; Renata offered her a sheepish smile.

Dalton had come to such an abrupt halt, it was a wonder they hadn't bumped into him. Despite the obvious tension in his neck and shoulders, he hadn't dropped his array, which was a small miracle in itself.

The explosion was so close, Renata felt the reverberation of it in the soles of her feet *and* her chest this time. It had come from *inside* the town center. A thick plume of black smoke shot into the air then, and the acrid scents of burnt plastic and something sharp and chemical wafted past Renata on the breeze.

Given the general location of the explosion, plus the one from earlier, her gut was telling her that whoever had attacked the hub was now targeting the telepads. The intruders wanted the residents trapped here. She supposed people could start running through the veil to get out, but the pain would be debilitating—if not outright fatal—if they didn't have the right talismans to bypass the heavy-duty veil magic. Renata's own emergency travel talisman was in a drawer in her apartment, clear on the other side of the hub. She'd have to get through or around the town center to get there.

Another explosion thundered, pulling a startled yelp from Renata. Dalton's shield array flickered for only a second before he reinforced it. Paola unleashed a string of what Renata assumed was Italian profanity.

"All right," Paola whispered in her decisive way. Paola being a handful of years older had never felt that significant before today—now Renata felt both humbled by Paola's life experience and grateful for it. "New plan. We're going to back up and head down Elsher's Loop on the eastern side of the town center. Maybe the telepad station in the residential sector hasn't been blown up yet."

Though Renata had also concluded that the intruders were targeting the telepads, she didn't like how confident Paola was in the exact same assumption. Their options for getting the hells out of this situation kept dwindling by the second.

Without a word, the trio backtracked. Once they were behind the buffet restaurant, Dalton dropped his shield and shook out his arms.

Paola got a solid grasp on her fire extinguisher, crouched, and then took off toward the garden installation. Renata wasn't sure how crouching would help, but she mimicked Paola and hurried after her. She tried not to look at the dead man still being picked apart by the crow.

The eastern stretch of Elsher's Loop was deserted. The halfway point was marked by a stretch of scorched earth that was clearly visible from a distance, the sight all but confirming the telepad station had been destroyed. Because of the complicated magic and technology that kept telepads running, Renata could only imagine the damage that had been sustained by the neighboring buildings. It wouldn't be as bad as a meth lab exploding, but it wasn't far off. What would have happened to someone who had been mid-teleport when the station blew up? She swallowed down the bile that clawed up her throat.

As they reached the burned-out space where the station had once stood, Paola slowed again. Renata eyed the burst of soot that fanned across Elsher's Loop and into the barren land of Testing Sector 1. A string of debris stretched a good twenty feet from the blast site. Shattered glass, large chunks of twisted metal, and ... body parts. Severed hands, feet, a whole leg from thigh to ankle. Her stomach heaved dangerously.

She didn't dare look through the gaping space. Dalton appeared too focused on the severed hand lying nearby to take a gander either.

Paola hinged forward. *"Jeeesus ..."* she muttered, stretching out both syllables.

Against her better judgment, Renata peered around Paola. She had a clear view of the town center; not even the building's supports or the telepad station's foundation remained. Renata watched in horror as pure chaos ensued. Even more upsetting than the people running for their lives, only to be taken down by ferals, was that, standing near the fountain in the middle of the town center, were four people who appeared to be having a casual chat. They weren't just any people, either. What in the hells did *elves* want with Elsher, and why weren't the ferals attacking them?

There were two men and two women, all dressed in jeans and T-shirts, as if they were tourists who had gotten lost and were regrouping in the town center. The men's short hair ensured their pointed ears were prominent. One of the women's ears was covered by her mop of thick, chocolate-colored curls. Renata supposed this woman might be something other than an elf, but they all bore similar-enough facial and body structures to peg them as belonging to the same species.

Renata's gaze kept lingering on one man in particular. Even from afar, she could tell he was incredibly beautiful, but in that off-putting, preternatural way. The others were focused on him the most, as if he led the conversation, and they were only asking clarifying questions when necessary. She guessed he was in his fifties or so. His left arm was missing from the elbow down.

A feral interrupted their conversation by unceremoniously tossing a person at their feet. The one-armed man took a startled step back. His nose wrinkled as he took in the emaciated feral whose tattered clothing was covered in blood and gore. The person at the elf's feet was, somehow, still alive. Was this like a house cat who brings a mangled lizard into the house as an offering to its owners?

The feral scuttled backward a few feet on all fours, its head bowed.

The elf kicked at the fallen person on the ground, knocking her onto her back. The surrounding elves produced folded pieces of paper or small notebooks from their pockets. After consulting their papers, and a few nods in the affirmative, one of the female elves grabbed the fallen woman by the elbow and yanked her to her feet. She tossed the nearly unconscious woman over her shoulder and then strode out of sight.

The one-armed elf barked an order at the prostrate feral, who, quick as a snake, took off again, galloping away on hands and feet like a mutated wolf.

"They're collecting certain people," Renata whispered out loud to herself. "They knew the identities of everyone before they even got here. How?"

Renata already knew the answer, though.

Through gritted teeth, Dalton said, "Someone inside Elsher sold us out."

Paola abruptly stood straight and pressed her back against the charred wall. The blood had drained from her face, her lips going a little gray. She looked like she might faint—or throw up. Placing a hand on her stomach, she eyed Renata and Dalton in turn. "I hope you two won't think less of me ..."

Something in her tone sent Renata's heart racing again.

"This isn't the kind of person I want to be. Praying for forgiveness might not be enough," Paola muttered.

Renata eyed her warily. Was Paola about to admit to something unthinkable? None of this could have been *her* doing, could it?

"Wh-what do you mean?" Dalton stammered, looking as concerned as Renata felt.

Paola swallowed hard. "My savior complex has dried up. We have to get the fuck out of here and never look back. You two are the only ones I'm worried about now. The telepad in the residential district or travel talismans are our only hope."

Renata let out a shaky, relieved laugh. She doubled over, hands on her knees. Dalton rubbed her back as she took in large gulps of air.

"We're at the bottom of the totem pole as far as breakthrough research goes," Paola said, either unaware of Renata being on the brink of mental collapse or not caring. "There's no way we're on that list. We're not important enough. That woman they took away? That was Joan Calder."

Dalton gasped softly. "You're kidding!"

Renata stood up so fast, her head swam. She knew what the woman looked like, but that beaten and bloodied person who had been dumped on the ground hadn't been recognizable. Calder's words, though? *Those* Renata knew. She'd read and re-read Calder's research papers so often, she practically had chunks of them memorized.

Though Elsher was a small community, it wasn't necessarily tight-knit. She'd had no idea Calder was in the hub. She had to admit that was a pretty big secret, though, even for Elsher.

Paola said, "She got here a couple of weeks ago. I only know because a friend cleans the offices on Calder's floor. Supposedly, Calder recently opened a stable portal. It was small, but she was able to reach in and pluck a beetle from the other side. Crazy, right? The portal stayed open for a full minute before she manually closed it again. Nothing we were working on could even hold a candle to that."

Renata's mouth dropped open. Not in shock, but utter disbelief. It had been a *flower*, not a beetle.

Dalton awkwardly cleared his throat. In a tone Renata instantly recognized as forced, he asked, "What or who did she have to sacrifice to get it to stay open for that long?"

Paola didn't seem to notice Renata's or Dalton's discomfort. She shook her head. "Nothing. All she used was perfectly crafted rune arrays—focusing on distilling a whimal chain down to its base parts before restructuring it with dystilian loops and frybol underpinnings. That's a small part of it anyway. It's complicated stuff. Genius, honestly."

Renata glanced up at Dalton. She assumed his pinched expression mirrored her own. The journal pressed to the small of her back felt like it weighed a million pounds. Had Calder stolen Renata and Dalton's theories and claimed them as her own? Or was it simply a coincidence?

Renata had sent that fan letter only a month ago. Calder's questions had made it clear she hadn't been anywhere close to making the same breakthrough. Renata hadn't revealed the entirety of her research to Calder, of course. Especially not in an email. There was no way, as brilliant as Calder was, that she would have been able to take what she'd gleaned from Renata's messages and fill in the plethora of missing components. Maybe in a year, or possibly six months with a team to share the workload, but not in a mere month.

She and Dalton had been working on their theories for years. While their peers were out on the weekend getting into teenage mischief, she and Dalton had been reading, studying, testing, postulating. The fact that the rigors of the sorcery academy had gotten close to breaking them both despite their studious backgrounds said a lot about the schooling. But those same rigors had made them knuckle down even more. It had resulted in them opening a portal that didn't require spilled blood or extreme expenditures of magic.

Death and violence so often resulted from people forcefully tearing open portals between worlds. Renata and Dalton's approach had been gentle. They had politely asked magic to show them a glimpse of another realm, and the magic had listened.

Renata had no proof, but she and Dalton had both speculated that the Glitch was caused by someone—or many someones—asking too much of magic, and that magic had retaliated before shutting the doors for good.

And yet, some deep part of her soul was positive she'd seen a small glimpse of the lost fae realm.

The small smile that automatically inched onto her face every time she thought of that iridescent purple-black flower only lasted a moment before falling away.

If whoever had infiltrated Elsher grilled Calder for information, they'd quickly learn she wasn't as knowledgeable as she claimed. She couldn't even remember that Renata had said the petals of the flower sparkled *like* the iridescent shell of a beetle, not that a beetle itself had been pulled here from another realm, for Goddess's sake!

If grilling turned to torture, would Calder give up Renata's and Dalton's names to save her own skin? Renata had been stupid enough to trust her idol with the name of the research hub she'd been working in. Her pride had gotten the better of her; she'd wanted her hero to know that she'd been accepted to an institution as revered as Elsher. And then, weeks later, Calder had not only secured clearance to travel to the facility, but she'd touched down in the hub.

Renata's stomach churned.

While Paola had been wrong about their research not being revolutionary enough for them to end up on that list, she was right about something else: They needed to get the hells out of here.

CHAPTER SIXTEEN

RENATA

On Paola's suggestion, the trio opted to trek across the barren expanse of Testing Sector 1 toward the edge of the hub before running alongside the veil until they reached the residential sector. They could have gotten there quicker if they followed Elsher's Loop, but the pandemonium of the town center almost guaranteed they'd be spotted sooner rather than later.

They kept silent as they jogged in a single-file line with Paola in the lead and Dalton bringing up the rear. Renata kept the flat head of her broom-turned-weapon facing the humming veil so she could hopefully knock any ferals back who might be on the other side trying to get in.

The fact that she couldn't see what lay beyond the veil usually comforted her. It was akin to being in a protective, impenetrable shell. Now she felt like a bug trapped under glass.

She stared at the back of Paola's head, her short brown pony-tail swinging. Before leaving the safety of her research lab, Renata had assumed she'd be collateral damage at best. The bottom of the totem pole, as Paola had said. But knowing Joan-freaking-Calder herself was here had drastically altered Renata's outlook on her situation. Now she operated under the fear that she and Dalton were on that master list, while Paola was not. Renata couldn't bear the thought of getting caught in either scenario. It was probably a death sentence for them all, either way.

Getting all three of them out of Elsher was the only option Renata could live with.

She frantically scanned the looming residential sector, hoping she'd spot any potential danger before it spotted them. She and Dalton lived close to this side of the sector in Kensey Towers, each in a one-bedroom apartment. It was one of several high-rise dorm-like buildings in the southeast corner of the hub. Paola's years as a Collective employee had allowed her to enter—and win—a lottery for one of the small cottages in a neighborhood close to Elsher's Loop. Normally, it was a most coveted location. Currently, there was a good chance her place had been overrun by feral vampires.

They stayed light on their feet and crouched low for reasons Renata still didn't understand. But Paola had been in the field before, so Renata trusted she knew what she was doing.

Something like hope started to bloom in Renata's chest the longer they went without an altercation. The sounds of battle grew softer in the background. Maybe the telepad here was still functioning, and they could get out.

They quietly slipped into the neighborhood that shared a border with Testing Sector 1, now jogging on paved sidewalks instead of hard-packed earth. A full minute went by without incident. It felt eerie, though; the sector was deathly silent. Granted, the breach had happened in the middle of the day, when almost the entire hub was at work. The residential sector would have been nearly deserted at this hour, anyway.

Which had likely been intentional.

Dalton's words from earlier rang in her head. *"Someone inside Elsher sold us out."*

The intruders had shown up with a plan that so far had been executed with ruthless efficiency despite using savage monsters as their primary weapon. How long had this been in the works? Why was it happening now?

Renata crashed into Paola's back, sending the other woman stumbling forward. Dalton caught Renata by the arm and wrenched her backward to prevent the women from going down in a heap. Paola righted herself and whirled around to shoot a death glare at Renata, who shied away. Paola pressed a finger to her lips and hunkered down behind a hedge. The butt of Paola's fire extinguisher clanked lightly on the cement. Renata swallowed her snarky comment about Paola and her fluctuating mood swings when she finally heard the snarling. She dropped to her knees, propping the wide head of her broom on the ground and keeping a death grip on the handle.

The sidewalk they'd been running down was flanked on either side by four-foot-high, well-tended hedges. The back of a house was to their left. Renata crouched just below the windows of a kitchen. She craned her neck to check if anyone was inside the house, but all she could see were faint snatches of sunshine-yellow paint on the walls and drawn-open gauzy white curtains.

Renata could tell at least one feral was nearby, but she couldn't gauge where the sound came from—ahead of them, behind, from within one of the quiet houses? The snarling reminded her of both a zombie movie and a ticked-off bear. Renata had always harbored an irrational fear of zombies, telling her sister and Dalton on numerous occasions that if the planet were ever overrun by the undead, she was sure to be one of the first casualties. That fear didn't seem quite so irrational now, but she hoped her odds continued to fare better than previously assumed.

Goose bumps sprang up on her arms as a series of chitters echoed off the walls—perhaps off the nearby veil, too—sending the nightmarish sounds bouncing, disorienting her. She flashed back to the ferals who had broken into the lab. The ferals she'd helped kill. They'd been so fast. If she and her companions were caught by surprise, they were toast.

She closed her eyes, willing her heart rate to slow as she attempted to figure out which direction the creatures were coming from. A chitter, a snarl, an answering call—and then a staccato burst of sharp inhales. It was sniffing them out.

Her eyes popped open, and her head snapped back. She saw the thing mere moments before it moved. "Above us!"

Thankfully, Dalton and Paola didn't ask questions. Paola lurched forward, Dalton skittered back, and Renata darted to the other side of the sidewalk, her back pressed against a hedge.

She was ready for the feral this time. Before its feet even hit the cement, Renata was already swinging. She knocked the beast back a few inches, disorienting it.

The feral recovered quickly, shaking her head like a dog to clear the stars in her eyes, but instead of lunging for Renata in a rage, she merely stared at her. The jolt seemed to have knocked something loose in the feral because something like clarity or recognition flashed through her eyes, which Renata found incredible, considering they were black voids. The feral opened her mouth, but instead of snarling incoherently, she said something that very much sounded like *"Please."*

Renata froze. *"What?"*

"Don't just stand there!" Paola said from several feet away, having darted further afield than necessary. She ran toward them, fire extinguisher held at the ready.

Dalton wrenched his fire ax from his belt loop, issued a battle cry, and charged forward. Some part of Renata wanted to shout "No! wait!" A small smile graced the feral's face at the sound of Dalton approaching from behind. The feral closed her all-black eyes.

Dalton swung and chopped the feral directly in the middle of her skull. Blackish blood splattered across Renata's shirt and face, startling her out of her stupefied silence. The blade embedded itself all the way to the monster's nose, as if its skull had been an overripe cantaloupe. Renata watched the life go out of her limbs before she toppled with a meaty *thunk*. Renata wiped her cheek on her sleeve, disgusted by the stench of the blood. Chunks of brain matter and dark blood oozed out of the feral's split-open skull, seeping into a sidewalk crack.

Renata's heart still raced, and her palm was sweaty under the death grip she had on her broom's handle. She knew they needed to keep moving, but she couldn't stop staring at the feral's prone body. And not because she was having an existential crisis over facilitating the death of something that looked this close to a human. Something that ... *who* ... had spoken to her.

"*Please*," she'd said.

She'd *wanted* to die.

Dalton placed one foot beside the feral, and the other on her back, then easily pulled the ax free. He wiped off the gore on his pant leg.

Renata squatted next to the body, careful not to get the stinking black blood on her tennis shoes. Distinguishing former ethnicity seemed impossible, as whatever changed them into monsters apparently stripped away any pigment in their skin and morphed their features into something more skeletal than anything. But despite the feral being as filthy and gaunt as the others, this one seemed ... different. And not just because she'd spoken. Black veins snaked under the feral's translucent skin, but her fingers *weren't* reminiscent of dark claws. They appeared to be dusted with soot, rather than digits ravaged by necrosis. Had she turned more recently than the others Renata had encountered?

Paola said, "I get that we're all scientists at heart, but there's a time and place for data gathering, Ren, and this isn't it."

Remaining crouched, Renata quickly rattled off what she'd discovered—and what she'd heard. In moments, Dalton had dropped into a squat on the other side of the feral, peering at the hand that lay palm up on the cement.

Though she clearly wanted to get the hells out of here, Paola's curiosity pulled her toward the body now, rather than resuming her frantic glances around the corner of the house. "You're *sure* she spoke?"

"Positive," Renata said. "The sound has kind of been burned into my mind."

It had sounded like rocks rubbing together—a grating, almost painful sound.

Paola chewed on her bottom lip. "This thing was way too far gone to be a hybrid. It was definitely a feral. I—" Her gaze snapped toward Dalton. "Rethink your plan. As fascinating as this is, we do *not* have time for you to remove her ratty-ass socks to check the state of her feet."

Shamefaced, Dalton stood, dropping the hold he'd had on the feral's socked foot. The tips of his ears went pink. "It might be useful information to have."

Paola passionately disagreed.

Renata only heard part of the argument, though, because she was picking up a new sound. Pounding footsteps. Paola luckily heard it, too. She cut herself off mid-rant, whirled, and thrust the butt of her fire extinguisher at a figure just as it rounded the corner of the house.

"Oh shit!" the guy yelped, ducking in time to avoid a broken nose.

Paola had lucked out, too, because the guy was brandishing an honest-to-Goddess spear with a wicked-sharp tip crackling with bright-green magic. He dropped it with a clatter, where it rolled off the sidewalk and under a hedge. Renata had never seen a weapon like it.

The pair stared at each other for a moment, heaving. The guy moved first, throwing his arms around Paola's middle. She sagged in the embrace, though she kept hold of the extinguisher. He was a good-looking middle-aged guy. Probably a solid ten years older than Paola. He had dark-brown hair smattered with flecks of gray, a graying beard, and prominent laugh lines. He was an inch or two shorter than Paola's five nine.

"I'm so glad to see a friendly face," the guy said, breaking the hug as quickly as it had begun, hands on Paola's shoulders. "I've been chasing that asshole for ten minutes," he said, jutting a chin at the dead feral. The guy seemed a little manic, talking quickly. "It had just killed one of the Bentley twins and was going after the other. They lived next door to me. It happened in the hallway right outside my apartment. I somehow survived getting back to my place from the town center, felt safe for all of five minutes, and then this monster was tearing apart a teenager in my Goddess-damned hallway—a monster I wasn't supposed to have to deal with anymore if I was living in a place like Elsher, mind you. I sort of snapped."

Paola finally seemed to get her bearings. "Do you know what the hells is going on, Joe?"

He blinked rapidly and took a step back, clearing his throat. He suddenly seemed a little embarrassed, and Renata figured the mania was more situation driven than how the guy normally acted. "I know more than most, probably. But we need to get inside somewhere. Any of you live close?" He directed the question at Dalton and Renata. "I think my place is too close to the Loop. Compromised for sure by now."

"That's where we were headed," Paola said. "They're both in Kensey Towers."

Joe nodded vigorously. He unearthed his spear from where it lay below the hedge. An unsettling dark acrid smoke had started to waft up from the bushes where the spear had been lying. Renata decided to ignore it.

Paola turned to motion at Renata and Dalton. "This is Renata Bernard and Dalton Edwards. They work—worked?—with me in Lab 9. Guys, this is Joe Taylor. He was involved with the Vampire Hunters of America for a long time. We'll be safe with him. He's got connections both inside the hub and out."

Renata eyed him. The guy looked dubious at best about the accuracy of Paola's introduction, but he didn't correct her. She figured the guy would agree to anything in exchange for company. He had a haunted look in his eyes. Considering that ferals wouldn't have been an unknown entity for him before all this, it didn't speak well to what he'd seen while in the town center.

"Do you know if Chancellor Thorpe is still alive?" Paola glanced at Renata and Dalton in turn. "Joe works in her office. If anyone in this hub knows what the hells is going on, it's the chancellor."

"Oh, she knows everything all right." The furrow of Joe's brow deepened. "She's the one who gave Lachlan Shade the blueprints to get in."

CHAPTER SEVENTEEN

KAYDA

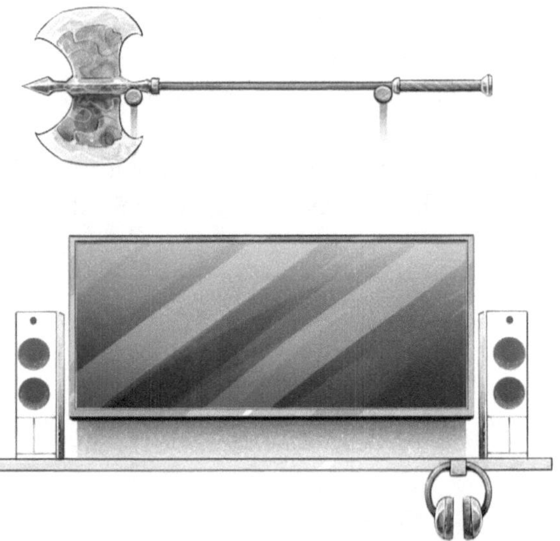

The jump from Montclaire to the hub of Thero just outside Vancouver was pretty mild as far as telepad rides went. It felt a little like being on a torture rack, where Kayda's top half was being pulled from her lower half like she was made of taffy instead of flesh and bone. As she teetered on the edge between "does this hurt?" and "Goddess above, this hurts so much, I would prefer death!" suddenly she was at her new destination. Kayda assumed that if one ever tried to jump too far, they'd definitely end up on the wrong end of that pain spectrum. She'd never chanced it.

Stumbling from her inbound tube, she found Marisol and a few others clustered in the middle of the lobby. The telepad station was housed in a building akin to an airplane hangar—high ceiling, smooth cement floor, metal siding for walls. It was chilly and sterile. Aside from the long row of telepad tubes lining the back wall—including two large vehicle tubes in the far-left corner—there were a few scattered seating areas, but they looked more functional than comfortable. A receptionist desk sat off to the far right, with signs promoting "INFORMATION" and "RENTALS" hanging above the heads of the bored-looking workers behind the counter. A pair of softly humming vending machines stood nearby.

Kayda checked herself over as she walked toward her group, making sure her hooded battle-ax was still strapped tightly to her torso and all her limbs were accounted for.

Marisol offered her a tight smile. "It'll be a few minutes before everyone gets here. Then we can make the second jump." She went back to furiously typing on her phone.

Grabbing her own phone, Kayda set up a group text between herself, Henri, and Harlow. She added Welsh purely out of selfish hope that he might answer. She hadn't had enough time in all the hoopla to tell any of them what was going on. The last she'd heard, Caspian, Harlow, and her mom were headed to the Collective's Tower for some meeting or other. Kayda hoped no news was good news.

Kayda
Lachlan Shade is in the Elsher hub in Canada.
I'm also in Canada. This is an "asking for forgiveness instead of permission" situation

Welsh
Elsher as in the top-secret research place?

Kayda
Holy Goddess, you answered! How are you?

Welsh
I feel like I was chewed up by a hippo, spat back out, run over by a steamroller, and then sat on by the hippo

Kayda
So…good then?

Another number was added to the group.

Unknown
Hi?

Welsh
So what's this about Elsher?

Kayda
Guess I shouldn't be surprised you know about the place

Henri
I didn't know there was a top-secret research hub. But I don't even know who the other two numbers in this thread belong to…

Welsh
Use deductive reasoning, Henri. I know you're capable

Henri
Thanks. Deductive reasoning tells me to program that one in as "Douche canoe."

Henri
I hope you're okay, by the way

Welsh
Blood poisoning 0/10. Do not recommend

Henri
Guess I'll take that off my bucket list

Unknown
Was I added to this by mistake?

Unknown
They treating you okay, Welsh?

Welsh
This is the first time I've been awake for longer than ten minutes. They bring me human food instead of blood so that's a plus. They put me in a little cottage, so I have the place to myself. I'm not in the cathedral, so at least I haven't been forced to see Roch's punchable face yet.

Henri
If it makes you feel better, Probably Caspian, I don't have the first clue what's going on either. I'm just happy to be included

Kayda programmed in Caspian's number.

Caspian
I have limited reception here, so I apologize if I don't answer promptly. I'm unsure why Harlow isn't replying. She's in a different part of the armory at the moment.

Henri
I'm so confused. What the heck are you doing in an armory of all places? (Though Welsh being in Tercla is way weirder.)

Welsh
Word.

Kayda briefly considered dropping her phone in a trash can. Why did group texts always go sideways immediately? She glanced up and found that Marisol had taken a call and was huddled beside one of the vending machines, a finger stuck in her opposite ear to better hear the person on the other end. The constant whooshing of the telepads wasn't loud so much as constant.

Doing a quick head count, Kayda noted that they were still waiting on one more VHoA member to make the jump here from Montclaire. She returned her focus to her phone. The conversation had derailed even further in the short length of time her attention had been diverted.

> **Kayda**
> I think there are Shades in the Collective

That stopped the conversation in its tracks. A conversation which had, inexplicably, moved on to everyone's favorite horror movies. Welsh's number one was *The Notebook*, and thankfully Kayda's statement had stopped Henri from asking him to elaborate.

Kayda told them Joe's implied theory that Lachlan must have connections in the Collective to even know about Elsher, let alone be armed with the information necessary to breach the veil.

In the midst of Kayda's texting spree, Marisol had returned to the group. What Kayda overheard Marisol tell everyone made her look up sharply.

"All of them?" Kayda asked.

Marisol sighed. "Three are confirmed destroyed. The fourth one, the one in the residential district, is offline. No one is sure if that means the spells on it are working a little too well, shielding it from detection to the point it looks like it's not functional, or if that one is gone, too. Until we know, it's too risky to even try attempt try it. And, of course, real-time communication is iffy. It could be a while until we hear anything."

> **Kayda**
> I just found out that three of the four telepads in Elsher were destroyed, and the fourth is out of commission. We can make an additional jump to Alberta, but then there's no getting into Elsher other than the old-school way. It could take as long as 14 hours by car

Her phone started buzzing with a flood of replies, but she was too defeated to read them. She stuffed her phone in her back pocket and crossed her arms.

There were two *thousand* people in Elsher. People who weren't even cut out for a run-of-the-mill fight. They definitely weren't prepared for a war against feral vampires, the ferals' masters, and Lachlan Shade. They were like bugs trapped under glass that was slowly filling with poison.

The horrifying footage from Mulgrew's breach replayed in Kayda's head. She knew that what was potentially—*probably*—happening in Elsher was worse. She wasn't sure if she wanted to punch something or cry. Maybe she could try them simultaneously.

Someone asked the question Kayda was too scared to voice herself. "What about the werecats who went ahead of us? The regular-size telepads were still functional when we left Montclaire …"

Kayda's stomach knotted at the thought of what could happen to someone who was being teleported across hundreds of miles, only to have their destination cease to exist mid-jump.

Marisol shrugged hopelessly. "I don't know. Jasmine's phone goes straight to voicemail."

Marisol's phone pinged, and she hurriedly yanked it out of her pocket. "It's Ben," she said, gaze glued to the screen. "There are reports of at least four other VHoA teams across the country who've had people drop off the radar—people who made it to Elsher *and* ones who were in transit. One team sent a van with seven people in it that left seconds before the large vehicle pad was destroyed." Her jaw clenched. "*Shit.*"

Kayda balled her fists. "Let's jump to Alberta and then drive the rest of the way. It'll take hours, but if we drive in shifts, we could get there faster than anyone else. We can adjust on the fly if someone comes up with a better plan later."

Cathy, who was sporting two black eyes thanks to Kayda accidentally elbowing her in the face earlier, crossed her arms. She kept her gaze focused somewhere beyond Kayda's shoulder. "Fourteen hours is a long damn time. It might be too late by then."

"Too late for what?" Kayda snapped. "You say that as if we know what in the hells Lachlan is doing. For all we know, he thinks Elsher would be a good vacation spot, and he's using ferals to clear the place out. We either head there and hope we can get there 'in time,' or we go back home and just accept that we gave up on a town's worth of people."

Marisol groaned. "*Dammit*, Kayda. Let me make sure we can jump to Alberta; that station isn't used as often. Gotta make sure we can get a car there, too ..."

She stalked off. The pair of bored workers who'd been staring into space behind the reception counter perked up at Marisol's approach. Kayda knew some telepad stations, like airports, had attached parking lots—either for parking one's own car or renting one. As was evidenced by their current predicament, sometimes telepads could only get you so far, and then mundane travel had to pick up the slack.

Kayda's phone had been buzzing incessantly in her pocket a few minutes ago, but her friends had clearly given up. Something Joe had said crept back into the forefront of her mind, though, and she pulled her phone back out.

Kayda
Hey, Caspian?

Caspian
Yes?

Kayda
Your eagle is an aeorci, right?

Caspian
He's a falcon, not an eagle. You can tell by his wings. They're more sharply pointed than an eagle's. But, yes, Rory is an aeorci. Why do you ask?

Kayda
Do you think you could send him ahead of us to scout what's happening in Elsher? He can get there faster than we can by car

Caspian
That's an excellent idea, but I'm currently sequestered in the Tower so I can't communicate with him.

Kayda
Dammit

Welsh
Henri could talk to Julip

Caspian
That could work. No one should be loitering around my house now if we're all currently in the Tower.

Henri
Who's Julip?

Caspian
She's an earth pixie who essentially runs my household. Tell her I sent you and that I need her to tell Rory to fly to Elsher and scout the place out.

Welsh
I'll send you a separate text, Henri. It'll have Caspian's address and the rough coordinates of Elsher. It won't be exact, what with the hub being secret and all

Henri
If it's a secret, how do you know about it?

Welsh
You know I'm not going to dignify that with a response, right?

Kayda mentally whimpered. Why couldn't they just have a normal conversation? And where the hells was Harlow? She was better at herding cats than Kayda was. She wrinkled her nose. Harlow being added to this conversation probably would have made it go even further afield.

Welsh
Hey, I've got an off-the-wall idea, Kayda. You mentioning Rory got me thinking…

Kayda
I'm scared to ask

Welsh
What do you think about getting some help from the residents of Navolt? You wouldn't need security clearance so much as the go-ahead from the FDMA to get on the guest list. Very few people go to that hub on purpose, so I can't imagine they're swamped with paperwork

Caspian
That's probably because the residents are wildly xenophobic. My parents have had to deal with a few of their representatives, mostly over issues of air traffic regulations.

Henri

Navolt? The all-avian hub? How would contacting them help anything?

Welsh

For a fee, I bet they'd fly Kayda's crew to Elsher. Veil magic doesn't work on the avians as well as it does on others. The line separating sapient and non-sapient is blurry for them

Caspian

An intriguing idea! In the early days of the hub system, flying by avian was even more common than telepad use is now.

Kayda had spent a good amount of time dreaming about regaining her ancestors' ability to shift into a dragon and fly. Gaining flight by way of sitting on the back of a human-turned-bird hadn't been what she had in mind.

Henri

Did the practice go out of favor because mundanes freak out if they see car-sized birds flying around?

Caspian

That, and avians get ornery when they're exhausted or hungry. If a rider wasn't keeping their mount well-tended-to while in the air, the avian had a tendency to dump their cargo while in mid-flight regardless of location or distance from the ground.

Welsh

Also, avians with geese or swan bloodlines are best suited for longer flights, but geese and swans are bitey even on good days. Getting bitten by a car-sized goose is guaranteed to ruin your week

Kayda hated all her current options. All she knew about the FDMA was that it was the government program in charge of determining the magic levels found in foodstuffs and items. The system was in place in large part to make sure humans didn't consume or use anything over a Level 4, as the side effect was often a horrific death and/or severe maiming.

Henri
What's the connection between the FDMA and Navolt? It's not some messed-up reason, is it? Like since we can technically eat birds, and they're in bird form more often than not, they're classified as foodstuff?

Kayda
I'm not sure if I'm proud of that line of thinking or horrified

Henri
Aw, thanks, babe!

Caspian
The M in FDMA covers a very broad range of magic-related policies and regulations. There was an entire semester at the academy dedicated to it. There's a branch of the FDMA called Parks Management that deals with sentient and sapient animals. Because of the avian's lifestyle…culture…whatever you want to call it, they're considered "sapient beasts," even if they're technically human.

Caspian
Zander! If you go on a tirade about how it's degrading to call fae "human," I will leave the chat.

Welsh
Don't threaten me with a good time

Kayda groaned.

Kayda
I'm not saying this is a good idea, or even a plausible one, but how would we get in contact with someone at the FDMA? Marisol's got the most clout of all of us here, but I don't know how far that'll get us. Calling in another favor from the Collective doesn't seem possible now that our personal werecat is MIA. It also might be a terrible idea if Shades have really taken up root with the sorcerers

Caspian
I haven't spoken to my parents in over a year, but I could ask if they'd be willing to reach out to their contacts. They'd probably listen to me for once, given the circumstances...

Welsh
Let's avoid that can of worms. I've got a veterinarian contact in another hub. He's obsessive about magical and sapient animals and specializes in exotics. If he doesn't have a contact within the FDMA, he'll know someone who does. I'll be back in touch if I get any info. Not like I can do much else but convalesce and make phone calls. I'll avail you of my services until I'm once again so sick I start hallucinating

Kayda frowned at her screen.

Welsh
Stupid Vaughn might have some stupid ideas, too. Assuming I can stomach being in his stupid presence long enough to ask his stupid opinion

Henri
I'm getting the impression you don't like your new roommates

Welsh
Astute

Kayda
Thanks, guys. This was…helpful isn't the right word. This was something.

Henri
The word you're looking for is "lively"

Welsh
I'm off to do some research, then. If Harlow materializes, tell her I said hi

Caspian
You mean she wasn't lying? You *actually* told her you missed her?

Welsh has left the group.

CHAPTER EIGHTEEN

HARLOW

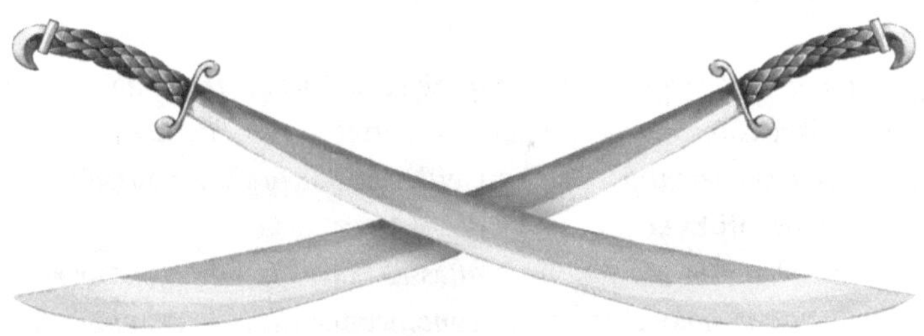

I religiously checked the time on my reception-less phone for ten solid minutes, hoping Sorcerer Avery would realize locking me in here was a dick move and he'd open the door, calling, "Just kidding!"

What I got was worse.

"*I assume you're sulking. Sulking is not conducive to success. Your success helps the greater good.*"

"Fuck you, Avery!"

A pause.

"*I also assume you just uttered something uncouth. Perhaps about my mother, Goddess rest her soul. No one can hear you. You might as well use your time wisely. Blackthorn is deep in a monologue about judlam runes, so he won't come to your aid any time soon. He seems to be caving to Miss Barden's feminine wiles faster than a sandcastle crumbles to a tsunami, so I'd hurry this along if you hope to impress him before she does."*

I pitied every human student at the academy who'd had to put up with Avery and his mental assaults. He couldn't even see me! Unless …

I scrambled to my feet from where I'd been sitting against the door. I scanned the corners of the ceiling for the telltale sign of cameras. I searched every inch of the place but found no wires, nor the sheen of lenses.

Which might just mean I was predictable enough that he guessed what I was thinking or doing. How annoying. I was as unpredictable as Mother Nature, dammit!

"No, I can't see you. Stop acting paranoid."

Ugh.

"To my knowledge, no one in quite some time, perhaps not since the likes of Likho Kamen, has been able to control the sentient weapons as … I won't say competently … let's go with adequately … as yourself."

I flipped off the door.

"For whatever reason, the cutlasses have deemed you worthy. I believe you and your charges can convince the sickle to acquiesce to the cause." He paused. *"I've yet to decide whether I'm impressed or not that you snuck in a second one under all our noses. Be glad Sorceress Rhiannon thinks so highly of your mother. It's my respect for Rhiannon that's kept truth serum out of your bloodstream. If it were up to me, you and Mr. Haskins would be neighbors."*

I truly was unsure if Avery was a tough-love kind of instructor —who used mental attacks to berate his unwilling students into accomplishing more than they would have had he not pushed them so hard—or if he'd gained Rhiannon's trust because he could act one way on the outside while secretly being an unadulterated jackass telepathically to everyone else.

Arms crossed, I glared at the box where my dormant sword and the sickle lay harmlessly on the black velvet pillow. Tim was still in power-down mode atop the box. If he wasn't going to help willingly, then he'd have to deal with being used as a mere tool. I angrily stomped toward Tim, intending to grab the sword and then bash it mercilessly against the glass until one of them broke.

The moment my hand closed around the dark hilt, though, a voice bellowed in my head. *UNWORTHY!*

I shrieked and stumbled back, leaving Tim on top of the box. I unleashed my frustration in a very cathartic full-body scream. Through clenched teeth, I said, "I'm never going to forgive you for this, Timothy."

Your survival will determine your worth.

"If I survive," I said slowly, "I'm going to get Cas to melt your ass down and turn you into sentient cufflinks, so you'll be forced to listen to boring board meetings all day. You'll never taste blood!"

I swore I could feel Tim hesitate in my mind, but he didn't say anything else.

Groaning, I refocused on the task at hand. Avery either didn't comprehend what I'd told him about my sword, or he didn't care. I didn't do anything to get my sword to "acquiesce." I clearly had even less control over Tim.

I didn't possess latent magic that reacted to my sword's. I wasn't a long-lost dragon princess who had been sequestered in the earthen realm until the moment it was time to take back my crown.

I was a thief who'd pilfered the wrong item, and now I was paying the price.

Maybe that explanation was too simple or too lacking in conspiracy for Avery to accept. Perhaps the sorcerer couldn't live with the notion that one of the Collective's best defenses against Lachlan and his grand nefarious plan lay in the hands of a petty criminal with exceptionally bad luck.

Either way, the only two ways out of here involved me either waiting until my mom or Caspian got word of this development and came to my aid or I learned how to speak sickle.

I made my way back to the still-open door on the box; I'd never been very good at waiting.

Plus I'd have to pee sooner or later, and I'd rather not have to pop a squat in a corner.

"Have you met your untimely demise, Fletcher child?"

I vowed that my sword's first line of business once we got out of here would be to divest Avery of a limb or two.

I peered through the open door at the sickle, searching for clues. About what, I didn't know. Since the blade was cool, I couldn't see the runes that must be etched on the metal. There were, however, a few small but deep scratches on the blade, as if someone had gone at it with a nail file.

There was no way to know how much clearance from the alloy powder the sickle needed before it woke up. Hopefully, as long as it was *in* the box, it would remain snoozing.

I shoved my arm through the door, grabbed hold of the sickle's handle, then thrust my arm as far as it would go, trying to hook the curved blade around my sword. It took half a dozen tries —my heart rate dangerously fast—before I finally snagged the sword and pulled it toward me. I dropped the sickle onto the velvet pillow, grabbed my sword instead, and tossed it out of the box.

My sword woke up moments before it hit the cement floor and immediately harpooned for the door to our prison. It harmlessly clanged off the metal, as if the sword had been no more threatening than a plastic spork. It hit the cement with a clatter but was back up again a breath later. It buzzed angrily, its blade cherry red, as it threw itself at the door and walls. I walked around the stand to rest my back against the box, arms crossed, as I watched the sword lose its shit. I knew how it felt.

I let it work out its rage before I spoke.

It took … a while. Which was good, because it let me think.

"Sword, I'm going to need your help."

It zipped toward my face, stopping only a few inches away before it launched into another mostly silent tirade about the depth of its anger. I didn't understand the details of this meltdown any more than the last one, but I got the gist.

I held up a hand to quiet it. "Let's put it in perspective, okay? You were only trapped in there for twenty minutes, tops. Who knows how long the sickle's been in there. If anyone can calm that thing down, it's going to be you."

It darted back a few feet, took on my likeness, and began to wig out anew. This bout of charades was somehow even more nonsensical. When it started doing a very stabby rendition of the Funky Chicken dance, I held up a hand again.

"I'm not making any decisions on what to do beyond getting the sickle out of that box," I said. "If it's anything like you or the Winchells' ax, I don't want it trapped in there forever. If the thing doesn't kill me—"

The sword vibrated so hard its entire being blurred.

A soft whisper sounded in my head. *UNACCEPTABLE*.

I refused to smile at that. It was good to know Tim wouldn't let the sickle murder me, but it was still annoying as shit that he only actively helped out when he felt like it. Hopefully he'd be more agreeable to whoever he eventually deemed as worthy.

"Assuming the sickle doesn't try *too hard* to kill me," I amended, "maybe the three of us can work something out. I'm in a tight spot, okay? I want us to have the best chance possible against the Shades, but I also don't want you and your … uhh … siblings to get turned into scrap metal to do it." *Except for Tim. Fuck Tim.* "But we need to appease Avery so he'll let us out."

The blade glowed the prettiest shade of blue. I wasn't sure which part it liked the best, but I welcomed the abrupt change of heart.

As one, we took up positions outside the open door of the box. My sword hummed nervously.

"Ready?"

Tap.

"All right …"

I jammed my arm into the box and grabbed the sickle's handle.

I blew out a long, slow breath. Condensation formed on the glass in a thin layer around the splayed fingers of my free hand. With a silent prayer to whoever or whatever might be listening, I pulled the sickle free and chucked it like a frisbee toward the other end of the room with such force I tweaked my rotator cuff. The sickle regained consciousness just before it reached the second empty box. It came to a complete halt, hovering in midair like a drone. I darted to the far side of the stand and cautiously peered around it.

My sword hung in the inverted position halfway between me and the sickle. It was issuing a bizarre series of notes I hadn't heard before. Whatever it was, the sickle was at least mildly intrigued by it. It, too, adjusted itself so it floated with its blade to the ceiling and its handle pointed at the floor.

Now that the thing was "awake," I could tell its handle was coated in the same kind of dragon scales that covered my sword's hilt. It was just a matter of whether the sickle had "wanton free will" like my sword, if it was an obedient tool like the ax, or if it was a condescending jackwagon like Tim.

After my sword quieted, and the sickle didn't move, the sword slowly floated toward the other weapon, blade first. The act didn't strike me as threatening, especially since my sword moved so slowly it was practically going backward. But after only a few seconds, the sickle shot past my sword and slammed itself ineffectually into the metal door. I flinched.

The sickle tried a few more times, but the door was impenetrable. I guessed it was covered in runes that weren't visible to humans or sentient weapons.

It searched for weak spots in the walls and corners, just as my sword had done. I did my best to stay out of the sickle's view, running around the stand to squat out of sight. The thing was bloody fast, though, and I knew it was only a matter of time before it spotted me.

My sword trailed after it, humming and buzzing, trying to either get its attention or talk it off the proverbial ledge, I guessed. Perhaps my sword would have a shred of sympathy now that it was experiencing the exhausting task of trying to talk reason with a thing that didn't want to hear it.

In one of my mad dashes around the stand, the sickle changed direction at the last second. It stilled so completely, I knew the jig was up. I'd always prided myself on being a flight kind of girl when faced with danger. But I knew at that moment that no amount of speed would save me. I slammed my eyes shut and held onto a corner of the stand for dear life.

The clang of metal that sounded a millisecond later was so loud, and the blast of heat that pummeled my face was so hot, I yelped and fell onto my ass. The sword and sickle were locked together, both of their blades glowing like embers. The angle of the sickle told me it had been going for a sideways swipe, as if my neck were a stalk of wheat that needed threshing.

Heart hammering, I scrambled backward on my ass like a crab until I hit a wall. I idly scratched at an itch on my neck and let out a shuddering exhale when I found my fingertips wet with blood. In the time it had taken me to close my eyes, the sickle had moved from one end of the room to the other. My sword had just barely stopped it from killing me.

"You fucking *suck*, Avery!" I yelled at the top of my lungs.

The sound of my voice distracted the sickle enough that my sword was able to propel the weapon up and away. It rocketed toward the ceiling again, spinning like a boomerang. It stopped its own momentum so quickly, it was as if someone had hit a pause button.

I kept a hand pressed to my neck, feeling my own heartbeat thrash under my palm. The cut wasn't deep, but the fact that it existed at all had weakened my knees. Even at the height of my sword's rage, I realized I'd never felt truly threatened by it. I'd been scared of it initially, of course, because I hadn't known what it was capable of, but it had *never* tried to hurt me.

The sickle felt no loyalty to me. And now that my sword had intervened against its attack on me, it didn't seem terribly pleased with my sword either.

My sword took on my likeness and whirled toward me. It mouthed *"OK?"*

My gaze shot to the quivering sickle. "I'm okay," I said, hand still to my neck.

Snarling with all the ferocity of a feral, my likeness pivoted and sprinted for the sickle. The image of me dissolved as my sword shot straight for the other weapon. They slammed into each other. They sliced and slashed and clanged. They moved so fast, I could hardly track where one ended and the other began. Sparks flashed. Their blades glowed bright red, vibrant green, and sickly yellow.

Every once in a while, the sickle seemed to remember I was in the room, watching the spectacle with a hand to my neck and my heart in my throat. I hadn't moved from my spot against the wall. The sickle would shoot toward me, and the sword would knock it off course—sending it windmilling into walls, the glass cases, to the floor. Every time it happened, the sickle grew even more pissed off.

I knew my sword's energy was finite—it *would* tire eventually. Question was, would it last longer than the sickle? I was in deep shit if the answer was no. Seeing as Tim hasn't twitched a scale to join the battle, I knew I couldn't rely on him, either.

When the weapons both began to flag what felt like half a century later, I finally got to my feet. I stuck to the perimeter as much as I could to stay out of their way while also desperately searching for an opportunity I could take advantage of to help my sword.

I still had no idea what it was about me that had made my sword decide we were allies instead of enemies. But whatever it was, it had gained information about me—just as it had gained information about Oliver Randal—through touch. I had to show the crazy sickle that it could trust me. Which meant I had to grab it and hope it didn't use my own hands to plunge the hooked blade into my gut.

If Mom didn't try to kill Avery after this bullshit, Caspian probably would. Then we'd be on the run *again*. I was never going to be able to hang out with Kayda in person at this rate!

"Sword!" I called out as I crept along the perimeter. "Remember Sweeney and how—ahh! *Shit!*"

I dropped to the floor, flat on my stomach, when the sickle hurtled itself toward me at the sound of my voice. Metal clanged, followed by a loud thud. I figured it had just been flung into the door—again. I scrambled back to my feet.

"You kept Sweeney occupied while I interrogated him," I said, wild gaze fixed on the warring weapons and hoping it understood my purposefully vague suggestion. "Can you do that again?"

The sword buzzed a quick series of notes that somehow sounded both frustrated and confused—*with me*. It had the audacity to think *it* made any more sense than *I* did?

A few seconds later, it was clear my sword had understood the assignment after all. Perhaps the frustration was more *"and how do you expect me to pull* that *off?"* Especially when it was already so weary and probably worried about what would happen to me if it failed to stay two steps ahead of the sickle. Clearly, my sword had no faith in Tim, either.

The sickle, though it had visibly slowed, was a ball of rage. The blade was bright red more often than not, and a persistent hum issued from it, as if it was shouting an unending battle cry. That blind rage meant it didn't pick up on the fact that the sword's next few slip-ups and fumbles were on purpose, giving the *illusion* that it was losing its edge. Metaphorically speaking, anyway.

So when the sword eventually dodged a hit from the sickle, only to glance off the edge of one of the glass boxes and go careening toward the wall like a helicopter that had just lost control, the sickle fell for it. The curved blade flashed a triumphant blue before it shot straight for my sword. Even though *I* could tell my sword was pretending, I still held my breath, my fingernails digging into my palms.

At the last possible second, my sword switched direction and rocketed straight up, flying parallel to the wall. Its hilt came so close to the cement, I heard the faint scrape of dragon scale against it. The sword issued a sharp, frantic buzz that I somehow knew meant "*Now!*"

I took off at a dead sprint.

The sickle had been flying so fast, with its blade so hot, that it slammed directly into the wall, unable to react to the sword's change in direction. An inch of its blade sank into the cement. I reached it before it could pull itself free, and I grabbed hold of the handle with both hands.

We don't want to hurt you! I screamed in my head, hoping somehow that the sickle could hear it. The handle warmed under my palms. If it went scalding, I'd be forced to let it go. I could feel it trying to yank itself from the wall, but for at least the next few seconds, it was wedged in there good. *Tell us what you want, or why you're so angry, and maybe we can help you.*

When my sword and I went into battle together, it also pumped my system so full of magic, I could only handle the contact for twenty minutes or so, and then I was wrecked for hours afterward. I thought, belatedly, that the sickle could do the same thing to me now and turn me into its puppet to go after my own sword.

I'd never experienced Tim's magic, solely because he hadn't let me—hadn't let anyone. Even if all of the weapons had been granted sentience via a happy accident in rune construction, Tim had clearly been crafted differently. Caspian would know the difference better than me. Not only had he understood the technical jargon Ronan Doherty the siren had been spewing, Caspian hadn't spent most of his time with the siren being magically coerced into flirting like I'd been.

The sickle's magic didn't flow into me the same way it did with my sword. While I *did* feel the sickle's magic, the sensation was wholly different. Despite the fact that the sickle was rage incarnate, its magic felt airy and light. For some reason, I imagined myself like a bird caught on an air current, drifting high above a field of tall grasses, gently buffeted by a breeze.

My vision went white.

I instinctively squeezed the handle tighter, as if it were a railing that would prevent me from toppling off a cliff. I was vaguely aware of the hard cement floor beneath my feet and of my sword humming erratically in my ear, like an irate mosquito. That awareness was the only reason I didn't let the sickle's handle go. If magical-slash-informational osmosis was what resided at the heart of my relationship with these sentient weapons, then I needed to hold on. Even if my loss of sight was so profoundly terrifying that saliva flooded my mouth and tears pricked my unseeing eyes.

An image snapped into view, like a movie projected onto a white screen. Blinking my eyes or turning my head didn't change the scene playing out in my mind.

The angle of the view was odd, as if I lay on my side on a table. The surface was worn and wooden, and I felt the pressure of something lying on my lower half. Something else touched my spine.

Someone swam into view, but it was a series of shapes and colors more than a discernible face. It was a middle-aged man, the best I could tell. He had a thick, scraggly beard and a receding hairline, and he wore a dusty pair of overalls. He patted my side and spoke to me. I didn't know the words, or maybe I just couldn't hear them properly, but I understood them all the same. I slowly rose from the table, gave myself a shake, and then I was streaking through the air at the speed of a torpedo.

My stomach pitched. I'd never been on a roller coaster, but I imagined this was what it was like—hurtling forward with no control over what happened next, with no safe way to get back on solid ground before the ride was over.

I slowed—*finally*—once I reached what appeared to be a field of corn. Tall, bright-green stalks poked into the air, some of their smooth leaves reminding me of a dog's floppy ears. I got the impression that I was scanning for something as I glided over the field. Unnatural movement among the stalks would cause me to turn on the jets again, and I'd dive into the rows. I scared off several wild hogs and injured another. Its startled squeals echoed in my head as I rose above my domain again.

I somehow experienced days of this—keeping an eye on the crops, scaring off wild animals, and reporting back to the man in the overalls when I spotted something I couldn't handle myself. Like the time a trio of drunk teenagers crept past the barn I rested in at night. They'd been wearing ski masks and had been armed with bats and crowbars. The man in the overalls, once I'd awoken him from sleep, had stumbled outside and fired his shotgun into the air, frightening the boys so badly that one peed his pants. They'd taken off at a dead run and had never come back.

One evening, someone new had snuck into the barn where I often rested. While the farmer was big, burly, and forever coated in a fine layer of dirt, this man was lithe, dapper, and instantly put me on edge. I needed to get the farmer. He'd chase him off with his shotgun. But no sooner had the thought entered my head, it was gone again. Every thought I had, every attempt I made to leave my perch on the worn table, was snatched away. I was trapped in my own mind, my own body, as the blond man found me, plucked me from my resting place, and took me. I desperately tried to break away from him, to tell the farmer that I hadn't left of my own volition. But I'd been powerless to stop it.

The human part of me realized the blond man had been Likho Kamen.

Memories after that were a fast-moving jumble of half-formed thoughts. I was used as everything from a party trick to a vehicle for murder. The alloy powder kept me from fighting back as I wanted. A friend of the blond man scratched at my markings, further hamstringing my ability to resist his demands. The more the powder was dusted over me, or stuffed into an added compartment of my handle, or used as lining in my plentiful prison boxes, the angrier I became. It was a deep-in-my-bones kind of anger that persisted and festered, even when my world was dark for mind-numbingly long stretches of time.

The next memory wasn't the clearest, so much as familiar. Familiar to the *actual* me, and not the me sharing a mind with a sentient sickle. I saw myself creeping around Haskins's basement. I watched as I stuffed odds and ends in my backpack, turned to leave, and then crept back toward my sword. This very sickle had hung on the wall catty-corner to the sword. I hadn't noticed it.

The sickle somehow showed me that the hooks lining the pegboard holding the weapons were crafted with the alloy. There was just enough alloy in them to keep the sentient weapons from moving on their own, but they were still awake, still aware of their surroundings.

It had watched as one of its siblings was freed while it had been left to rot away in a waking nightmare. Until werecat guards showed up and raided the basement anyway. Which explained how the sickle had ended up with the Collective.

The image in my head dissolved into pure white.

I wondered why the Collective hadn't "dismantled" this one, as they supposedly had with the other sentient weapon in their possession. It would be infinitely easier—and safer—to study the sickle when it was incapacitated. But I remembered that the runes that gave these weapons life were only visible when they were heated—potentially only from within. Maybe the Collective had learned the hard way that the only way to get the information they needed from the weapons was if there was an alliance of sorts, like the one I had with my sword.

My supposed murder rampage through Luma had possibly served as this sickle's stay of execution. Because even if the Collective truly believed the sword was under my control and was helping me cut down my enemies—it being under my control was the part they were most interested in. They'd used their go-to method of brute force to get the information they wanted out of the sickle and had failed.

Hence luring Caspian, Mom, me, and my murder sword back to Luma. They needed us all for one reason or another.

The Collective truly *was* desperate, as Caspian had guessed. They were terrified enough of Lachlan and his Shades that they believed they were currently outmatched. The most powerful magic-wielders in the earthen realm needed clueless-ass me to succeed.

We really *were* fucked.

Blowing out a breath to expel the doom and gloom, I pushed my next thought into the sickle as best I knew how.

I'm sorry I didn't take you, too. You didn't deserve whatever's been done to you. Talk to the sword, if you can. If you're mad at it for not making me go back for you, I doubt it turned its back on you maliciously. It's been very upset about others like you being trapped here. The alloy powder, as best I can guess, doesn't just knock you out. I think it messes with your memories. The sword might not have even known you were in the same room. And even if it did, it's trying to make up for it now. Give it a chance.

I held my breath, unsure if the sickle could "hear" me the same way Stabby and Tim could—assuming it could understand me in the first place. Three beats of silence ticked by.

The warmth of the handle in my hands cooled, and my vision slowly returned. I appreciated that it came back in stages—from white, to gray, to muted colors, to full vision.

"I'm going to help pull you free now, okay?"

The sickle hummed in response, and a small shower of dust sprinkled the toes of my boots as a result. I placed one of those boots on the wall, counted to three, and yanked. The sickle came loose, and I stumbled backward, letting go of the handle. Somehow, though, I didn't land on my ass or brain myself on the stand behind me. Under one armpit was a dragon-scaled hilt, and under the other a dragon-scaled handle. As one, the pair of weapons gently lifted me until I could stand on my own two feet.

The two weapons floated a few feet away. They eventually touched blades, just as the sword had done with the Winchells' ax.

I hoped they were having that chat now and that I no longer needed to worry the sickle was going to try to kill me.

I felt Tim's sudden presence behind me. *WORTH—*

I held up a hand. "I don't want to hear it. You're on my shit list."

He grumbled something unintelligible, but I had a sneaking suspicion he actually felt some remorse. I refused to acknowledge it.

After only a few minutes, my sword and the sickle floated back over, hovering before me in the inverted position.

"All good?" I asked them in turn.

I got a tap from each in response. Tim slowly drifted from behind me to hover with the other two.

"Good," I said. "Now, we need a plan to make Avery regret ever locking us in here."

Two blades glowed blue.

Tim sighed in my mind, then his blade flashed a muted white for a moment. The whole sword shook a bit afterward, as if shuddering at the horror of being forced to assume the customs of common riffraff.

I frowned at him. It wasn't like I needed the thing to be a dutiful automaton—and it wasn't like I had the power to force that on him anyway. But I didn't know how to get him to see that I was on his side regardless of how worthy he found me.

I ... UHH ... Tim said, sounding unsure for the first time.

I waited him out.

MAY HE CHOKE TO DEATH ON ONE OF HIS BELOVED PEPPERMINTS, AND HIS BODY BE USED TO FERTILIZE THE SOIL THAT FEEDS THE CROPS THAT NOURISH YOUR OFFSPRING, GIVING THEM THE STRENGTH TO WIPE ALL OF HIS LOVED ONES FROM THIS EARTH.

I stared at Tim for a long beat. I supposed he *was* trying. Kind of. I didn't forgive him for essentially abandoning me and Stabby, but a little encouragement probably would help his growth. Or something. "Uhhh ... I appreciate the passion."

Tim's blade, though briefly, glowed blue.

CHAPTER NINETEEN

CAMILA

The feral testing facility was on Floor J. Camila had never traveled this far into the bowels of the Tower when she'd been a bounty hunter. Speculation had always run rampant among the hunters—and even some of the cats—about what all was on the lower levels. The cats had a gym on Floor F, if she remembered correctly, but beyond that, she was clueless.

When the doors slid open on Floor J, Camila warily eyed the narrow, sparsely furnished lobby and the sea of industrial steel tables beyond. There had to be at least fifty of them, and half had a white-coat-clad scientist standing or sitting beside each doing Goddess knew what. Some tables had a fire crackling merrily in its center. Metal contraptions held various items over the fires— flasks filled with bubbling liquids, crucibles, small glass cubes filled with wafting smoke, balls of vines that wiggled like earthworms. Other scientists were consulting notes or books or typed away on laptops.

There was a subtle, ever-present scent of burnt plastic in the air. Camila hoped they weren't inhaling anything they shouldn't. All the busy scientists—even the ones not sitting before a crackling fire—wore masks.

Camila held the small carrying case with the three vials of attractant tucked inside. She remembered that Vaughn had said the stuff smelled like pungent garbage left to roast under a summer sun. She willed the case not to slip from her clammy palms. She'd somehow felt less nervous about being in the presence of the stuff when Harlow had been in possession of it. Probably because Harlow had two swords who could cut down an incoming horde of ferals faster than the rest of them should there be a mishap with the attractant.

Rhiannon led Soren and Camila in a single-file line down the wide center aisle made by the tables. The trio was largely ignored, but occasional curious glances were thrown their way. Most, Camila noted, were aimed at her specifically. She kept her attention focused on a spot just above Rhiannon's head.

Directly in front of them, past the tables, stood a glass door embedded in a cement wall. Rhiannon's unwavering path suggested that was their destination. On either side of the door and along the far side of the room on each side stood floor-to-ceiling shelves stuffed with books, binders, and lab equipment. Camila had known that one of the lower floors housed a testing area, though the Soul NDA had kept her from telling her daughter, Caspian, or Soren about it. It was the *how* ferals were brought into the Tower that had eluded her all these years.

Upon reaching the door, Rhiannon grabbed hold of the blue plastic card that hung from her neck by a lanyard and waved it before a card reader on the wall. A small light on the boxy device flipped from red to green, and a mechanism in the door unlatched.

Rhiannon yanked it open and stepped through.

The only view into the room had been supplied by the door itself, so Camila wasn't prepared for what awaited her. She stopped in her tracks so abruptly that Soren collided with her back. He let out an "oof" and grabbed hold of her waist to keep her from pitching forward. Thankfully, she didn't lose hold of the attractant case, which she clutched to her chest like a life raft now. His question about her well-being died when he presumably registered their surroundings, too. He softly cursed like a sailor.

On the left side of the room, four columns of tubes—the rows a dozen deep—held ferals. The containment units were identical to Roch's. Camila presumed there weren't too many places in the world that manufactured reliable feral-containment tubes, so either the Collective and Roch ordered from the same supplier, or the Collective had sent a few of these to Roch. Camila couldn't remember a "feral prison" section of the Pact, but she had no doubt provisions had been added to the living document since the last time she'd read it several years ago.

The Pact, she remembered, had focused more on aspects of the population's safety—fae and mundanes alike—from the pures. The biggest items were the monthly kill quota for pures, a stipulation that children under eleven couldn't be used as a food source, and a promise that "vampire culture" wouldn't spill out beyond the veils of their enclaves beyond necessary hunting. There were a host of other minutiae, but that was the gist of it. In exchange, the Collective as a whole agreed to create safe havens—enclaves—for the pures and that they'd maintain the enclaves' veils to further shield the mundane population from the things that go bump in the night.

Runes specific to hybrids had been added to the obelisks surrounding hubs well over eighty years ago. After an incident in a small enclave in Nebraska, there was an added stipulation that when the Collective updated the protections on hubs worldwide, they upgraded the ones for the enclaves as well.

The Nebraskan enclave that served as a cautionary tale had been unknowingly infiltrated by a hybrid. Within days, two of the pures had gone inexplicably feral and slaughtered the whole enclave. Camila wasn't sure if that was a true story or a campfire tale that had evolved over the years. Either way, the Pact included specifics about helping to protect pures from hybrids.

As far as she knew, finding a solution to keeping ferals out was an ongoing effort. Non-sapient biological life was so abundant, it would be nearly impossible to add enough runes to exclude every potential entity that may interact with a veil. It was too complicated to keep out weeds sprouting near the edge of the veil or a swarm of insects or a wandering deer. The veils would fail constantly in certain areas if the runes were designed to keep out *everything*, so plants, insects, and animals were exempt.

Ferals proved to be a conundrum. They existed so thoroughly in the gray area between vampire and animal that the veil magic didn't know how to treat the monsters. The magic seemed to cause the beasts enough discomfort that they often avoided crossing the veil, but they could do so while sustaining only minor injuries. Camila glanced down at her own left arm. Though most of it was covered by the three-quarter sleeve of her shirt, the twisted, ropy skin of her forearm—thanks to her own attempt to cross the veil after she'd been exiled—was still visible. If a veil was magically altered to keep you out, it did a hell of a job at it.

Which was why the Shades being able to tear holes in the veil was so damn terrifying.

As Camila swiveled to the right, she found more ferals. These were in larger glass boxes, some of them even furnished for reasons she couldn't fathom. Nearest Camila and Soren stood a row of what looked like industrial freezers. Masking tape slapped on the front of the freezers had labels written in black ink.

Female Torsos

Male Left Legs

Right Hands—Mixed Genders

Camila had killed more ferals than she could count. She knew that once a hybrid went fully feral, there was no coming back from it. Regardless of whether the feral had once been a human or a born vampire, they were now monsters that would kill indiscriminately unless under the command of a hybrid. And hybrids usually had dubious moral values. Putting a feral down was a mercy, as far as Camila was concerned.

Research into what made ferals tick—biologically speaking, anyway—and understanding the ins and outs of their necrosis and how their bites and scratches killed pures so easily … all of that was vital in the fight against the monsters. Camila knew that and believed the work both the Collective and pures like Roch were doing was important. Imperative, even.

And yet, seeing so many of them caged like this made her stomach pitch uncomfortably. Camila didn't know what the alternative was—it wasn't as if the things could be tamed by anyone other than a hybrid.

She recalled the three ferals in Roch's lab and how the attractant had turned the monsters against each other—had forced them to tear each other to pieces in a matter of seconds. Was the Collective working on similar experiments here? How close were they to creating their own attractant? Clearly, multiple entities were interested in the stuff—including the Vampire Council. The case in her hands felt heavier by the minute.

Roch had had his falling out with the council some thirty years ago. Most of it was mired in bullshit vampire politics and culture that Camila understood well enough to know it sounded like the grumblings of wealthy socialites with too much time on their hands. Usually when Roch started in on a rant about it, she'd shoved her hand down his pants or her tongue in his mouth to shut him up. It was a flawless method.

Now she wondered if she should have asked more questions. Roch had been working on the feral attractant back when they'd been … involved. *That* was a subject she'd actually been interested in. She'd even been the one to suggest trying goblin blood as the attractant's base, as hybrids and ferals alike had an affinity for their blood. So much so that most goblins living outside the hubs had been eradicated by the vamps.

In the years after the Glitch, once hybrids and ferals became something of an epidemic, the Collective and VHoA had assumed that lesser fae would be hunted to extinction by hybrids simply because they'd be easier to catch—both due to their size and being weaker magically. Yet some lesser fae populations were largely ignored by the vamps unless they were starving. Goblins, though? Those poor little bastards were picked off so thoroughly, the early iterations of the Collective had created task forces geared specifically toward getting goblins behind the veils.

Camila had felt a little guilty about suggesting goblin blood as a base, but she knew Roch could be merciful when he wanted to be. It was possible to take blood samples without draining the poor things dry, after all. And it wasn't as if the pures would want to feed on the goblins anyway. Roch had even assured Camila that he'd paid the goblins for their donations.

Besides, even if a few goblins had met their end during the donation process, getting a stable, effective attractant not only developed but mass produced was important enough to make it worth the cost. Camila had agreed to return to Tercla, despite how awkward it would be, in large part because she'd wanted an update on his progress. She'd been quietly elated to learn he'd actually been successful.

Watching the attractant in action had been horrifying, but she'd witnessed far worse experiments in Roch's labs over the years. As violent as the attractant made the ferals, the effects were as fast as they were deadly. Between having an army of sentient weapons that could be sent out into battle and an attractant to lure the ferals to designated locations, there might actually be a chance to stem the tide of the beasts.

If they could cull Lachlan's army, hopefully it would weaken his efforts enough that the Collective, VHoA, and the cats could stop the psychotic elf once and for all. Once they figured out what exactly he was planning, anyway. Harlow's friend Samar was under the impression that Lachlan wanted to get the portal pathways open and the Shades to have a monopoly on portal magic, eventually turning this realm into a waystation for his drug and travel empire.

It was as good a theory as any, but Camila feared Lachlan's agenda had at least a small revenge component. The elf was pissed at the Luma Collective in particular—he'd told Kayda as much when he crawled out of the portal—but Camila had to assume no love was lost for the small group who had been witness to Lachlan's exile.

Of which she was one.

If she was honest, she was worried that Lachlan would target Harlow specifically to get back at Camila for her role in the whole thing. Lachlan had somehow been aware that Camila was pregnant—and with a girl—even when Camila herself had only just found out about her condition days before.

She'd do whatever was necessary to make sure Lachlan was eliminated, for Harlow's sake above all else. There was no way Camila would be back here otherwise. Regardless of Rhiannon, Avery, and even Macrae being trustworthy, they were still Collective sorcerers—and the Collective had taken Nelson from her. The organization had essentially put out a hit on her, Nelson, and Naomi using the kind of monsters that were locked in these cages. Camila was the only one from that op who was still alive. And they'd tried damn hard—were still trying—to take her down, too.

So, no, trustworthy or not, these people were not her allies. They were a means to an end. Once she was sure Harlow was safe, Camila was out of here—out of Luma, and out of the hub system. Ideally, Harlow would come with her, but that would be a separate battle.

At the same moment that a muted roar sounded in a distant part of the lab, the lights flickered. The electricity couldn't have gone out for longer than four seconds total, but it was enough that the row of freezers shut off and then came back to life with a series of protests from their compressors.

That snapped Camila out of her musings, and she scanned the room, finding Rhiannon, Soren, and a lab tech standing before one of the furnished glass boxes. None of them seemed alarmed. Steeling herself for whatever this shitshow was, she slipped through the space between a freezer of male left feet and female right ones to join the others.

Soren glanced over his shoulder and arched a brow at her in question. She nodded once. They both knew she'd talk his ear off about it later when she was ready.

Her conversation with Harlow outside Tercla came back to her then.

"Soren has got it bad *for you,"* Harlow had said.

Camila had winced. *"I suspected, but I didn't realize he ..."* She'd trailed off, not knowing what to say. In Camila's early days post-exile, she'd met Soren. They'd had a few drunken hookups that Soren had wanted to become something more—he hadn't said as much, but Camila could tell.

Soren had lost a lot of his inhibitions when he'd fallen under the Tercla protection spell. Harlow had said, *"Maybe he won't remember all the nicknames and ogling when he wakes up..."*

"He'll remember. Part of the 'keep-out' spell is that the person

remembers this place is bad news. He'll remember enough of that interaction to make sure he wakes up embarrassed."

And he *had* remembered. Once the kids had left on their trip to Lake Nacimiento and Soren and Camila were alone, he'd sat her down in Caspian's backyard. With the pixies no doubt listening in, Soren had told her how he felt.

In his serious, sincere tone—one very few others got to hear—he'd said, "I know I was a rebound in a lot of ways when we first met. But now? You're the person I call when I need to talk. I know I'm that for you, too. No matter where we are, you're home for me. I'll never replace Nelson. And I'll probably never have the stamina of Roch."

Camila had cackled at that, if only because he'd caught her off guard. He was good at that. He could always make her laugh—a trait he shared with Nelson, if she was honest with herself. She'd told herself time and time again that her reluctance to pursue anything with Soren was because it was too soon—that it was somehow unfair to Nelson to move on. But now she wasn't sure if that was a barrier she'd put in the way of her own happiness just because she was scared.

"But I hope you know that I'd move mountains for you if you'd let me, Cam," he'd said.

She'd sobbed on his shoulder after that but hadn't given him an answer either way. The ball was in her court. She just didn't know what to do with it. Soren's unwavering patience was yet another trait he shared with Nelson.

Infuriating.

Soren and Rhiannon silently made room for Camila, and she stepped into the space between them as the lab tech continued chatting about the subject behind the reinforced glass of the furnished cube. A cot was bolted to the floor in the middle of the space. A full bookshelf sat along the back wall, its three shelves stuffed with paperbacks. A small dresser rested against the wall to the left. A vase with a single wilting red rose sat atop it.

The feral, unlike the ones in the tubes, wasn't paying its

onlookers any mind. It was also clearly a young adult female. Her stringy brown hair was pulled into a ponytail, and she wore a T-shirt and sweatpants. The loose clothes did little for her rail-thin figure and made her gaunt face seem almost skeletal. Yet it was still somehow clear she'd been in her late teens or early twenties when she turned. She roamed a bit aimlessly, her arms hanging loosely by her sides. Her wall-to-wall black eyes didn't appear to be focused on anything in particular, but it was hard to tell.

That uncomfortable feeling in her gut resurfaced, and Camila desperately hoped that this young girl—no, *feral*—wasn't going to be one of the test subjects for the attractant. She seemed so docile. But perhaps that was the best kind of test subject—it would show how quickly the attractant worked.

"... extensive gene therapy treatment," the lab tech was saying. "Survival rate is currently around seven percent, but that's up from last year's two percent, which is quite astonishing, all things considered. During the transformation, the amygdala is eroded almost immediately, which erases the rage so many of them seem to possess. Jill 6 here has been given a slate of tinctures, and some of the runes you see on her body are meant to help increase her brain's neuroplasticity. Unfortunately, because the survival rate once they've gone feral is so low, their treatments are meant to teach *us* more than find a way to heal them."

Which was a diplomatic way of saying they were lab rats.

After the tech offered a bit more information about Jill 6, Rhiannon thanked the tech and once more headed for the wide aisle that bisected the room.

However, the diminutive woman set off toward a door opposite the one they'd come in. "I apologize for the pit stop. I wanted to check in on Jill 6. She's been one of our more promising subjects as of late. Unfortunately, she hasn't eaten in nearly three days. Refusing to eat, followed by idle wandering, usually means they'll be dead in a week. Pity."

Camila and Soren shared a pensive glance. She couldn't read

his expression; she was sure he couldn't read hers, either—not even *she* knew how she felt about this.

Another scan of Rhiannon's key card got them out of the feral holding facility and into a hallway that split off into three directions. The walls were made of a much darker material here than the smooth concrete that dominated most of the floors. It felt colder here, and it was the first time Camila was truly aware that they were deep underground. The walls weren't weeping with moisture or anything, nor was moss dotting the walls, but the rows of LED lights housed in plastic that ran along the top and bottom of the walls did little to supply any warmth or chase away Camila's mounting heebie-jeebies. The lights flickered again, and she instinctively grabbed hold of Soren's arm.

"Jumpy?" Soren asked right by her ear and she, well, jumped. He chuckled.

"Not funny," she said, unhanding him.

The lights went out again a breath later, causing her to latch into his arm again. This time the electricity stayed off for a full three seconds—just long enough to send her heart into her throat and make her fear the lights would stay out.

Rhiannon stopped just outside the threshold to consult a device that looked a lot like a cell phone. The screen bathed the woman's face in a splash of white light. "Nothing to worry about. The electricity often glitches down on the lower levels. The backup generators have backup generators."

The lights came back up.

"What about the ferals' pods?" Camila asked, the case of attractant tucked close to her side. Harlow's question to Roch about ferals getting loose in the lab had burrowed its way into Camila's head. Other than the daggers strapped to each of her ankles inside her boots and the switchblade in her pocket, Camila was unarmed.

"Each one is programmed to lock upon the loss of electricity. They all have their own backup battery power as well, which has enough juice to make sure they have a day's worth of oxygen should something catastrophic happen," Rhiannon said, without a hint of distress in her voice and without even bothering to look up from the device she was tapping at.

This hallway was much busier than the ones preceding it, though most everyone seemed to be headed in the same direction. Werecats and sorcerers walked by in groups of twos and threes, none stopping their conversations as they moved past, but most cast curious glances at the group—namely at Rhiannon. None seemed bothered by the glitchy electricity, either.

Soren placed a hand over hers, which still clutched his forearm. He offered her a warm, comforting smile when she glanced up at him.

Camila nodded once, then let him go. She *was* jumpy. She needed to get ahold of herself.

"Okay, we'll be heading to Theater 2—they've prepped a room for us," Rhiannon said, either oblivious to or not caring about the attention angled her way, before stowing her device in her pocket. She turned to stare up at Camila. "The attractant is a game changer. Nothing out of our labs has come anywhere close to what you describe. If it's as effective as you say, it may be enough to put the kibosh on the faction war—at least for now. Word about the attractant went out about half an hour ago. An audience is assembling now. No pressure or anything, but I need you to convince them all that their efforts need to be focused on the many ways we can use the attractant if we're to have any chance against the Shades and their feral dogs."

Camila huffed a laugh. "I didn't exactly prepare a statement."

Rhiannon smiled softly. "You'll be fine. You were always good at thinking on your feet."

Without another word, Rhiannon turned on her heel and began heading in the same direction as the dozen other people who'd passed them.

The lights glitched once more, but for only a second, during the trio's meandering journey down a seemingly endless path of identical-looking hallways.

Rhiannon eventually stopped at a nondescript metal door with a plaque beside it reading Theater 2, which sat above another key card reader. The tiny sorceress turned to Camila and Soren. "We're entering through the back entrance of the theater. Several of my colleagues have been prepping the space for this occasion. Don't be alarmed by the presence of the cats. They've been hand selected. We employ an abundance of caution when dealing with ferals." She checked her watch—an old-fashioned piece with a chunky gold band. "We still have a good fifteen minutes before we're scheduled to begin. We'll coordinate with the containment technician about how best to utilize the attractant. Containment boxes are built with backup mechanisms that allow for the gassing of occupants, so it shouldn't be a problem to use those for our purposes today. I hope to show the audience at least three uses for the attractant—brainstorm ways that will kill them the quickest. The last batch of our house-made attractant ended up acting more like a nerve agent. The feral's brain cooked after inhaling the concoction. Its eyes wept black blood for quite some time before the feral lost what was left of its sanity and then barreled into the wall over and over until it managed to break open its own head like a jack-o-lantern a week after Halloween."

Once again, without allowing time for comment, the sorceress turned, swiped her key card, and then yanked the door open after the light on the box flipped from red to green.

"I'm man enough to admit that tiny lady creeps me the hell out," Soren whispered.

Camila shot him a grin. "I'll hold your hand if you get too scared."

His return smile was sad. "Promises, promises ..."

Rhiannon poked her head back into the hallway. "We're on the clock, Camila. If Mr. Larsen is going to be a distraction for you, I'll have him sit in the audience instead."

"I'll behave, ma'am," Soren intoned gravely.

Rhiannon's lips puckered minutely before she huffed an

annoyed breath out of her nose and then disappeared inside again. Camila and Soren quickly followed her.

The area they stepped into was dimly lit and reminded Camila of the time in college when she and some friends had been allowed backstage at a concert. The space was a hundred feet wide or so, and thick black curtains lightly fluttered against the two side walls. To the right side of the room were several feral tubes that looked to have been wheeled in on giant dollies. Runes likely lined the dollies, making them easier to maneuver. Though the ferals inside their capsules thrashed as violently as the one in Roch's lab, Camila couldn't hear their snarls, or even the sound of them slapping their necrotic hands against the glass. She did her best to ignore them.

Half a dozen werecats in their feline forms prowled around near the capsules, keeping an eye on things so they'd be able to spring into action should something go wrong. Camila ignored them, too.

Ahead and to the left, a pair of workers—containment technicians, Camila assumed—stood before an impressive array of electronic equipment. A large trifold table was topped with two flatscreen monitors accompanied by computer towers, a series of smaller screens with moving graphs and charts Camila didn't understand, and a host of other devices that issued soft pings and showed periodic blinking lights in a variety of colors.

As Rhiannon approached, the two male techs turned around. Camila was distracted by what stood at the far end of the room. A towering glass box—like the ones she'd seen in the feral testing lab—was straight ahead. The lighting was even more sparse there, but the box itself appeared to be glowing from within. This box was at least three times the size of the furnished enclosures she'd seen, and this one was rectangular instead of a perfect cube.

"Camila?"

"Sorry," she said, offering Rhiannon an apologetic smile.

"This is Isaac and Aaron," Rhiannon said, gesturing to the men. They were dark-haired, dark-eyed, fair-skinned, and in their thirties. One was older than the other, but at first blush, they could be twins. The only way Camila was able to tell them apart was that Isaac, the younger one, had frosted tips, which was … unfortunate.

"Can we see the attractant?" Isaac asked.

Camila nodded tightly, then opened the case she'd been carting around for what felt like hours. She held the open case toward the men, and they leaned forward to peer in at the three vials. The silvery strands in the nearly clear liquid glistened softly in the light pouring off the equipment.

As Aaron reverently took one of the vials from its foam indentation, Camila started in on an explanation of how it worked and Roch's recommendations about how much to use, and she described the demonstration she'd witnessed. The brothers asked a lot of chemistry-class-level stuff Camila couldn't answer, but she was comforted that the guys seemed most interested in the science of the attractant and not reveling in what the stuff was going to do to the monsters behind them, snarling relentlessly in their glass enclosures.

She didn't blame anyone in the Collective or VHoA for despising the ferals, but when hatred of the beasts was one's motivating force for eliminating them, things got dicey in the field. Killing and experimenting on the ferals should be a means to an end—not a sport.

Within ten minutes, the group had come up with three ways that Rhiannon deemed worthy to demonstrate the attractant.

"You boys finish up the last few details," the sorceress said. "Camila, if you'd come with me?"

Rhiannon moved fast on those short legs. Camila hurried to keep up.

As they neared the box, Camila realized it was two cubes sandwiched together. The front cube sat on a stage, and the back half was propped up four feet on an additional platform. A short ramp led to the box's door. A keypad sat beside this door as well, the light on it red, glowing in the dim room like the single eye of a malevolent pixie.

The thickness of the reinforced glass—or heavy-duty plastic?—meant the details of the interior looked distorted, especially from a distance. As Rhiannon led her to the left of the rectangle, though, Camila noted that the connecting section of the two cubes *was* distorted. Inside the box, two support pillars coated in runes stood on the seam between the two cubes. Between the pillars, just like with the obelisks that ringed hubs and enclaves, was a sheet of rippling air. A veil. One she guessed that had been designed specifically to only allow a feral one-way passage through the wall of magic. With conditions being this contained, they could craft more highly tuned veils.

A set of five stairs led to the stage, where the other half of the box was hidden from Camila's view. The stage's thick black curtains were drawn closed and appeared to be tailor-made to accommodate for the box, completely shielding the audience's view of the backstage area. Camila could only see a sliver of light peeking between the curtains.

"On the stage is a cube identical to this one, except it doesn't have a door," Rhiannon said, stopping just short of the stairs and reaching up to place a hand on the wall of the cube beside them. "It sits on a circular stage that's ringed by three rows of amphitheater seats that are currently filling up."

Camila's stomach knotted. She wasn't a fan of public speaking, especially not to *this* audience. If their hastily cobbled together demonstration wasn't convincing enough, then what? They'd thank her for her time and send her back into Luma to do as she pleased? Would they throw her in a cell for being an "enemy of the hub"—that was one of their favorite accusations—thereby cutting her off from Harlow again?

If it wasn't for Rhiannon vouching for her, Camila wouldn't have made it past the parking levels. None of the sorcerers would even have humored her claims that her elder vampire contact had crafted a viable weapon against the ferals. Hells, without Rhiannon, Camila wouldn't have been let back into Luma at all.

Suddenly it felt like too much pressure—needing to perform for these people like a trained monkey and hoping that her performance was good enough that she'd be thrown a few scraps—and then be expected to thank them for the opportunity.

"Come back down to Earth, Cam," Rhiannon said gently, giving Camila's arm a squeeze.

Camila gusted a sigh and rolled back her shoulders. She needed to get her emotions in check, or she was going to fuck this up before she even made it to the stage.

"We've been running demonstrations of various concoctions in the theaters for several years now," Rhiannon said. "Everyone out there knows the drill, and the containment technicians have the routine down pat, even with the new attractant as part of the deal."

Camila nodded. "Okay. How does it work?"

Rhiannon turned so her back faced the stage. "There's a rune array on the door of the cube that matches one on the lid of the canisters. We can seamlessly load the ferals into the cubes like plugging a phone charger into a socket. There are a series of trap doors, hatches, and pipe systems within the cubes. Luring the feral through the veil wall and into the cube on the stage is never where the problems arise. You and I will be on the stage explaining how the attractant works and how Roch's iterations have changed over the years."

She paused for so long, Camila grew concerned.

In a gentle tone, Rhiannon said, "Regardless of how … complicated your departure from Luma was, you *are* well respected among many here. Seeing you will bolster the sorcerers and werecats in my faction. Looking beyond the Collective's outdated rules, seeking assistance from unlikely sources such as the pures, and trusting in the expertise of someone like you when we are outmatched are all things I advocate for. I'm not the only one. I truly believe what is said on that stage is not nearly as important as the person saying it."

Camila stared at her old, dare she say, friend for a long beat. "You're such a softie."

Rhiannon waved the comment away, but a small smile graced her face, nonetheless. "You're on board then?"

"Yeah, let's do it," Camila said.

"Excellent." Rhiannon adjusted the plastic headband pushing back her frizzy reddish hair. She always looked a bit like a frumpy, slightly disheveled librarian. "Let's go scare the shit out of everyone."

CHAPTER TWENTY

CAMILA

Camila squinted as she pushed aside the curtains beside the cube and stepped cautiously onto the stage. The rows of seats that ringed the stage would probably hold upward of a hundred people, but only about half were filled. The lights on the stage were so bright, her audience looked like blobs rather than people. Camila wasn't sure if the lack of a full house was a sign that people didn't care to see yet another experiment conducted on ferals or that Rhiannon's faction wasn't as substantial as Camila had hoped.

The cube stretched two-thirds of the way onto the stage and was currently blissfully empty. If a feral had been thrashing around in the cube behind her while she attempted to get through her introduction, her concentration would have been broken for sure.

She'd just brought the microphone to her mouth when she glanced behind her and *didn't* see Rhiannon. She'd left Camila to take the stage on her own first—to be the voice and face of change or whatever she'd claimed in her motivational pep talk.

"Good to see you, Camila!" someone shouted from the first row.

"Didn't think I'd ever see you again."

"I was sorry to hear about Nelson."

"You still owe me five bucks for stealing my yogurt from the fridge!"

Camila grinned. She instantly recognized that last voice. She used her hand as a visor—whoever was in charge of the lighting needed to turn up the house lights. "No one was stealing your nasty root beer–flavored yogurt, Gregor!"

The lights adjusted and she was finally able to see her audience's faces rather than just shadows. More familiar faces than she'd anticipated stared back at her—people she'd worked with for years. People who had attended Harlow's early birthday parties and had brought their own kids. People who had known Nelson even better than they'd known Camila. People who, like Artie manning the guard kiosk, hadn't believed the message that had been etched across their bounty mirrors declaring that Camila had gone AWOL after Nelson had been killed in a drug bust gone bad.

Camila's chest tightened at the sight of them. Perhaps Rhiannon's faction wasn't a veritable army of like-minded sorcerers, hunters, and cats, but from this showing alone, the number was higher than she'd thought. Maybe Camila had allies here after all.

Rude of Rhiannon to be insightful.

There were hostile faces in the crowd, too, though. People who probably hoped that the claims about this powerful attractant—a gift from the much-maligned pures—would prove false, that Camila would fail.

Camila launched into her spiel. She wasn't a skilled orator by any stretch, but she could get a good froth going if the subject interested her.

Before long, Rhiannon had joined her on stage. With a cue from the diminutive sorceress, an aerosolized mist of attractant hissed through tubes in the cube and filled it with a white haze. Within seconds, a feral came charging into the cube through the wall of veil magic. Since the magic was a rippling opaque sheet, it looked as if the crazed feral had materialized out of thin air. It skidded to a stop on all fours in the middle of the cube, frantically sniffing the air.

"As you can see," Rhiannon said, gesturing to the feral, "unlike in every other demonstration we've done, even if the feral was drawn to the scent of our attractant, it was never potent enough to fully ensnare its focus. It hasn't seemed to notice that two warm sacks of food are mere feet away—especially one as delicious as me."

The crowd chuckled.

With another hand signal, a second feral came charging into the cube.

Hissing issued from the cube as the aerosolized mist was sucked back out. Within ten seconds of the fog being pulled from the room, the ferals' behavior changed. The change was so sudden, it even startled Camila. Neither she nor Rhiannon had truly known how the ferals would react to these experiments, as these were the first of their kind. But if Rhiannon was caught off-guard, she didn't let it show. Camila had a theory that Rhiannon was skilled at freezing time in awkward situations so she could compose herself before turning time back on. It would be an incredible waste of magical expenditure, especially with this many people in the room, but the thought made Camila feel a little better about Rhiannon's seemingly supernatural composure.

In unison, the ferals lunged toward the side of the cube nearest Rhiannon, as Camila had predicted they would.

Rhiannon didn't flinch. "See? Delicious."

That earned her another round of chuckles. Perhaps she froze time to test out her comedic material, too.

Into her microphone, Camila said, "The mist was distracting enough for them that they were solely focused on finding the source of the smell—the promise of a buffet-sized meal—especially since the fog surrounded them. Even though the fog has been removed, a layer of the attractant is now covering each of the ferals like a film of sweat. The longer it sits on their skin, the more potent the smell will become."

As if on cue, one feral caught a whiff of the attractant coating its cube-mate—the scent was now localized to a targetable entity. The feral issued a few short barks, then lunged. Bloodlust overtook the second feral a breath later, causing it to attack with just as much ferocity. They tore each other apart in the matter of the few seconds of frenzied savagery.

Stunned silence filled the theater.

"Demonstration two will begin once the cube is sterilized," Rhiannon said matter-of-factly, then turned on her heel, her rubber soles squeaking on the stage's polished wood surface, and headed for the set of stairs on her side of the stage.

Camila quickly headed for the staircase on her side. She tried not to flinch when a clank sounded in the cube. The floor abruptly fell away, taking the shredded feral bodies with it. Once the cube's floor was back in place, a cascade of runes skated across the walls of the cube. Blue-white flames erupted inside moments later. Roch had told her that fire—the hotter the better—would burn away most residue of the attractant, and a good powerwashing with mundane soap and water would get rid of the rest.

Backstage, the activity level had ratcheted up. A few more feral canisters had been wheeled in, as the third and final demonstration would require at least half a dozen of the monsters. The ratio of cats to ferals for safety's sake, was two to one, so three additional felines roamed the space now.

Rhiannon and Camila rejoined the guys at the table of electronics to make sure the plan for the second demonstration didn't need any alterations in light of the results of the first one.

Soren sidled up next to her. "How'd it go? The folks in here seem pretty jazzed about it. I'm kind of creeped out by this whole thing, but I'm not sure why. Seems hypocritical for a vamp hunter to clutch his pearls over the manner in which the things are executed, but that's where I'm at."

"It's not just you." Camila had an itchy feeling between her shoulder blades—it was a feeling she got when something bad was about to happen. Harlow called it her sixth sense.

Camila couldn't tell if it was her instincts reacting to being in the same room with ferals and the possibility that one could get loose—or something else. Then again, she'd been on edge since they'd headed to the Tower this morning. Not knowing what was going on with Harlow and Caspian wasn't helping, either, but how much trouble could the kids have gotten into in only a few hours?

Other than a three-second-long electricity blip just as Camila and Rhiannon made it back onto the stage, the second demo went off without a hitch. The audience had grown in size, too.

Feeling buoyed by the reception the attractant's effectiveness was getting, Camila hardly flinched when the bottom of the cube dropped away and the four dead ferals dropped out of sight. One more demo to go, and then she could check on Harlow. Hopefully Avery and Macrae were behaving themselves.

She resisted the urge to pull out her phone to text Roch to tell him the deal was as good as signed. The Terclan pures would get the upgrades to their obelisks, which felt even more important now that Welsh was there. Their veil wouldn't be able to wholly keep ferals out of the enclave any more than Luma's could, but newly reinforced runes would help slow them down *and* assure that no hybrids could get in.

Roch would be getting paid in cash, too.

As Camila and Rhiannon prepared for the final demo back-stage, Camila felt something like hope stir within her. Sorcerers and cats alike thanked her—actually *thanked* her—for brokering a deal with the pures. One woman tearfully told Camila about seven members of her family who had been at the festival in Mulgrew at the time of the breach. Only one member had survived—a nine-year-old boy who had hidden with the animals in the petting zoo.

The effectiveness of the attractant, the woman said, loosened the knot of tension in her chest that had been plaguing her since she'd gotten the news about Mulgrew.

Two werecats who Camila had once been on friendly terms with approached her separately, each telling her that they had additional ideas about potential uses for the attractant and that they hoped Camila could help get them an audience with Rhiannon.

After the second werecat walked away, Camila grinned over at Soren, who had been watching her. He stood with Aaron, Isaac, and Rhiannon. The brothers were busily pointing something out to Rhiannon on one of the small screens on the table, probably working through a few last-minute tweaks to the big finale.

Soren had only taken one step toward Camila when the power blinked out. Only this time, it didn't come back on after a few seconds.

There was a flurry of activity in the dark—crashes, muted grunts, the sound of shattering glass.

Oh, Goddess! she thought. *Shades are here. They're going to set the ferals loose.*

No sooner had she thought it, the dark room lit up with hurtling rune arrays, like tiny colorful comets streaking through the night sky.

More bodies hit the floor, including hers. She was paralyzed, only able to move her eyes. She couldn't scream, couldn't call out for Soren or Rhiannon.

If the Shades cracked open those canisters now, Camila knew she was as good as dead.

Her already thundering heart took off at a gallop when she was suddenly lifted off the floor. Someone stood behind her, their arms wrapped around her torso and their chest flush with her back. She hung there, helpless and terrified.

"Wanted to make sure you had a front-row seat," a male voice said in her ear. She would have recoiled from it had she possessed control of her body.

A few seconds later, the lights snapped back on. Camila watched in horror as a male sorcerer, who'd just finished drawing runes on his bare arms, morphed into—her. He'd been in his forties, tall, fit, and light-skinned. His hair, which was going a little gray at the temples, had been jet black. And now he looked like a mid-fifties black woman with short, curly, dark-brown hair. He even wore the same clothes as her. Had they been watching her and studying her so they could tailor the runes to mimic everything about her, down to the color of her shoelaces? When had this part of the plan begun? As soon as she'd walked into the Tower? When Rhiannon had frozen everyone in the lobby, had someone been on a higher floor, watching the frozen scene and taking notes on Camila's posture, attire, and mannerisms?

Harlow had told her about a man, Leon, who worked at the Ghost Lily. One of Leon's first tasks when he was assigned to the bar was to help dispose of Oliver Randal's body—the caracal shifter Harlow's sword had killed. According to Leon, a sorcerer with a proclivity for illusion and/or glamour magic had covered himself in runes and then assumed the likeness of Harlow to frame her for Randal's murder.

This man could very well be the same sorcerer.

Camila tried to turn her head, desperate to know how Soren and Rhiannon had fared in all this.

What she got was much worse. She watched, helpless, as two cats carried an unconscious Rhiannon up the ramp to the back half of the cube. They unlocked the door and bodily tossed the tiny woman inside. A trickle of blood ran down her forehead and toward an eye, suggesting she'd been knocked out in the dark. Which meant they'd not only had to be quick, but they'd had the blackout timed down to the second—each second counted when tangling with a sorcerer who could control time itself.

Any hope Camila had that Rhiannon could freeze time and free herself once she regained consciousness was dashed when Camila saw what ringed the woman's small wrists. What looked like jade-colored bracelets wrapped around each one, with a tendril of blue magic crackling dully between them, like a translucent chain—magic-suppressing cuffs usually only meant for the worst of the magic-touched criminals.

Soren! Camila screamed in her head, as if he could somehow hear her. She *willed* her limbs to work, to thrash their way out of this man's hold. Tears pricked her eyes when no part of her reacted, as if she were a rag doll that had just gained consciousness. *Fuck!*

Her mind stuttered.

If this was happening to her, what in Goddess's name was happening to Harlow right now? Her stomach heaved. She was going to pass out from the sheer stress of not knowing what was happening.

A canister was wheeled into Camila's periphery. The feral within pounded its fists on the glass, snarling like a rabid animal.

There was a flurry of activity in the room and a sea of voices all talking over one another. Blood pounded in Camila's ears, whooshing like a rushing river and drowning out details. It wasn't as if she could do anything, anyway. She didn't even feel the telltale tingle in her extremities, the signal that her nerves were waking back up.

The sorcerer wearing Camila's likeness had been talking to a fellow female sorcerer for a couple of minutes now.

"Goddess speed," the young blond woman told Fake Camila. "We're right on schedule, so don't fuck this up."

Fake Camila turned toward the real Camila then and smiled. "How do I look?" She gave a little twirl. This over-the-top display wasn't reflective of herself *or* the sorcerer's natural form. That somehow made it even more infuriating. It was bad enough that this asshole was impersonating her—now he was making a mockery of her, too. "Oh, right. Can't talk right now. Never should have come back to Luma, Fletcher. And now your kid is fucked, too."

Bile clawed its way up Camila's throat. If she threw up, would she choke on her own vomit since her goddamn mouth didn't work? Her vision went black at the edges.

Soren!

"Showtime, everybody!" Fake Camila said, then headed for the stairs.

She lost her sass bit by bit as she took the stairs, as if this personality was chipping free with each step, revealing Camila's stolen one beneath. She disappeared behind the curtain.

"We have one demonstration left," Camila heard her voice say. "This one really showcases what the attractant can do—how I think it should *actually* be used."

Camila's aching eyes flicked back toward the cube, her breath catching when she found that Rhiannon was not only awake but staring right at her. She had her palms pressed to the glass, her hands close together thanks to the cuffs. Even if her old friend could speak, Camila knew she wouldn't be able to hear her. Camila read the regret in the sorceress's eyes loud and clear, though.

I'm sorry I asked you to come back, her eyes said. *I'm sorry my trust in my colleagues was misguided. I'm sorry I was duped. I'm sorry I pulled Harlow, Caspian, and Soren into this.*

I'm sorry this is how I'll meet my end.

Tears slid down Camila's frozen face. They fell freely from Rhiannon's as well.

The two women didn't break eye contact until the top of one of the canisters—hefted by four of the cats—was placed just beside the door of the cube. Rune arrays flared to life in a cascading swirl of blue symbols on the canister's lid and the cube's door. Rhiannon clawed at the hole that irised open in the glass as if she could crawl out and scurry to freedom. The canister was shoved into place before Rhiannon could escape.

The sorceress stumbled back, silently shouting for help, or cursing her colleagues, or pleading for mercy. Maybe all three. The material of the cube fused with that of the canister with frightening speed. Within seconds, the top of the containment vessel clattered inside the cube, like a hot knife slicing through butter.

The feral, on all fours, slowly crawled out of the canister and into the cube. Camila recalled all the times Nelson had captured spiders that had gotten into the house, trapping them under glass before dumping them outside into the hedges. The human-shaped spider scuttled slowly toward Rhiannon, as if it were just as baffled by its new environment as the sorceress was.

As one canister was disengaged from the now closed hole, another was added.

With one last desperate glance at Camila, Rhiannon turned and fled through the veil wall, vanishing from view.

The feral had given chase but came up short when it reached the veil. It shied away from the magic, suggesting the magic either hurt it or had a strong enough "keep-out" spell to discourage it from moving forward. It was further proof that, at least in a controlled environment, veils *could* be crafted specifically to keep ferals out.

Camila listened to her imposter talk to the crowd. Shouts of alarm hadn't risen from the audience at the sight of Rhiannon rushing into the cube. Either the composition of the crowd had changed, or the stage lights had gone dark.

Camila's captor turned her body so she was facing the back of the stage, rather than the cube slowly filling with confused ferals.

"The elder vampire, Vincent Roch, who gifted me this attractant, had a condition," Fake Camila said onstage. "He and I bonded over our mutual hatred of the Collective. He thinks the rules of the Pact are too authoritarian. I think the sorcerers are elitist pricks who have let their power go to their collective heads. Roch promised to help me stage a coup in Luma—and where better to start than in the Collective's Tower?"

The crowd was grumbling now, but Camila guessed the cats and sorcerers in the other faction were preventing Rhiannon's supporters from retaliating. Sowing uncertainty helped, too. It was difficult to rally against something when you weren't yet sure what that something was.

"Ut, ut, Thompson," Fake Camila said sharply. "You can't see it, but I'm holding a full vial of attractant. If that earth array hits me and this vial goes splat, you're all screwed. There are a few ferals backstage that are being restrained by nothing but shock collars—much like reactive dogs. If those collars are turned off, your entrails will be on the floor before you can reach a door."

"*What do you want?*" someone shouted.

"I was getting to that before Thompson tried to be a hero," Fake Camila said, resuming her villain monologue. "As I was saying, Roch agreed to help me stage a coup if I gave him proof I was serious and that my plans weren't just idle pillow-talk musings. If I use the attractant to kill a Luma sorcerer in their own house, he'll give me as much attractant as I need. Can you *imagine* what would happen if a loyal hybrid gained access to the secret tunnels, made their way onto this floor, and set the ferals free? What would happen if the attractant was dumped into the sprinkler system? What if the power was deliberately cut like it was earlier and all the doors were sealed? How well do you think you'd fare in the dark in these hallways, covered in attractant, and being chased by a feral monster?"

The slivers of space around the curtain brightened. A series of gasps went up from the crowd. They shouted Sorceress Rhiannon's name. A scuffle sounded, but it was short-lived. A lion roared.

Fake Camila asked, "Who better to choose for my sacrifice than the sorceress who was gullible enough to revoke my exile status?"

A mechanism on the back side of the stage whirled to life, hissing and chugging. When the ferals all stilled in Camila's peripheral vision, then charged forward like a sea of fish, she closed her eyes. It was the only control she had.

It did little to quiet the shouts of horror. Cats roared, magic whizzed through the air, and people screamed. Tears slid past Camila's closed lids.

I'm sorry, Rhi. I'm so, so sorry.

Her only consolation was that she didn't have to witness her friend being torn to pieces on the other side of the veil wall.

"Camila Fletcher, stand down!"

"We have your daughter! If you ever want to see her again, you'll surrender the attractant!"

Camila's eyes flew open.

A few agonizing seconds later, two werecats bodily dragged a flailing Fake Camila down the stairs in handcuffs. The sorcerer's false sassy personality reemerged as she stopped in front of Camila. One of the werecats was behind her, unlocking the cuffs.

"Pretty good, right?" Fake Camila asked. "Maybe I missed my calling as an actor."

By the time the werecat had removed the cuffs, someone had run over to Fake Camila, a small bottle and rag in hand. The stuff was pungent—crafted from rubbing alcohol, lemons, and something earthy. Fake Camila poured a generous helping on the rag and then rubbed furiously at her arm, though no runes were immediately visible; they'd dissolved into her skin once the arrays were complete.

Once the first array was broken, the runes were visible once more, and so was the sorcerer's original form. The forty-year-old light-skinned man with salt-and-pepper black hair was back. He stood a few inches taller than her.

"I can't thank you enough for being here," he said, still rubbing at the runes on his arms and neck. "You weren't part of the original plan for Rhiannon, but you showing up made it a hells of a lot easier for us."

Where is my daughter, you asshole? she screamed in her head. Her lips didn't even twitch. She hoped she conveyed her hatred with her glare.

From outside her range of vision, someone asked, "What should we do with the other vamp hunter?"

Soren? Soren was still alive?

"Toss him in a cell, too," the man in front of Camila said, his neck pinking where he scrubbed at it, never taking his eyes off Camila. She didn't know the guy, but he seemed to have a host of unpleasant opinions about her, if his sneering was any indication. "We'll get clearance for a serum treatment—he'll have good intel on VHoA for us."

The man glanced toward some spot over Camila's shoulder, likely at her captor, who still held her to his chest. "Take her to a cell. She's assigned to 9-B. The door is already spelled and was left open. Hurry, though. That spell on her will wear off in twenty minutes or so."

Without a word, her captor easily tossed her over his shoulder like a sack of potatoes and headed for the door. Camila frantically scanned the room from her new vantage point. Two cats hefted Soren off the floor. Aaron and Issac lay crumpled near the table of electronics. Camila couldn't tell if they were paralyzed or dead.

The woman, a shifter, who had told Camila about her family being killed in Mulgrew lay slumped against a feral canister that still had a thrashing monster inside. She'd thanked Camila for giving hope to the hubs—for giving them a way to combat the ferals who'd threatened her safe life here in Luma. The smoking hole in her chest proved she'd been threatened by the monsters inside the hub more than the ones outside it. Camila's heart broke for the nine-year-old boy who would have to learn that yet another member of his family was dead.

"Quickly and quietly, people!" someone called out. "We've got to get this contained. The leaders of the other hubs will be here this evening. It's gotta look like business as usual by the time they get here."

Camila tried to kick her feet or pound her fists into the back of the behemoth who carried her. But her arms hung loosely behind him, flopping like noodles. She'd only felt truly helpless a handful of times in her life—this was certainly one of them. How was she supposed to talk to Harlow or Soren? How had this gone so bad so fast? Her vision was starting to tunnel again, crackling black on the edges.

After leaving the backstage area, the guy carrying her started to jog, jostling her violently on his shoulder. She couldn't get her bearings. She had no points of reference, especially not from this angle.

She had no idea how she was going to get her, the kids, or Soren out of this. None. She'd failed Harlow—again.

When her vision went fuzzy once more, saliva flooding her mouth and sheer anxiety overloading her system, she let it win.

She passed out.

CHAPTER TWENTY-ONE

HARLOW

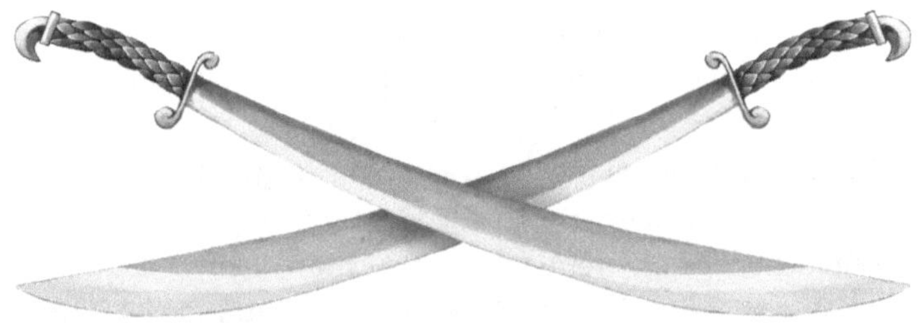

I was in a fierce debate with myself over whether it would be better to relieve myself in a corner or in one of the drawers below the glass-topped stands when a great metallic groan startled me *and* my bladder. My sword and sickle had been locked together in another one of their silent weapon "conversations," and at the jarring sound, they'd yanked themselves apart like a pair of forbidden lovers caught in a tryst.

Tim hovered near, not talking to or interacting with the other weapons.

The weapons and I huddled before the slowly opening door. My sword and the sickle hovered on one side of me, while Tim floated by my other shoulder. My sword hummed up a storm, preemptively furious. The sickle was deathly quiet, which alarmed me even more. I trusted the sword not to go homicidal maniac, and Tim was polite in that he asked for permission before partaking in slaughter. The sickle might have decided *I* was okay, but I couldn't say the same for anyone else. I'd described Caspian to it half a million times, but who knew if the damn thing had been listening. My sword might be able to move in time to stop the sickle from killing the first person it saw. I sure as hell couldn't. Tim would probably outright refuse to participate again.

The door had only trundled a couple of feet into the ceiling before I could make out voices on the other side. There were several people talking over each other—more agitated than excited. I couldn't understand what was being said, and the door's snail-like pace was setting my frayed nerves even further on edge.

I wondered if Avery had anything to do with this new annoyance. The door hadn't had any problem quickly slamming into place earlier, locking me in here.

"Oh, this is ridiculous," came Caspian's familiar voice, and then he rolled into the room under the gap in a very undignified manner.

My sword caught the sickle by the hook and flung it backward. I wasn't sure the sickle had even moved, but I supposed my sword didn't trust the sickle's impulse control, either.

I grabbed Caspian under an arm and helped haul him to his feet. "Cas?" I swatted dirt off his shirt. "What's going on out there?"

"Out *there*?" he asked, incredulous. He took my face in his hands and turned it this way and that. He patted my arms, then poked at my torso. He cursed very colorfully when he discovered the scratch on my neck. It had stopped bleeding a while ago, but the spot was still a little sore.

I gently swatted his hands away. "I'm fine! I want to strangle Avery, but that was already the case. Everything okay out there?"

Caspian's pupils were blown. While I didn't doubt he'd been worried about me, trapped as I'd been with an unknown sentient weapon, and he likely felt guilty that he hadn't tried to get me out sooner—this panicked look on his face was something else.

"Cas …" I said slowly, my stomach twisting. "What's wrong?"

A new sound reached my ears. A sound that might have been present the entire time, but Caspian's fussing had distracted me.

It was the distant blare of a siren.

"*Caspian*," I snapped. "What. Happened?"

"We don't have the details yet," he said slowly—*too* slowly. "But your mother—"

"*Has gotten herself into a bit of a bind,*" a voice said in my head, crowding out whatever Caspian had said.

The door was fully open now. Avery, Macrae, and Caspian's gaggle of new interns stood in the doorway. I noted that the interns stood farther back—using the older sorcerers as meat shields lest the weapons in the room start hacking off limbs.

"And what the fuck does *that* mean?" I asked, glaring over Caspian's shoulder at Avery.

Several interns flinched at the vehemence of the question, especially when they hadn't heard the statement that prompted it.

"*I would suggest—*"

I stalked past Caspian and stopped in front of Avery. "You'd suggest *what*?"

A trio of buzzes sounded beside me. I didn't need to look to know the weapons had flanked me again. We hadn't gotten far in our discussion about how to deal with the Avery problem, but they'd all agreed that if I was clearly pissed off at someone and didn't instruct them to back down, they were allowed to come to my aid. I just hoped the sickle took cues from my sword and didn't stab Avery in the gut before I could get information out of the old bastard.

The faint siren still wailed in the background.

"I can see you're all on edge," Avery tried.

Caspian sidled up next to me. "I'd drop the diplomatic bull-shit, Avery."

Macrae took up a position beside Avery. His pinched face

pinched further. His glasses sat low on his nose, and he angled a disappointed glare at Caspian over the top of his lenses. "That's no way to speak to your superiors. I suppose I shouldn't expect something as basic as respect from the likes of you, though."

"What are you, five?" I snapped at Macrae.

Much like a petulant child, he crossed his arms and ignored me.

Avery huffed a peppermint-scented breath. And yet, what he said next was *in* my head. The way Caspian stiffened slightly told me he was hearing it, too. *"I know you have no reason to trust a word I say, but I don't want to say too much out loud. Camila and Soren were with Rhiannon in one of the feral testing theaters. Our scientists wanted to see the effects of the attractant firsthand before making plans on how best to implement it."*

I had no idea where this was going, and I already knew I'd hate where we'd eventually end up. My pulse thundered in my ears. Tim, which had been floating between Caspian and me, suddenly moved backward a couple of inches. A moment later, Caspian hooked his pinky around mine.

"According to the report we were just given, Camila and Rhiannon planned to give three demonstrations on the attractant's uses. The first two went fine. But for the third, Camila appears to have gone rogue. She seems to have orchestrated Rhiannon's murder via ferals, using the attractant to ensure the job was completed successfully and in a very public way."

I started shaking my head halfway through his claim, unsure what I found more unbelievable: that Rhiannon was dead or that anyone could believe my mom would have the woman killed.

Rhiannon was dead? She couldn't be dead. I'd just seen her.

My knees buckled but Caspian was there to grab me under the arms before I hit the floor. My sword, its blade bright red, buzzed in my face. I idly waved it away.

I could only imagine what the interns thought of this silent conversation. Macrae had been standing resolutely nearby this whole time, his expression blank for once instead of sour.

Avery soldiered on. *"Camila was tackled on stage after Rhiannon was killed and was carted away by werecat guards. She and Soren are being taken to cells now to await … interrogation."*

That last part almost took my legs out from under me again. Interrogation meant truth serum. Truth serum meant everything Mom knew about VHoA, about Vincent Roch, and who knew what else, could be plucked from her head.

Monumental privacy violation aside, this was bad. *Really* bad. Was *this* the reason the Collective had wanted Mom back? They hadn't wanted to pick her brain about her wealth of knowledge about vampires—they'd wanted to pick it clean … to have access to *everything* in her head.

Haskins's toadlike face popped into my head. *"You ripped everything out of my brain already. You said yourself that another dose would turn me into a slobbering idiot,"* he'd said, then angrily poked the side of his head. *"There's nothing left in here for you to take."*

I couldn't let that happen to Mom or Soren. Not only for the obvious reasons, but for the added horror that Haskins believed people who had been truth-serumed had what amounted to a tracking device etched onto their skin. Mom and Soren would lose their freedom on top of having their brains scooped out like melons.

Caspian jabbed a finger in Avery's face. "Give us a minute or two."

Without waiting for a reply, Caspian grabbed me by the elbow and dragged me into a far corner of the room. I figured Avery and Macrae would still be able to hear whatever Caspian said next. Instead, he pulled his phone from his pocket, swiped at the screen, then started typing. He handed the phone to me. On the screen was a single statement typed in the Notes app.

Kayda thinks there are Shades within the Collective.

My gaze snapped up sharply to Caspian's. I'd ask later when he and Kayda had spoken. I wished like hell at that moment that *we* could communicate telepathically. Two very fucked-up thoughts were circling each other like caged tigers in my mind, each one fighting for dominance. I desperately needed Caspian to tell me they were both ludicrous.

Thought one: Mom and Soren were going to be tried, interrogated, and exiled to the Antarctic hub for a litany of crimes ... conspiracy to commit murder, masterminding Rhiannon's demise, treason. There was probably some bullshit condition of her Soul NDA that was now in violation, too.

I knew beyond a shadow of a doubt that Mom hadn't done this. The same sorcerer with a penchant for glamour or illusion magic who had worked so hard to frame me for Oliver Randal's murder was likely the same asshat who was now setting up my mom. But that would be my word—the word of a fugitive, a petty criminal, a woman driven mad by dragon magic—against the Collective and their werecats, who already hated me.

The worst part, though, was that a truth serum blast would tell them Mom *hadn't* committed the crimes. Yet that wouldn't matter if the ones conducting the "interrogation" controlled what truths were worthy of ending up in official reports.

I glanced across the room to where Avery and Macrae appeared to be having a one-sided silent conversation. A few of the interns had wandered off.

The other even more distressing thought was that, if I was right about Rhiannon being an ally—and that she'd selected Avery and Macrae to meet with us separately because she trusted them—it meant those two jackwagons were currently our best bet for both freeing Mom and Soren with their brains intact and getting all of us out of this tower alive.

I had to imagine the pained look I sent Caspian mirrored the one on his own face.

"We'll figure it out," he said softly, the only words either of us had spoken out loud since he'd pulled me over here. I kind of wanted to hug him, if only because he'd known I'd need some time removed from the sorcerers so I could calm down enough to get my thoughts in order.

I nodded once, signaling I'd at least partially gotten back in control of my racing thoughts, and then we made our way back to the pair of elderly sorcerers. The last of the interns had wandered away, either out of boredom or after being ordered to return to work. For the moment, it was just the four of us.

Well, seven if the weapons counted. Tim still hovered where I'd left him when Caspian had dragged me away. My sword and the sickle were having their own tête-à-tête in a corner of the ceiling. I still didn't know how I felt about my sword having a playmate. Given how often they literally clashed, I guessed my sword also didn't know how it felt about this new development.

"You're right," I said to Avery. "I don't trust you. But you're currently all we've got. What do we do?"

The minuscule hike of his eyebrows said I'd surprised him.

A crackle of magic skittered across my skin, like phantom hairs tickling me from head to toe. It wasn't quite as bad as walking into a spiderweb, but it was close. I glanced sharply at Macrae just as his hands settled back at his sides. The faintest tendrils of gold dissolved into the air, like gilded dust motes.

"Soundproofing spell?" I asked.

His lip curled a fraction. "If you want to reduce the feat of climbing Mount Everest down to something as mundane as 'taking a hike,' then sure."

Avery angled a long-suffering glance at Macrae, then stuck a hand into one of his cardigan's oversized pockets. He pulled out not a peppermint, but a small chocolate-and-peanut candy bar. He all but thrust it at Macrae.

Dawning understanding loosened my tense shoulders. "Ohh, he's just hangry. We have one of those, too."

Macrae somehow looked even more aggrieved, and I didn't think it was because he was having a hard time freeing the candy bar from its wrapper. "What is … *hangry*?" He said the word as if it were an obscenity most foul.

"It's a portmanteau," Avery said, nose wrinkled in distaste. "It's one of the countless horrific things mundanes do to language. It's 'hungry' and 'angry' combined."

Macrae glowered at me as if I'd just backhanded a puppy.

"It's both efficient and an abomination," Caspian agreed.

I wagged a finger at all three of them. "Y'all need to get hobbies or get laid or something because this can't be the shit that gets a bee in your bonnet."

Caspian coughed a laugh.

"I've been spending too much time with you; now *I* sound like I'm ninety," I said, cheeks heating. "Let's focus, boys, okay? My mother and Soren are currently getting carried off to Collective jail, Rhiannon was probably assassinated, and there are Shades in your ranks. Shit has officially hit the fan. So, I repeat: What. Do. We. Do?"

Avery shot a meaningful look at Macrae, who, after several moments, nodded.

Macrae returned his focus to me. While he still looked like he'd just sucked on a lemon, his tone was almost polite. "Rhiannon has been kicking quite a few hornet nests over the last several years. She's been claiming for a while now that she believes the uptick in Shades attempting to open portals, the increase in Bliss flooding hubs, and our colleagues' wanton disinterest in the effect Bliss has on fae and mundane populations alike were related."

Now it was *my* brows that hiked.

Avery picked up where Macrae left off. "Any time Rhiannon filed a motion to start a task force to look into such matters, she was outvoted. There are many here who are sympathetic to Rhiannon, present party included, but we are the minority." For the briefest of moments, Avery looked apprehensive. "Rhiannon had been secretly working with your parents, Harlow, to figure out how Bliss was getting into Luma. We believe that someone

Rhiannon trusted in error, or someone who caught wind of your parents' last mission in Sacramento, was a Shade. We believe your parents had butted right up against the truth, and this Shade called in a favor to their allied vampires to take your parents out of the picture."

I clenched my jaw and fought the urge to rub at my itchy eyes. I'd always known, deep in my marrow, that someone in the Collective had tried to kill *both* of my parents. It took everything in my power not to send all three weapons after Avery and Macrae simply for having this information tucked away in a pocket like one of Avery's damned peppermints while I'd been floundering in the dark for years. For knowing all this and *still* assuming the worst of me. For standing by and allowing Mom to be exiled, Caspian's reputation to be dragged through the mud, and their trained cats to be set loose on me *and* Kayda ... all because that was easier than confronting the majority.

Maybe that was oversimplifying the rock and the hard place these two sorcerers were wedged between, but it didn't feel that way. It felt like they were only letting me in on these details now because it was convenient.

Though I supposed standing against the majority *had* gotten Rhiannon killed. Rhiannon, an elite sorcerer with the ability to manipulate time itself, hadn't been strong enough.

"Our best bet," Avery said, "until we can suss out who is a Shade and who isn't, is for us to continue with the plan. There's a group of sorcerers due to arrive at the Tower in an hour or two for the meeting Rhiannon circumvented. In light of Rhiannon's demise, it's possible the meeting will be postponed, but even if it is, it would likely be moved to this evening rather than a different day entirely.

"The interest in learning all we can about vampires has increased tenfold. Most sorcerers know little about how vampires occupy their time because, as long as they abide by the rules of the Pact, their actions don't affect us in the hubs."

"Until Bliss," Caspian said.

Avery frowned. "Yes, well …"

"Clearly we should have listened more closely to Rhiannon ages ago." Macrae cut me a sidelong look. "And, yes, your parents as well."

I would have been slightly mollified had that admission not sounded so reluctant.

"The other sorcerers aren't coming here simply to talk to Camila," Avery said. "Reports coming in from werecats and bounty hunters nationwide imply that the feral vampires are … mutating. That, or they're being turned in a different way. There are rumors of them being as ferocious as a feral but as lucid as a hybrid. A wild animal driven solely by base instincts can be thwarted by something like the attractant—it's a way of weaponizing that instinct and turning it against them. But if they retain enough of their cognitive ability that they can then throw off the shackles binding them to their hybrid masters?"

I shuddered a little.

"What if we're already too late?" I asked, looking at each sorcerer in turn. "Lachlan Shade clearly has been working to … I don't know … topple the hub system for a while. He's got his little spies everywhere. We're standing in a protective bubble in *your* territory because even the highest seats of power in Luma have been infiltrated. It's very possible we're only aware of what he's doing now because he knows the runaway train can't be stopped."

"A sobering thought," Avery said. "I believe we have two options. One, we attempt to get you two kids out, and you'll once again be wanted criminals. Macrae and I could devise a plausible lie to heavily suggest you two, plus the sentient weapons, outmaneuvered us." In an affected tone, he said, *"Goddess above, the magic in those blades is truly remarkable for it to allow a mere mundane to give the Collective at large the slip once again."*

I wondered how often they could use that excuse before their fellow sorcerers either began to suspect they were up to something or assumed the two had gone too soft in the head and needed to be retired.

Avery said, "It would behoove me to remind you that a substantial subset of the werecats have all but declared war on Harlow, and once she's no longer in neutral territory—"

I barked an incredulous laugh.

Avery huffed a little breath out of his nose. "When you're no longer in the Tower," he amended, "all bets are off when it comes to what O'Neill and his sycophants might do. I don't believe they're Shades. But I also believe that if the Shades charged the entrance to the Tower right this instant, those werecats in particular would merely step aside to let them pass."

Caspian said, "And option two is to stay the course?"

"Correct," Macrae said. "It would require you both to play dumb for a while."

"Don't pluck the low-hanging fruit, Macrae," I said, jabbing a finger in his direction.

He offered what might have been his first genuine smile since I'd met him. "Honestly, the only reason *we* know about Rhiannon's death and Camila and Soren's subsequent arrests is because we have our own spies. The spy in question believes the assassins hope to sweep the details of the attack under the rug so that word of it doesn't reach our guests. It's plausible that neither one of you would know what transpired downstairs, simply because you're not Collective sorcerers or employees of the Tower. You're here merely because you serve a purpose. We need Harlow and her ability to command the sentient weapons—"

My sword, from the corner of the ceiling, issued an offended buzz of protest at the notion of it being under my control.

Macrae didn't notice the interruption. "And we need Caspian for his runework prowess. Cueing you into the nasty business downstairs would distract you from your tasks at hand.

"Harlow can ask why her mother and Soren aren't in attendance at the meeting. Avery can cast a meaningful look her way, and then Harlow can *suddenly* go a little slack in the face. She can nod and agree that her mother is too busy at the moment to join us."

"And what about me?" Caspian asked.

"I would assume you'd be able to at least *fake* respect when you're in a room full of your betters, no?" Macrae asked.

Caspian's hold on my pinky tightened. "Of course," he said tightly.

"Excellent," Avery said. "I'll do what I can to keep you both mentally abreast of any red flags during the meeting or if we get word from any of our little birds. The guest list includes several prominent Collective members from various hubs."

I resisted the urge to ask how there were apparent hub leaders when the whole concept of the Collective was that it was an oligarchy. I supposed these "prominent members" could be more like liaisons or diplomats sent to represent each hub, and then that person would bring back what they'd learned to help their own hub make decisions, but I somehow doubted it worked that way. There was a hierarchy in the Collective, just as there was anywhere else. These two hiding out in a soundproof bubble because they feared being overheard by their colleagues spoke to how unequal things had grown in the Tower. A fully democratic ruling party made up exclusively of the most powerful fae on earth was one more thing to add to the long list of ideas that sounded great on paper but didn't work according to plan in execution.

"One such member is a sorcerer from Mulgrew," Macrae added, his bushy brows smashed together behind his glasses. "Most distressing."

After a beat of silence, I asked the one thing I'd wanted to ask all along but couldn't muster the courage. "What are the odds we can get my mom and Soren out? And, not that I'd expect you to, but don't sugarcoat it."

Avery said, "A solid twenty-five percent chance, but we have to play this right, or that drops to zero. We don't know who carried out the frame job on Camila."

I'd thought that much was obvious. "It was the Shades." I looked at each man in turn. "Right?"

Macrae shrugged. "It could have been someone within our ranks who had it out for Rhiannon in particular. She'd been spearheading several initiatives that would upset the applecart, as far as the status quo here. Camila's arrival today could have been the icing on the cake. In her day, Camila also upset quite a few members who were happy with the status quo. Two birds, one stone."

I shook my head. "But what happened sounds so … planned. Rehearsed, even. Someone had to know we were coming well before we got here. O'Neill's standoff felt like a knee-jerk reaction; his people didn't know to expect us. The werecats in the testing theater did. They were given a cue and jumped into action. Not even *we* knew we were going to pick up the attractant until we got to Tercla.

"Yet the plan to take out Rhiannon—a woman who can *manipulate time*—with the attractant went off without a hitch. Maybe the plan had always been to throw Rhiannon to the wolves—er, ferals —and they'd just been waiting for the right opportunity. The attractant showing up in its little carrying case might have been just that—the perfect gift wrapped with a big red bow. It guaranteed Rhiannon wouldn't stand a chance. With that many people involved, they had to know that anything could go amiss at any link in the chain. And they had to know that if Rhiannon suspected anything, she'd just turn time off and escape.

"All the players knew their roles and played them well, even when the attractant was added to the mix late in the game. Rhiannon didn't suspect anything until it was too late. Which has to mean people here knew we were coming. Did Rhiannon warn you that my mom was bringing the attractant here? Or was that a surprise, along with the revised timeline?"

Macrae pushed his glasses up his nose and frowned deeply.

Avery's pocket, where his hands were buried, gave off faint crinkles. I imagined a cellophane-wrapped candy dancing between his fingers like a magician might manipulate a coin. "I fear we are to blame for this. Camila called Rhiannon about the attractant while you were still on the road. Rhiannon in turn told Macrae, who told me. All three of us contacted the prominent figures in question, using our possession of the attractant as a way to lure them into attending. Someone we invited spilled the beans, so to speak."

These guys sure liked their food-based idioms.

Caspian said, "Whether that person is a Shade remains to be seen. The growing factions within the Collective might be developing independent of the Shades' plan. Perhaps the Collective is using the rising tension and uncertainty about the Shades as a shield for their own plans to clean house."

We fell silent for a long moment.

Sighing, I said, "People always get on my case for being paranoid and not trusting anyone—for thinking everyone has their own self-serving agenda. Is it still called paranoia when I'm right?"

Avery pulled out a peppermint but only stared down at it, clearly visiting a place only he could see. Perhaps a time and place where his friend Rhiannon was still alive. A friend who very likely expressed her own seemingly paranoid thoughts to him—thoughts he might have discounted. In a distant, contemplative tone he said, "I suppose not ..."

CHAPTER TWENTY-TWO

KAYDA

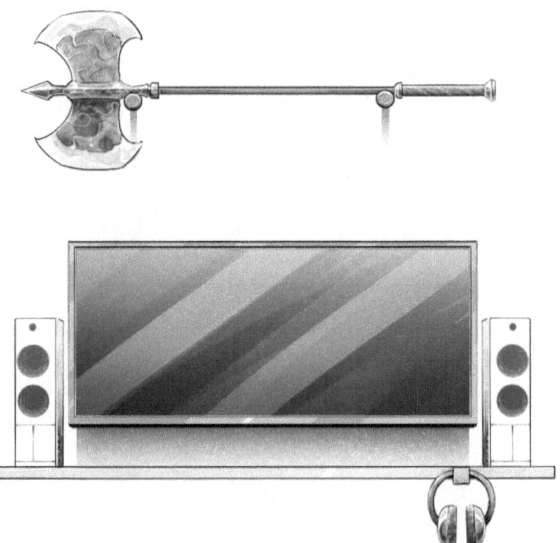

The only thing keeping Kayda sane at the moment was that she was the one behind the wheel of the rented SUV. They'd been driving in four-hour shifts and were currently deep into shift three.

They were still a few hours outside Navolt, traveling on a

makeshift road that supposedly led directly to the hidden avian city. It wasn't a tourist destination, so the road got little traffic, further evidenced by the occasional treacherously deep potholes. Kayda imagined environmental scientists were out here from time to time cataloging flora and fauna or whatever they did, but it wasn't exactly a busy place.

They were heading in the general direction of Yellowknife in the Northwest Territories, though their destination was beyond the human town. Well, mostly human. Apparently there was a small population of selkies who frequented Yellowknife's nearby Great Slave Lake.

While Kayda's group could have routed their trip to include hitting as many mundane gas stations as possible, Kayda had convinced them it was best to stock up on gas and drive straight through. Several passengers grumbled about not taking the well-paved highway, but Kayda hated the idea of their presence threatening any of the clueless mundanes using the highway for their mundane purposes. Kayda knew her mere existence could spell trouble if they had any run-ins with ferals. Ferals craved fae blood above all else. Everyone in the SUV, save herself, was human, but at least they were capable of fighting the monsters off, while the average Canadian citizen was definitely not.

Thankfully, detailed maps of the secret path to Navolt had been easy enough to find once they knew where to look, and her travel companions had agreed to her rules: no gas stations, no cafes, no sightseeing. Thankfully, Quaid had thought to clean out both vending machines in the lobby of the Vancouver station. The Alberta one was so run down, Kayda was shocked they'd survived the jump. The fact that they'd had a few cars available for rent had been even more shocking.

She knew she wasn't the best company. She had no patience for pit stops. They'd already had to pull over an unsettling number of times for people to empty their tiny bladders.

It likely would have been safer—and more enjoyable—for all involved if Kayda had traveled alone.

Given how bad her eyes itched from general lack of sleep, though, solo travel probably would have been even worse for her.

Kayda admitted to herself that the perpetual daylight was getting to her. There had been a few hours of twilight at some point, but it had never gotten fully dark. It was throwing off her circadian rhythm that dusk didn't hit until around eleven p.m., and it was daylight again a couple of hours later. She'd been unable to nap for any stretch of this so far twelve-hour road trip. That, and the fact that she was worried Lachlan and his vampire pals had already slaughtered an entire town of defenseless scientists.

One of her eyelids twitched.

She probably shouldn't have chugged that second energy drink, especially since it had been lukewarm.

Suddenly, she desperately missed Henri. His goofy, kind-hearted nature always put her in a better mood, even when she didn't want to be.

She glanced at her cell phone mounted on the dash. Still nothing. Reception had been spotty, if not nonexistent. Accessing VHoA forums on cell phones was a pain in the ass at best and an utter waste of time at worst. Other than the sporadic text messages that came through from Ben and Ingrid to Marisol's phone, they were flying blind. All Kayda knew was that they were destined for Navolt solely because all current known paths into Elsher were blocked, blown up, or being patrolled by ferals, hybrids, and/or homicidal elves.

She kept hoping for an update from Caspian with news from his aeorci about what in the hells was going on in Elsher. The falcon had to have made it there by now, right?

She imagined an explosion of brown and white feathers raining down like confetti as the bird met some horrible end. But if that happened, Caspian would have sensed it or something, right? No news hopefully meant just that ... no news. Her foot involuntarily pressed a little harder on the accelerator.

Marisol rode shotgun. The woman excelled at being present, at making you feel seen and heard, while managing to be glued to her phone or computer the rest of the time. With limited to no access to the internet, and only getting the occasional text reply from Luma, Kayda could tell she was antsy. She also looked exhausted. Everyone in the back seats was currently asleep, able to catch the much-needed rest that had been eluding Kayda and Marisol.

Kayda had never prided herself on being good at small talk, but she liked Marisol, so she found herself wanting to ease her discomfort somehow. This was the first time they'd been paired together up front. "Do you think Jasmine is dead?"

She winced internally.

Marisol huffed a sardonic laugh. "I'm holding out hope they were delayed or rerouted somehow. It would be an explanation for why all their phones are off— something other than being reduced to atoms. And if they were vaporized, wouldn't their phones be out of service entirely? I'm aware that the hopeful answer is the most unlikely, but ... right now I can't deal with the reality that I'm responsible for more deaths."

Kayda wanted to tell her it wasn't her fault—that Jasmine and the other werecats had *volunteered* to travel to Elsher. But she knew Marisol didn't want to hear that.

After a long, pronounced silence, Kayda awkwardly cleared her throat. "Did you get the travel clearance from the FDMA contact yet? Welsh and Caspian made it sound like the bird people aren't crazy about visitors, so it would probably be better to show up with an invitation."

"Oh! Yeah. Sorry. Did I not tell everyone that?" she asked, rubbing the bridge of her nose. "I had a few minutes of reception during our last stop and got the okay in an email. There's an old cabin about a mile out from the western entrance of the hub. We'll stop there, and a representative will make sure we can get into Navolt. We apparently don't need to call ahead because they'll, and I quote, 'see us coming from miles away.' I was told that I'd better hope my description of the SUV and all of us was accurate, as the welcome committee has been known to kick suspicious intruders to death and ask questions later."

Kayda shuddered. She'd always assumed she had an aversion to birds because they were small and delicate and she was not, but perhaps she had a phobia that was just now surfacing. Though she'd hope any sane person would be at least mildly leery about human-sized birds whose weapons of choice were their own feet.

"Sorry. I really thought I'd told everyone we got the clearance." Marisol peered into the back of the SUV for a moment, like a mom checking on her dozing kids. She sat forward again and crossed her arms. "To be honest, I'm not handling the Jasmine situation that well. There were eight of them, and now they're just … gone."

Kayda suspected Marisol hadn't—and would probably never—get over the Fresno job, either. She'd lost two-thirds of her team that night. It would be more alarming if that *wasn't* catching up to her. Marisol hardly ever let stuff like that show, but it had to be draining to keep it bottled up. If she wanted to unload on Kayda, of all people, she wasn't about to stop her.

Marisol angled her thousand-yard stare out the windshield. "What if they're the kind of gone where finding their bodies for a funeral is impossible? What if all of *us* had been in transit when our destination telepad was destroyed? All the telepads in Elsher are probably gone now. All of us could have been vaporized because people keep listening to me and trusting my judgment." She glanced at Kayda a moment, and Kayda tried not to react to how red Marisol's eyes were. Marisol looked away first. "I don't know what the fuck I'm doing any more than anyone else does. Showing up at Navolt could end with all of us getting killed."

"By murder-chickens, no less."

The laugh that spluttered out of Marisol was so loud and abrupt, she had to clamp a hand over her mouth. Kayda bit down on her bottom lip to keep herself from laughing and waking the others.

Once Marisol got herself under control, Kayda said, "I know

you already know this, but maybe you need to hear it again: No one is forcing us to follow you anywhere. You should know me well enough by now to know I don't do anything unless I want to."

"You sure do complain a lot for someone who sticks around voluntarily ..." Marisol muttered.

Kayda chuckled, shrugging a shoulder. "You've got a solid reputation, and you're in enough people's good graces that we got someone from the FDMA, sight unseen, to grant us clearance to Navolt. Obviously, someone out there thinks you're capable of getting the avians to help. I can guarantee you no one thinks that of *me*. I doubt it's because of anyone in the back, either. No one but you is casting blame. Cut yourself some slack."

Marisol was quiet for a few beats. "Should have figured you were a tough love kind of person."

When Kayda glanced over, she noted that Marisol's eyes weren't nearly as watery.

"Oh, you just reminded me," Marisol said, picking up her cell phone that had been lying on her thigh. "I really think I need a nap, but that high-octane jitter cola I drank earlier probably means I won't sleep for at least a week." She tapped and swiped at the screen. "So this all started with Welsh. He called in a favor to a contact, and that contact got in touch with a werecat, and that cat talked to the same Rhiannon lady who got Jasmine—" Marisol chewed on her lip for a moment. "Who got Jasmine the map of Elsher.

"I should be able to still pull up the email ..." Marisol said slowly as her thumb swiped up the screen. "Okay. Here ... the FDMA contact CC'ed me and a couple of others with instructions on where to go and all that, but then he sent a separate message just to me and asked if we could report back any odd sightings."

"Like what?" Kayda asked.

"It says, *The avians have been reporting a rash of disappearances lately, but most branches of the Collective are currently short staffed due to extenuating circumstances. I have a personal, vested interest in the goings-on in Navolt, as I have a nephew stationed there. Communication with the hub is often inconsistent, but the disappearances have me more concerned than usual. Any information you could provide would be deeply appreciated."*

Kayda cocked an eyebrow at Marisol. "That sounds … not great."

"I've been trying not to think about it, honestly," Marisol said. "I'm guessing the werecat guard Welsh contacted already knew this Nial Douglas guy had a personal connection to Navolt. My reputation may have helped a lot in getting us clearance, but not as much as an uncle worried about his nephew."

Kayda wondered all over again if this was a bad idea. They had no clue what they were driving toward, what Lachlan wanted with Elsher, or if Kayda and her friends had lost this fight the moment that first telepad had been blown to bits. She didn't feel any more prepared now to square off against Lachlan than she had the first time. In fact, she felt *less* prepared now.

But Navolt was the only other hub in this part of the country. Even if scores of VHoA members, werecats, and bounty hunters were on their way to Elsher, they had just as far to travel, and there was no guarantee any of them could get past the veils anyway. Kayda and her friends had a head start. Granted, the head start could just mean their deaths would serve as a cautionary tale.

Kayda glanced toward her phone again. While her screen stayed dark, an icon lit up on the dash. She sighed. "Gas light just came on."

Marisol nodded. "Pull over, and I'll get the can out of the back."

Kayda pulled partially off the road and threw the SUV into park, then popped open the gas tank door and the door to the rear cargo area. She grabbed her phone off the dash and pocketed it, more out of habit than anything. Jittery and on high alert, she scanned the foliage as she climbed out of the car and quietly closed the door behind her. It was an unnecessary gesture; her sensitive hearing had registered that almost everyone who had been asleep in the back was stirring now that they'd stopped moving.

Marisol met her on the side of the SUV with the gas can. As Kayda got to work filling the tank, Marisol wandered off, cell phone pointed toward the sky. The fact that she kept changing directions every few seconds told Kayda that the reception situation hadn't suddenly improved.

Kayda had just pulled out the nozzle when she heard a chitter so familiar she stilled, pulse immediately taking off at a gallop. She whirled around, scanning the shoulder of the road. The left side of the road opposite where they were parked was densely packed with trees—firs or pines, she guessed. The right side, however, had a wide stretch of bare earth dotted with clumps of moss. Beyond that was a wall of trees.

Her gut told her the chittering had come from there. Something watched her. She placed the empty gas can on the ground without breaking eye contact with the trees and closed the fuel tank door with a quiet click.

Marisol still tried in vain to catch a signal, if her muffled curses were any indication. No one in the SUV behind Kayda seemed to have sensed anything amiss, either. The only person with a jack-hammering heart was herself.

Kayda knew, obviously, that there were ferals in this part of Canada. She was on this too-long road trip because of the damn things. Navolt was still hours out from this particular location, and farther still from Elsher. Ferals were fast, but had they strayed this far east? Had they strayed because there was no one left to eat in Elsher? Maybe this one had been on the way to the research hub and gotten lost.

There could also be an established nest in the wilds of the Northwest Territories, she supposed. Other than the selkies, Kayda didn't know what species of fae lived out here. She doubted there were enough to keep a large nest fed.

The chitter sounded again, and Kayda involuntarily took a

step toward it. Despite knowing everyone with her was more experienced in dispatching ferals than she was, she also knew that ferals probably wouldn't be lurking nearby if she hadn't been here. Her hooded battle-ax was in the back of the SUV, wedged between two duffel bags.

"Kayda?" Marisol asked behind her. With Kayda's auditory dials tweaked this much, Marisol's faint whisper sounded like she was shouting in Kayda's ear. "What are you doing?"

The feral's breath hitched. Then it chittered again, louder this time. It was sniffing the air now, like a wolf scenting prey.

A second chitter joined the first. After a few moments, both monsters crept forward. So much for the hope they'd get bored or decide they didn't like their odds and ran off. Kayda and her companions would have to either scare the ferals away or kill them; no other options were safe. The last thing Kayda needed was to try to make a hasty getaway, only to have one of the ferals land on the windshield like a splattered bug. When ferals had their sights set on their next meal, there was no stopping them, speeding cars be damned. They would pry at doors and windows until they got what they wanted, to the detriment of their own well-being. Kayda would rather not end up in a ditch or crashed into a tree.

Shit.

"Mari," she said slowly. "Go get my ax."

It said a lot about Marisol that her first question was "How many are there?" and not a time-wasting "Why?"

"At least two," Kayda said, gaze still locked on the trees ahead. There was some comfort to be found in that hundred feet of patchy dirt separating herself from the ferals' hiding place—but not much. There was still no telling how many more were nearby. But given what she was hearing now, these two were gearing up for an attack.

It was somewhere near two in the morning; perhaps this was their prime hunting time. They were technically vampires, after all.

Marisol darted around the SUV and lifted the rear door, leaving it open. Confused questions from the others spilled out. Without looking away from the trees, Kayda thrust her right hand back. Two seconds later, the familiar haft of her battle-ax was in her palm.

She whipped the weapon around in front of her, then snatched off the magic-dampening hood and shoved the leather into her back pocket. Crackling blue lightning danced over the gleaming blade.

Red magic sparked to life in her periphery, and she found Marisol standing beside her with her favorite spear in hand.

Kayda felt inclined to tell Marisol to stay back with the others, but she knew that would only insult her friend, so she kept her protests to herself.

"Can you see or hear what they're doing?" Marisol asked.

It still sounded like the bastards were doing a risk assessment. Agitated chittering, pacing, sniffing. Kayda eyed the ground around her, spotted a rather substantial rock, and used the toe of her boot to pry it loose. While keeping the ax held firmly in one hand—which was a chore; despite her extra training, the thing was still heavy as shit—she chucked the rock into the trees.

A muted scream told Kayda she'd hit her mark. The beasts galloped toward them.

"Well, that's one way to get their attention," Marisol said, then sprinted to meet them.

The others still in the SUV had figured out what was going on and scrambled for their own weapons. By the time they'd piled out of the car, though, Kayda had lopped the head off one feral, while Marisol had punctured the neck of the other.

They were both scrawny, even by feral standards. What was most unusual about them was how ... fresh they looked. Their clothes hung off their too-thin bodies, as was common with all ferals, but while their clothing was dirty, it wasn't in tatters. Their hair was matted and filthy, yet it wasn't falling out in clumps.

Reluctantly, Kayda walked the few feet to where the severed

head lay in the dirt. It had fallen face down. With a wince and a gentle nudge from her boot, she rolled the head over. Its light-brown hair had been shoulder length, and several strands were draped over one wall-to-wall black eye. It had been a young woman—a *very* young one. Possibly no older than fifteen.

"Dammit," Marisol muttered from where she squatted beside her own kill. "They were just kids."

Kayda hadn't realized until now that every feral she'd encountered had once been a human adult. She knew now, thanks to Welsh and Kessler, that shadow vamps were a thing. She supposed she should be grateful this was a standard feral and not an elephantine one.

She got lost in the very horrifying image of a feral orc. The non-feral one Harlow had faced sounded huge—and he had been a more-than-equal match for the sentient sword. She shuddered.

Turning fully toward Marisol, who had been joined by the other VHoA members, Kayda asked, "You've never seen ferals this young before?"

One of the guys spoke up. He was in his fifties, six feet tall, lean, and his salt-and-pepper hair was cropped short. He rarely smiled. "I've bounced around the country to at least a dozen hubs and have been working with VHoA for the past ten years. I've never seen a teenage feral."

Kayda was almost positive his name was Hank. Or maybe it was Will? There were a couple of guys who mostly went on outside-Luma patrols at night and worked closely with the were-cats. Marisol had said that particular group of hunters were the most lethal when it came to feral takedowns.

Kayda asked, "Do you think the fact that they're so clean, relatively speaking, means they're recently transitioned?"

The question seemed to flummox the group as a whole. Ferals, in Kayda's limited experience, all looked the same: middle-aged, gaunt, full-black eyes, and clothed in tattered rags or nothing at all. She hadn't thought much about why that was. She supposed in hindsight she was glad she hadn't needed to cut down ferals who looked like sweet little girls in pigtails or someone's Grandpa Bob.

Marisol was the only one who hadn't been silenced by Kayda's question.

"There's, uh … a theory about teenage ferals …" Marisol said, not sounding like her usual confident self.

Quaid groaned, which was echoed by Cathy. Cathy still sported two black eyes, but the discoloration had faded, and concealer covered up the rest. Kayda realized then that Cathy hadn't made direct eye contact with Kayda since the incident. Was Kayda supposed to send her an apology fruit basket or something? It wasn't like Kayda had elbowed her on purpose.

"Not this again, Mari," Cathy said. "That corner of the forum is a timesuck, and almost every theory in there has been debunked or will be."

Quaid shrugged. "I dunno. I still like the theory that ferals are created in a lab using the DNA from dead celebrities."

Hank-maybe-Will said, "My favorite conspiracy theory about the conspiracy theorists is that the nonsense in the forum is posted by Collective spies trying to discredit VHoA even further."

Kayda could actually hear Marisol grinding her teeth. "What's the theory, Mari?"

That finally got Cathy to look at Kayda directly. Though it was more of a glare.

"It's not that teenage ferals don't exist," Marisol said, mostly focusing on Kayda. "It's that the combination of the fae-blood poison and spiking hormones kill the kid before they can transition from hybrid to feral. It's like giving heroin to an infant. But if the transition actually holds, they're stronger, faster, more deadly. The theory is that homeless kids are getting plucked off the street to be used as fodder for experiments to turn them into feral super soldiers."

Everyone, including Kayda, glanced down at the dead teen ferals at their feet—teen ferals who had been easier to kill than any feral Kayda had squared off against before.

Cathy gusted a sigh so loud, Kayda didn't need heightened senses to hear it. She managed to keep her tone more neutral than condescending when she asked, "If they're so deadly, why haven't any of us ever seen one until today? Why don't reports of these supposed super soldiers ever pop up on the main forums?"

"Because everyone who runs into them ends up dead and can't report back about what they saw," Marisol said, but she'd clearly lost faith in her own statement halfway through.

Slowly, Cathy asked, "If no one survives the encounter, then where are these theories coming from?"

Brow furrowed, Marisol idly toed the side of the feral in front of her. Dead as a doornail. She seemed disappointed, perhaps worrying that Cathy was right and that all the wild theories on the forum she spent so much time poring over were just that.

A rustle made Kayda's head snap up. She took a few steps away from the decapitated feral and eyed the wall of trees. Squinting, she adjusted her vision, scanning the shadows.

A shape solidified. Another young feral from the look of it. It was sniffing the air much like the others had, reminding Kayda of a curious chipmunk more than a prowling wolf.

"Hey!" Kayda yelled at it, causing her companions to flinch or whirl around.

Then, in a very un-feral-like fashion, the monster … ran away.

Kayda took off in a dead sprint after it.

CHAPTER TWENTY-THREE

KAYDA

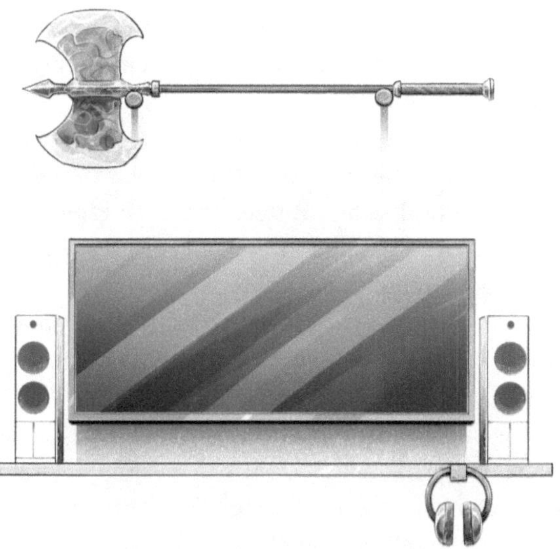

Kayda charged after the departing feral. She kept hold of her battle-ax, the sparking blue magic flashing in the corner of her eye every other second as she pumped her arms—arms that were already beginning to ache from the strain of holding on to the bulky thing, but adrenaline kept her going.

The feral loped on all fours, and while it was faster than a mostly human had any right to be, especially when galloping like a dog, the thing wasn't markedly faster than her. Ferals were typically like cheetahs on steroids. There was definitely something off about these younger ferals, but whatever intel Marisol was getting was faulty.

Kayda was distantly aware that at least three VHoA members were crashing through the trees behind her. She figured one or two had been ordered to stay with the car and/or dispose of the bodies. The odds of there being much traffic on the road—especially at this hour—were slim, but a lost traveler would get the scare of their life if they found two murdered emaciated kids lying in the dirt while their murderers loitered nearby.

Her phone vibrated in her back pocket, followed by several more buzzes in quick succession. A discordant series of chimes sounded in the distance, and she figured their reception problems were temporarily resolved.

Fifteen minutes of sprinting through the woods eventually dumped Kayda and her quarry into a stretch of open terrain. It looked as if a vertical swath of trees had been removed, leaving a wide, semi-flat area hemmed in by walls of pine. About a mile to the left, where the feral was heading, Kayda could make out what looked like a small village. Maybe "hamlet" was more accurate, though the word implied cozy, and any place infested with ferals was anything but.

It was the sight to the right, though, that almost made her trip and face plant. She managed to slow to a semi-graceful jog before stopping altogether, chest heaving. The feral peered over his shoulder, and though he clearly saw he was no longer being pursued, he picked up his pace, sprinting for the hamlet.

Kayda knew she should be more concerned with whatever fresh hells awaited her in that direction and how many ferals might be lurking in or around the few stone structures, but her gaze was continuously pulled back to the massive, hulking body. As she slowly crept toward it, she extracted the ax's hood from her back pocket, shielded the weapon, and slung the ax into the reinforced loop on her belt. The sounds of heavy panting and crunching pine needles told her that her companions would catch up soon enough.

Before her was a completely flattened expanse of earth, most likely achieved via farming equipment or magical intervention. The natural terrain was littered with small rocks, tough weeds, and prickly bushes. Kayda wasn't sure what was more alarming about the cleared-off spot—the detailed rune array that appeared to be burned into the ground, or the gigantic carcass lying on top of it. The wind shifted and brought with it the pungent stench of rotting flesh. Kayda wrinkled her nose. She'd dialed up her hearing and sight so much that she'd inadvertently turned her sense of smell nearly off to compensate. The fact that the pungent aroma still assaulted her only further confirmed that the carcass had been here a long time.

She wondered why the body hadn't been picked clean by scavengers yet.

A scrabbling sound pulled Kayda's gaze toward the ground. If the circle was a clock, she stood at the six, while the soft noise came from the three. A moment later, a tiny field mouse emerged from a low scrubby bush. Kayda held stock still, watching as the mouse cautiously hopped toward the enormous carcass, tiny nose twitching. To the rodent, the pile of meat must have looked like a buffet fit for a queen. The mouse stood on hind legs at the edge of the rune array for a few more moments before hopping forward minutely. As soon as its feet hit the scorched earth of the array, though, the mouse screeched, flinched, and ran back the way it had come.

"Guess that answers that," Kayda muttered to herself.

A few seconds later, her companions finally reached the clearing. Their voices had been background noise in her head for a while. They'd mostly been gagging, asking each other what they believed was the source of the stench. "A mountain of human bodies" had been the most common guess—mostly voiced by Quaid.

Marisol reached her first. "What the hell is this …" Without waiting for a reply, she started to make her way around the rune array, heading for nine o'clock. "Think this qualifies as an 'odd sighting'?"

"If this isn't odd," Kayda said, folding her arms across her chest, "I don't know what is."

Cathy reached them next. "Oof. That's a smell we won't be able to get out of our clothes …"

Hank-maybe-Will was the last to arrive. Everyone had either stopped beside Kayda or took a slow cruise around the rune array.

Hank-maybe-Will said, "Fine, I'll ask. Do we think there's a sorcerer living in that village? Is this a food trap for the ferals?"

Kayda eyed the giant, dead, school-bus size Canada goose. Its long neck reminded her of the curling serpentine body of a boa constrictor rather than anything belonging to a bird. Its monstrous head lay near Kayda, like a misshapen boulder. Its black beak, nearly as long as Kayda's leg, was cracked, as if someone had punched a hole straight through, revealing a pink tongue writhing with maggots. Though animals were apparently repelled by the array, insects had slipped past the magic. As people moved around the body, great plumes of bugs were startled into the air.

A good portion of the body's meat had been carved away or eaten, but entrails oozed out of the bird's torn-open chest cavity, spilling onto the array. Though the beast had to have been dead for a while, as the blood had congealed into a thick, blackish sludge, the array clearly still functioned as normal; the viscera hadn't eroded the runes. What had it been burned into the earth with that it held this well?

While her companions discussed whether they thought there was enough fae blood in a bird this large to sustain a hamlet of ferals, Kayda glanced skyward. She scanned the treetops, straining to hear distant honking of other geese. The sky was a clear blue. Not even mundane birds winged by. Had the array not been repelling scavengers, the sky above them would have been filled with dozens of slowly wheeling vultures.

She pulled her phone out of her pocket and took as many pictures of the runes as possible, doing her best not to actually touch any part of it. She dumped the series of pictures into the group chat and re-added Welsh. She realized two things the moment she hit send. First, it was after one in the morning back home, and she might have just woken everyone up. Second, she should have just sent the pictures to Caspian, as she was almost immediately hit with a flurry of replies.

Henri
Hi. I'm never eating again.

Welsh
The sound that thing must have made when it hit the earth …

Harlow
ZEEF WELLINGTON! I was indisposed when y'all were talking earlier. Hi!

Welsh
Hi, Harlow

Caspian
That runework is incredible! Is that tourmalinic char? Without touching the array, can you get close enough to inhale the aroma wafting from the runes?

Henri
You want her to SNIFF the runes?

Harlow
How could anything within a mile of that smell like anything other than Very Large Dead Bird?

Kayda groaned internally, amazed once again at how quickly they all could get off track.

> **Kayda**
> What do the runes say, Caspian?

A full minute ticked by without a reply.

> **Welsh**
> Give it to her in layman's terms, Blackthorn. She's no doubt on a time crunch and literally no one—NO ONE—wants to hear anything that comes after the "Well, actually..." that you're in the process of typing

> **Harlow**
> I can confirm he just hit the backspace button roughly 90 million times

> **Caspian**
> Best I can tell, this is an array that includes spells for confusion, loss of sight, and a gravitational shift. There's more nuance than that, but basically it's a trap. My guess is, the goose unknowingly flew over the array and was yanked down to its death. Are there other arrays in the area? Perhaps there's a series of them that the goose flew over that worked in tandem to create a compounding effect. Even with runes as powerful as these, it would take a lot to down an animal that large with only a single array.

Kayda stepped away from the carcass and headed a few feet in the direction of the hamlet, scanning the ground. She couldn't tell for certain, but there *did* seem to be another section of unnaturally flattened earth half a mile away.

Kayda
I think so. Thanks. If you figure out any more details from studying the arrays, let me know

Caspian
Will do, but we're still in the Tower. I have limited research materials as it is. It's well after midnight and the planned sorcerer meeting hasn't even started yet. We're locked in an office.

Kayda
You doing okay, Low?

Harlow
Not even a little bit

Welsh
Lot of that going around lately

Henri
Oh, Caspian? Your pixie gang is pretty scary, but Rory is nice. He was very polite to me before he took off on his mission

Harlow
Wait a hot damn minute! Rory as in the telepathic eagle? He talked to you?

Henri
Does he not talk to everyone?

Caspian
For the millionth time, Harlow. He's a falcon. Not an eagle.

Harlow
Are you sure he's not an eagle?

Caspian
Slitted-eye emoticon

Harlow
OMG. We've been through this! You SELECT an "emoticon." You don't DESCRIBE it. And the word is emoji!

Caspian
Rolling-eye emoticon

Henri
Laughing so hard I'm crying emoticon

Harlow
Henri! Don't encourage him!

Kayda
I'm once again filled with regret over the existence of this thread

Welsh
Same.

Welsh
Rory speaks to me telepathically as well. He will typically only choose people of noble heart and character, though. I can't say I'm surprised you're not on his list

Harlow
You're on MY list...

Welsh
Kissy face emoticon

Caspian
asterisk, I am guffawing, asterisk

The conversation was a flurry of nonsense chatter for a few more minutes before everyone more or less decided they'd try to get some rest. Kayda was a little concerned that sleep seemed to be eluding Henri and all of her friends.

She was about to stick her phone back in her pocket when she got a text from Henri in their personal thread.

> **Henri**
> Hi

She smiled to herself, despite the fact that she had a rotting goose nearby and could hear the distant chittering of ferals coming from the general direction of the hamlet.

> **Kayda**
> Hi

> **Henri**
> I need you to come back in one piece, okay?

> **Kayda**
> I feel like you said the exact same thing to me mere days ago

> **Henri**
> It was a copy and paste message

> **Kayda**
> I'm a terrible girlfriend

> **Henri**
> I've had worse

> **Kayda**
> asterisk, gasp, asterisk

> **Henri**
> 

> **Henri**
> Just keep in contact, okay? Being out of the loop stresses me out

> **Kayda**
> I will. I'm trying to do better. Promise

> **Henri**
> I know you are

> **Kayda**
> We'll talk soon, okay? I have to strategize about dispatching a feral horde

Kayda pocketed her phone before she could see Henri's reply, which arrived moments later. The snarling and chittering were still a way off, and she was fairly positive they hadn't started moving toward her group yet, but the ferals were definitely congregating. She closed her eyes, funneling all her focus into her sense of hearing. If she had to guess, there were less than ten. She couldn't pick up the sound of normal speech that could help confirm the presence of either hybrids or a sorcerer. That didn't mean they weren't out here, though—just that she couldn't hear them.

Marisol's voice sounded beside her. "How many we got?"

"Seven is my best guess," Kayda said, eyes still closed.

"Do you think that other one ran away to get reinforcements?" Marisol asked.

Kayda mulled that over.

"I think they're weak," Kayda said, glancing down at Marisol. "Maybe they have food traps out here because they can't catch stuff themselves. Maybe your conspiracy theories hold some weight, and these teen ferals are weak when they're first transitioning but turn into super soldiers after a certain gestation period or something. Either way, I say we take them out before they become a bigger problem."

Marisol nodded. "We're all armed. Let's go." She called out for the others.

Hank-maybe-Will had been the one assigned to watch the car, but he'd refused. He'd apparently stashed the bodies and then joined the group, so the whole team was here. They fanned out across the wide expanse as they walked in a horizontal line. Kayda took up the position on the far left of the wide clearing, while Hank-maybe-Will took up the right. Marisol, Quaid, and Cathy were in the middle. Kayda kept one ear tuned to the forest beside her, hoping there weren't stronger ferals hidden among the shadows of the trees, waiting for an opportunity to strike. But other than the occasional scrabbling of a rodent or call from a bird, it was relatively quiet.

When they reached the halfway point between the goose carcass and the hamlet, they did indeed come across another massive rune array burned into the earth. No carcass lay here. They halted their march forward so Marisol could take several photographs of the array. Once she gave the thumbs-up that she was done and they'd started walking again, Kayda's phone vibrated in her back pocket, probably meaning Marisol had forwarded the pictures to her to send to Caspian later.

Despite Kayda being able to hear the ferals' growing agitation at their approach, the ferals didn't attack. They paced the edge of the hamlet, snarling and chittering. It even sounded like they were starting small skirmishes among themselves, but they made no effort to advance.

Kayda's companions regrouped once they were a mere hundred yards from the hamlet. There were still no signs of other ferals hiding among the trees, nor lurking hybrids or sorcerers.

From here, it was clear there were only three small stone homes, a pair of pig troughs, and two fence-enclosed areas that might have once been meant for horses. One area was dotted with training dummies, while the other was scattered with what looked like upsettingly large bones. She decided she didn't want to know what had happened in there.

Only half a dozen ferals, not seven, lingered on the edge of the hamlet. A few stood upright, while some were on all fours. Kayda noted that they weren't all at the same point of the transition process, though all their eyes had gone black.

Scratch that—there *were* seven ferals. A very young girl, who looked no older than twelve, crouched behind one of the larger boys. *Her* eyes still looked human.

"This is weird," Cathy said, tone low. "I don't see any runes or obelisks anywhere. They almost act like they can't leave that area. Since when do ferals—especially in a group—not attack?"

Kayda, arms crossed, watched the ferals over the heads of her companions. The ferals' heartbeats were erratic, their chittering was more nervous than hostile, and she detected a faint musk. They were sweating bullets, these kids. "They're scared."

The VHoA members all turned their attention to her.

Cathy scoffed. "You almost sound sympathetic. Going soft on us, draken?"

Kayda wasn't sure why Cathy thought now was the time to pick a fight, but Kayda refused to take the bait. "Seems like the theory about teen ferals being fighting machines is the exact opposite—they *can* be turned, but they probably get killed off in droves because they're like baby birds who just fell out of the nest."

"Easier to kill," Hank-maybe-Will said.

"Dark," Quaid said. "But accurate."

Marisol and Cathy muttered their agreement.

Weapons were pulled from sheaths, and magic-dampening hoods were pulled off blades. Kayda, however, didn't budge.

"You kids out here alone?" Kayda called.

Several of the ferals cocked their heads to the side, like curious dogs. A couple of them sniffed the air. Another pawed at the ground with their foot like an agitated bull itching for a fight.

"Talking would be a lot less fatal of a choice!" Kayda shouted.

A feral tossed its head back and chittered. The others answered in unison, and without hesitation, they charged.

Kayda muttered, "So much for the diplomatic option ..."

The group, save Kayda, raced forward, magic crackling off spears, a baton, and a short sword. Kayda merely watched them go, curious how the ferals would react. The ferals lashed out with fang and claw with the same ruthlessness she'd grown to expect.

After several long seconds, however, the youngest one rabbited in the other direction. Kayda took off after her.

Though the ferals Kayda's companions fought against were scrappier than the ones she and Marisol had taken out earlier, Kayda felt no guilt about skirting the battle and leaving the others behind. She wove around the fenced-in area littered with bones, past a stone house, and caught the feral girl by the back of her shirt just before she slipped past the farthest edge of the hamlet. The kid thrashed and kicked, but Kayda was able to hold her out at arm's length, remaining safe from the kid's feeble attempts to get loose. After only a few seconds, the fight went out of her. She hung there like a sopping-wet kitten.

Kayda twisted her wrist to swing the kid's face into view. No black swam in the whites of the girl's green eyes. Faint tendrils of necrosis crawled along her temples and in the veins of her fore-arms. Her fingertips were more of an ashen gray than the deep black of frostbite. The girl snarled at Kayda, revealing needle-sharp fangs, confirming the vampire transformation had taken hold, even if she hadn't gone feral yet. Kayda still couldn't muster up any fear, though. Now the kid just looked like a sopping-wet kitten trying to roar.

"Can you talk?" Kayda asked the girl.

The kid pursed her lips and crossed her arms, brow furrowed. Kayda might have been wrong about the age. Maybe she was closer to ten. What kind of monster tried turning a ten-year-old? She couldn't have weighed more than sixty pounds. Hybrids used ferals like scouts and attack dogs—this little thing couldn't hope to be anything more than an ankle-biting chihuahua.

The false bravado slipped off the girl's face a moment later, and her focus shifted to something behind Kayda. Kayda's companions had found her. Their casual chatter told her they hadn't run into much trouble squaring off against the six others.

"Your friends are dead, kid," Kayda said, redirecting the girl's attention. "Now's a good time to let me know if there's any human left in you. Otherwise, you're going to end up just as dead as the others."

The little girl swallowed. Her fangs had retracted by the time she said, "I can talk."

She sounded … normal. Her voice was a bit hoarse, but Kayda thought that was more from disuse than anything.

"What's your name?" Kayda asked.

"We don't have names here."

"When you *had* a name, what did they call you?"

The little girl's gaze flipped from Kayda to a spot past one shoulder, then the other, and back again. "Alyssa. I like Aly better, though."

"Hi, Aly. I'm Kayda."

Cathy scoffed.

Ignoring her, Kayda asked, "Is it just you kids out here, Aly?"

"Yeah," Alyssa said. "Adults come check on us once a month. That's what Johnny said. I've only been here for two weeks, so I haven't seen any grown-ups until today."

"How old are you?" Kayda asked.

"Eight."

Quaid cursed.

Kayda asked, "How'd you get here? Your parents—"

"I don't have parents," Alyssa said, once again taking on a brave air that belied her size. She sounded less and less froggy the more she spoke. "I was living in a group home, and a bunch of the kids hated it there, so we all left. We could take care of ourselves better than the adults did."

Given their current situation, Kayda had her doubts. Something clearly had gone even further awry for these kids after they'd fled the group home.

Kayda recalled the details of Marisol's conspiracy theory from earlier. There were probably nuggets of truth in there, buried among the nonsense. "Did an adult find you while you were living on the street? Maybe someone who offered you a place to live?"

Alyssa's eyes lit up as if Kayda had just performed a magic trick. "Yeah. How'd you know?"

"I'm a good guesser. Tell me about the people who found you."

"Umm ..." she said. "It was just one person at first. A grown-up lady. She said if we wanted to make some money working for her, she had a job. She brought us to a house where a bunch of other grown-ups lived. She said if we helped clean her big house and pull weeds and stuff, then we could live there for free."

Marisol chimed in, taking up a spot beside Kayda. "After a while, did the rules at the big house change?"

Alyssa, despite still being held in place by the back of her shirt some four feet off the ground, nodded vigorously. She seemed happy to keep chatting now that she had a rapt audience. Maybe she'd figured out that she had a better chance of surviving if she cooperated. "Some of the grown-ups would do weird stuff, though, and, like, bite the kids? And sometimes they'd make us drink this really gross red drink that smelled like metal. If the kids drank too much of the drink, they started to change. Not like an alcohol drink when if you drink too much you throw up and fall down a lot. But, like, their eyes got all weird and stuff? It would look like black smoke was flying around in their eyeballs. And sometimes it would make the kids bite people, too." She frowned. "But other times, if they drank too much of the red stuff, they'd flop around and not wake up again. That's how my big sister died a while back. She wasn't my *real* big sister, but she looked after me a lot and would keep the bigger boys from bugging me too much."

Kayda didn't know how to process any of that. It didn't sound like the kid even *knew* she was a vampire. "If I put you down, do you promise not to run away?"

Alyssa scrunched up her face. Her gaze flitted between the assembled armed people who had just killed everyone the girl considered friend or family, then settled on Kayda. "Promise."

Kayda deposited the girl onto her ratty tennis shoes, then

shook out her own arm. Alyssa's shirt collar was bunched up and stretched out at the back of her neck, but she otherwise looked all right.

Marisol said, "Watch the kid" to no one in particular, then pulled Kayda away from the group.

"The draken is going to get us killed," Cathy muttered, but Kayda's hearing still picked it up.

When she and Marisol were out of human earshot, Kayda cast a glance back at the others. Hank-maybe-Will, despite looking like the kind of guy who was allergic to happiness, was hinged at the waist in front of Alyssa, hands on his knees. He made a goofy face at the kid, and she cracked up even though she'd clearly tried not to. Cathy stood nearby, scowling. Quaid was busy scanning the hamlet, checking for other threats. Kayda returned her focus to Marisol.

"I shouldn't have to say this, but we can't keep a vamp with us, Kay—kid or not," Marisol said, hands on hips. "She might *seem* sane, but we don't know enough about gestation periods in kids to know what's going on with her. She's a hybrid. We don't know if she's going to suffer withdrawal from a lack of fae blood. We don't know what kind of bond she's got with ferals. I doubt she knows, either. The last thing we need is for her to turn fully feral in the back seat and tear out throats before we can pull over. Maybe ferals are instinctively drawn to hybrids, and we'll be like a beacon, calling them to us. Maybe they all share a hive mind. Too much about her is an unknown."

Everything she'd said made logical sense, and yet Kayda was surprised at her friend's willingness to write Alyssa off that easily.

"What are you suggesting?" Kayda asked. "You wanna take an eight-year-old kid out back and shoot her because she *might* pose a threat? The others were too far gone, or close to it. There's still hope for Alyssa."

"I can't be responsible for—"

"Think about what you know about vamps in general and ferals in particular," Kayda said, interrupting another of Marisol's pity parties. "You know as well as I do that, even if vampirism isn't reversible, going feral *is* if you catch it in time. The kid's only eight, and the chance of her ever having a normal human life is already forfeit. But she *can* be rehabilitated and *can* live in a place like Luma. There's gotta be a community of rehabbed vamps that would take her in. Not every vamp ended up that way by choice. There would be sympathy for a kid who got forced into this."

A peal of laughter pulled their attention toward the others. Hank-maybe-Will had slung the tiny girl over his shoulder and was sprinting around one of the stone buildings while Quaid chased them. Alyssa cackled, her blond hair flapping behind her.

Kayda looked away first, finding a small smile on Marisol's face. "I'll go along with whatever you decide, but make your choice based on what *you* think is right. Don't let the doubts in the back of your mind win. Don't let the others tell you what to do."

Marisol stared at Kayda for a beat. "You mean I should let *you* tell me what to do but not Cathy."

Kayda shrugged. "Well, yeah. I'm right, and Cathy's an asshole."

Marisol spluttered a surprised laugh. "Cathy's just looking out for me. We've been friends a long time. But … she's also a little … anti-draken."

Kayda cocked a hairless eyebrow.

Marisol took a step forward and pitched her voice low. "You didn't hear this from me, but her dad and a draken got into a bar fight several years ago. The draken punched him so hard, her dad had to be put into a medically induced coma. He woke up and is able to function on his own and everything, but he never fully bounced back. Can't hold a job. He had a drinking problem before and now is a full-blown alcoholic."

Kayda felt a little worse about the accidental broken nose. Still, it wasn't fair for Cathy to write off an entire group of people because of what had happened to her dad.

Marisol asked, "Are you willing to be the kid's personal vamp-sitter until we figure out what to do with her? If you get bitten, the chances you'll turn are much lower than the rest of us."

"Sure," Kayda said without hesitation, knowing some part of her—maybe *most* of her—was still searching for a miracle cure for Welsh. "If this plan goes sideways, you can throw me under the bus instead of blaming yourself. Cathy would love that."

Marisol chuffed another laugh, then started heading toward the rest of the group. "Let's check out the houses and see if there's anything useful. Don't forget: The kid's going to need a blood meal eventually." She turned around, walking backward. "You'd better hope there are prepared sippy cups or something because keeping the tiny vamp fed is now in bold letters at the top of your new job description."

Kayda sighed. She didn't regret getting a stay of execution for the tiny vampire, but she also knew there was a kernel of truth in Cathy and Marisol's misgivings about keeping a hybrid like Alyssa alive.

Maybe grouchy Cathy was right about something else, too.

Maybe Kayda *was* going soft …

CHAPTER TWENTY-FOUR

FELIX

Over the last couple of weeks, there were a number of things that had struck Felix as odd about the Naomi West case, the first being that the official report about Naomi's death had been heavily redacted sometime between last year and now. He'd read the printed reports so many times, he practically had them memorized, but after his meeting with Denise two weeks ago, he'd gone back into Naomi's digital file to double-check a few details, only to find the thing littered with black bars.

Clicking on the black bars caused an error box to pop up.

Warning!

You do not have the necessary clearance to view this report in its entirety. If you believe you've received this message in error, please contact Mundane Resources.

It was a warning Felix had seen countless times over the years, usually when he was poking around in cases that involved both humans *and* magic-touched or fae. The overlap usually meant the case was sent to the werecats, even if it made more sense to go to the hunters.

For the warning to come up on Naomi's file upward of four years after the fact was … curious. He'd eventually found the edit log on the file. That was where the second oddity about Naomi's case materialized. The last person to edit the file had been Sorcerer Jeffries. Sorcerers' names rarely, if ever, popped up in the edit logs. At least not in his experience, seeing as the vast majority of his cases involved humans or very low-level fae. Maybe sorcerers edited the werecats' case files all the time, but in his department, it was unheard of.

Felix didn't know much about Sorcerer Jeffries other than secondhand information via Bartholomew—usually in the form of complaints. The sorcerer was apparently a stickler for detail and was known to dock pay from werecats who didn't fill out their paperwork thoroughly. One of his top disciplines had something to do with time magic. On a small scale, he could see a minute or two into the future. On a larger scale—using rune arrays that took months to complete—he could see further into the future. This ability had turned the sorcerer into a perfectionist, always peeking a minute or two into the future to spot impending problems and urging people to fix their mistakes now to prevent future ones.

Since the "problems" were often small, inconsequential things, it meant Jeffries was the absolute worst micromanager in the history of the universe.

Why was a guy like that even *looking* at a cold case that had been relegated to the human police? And why was he redacting large chunks of it? There hadn't been anything in the official report that had been out of the ordinary, from what Felix remembered.

Oddity number three was that when Bartholomew logged in with his werecat clearance, he received the same error message.

What was in that file that Jeffries wanted hidden? Had he seen something with his future-cast ability that was connected to Naomi's case?

Felix was distrusting of his bosses on the best of days, but given the weird tension in the Tower as of late, and how the sorcerers had been making life hell for Harlow and her friends, his first thought was that Jeffries was covering either his own ass or that of a colleague.

Felix wanted to do right by Naomi and Denise, but if Naomi had raised the ire of corrupt sorcerers enough that they were still covering their tracks years later, Felix was in way over his head already.

Recalling the day he'd gotten beaten to a pulp by thugs in masks, he figured he'd been in over his head for a while. He'd always assumed the goons had been hired hands for someone in the Collective. Despite the elite sorcerers being his bosses, not even Felix knew how many made up Luma's Collective. The organization was so big and so secretive, Felix had assumed he'd never be able to put a name to his attackers—neither the ones who had wielded tire irons and threats on Harlow's life nor the sorcerer who had paid them or ordered them to do it.

The name Jeffries got him closer to knowing who was responsible. Even if Jeffries wasn't the one who had sent those guys after him—and possibly Naomi—Jeffries very well could know who had.

Denise had also given him another name: Tatton.

Tatton initially had sounded like a unique name, but apparently "Tatton" was to bear shifters as "Joe" was to mundanes. This fact was made worse by learning that Tatton no longer worked at the Ghost Lily. Over the past week, Felix had talked to at least eight waitresses and bartenders, and none of them had heard of the guy.

Felix was going to try his luck at the Ghost Lily again today. It was six in the morning, so the place would hopefully be dead, allowing him to talk to a bartender or two without needing to shout himself hoarse to be heard. He sat in his car in the parking lot of the bar, unable to get out just yet.

He was worried about Harlow—worried in a "something feels wrong" way more than an "I'm obsessed with my ex" way. She'd gone into the Tower yesterday morning, and he hadn't heard jack shit from her since. That was par for the course for them, which was honestly fine, but he had a bad feeling about her silence.

He'd gotten both yesterday and today off. Getting an email from his direct supervisor two nights ago telling him he could have two days off as a thank-you for all his hard work as of late had been so surprising, Felix's initial reaction had been suspicion. But he was drowning so thoroughly in his personal cases, he'd been grateful for the time off yesterday. He'd actually spent a good chunk of it sleeping, which was unheard of for him. Perhaps it was guilt that was eating at him now. Harlow and Camila could have needed him yesterday, and he'd spent it passed out in bed or working on his cases.

Today, with no news from Harlow, his suspicions had been roused once again. Was it a coincidence that he was being kept out of the Tower on the same days the Fletchers were invited in?

He was honestly more worried about how Camila was faring in the Tower than Harlow, if only because of that sword of Harlow's. The unhinged thing was almost guaranteed to act rashly and violate the neutrality law, but Felix was still confident the weapon, especially if Caspian was with them, could get them out if shit went sideways. The small werecat clan that was on a vigilante kick and headed by O'Neill would be a problem for her, but not even they were suicidal enough to violate the neutrality law.

Probably.

If the sorcerers had separated the Fletchers, as Felix suspected they had, it was probably Camila who would be in the most danger. She had more enemies in the Tower than she knew, and Felix couldn't warn her. The last number he had for her had been disconnected months ago. And the Soul NDA kept Felix from being able to say much of anything to Harlow to pass on to her mother.

Despite it being not even six in the morning, he finally broke down and texted Harlow.

> **Felix**
> Are you OK?

He debated about going into the Tower today, just to see if the rumor mill had any intel, but he almost immediately decided against it. He was swamped.

And yet, even Bartholomew was off today. The charismatic, gregarious werecat was up in everyone's business all the time, so he was often Felix's best source for office gossip. But the guy was probably passed out in a sunbeam somewhere, oblivious.

With no reply from Harlow, Felix grunted in annoyance at himself and got out of the car.

The Lily, as expected, was pretty dead. The restaurant had decent food, especially for breakfast, so there was still a stream of activity. He figured the greasy food helped everyone who was currently suffering from raging hangovers. Music played loud enough that you had to raise your voice slightly to be heard over it, but nowhere near as ear-splittingly loud as it would be by the evening. Half of the seats at the bar were empty, filled only with those who hadn't gone home yet despite the sun being up, blue-collar workers unwinding after an overnight shift, and the alcoholics getting an early start.

The woman working behind the bar was a draken who made Kayda look like a helpless kitten. Felix quickly learned that the woman, who went by Spike, had been working at the Lily for fifteen years and remembered Tatton well.

When Felix started peppering her with questions about the guy, Spike held up a large hand to quiet him. "I'll talk to you on one condition, pretty boy. You gotta promise to keep them orders coming, or Security is going to wonder why I'm letting you chat me up."

The guy working the front door was the only security guard Felix had seen. And "working" was … generous. The draken man had been passed out in a flower box when Felix walked in, and it looked like he might have thrown up on the bar's namesake—silver-colored lilies that grew in planter boxes and repurposed wine barrels scattered around the front of the building.

Still, Felix dutifully downed half his beer. "Isn't flirting with customers part of the job? Flutter those lashes and rack up the tips?"

Draken didn't naturally have much body hair, including eyelashes, but Spike had donned fake ones. She also wore a long black wig she'd pulled up into a high ponytail. The hair and lashes clashed with her otherwise hardened exterior, especially since a nasty scar running through one eye had clearly resulted in her losing it. Her glass eye remained unsettlingly still no matter how Spike moved. Her natural iris was brown, while the one in the glass eye was blue.

Spike leaned her massive arms on the bar top and smiled at Felix. At least four of her teeth were missing. "They'd understand why you're flirting with *me*, pretty boy. Wouldn't be the first time a scrawny little mundane thought he could handle Miss Spike. It's just that they know my preferences are more … caprine in nature. I don't waste my flirtations on hairless monkeys. Too breakable."

The woman had to be eight feet tall, was as wide as a refrigerator, and looked like she'd snap a caprine—fauns and their cousins —in half. Plus, draken were far closer to hairless than humans were. But maybe the furry ones got her hot and bothered simply because they were so different from her kind.

Felix asked, "What can you tell me about Tatton? Do you happen to remember his last name?"

"Tatton Fairchild. It's like naming your kid John Smith, as far as bear shifters go. Weren't nothing common about him, though. He was a *nasty* sonofabitch, I can tell you that much. Grizzly shifter. Competed in battle arenas when he was younger. Got into security as an adult—but he took side gigs, too."

"What kind of side gigs?"

Spike stood to full height and placed one of her massive hands on the bar top, the other on her hip. "You need another?" she asked, gesturing at his beer.

Felix sighed, polished off the glass, and motioned for her to refill it. She did so, then moseyed down the bar, checking on her other customers before returning to Felix.

She pulled a small white dishrag off her shoulder and mopped up a nonexistent spill. "He wasn't a mercenary exactly, but if someone had a job where they needed someone to get roughed up, they'd come through here looking for Tatton. He developed enough of a rep that he frequently got jobs with the Bruin Cartel. After one sketchy type too many came through here—the top floor started to look like a mob hangout—looking for Tatton, he got the boot. You know it's bad when management here thinks the crowd is getting *too* rough."

"Wait, did the Bruin Cartel raid happen *here*? I swear every time I hear that story, the location changes."

The raid was one of the biggest busts in Luma history—nearly urban legend status.

After an encouraging gesture from Spike, Felix reluctantly took a sip of his beer. He really didn't want to get plastered before noon, but this was apparently the only way to guarantee she'd keep talking.

"Yep. Tatton showed up here one night a few days after he was canned with a bunch of them sketchy Bruin thugs. It was mostly bear shifters, but a couple draken were with him, too. They were harassing customers. Causing a scene. The old owner—best boss this place ever had—called the werecats. Not only did the cats show up, but several elemental witches did, too. This place got *trashed*. It was wild. But a whole bunch of Tatton's new friends got arrested, Tatton included. Several others escaped. The Bruin Cartel dissolved—at least here in Luma. None of them came back to retaliate, so my guess is they either got scared straight, ended up in the Antarctic hub, or got exiled from the system."

Felix sighed, worried that meant Tatton was long gone—especially since this was upward of ten years ago. And that bust had clearly scattered the cartel's members and associates to the wind.

The story was so beloved among his coworkers because, instead of taking out the Bruin Cartel by raiding a compound after months or years of careful planning, the werecats had managed to capture over a dozen of the cartel's top players simply because the idiots had gotten too rowdy in a bar. Though sometimes it was a restaurant in the recounting. Or a casino. Or a kid's birthday party.

The cartel had been drunk on elfin wine or high on their own supply and had acted like they'd owned the place. The fact that most of the members had been in their late twenties and hadn't known how to handle suddenly having pockets full of cash probably had doomed the cartel from the start, anyway.

Before the raid, most folks had been too scared to snitch on the cartel, so they'd gotten away with murder—often literally. The owner of the Lily had only been at the job for under sixth months after his brother unexpectedly died, and the poor sod had had no idea that the young, boisterous, and reckless shifters causing mayhem in his bar had been blazing their way through Luma's criminal underbelly for several years. One phone call to authorities had cut the wildfire-like sweep of the Bruin Cartel off at the knees.

The tale got trotted out any time there was a large gathering of Tower employees in one place. Even though hunters hadn't been part of the raid, the story had even been turned into a skit performed during the bounty hunter conference Felix had attended in Kensey a couple of years ago. The script and acting had left a lot to be desired, but the costuming had been exceptional.

It was wild that Tatton had ultimately been the catalyst for it. Felix feared anew that the reason Tatton's name had been lost to history—hells, Felix hadn't even known the bar in question had been the Lily—was because *Tatton* had been lost to history.

"Did Tatton get his job back at any point after the incident with the cartel?" Felix asked.

Spike's good eye studied him for a long beat. "Nah, he was blacklisted."

Felix groaned internally. The intel Denise had gotten from that waitress only a few years ago had been a bullshit answer to get Denise to stop asking questions. Tatton had been long gone by the time Naomi worked here.

"Why you asking?" Spike placed her large hand on the bar top again, and her fist on her hip. "Figured you were a reporter or writer or something—looking for an anecdote to add to your piece. No one really comes asking about Tatton unless they already know at least part of the story."

Felix weighed his options. She might clam up if she told him he was a bounty hunter doing some sleuthing on the side. If he flashed her his newly acquired PI license, she'd probably refuse to say anything else. Talking about Tatton wasn't a crime, after all. She was merely telling a customer a bit of local history.

He knew better than most that, even if the owner from ten years ago had been a grieving man who'd been in over his head as he tried to honor his brother's wishes, the current owner was a different story. Jalen Graves let Bliss flow in and fae teens flow out of this place like a coursing river, and the Collective was letting him do it—or at least was looking the other way. People as flashy as the Bruin Cartel weren't running the Lily now. No, now the place was run by shadowy people who were better at covering their tracks—or making friends with people in high places.

If Spike feared what might happen to her if she started divulging info to a Collective employee, she might not only stop talking to him but also get him blacklisted the way Tatton had been.

"That's a mighty long hesitation, pretty boy," Spike said.

Decision made, he pulled his cell out of his pocket, scrolled through his pictures, and pulled up one of Naomi. Holding the screen up to Spike, he asked, "Do you remember her?"

Spike glanced at the screen for only a moment, then walked away without a word. She tended to a few more customers at the other end of the bar. He honestly wasn't sure if Spike was angry or if he'd just been summarily written off. After two full minutes of Spike ignoring his existence, Felix figured it was time to bail.

She finished up a flirtatious chat with a man with very impressive horns, then Spike reached below the lip of the bar, remained hunched there for a few long seconds, and stood with a landline phone pressed to her ear. After saying hello to whoever answered, she glanced at Felix for a moment before turning her back to him.

Gusting a sigh, Felix tipped onto his hip so he could pluck his wallet from a back pocket. He wasn't sure how much two beers would run him, but he figured a generous tip would let Spike know he had no hard feelings. Not even highly trained undercover cops fared well in here. Graves and the security guards had done a good job of breaking any rebellious spirit in the staff.

He left his nearly full glass of beer on the bar top and casually strolled for the door. The security guard was still passed out in the flower box. In addition to the smell of vomit that wafted off the guy was the scent of urine. The steady rumble of his snores at least let Felix know the guy was still alive.

He slowly walked to his car, frustrated that he was back at square one. Denise would be bummed when she called this afternoon and told her that the waitress had given her bogus intel.

"Hey! Pretty boy…"

Felix whirled, stopping in the middle of the rectangular-shaped parking lot, and cocked his head at Spike. She closed the distance and gestured with the lit cigarette she had wedged between two fingers.

"You know, you're the first cop who's ever come in here asking about Naomi," Spike said, taking a long drag of her cigarette as her good eye regarded him.

Even though Felix hadn't known until recently that Naomi had worked at the Lily, he doubted no one from the Tower knew that. Had Naomi's ties to the Lily—especially in light of what had been discovered about this place recently—been part of the redacted information in her report?

"How'd you know I was a cop? And what happened to the reporter theory?"

Spike smiled, her missing teeth prominent. "You move like a cop, talk like a cop. I threw that reporter thing out there to see if you'd lie to me. The fact that you didn't confirm or deny it *also* told me you were a cop."

Felix was consistently unsure if, at any given moment, Spike was fucking with him. "No one ever came in asking about Naomi?"

"Not that I know of. I know the girls in particular get twitchy about talking to anyone they don't know—cops are trying to infiltrate this place all the time. But we talk to each other. Everyone who worked with Naomi, even though it wasn't that long, all things considered, really liked her. Fucked us all up when she was found dead—but we suspected she wasn't coming back when she all of a sudden didn't show up for her shifts. She was as reliable as they come."

Felix knew the answer to his next question but asked it anyway. "None of you reported her missing?"

Spike pursed her lips and leveled him with a "you're joking, right?" look. "Girls go missing from here all the time, pretty boy." She pointed her cigarette at him. "And if you're going to start getting all high and mighty about that, asking why we'd work at a place like this knowing what we know, then I'll walk my fine ass right back inside. All the girls here, me included, work here 'cause our options are limited for any number of reasons. You either accept that or you don't."

Felix held his hands up, palms out. "Hazard of the job, all right? I deal with a lot of domestic violence victims and cases of missing teens. It's hard for me to know places like this exist and not be able to do anything about it."

"Ah," Spike said, taking another long drag before blowing a plume of smoke out the side of her mouth. "Bleeding-heart type. So, what, you somehow thought Tatton had something to do with Naomi's disappearance?"

He gave her a brief explanation of how that name had made his way to him. "I knew her. Naomi, I mean. She was friends with my ex. I keep investigating what happened because I really liked her, too. She was a good friend to us. I hate not knowing who killed her or why."

Spike stared at him for a long time, her good eye watching him closely and her glass one staring into his soul. Suddenly she grabbed him by the arm and dragged him to a far corner of the parking lot. She gently pushed him against a wall, then took several steps back. "All right, you didn't hear this from me ..."

"Hear what?"

She pointed her cigarette fingers at him again, but in appreciation this time. Keeping her voice low and conspiratorial, she said, "Graves took over about seven years ago. He's a slimy little weasel, but he pays well. *Too* well, you get me? It's hush money without being explicit about it. Anyway, Naomi was here two years after Graves started. By the time she started working here, it was already well established that if you wanted Bliss, you came to the Lily. For a long time, a lot of us actually thought *Naomi* mighta been a cop."

Felix reared back slightly at that. "Why?"

"She claimed she was new to town, but her casual questions

always felt a little probing. She had a bad habit of swooping in and sneaking the too-young ones away from the frequent fliers on the second floor. Pissed Graves off enough that he'd come out of his office and give her a lecture about respecting our customers' privacy—especially the high-paying ones." She took another drag. "Did you know Naomi was part faun?"

Felix nodded.

"I don't got proof, but I think she had faun or nature magic she used to get her ass outta trouble. That girl was ruffling feathers here all the time, but she never got fired. Girls have gotten fired—or disappeared—for a lot less. I think she pushed it too far one time too many, though, and Graves had one of his minions take her out."

Felix clenched his teeth. His desire to torch the place had rekindled.

"After Naomi went missing, the rumor going around was that she'd pissed off the wrong client and skipped town to avoid the guy's wrath. Then, a few days after she was found dead? Graves gave the staff 'bereavement bonuses.' The kind of money that can really turn shit around for people like us. It was still early days with him as the new owner, and we thought he was just taking care of us. He bought our silence, and we didn't even realize it." Spike took a final drag, then tossed the butt away with a flick of her thumb and middle finger. She shoved her hands into the pockets of her black cargo pants. "Not long after that, the bouncers, security, and drug runners started coming up with a code—we don't really use it anymore. They told the staff that if people started getting too nosy about the habits of Graves's guys, we were to give them a special number to call. Inquiries about the bouncers got sent to Mikey. For Bliss, the name was Drew. The names changed every month. The idea was that if the 'special number' got a sudden uptick in calls from undercover cops asking for Paul, it might reveal a chink in the chain of secrecy or something.

"Graves treated it as a way to make sure we were all staying safe, but in hindsight, he was just installing a semi-anonymous snitch system. The guy's pretty paranoid.

"Anyway, when it came to dealing with questions about the hot-button stuff—Naomi, Bliss, missing kids, any of it—we were supposed to deny knowing anything first, then give the code name and special phone number if we needed the person to back off.

"We have a runner who wanted a specific name tied to him, and he never changed it as far as I know. He chose 'Tatton.' Guy's actual name is Yuri Bruin. No relation to the cartel. He said he thought the name was funny, given the history."

"Bear shifter?" Felix asked.

"Yep. He's one of the runners who brings Bliss in from the outside. Been here nearly as long as me. *He's* the one who put the idea in my head that Naomi was a cop. He said she asked too many questions. He'd gone to Graves about her, too, and was annoyed that Naomi kept seeming to charm Graves out of firing her. Graves might be paranoid, but Yuri is ten times worse—he's accused *most* of the staff of being cops or spies at one point or another.

"He's so obsessed with keeping Graves's ass nice and kissed, I honestly didn't even consider until just now that Yuri might have been so spooked by Naomi that he'd hurt her." Spike looked truly troubled for the first time since Felix met her. "But if one of the girls used the name 'Tatton' to get Mama West off her back all those years ago, she could have only meant Yuri. The fact that Mama West wasn't given the number to call makes me think the girl was giving Mama West a clue the best way she knew how. And ... the only girl from Naomi's day who would have known that code name is Ella. Last name was Sellers, I think."

"Think she'd talk to me?"

Spike frowned. "She vanished about four years ago. I'd hoped she just got scared and left town. Her backstory was pretty tragic, so it would make sense. But now ... now I don't know."

Felix didn't like the implications of this. "Does Yuri still work here?"

"Kind of? He's in and out of here a lot, but he's mostly up on the second floor doing Goddess knows what or out running errands for Graves. That guy seems more like a mercenary than Tatton ever was—which also might be why he chose that for his code name."

Felix wasn't stupid enough to think he could tango with a paranoid bear shifter on his own and live to tell the tale. Research he could do, though—and he had a solid lead now.

"I really appreciate your time, Spike." Felix took out his business card case and slid one out to hand to the draken. "If you think of anything else that might help, please don't hesitate to call me. That's my cell."

Spike took the card and stared at it for a long beat, then slipped it into her pocket. She swapped the card for a pack of cigarettes and a lighter. "Haven't thought about Naomi in a long time. All these memories are making me anxious."

Felix figured she was a chain smoker regardless of her anxiety level but kept that to himself. He thanked her again, then started to head toward his car, intending to leave her to her prolonged cigarette break.

He'd only made it a foot or two past her when she asked, "Hey, pretty boy?"

He turned around and raised a brow in question.

She slowly turned to face him, her head bowed for several long seconds before she finally looked him in the eye. "Over the last fifteen years, I've convinced at least ten ladies to quit. I've dumped out countless drinks after someone slipped something into them. I've broken even more fingers. Last year, I started giving girls their drinks in cups with plastic-lined tops they can put a straw through to help prevent them from getting roofied or Blissed. It might seem shitty to you that I'm still working here, given everything I know about this place, but until people like Graves don't get preferential treatment, all I can do is help treat the symptom of a bigger problem. I know I can't save them all, but I worry if I leave, there will be no one left willing to try."

Felix smiled up at her. "Aw, you're a bleeding heart, too."

She pointed at him accusingly with her cigarette. "If you tell anyone, I'll kill you."

With a smile and nod in parting, he left Spike to her cigarettes and memories. He marveled at the feeling—possibly for the first time—of leaving the Ghost Lily *without* the overwhelming desire to commit arson.

CHAPTER TWENTY-FIVE

KAYDA

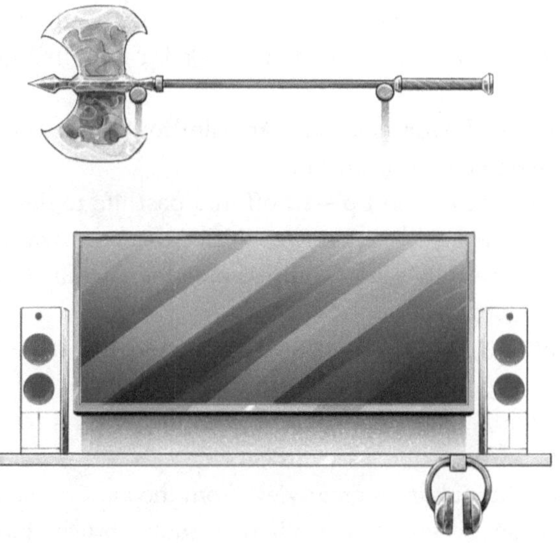

I t wasn't until Kayda, her Vampire Hunters of America companions, and her new charge pulled up to the small shack that was to be their meeting place with the Navolt avian liaison that Kayda remembered something Marisol had said hours ago.

"I was told that I'd better hope my description of the SUV and all of

us was accurate, as the welcome committee has been known to kick suspi-cious intruders to death and ask questions later."

Alyssa hadn't been included in that initial description. If getting kicked to death by a human-sized bird was in Kayda's future, she didn't want to get out of the SUV.

Seeing as none of her travel buddies immediately climbed out of the car, she supposed *no one* was looking forward to this. It was nearing five in the morning, so at least it seemed like ideal bird hours.

Kayda was currently smushed into the very back of the car with Alyssa—the terrifying vampire hybrid child who'd spent the entirety of the ride asleep with her head on Kayda's thigh. She stirred now, sitting up and stretching. Cathy turned in her seat to glare at them both.

Alyssa hissed at her, fangs on full display. Cathy flinched so hard, the car rocked. Alyssa then angled a fang-free grin up at Kayda.

Hand low, Kayda held out her palm to Alyssa. The little girl happily slapped hers against it.

"I don't know who I pissed off in a past life to deserve this," Cathy grumbled to herself as she whirled to face forward again.

Quaid cheerfully said, "You piss me off on a daily basis, so it's probably a long list."

Cathy laughed. If Kayda had attempted the same joke, she would have gotten knifed in the kidney.

"All right, gang," Marisol said from the driver's seat, punctu-ated with a wary sigh. "I see our contact."

Kayda didn't have a great view from the back of the SUV. The one-room shack sat in a patch of scrubby brush, the base so overrun with wild brambles and weeds that the door would be impeded from opening easily. She suspected the paint coating the building had once been bright red, but weather had worn it down to a very soft pink. Nothing else was out here but wilderness as far as Kayda could tell. She knew Navolt itself had to be nearby, but the veil surrounding it kept it hidden.

By the time all six of them emerged from the SUV, with Kayda keeping Alyssa behind her, two birds were easily visible coming in from the east. And they were visible because they were flippin' huge. Kayda was admittedly not well versed in bird types ... species? ... but her first thought was that they were cranes.

Kayda stood resolutely with one hand behind her, holding Alyssa in place. Given how badly the tiny vampire trembled, and how she had a handful of Kayda's shirt clutched in her fist, at least Kayda didn't have to worry about the girl giving away her hiding spot anytime soon.

The cranes' wingspan alone had to be ten feet. A few of her companions were muttering some version of "oh holy shit" under their breath. The underside of the birds was soft gray, while their necks, heads, and tips of their feathers were a vibrant blue. Their long black legs were as long as Kayda's. She eyed the birds' taloned feet warily.

Wind kicked up by the cranes' massive wings sent hair whipping around people's heads, made clothing flap, and sent dried plant debris into the air. Alyssa coughed behind Kayda, but the booming trumpet calls from the birds drowned out the sound. Kayda's sensitive ears rang, and she dialed down her hearing to prevent her eardrums from blowing out.

The group at large took several steps back to give the landing birds enough room. One landed with a soft thump on the ground, while the other alighted atop the overgrown shack. Kayda half expected the structure to collapse under the giant bird's weight, but it issued nary a groan of protest.

Though the crane stood a little shorter than Kayda's own seven feet, it was still entirely too large for a bird. A striking splash of white fanned from either of the bird's eyes to the back of its head, where white feathers flared out like low-lying ponytails. Its neck alone was a good three feet long. It swiveled its head on that long neck now so its red eye was angled directly at Kayda, even though she was standing at the back of the pack. She swallowed as she took in the sight of the bird's sharp yellow beak.

Kayda blurted, "Between the time of our last correspondence and now, we picked up an additional member of the party. We are now six instead of five. We had no way of informing you of this change sooner, as we've had limited means of communication."

She had no idea why she was speaking to the bird as if she were someone's stuffy butler.

Neither bird reacted to Kayda's declaration. Were they pissed? She wondered if she and her friends could get back into the SUV before any of them fell prey to the birds' talons.

In one fluid motion, the crane on the ground morphed into a five-foot tall human man. He wore light-gray linen pants and a loose-fitting tunic. His hair was composed of feathers in the same bright blue as his crane form, including a shock of white at either temple. As with most avian shifters, the transition didn't totally gel with human conventions for normal. His neck was too long, his nose was too pointy for his thin face, and his eyes sat too far apart—eyes that were still blood red. The oddity of their human forms was one of the many reasons the avians preferred their exclusive hub.

Beside Kayda, Quaid let out an instinctive *"yeeugh!"* at the sight of the avian-turned-human and got an elbow in the ribs from Cathy. The crane atop the shack stretched its neck to full length and unleashed a trumpeting shriek of contempt. Alyssa further buried her face against the small of Kayda's back.

They were going to get kicked to death in the middle of nowhere, and their bodies were going to get picked clean by vultures the size of a locomotive. Kayda was sure of it.

The avian-turned-man took a few steps to the side so he could better make eye contact with Kayda, now that he was a good foot shorter. "I appreciate your candor. Who is the stowaway?" His voice was haughty, like the kind of snooty guy you'd expect to meet at a wine-and-cheese party who only wanted to discuss esoteric literature. He'd seemed drawn to Kayda even before her confession about Alyssa. If he thought he got a hoity-toity vibe from her, he was sure to be disappointed.

Kayda nodded awkwardly at him, narrowly avoiding the urge to curtsy, and turned around to face Alyssa, prying the little girl's fingers from her shirt. With both of the girl's hands clasped in hers, Kayda bent low to look into Alyssa's wide eyes. "Honesty is the best policy here, okay? Just tell him your name and that we're looking after you until we can find a home for you."

Alyssa visibly swallowed, then blurted, "I got attacked by crows when I was real little."

Kayda blinked at her. "Oh. You're scared of birds."

"Super scared." Alyssa leaned to the side, presumably to eye the gigantic crane perched atop the shack. She quickly leaned out of the bird's view again. "I have nightmares about them eating my eyeballs."

Kayda tried not to crack a smile. "I'm a little scared, too."

Eyes the size of dinner plates, Alyssa gazed up at her in wonder. "*You?*"

"Me," she said. "But if you put on a brave face, I will, too. Then we can both pee our pants later."

Alyssa cracked up. "Okay."

With Alyssa's little hand in Kayda's, the pair turned to face the avians. The one perched on the shack shrieked in aggravation when it laid eyes on the tiny vampire. Alyssa instinctively hissing back, fangs prominent, didn't help the situation. The crane flapped its wings in agitation, kicking up dust and dried vegetation.

"She's under my care," Kayda said, projecting her voice as loudly as she could. The crane was honking up a storm, though. Kayda's mundane companions had all clapped their hands over their ears. "You have my word that she is no threat to you or your people—uhh ... birds. Avians? Winged comrades ..."

The avian-turned-human, who had remained completely still and impassive while his companion lost its ever-loving shit, raised a hand. The crane immediately quieted. It pulled its wings back toward its body, though its feathers were still ruffled. It kept a beady red eye fixed on Alyssa.

"I am Gagan Darshelle, and this," he said, gesturing to the still-irate crane, "is Fiza Indrelle, my mate."

"I am Kayda Verdan," Kayda said, sensing the avians liked their customs and appreciated having them respected. "And this is Alyssa … uh …" She leaned toward the girl and whispered, "What's your last name, kid?"

"Miller," Alyssa whispered back.

Kayda stood to full height. "And this is Alyssa Miller, my charge. Everyone, be honest in your introductions. The avians value transparency."

Gagan inclined his head, clearly pleased.

The rest of the group gave their full names, though, given the way they shifted their weight, the rapid thump of their hearts, and the nervous swallowing, they still felt uneasy.

Turned out that Hank-maybe-Will was in fact named Will, and in a burst of staccato rambling, he informed everyone that he was Marisol's mate. Marisol turned the color of a tomato.

"Oh. Shit. Um, that's not true. Not for months—like a full half year," Marisol hastily said. "I, um … we *have*, err, coupled before? You know, conjugally, but I'm seeing someone else exclusively. Maybe? His name is Felix Turner. But that doesn't matter because he's not here. We're mating. Well, actually, we haven't actually mated yet, but I want to. I think. We're not *mated*, though. Not the way you and Fiza are." She issued a pained whimper, then whispered, "Oh, Goddess, someone please kill me."

Will stared at Marisol as if she'd slapped him.

"As in *Harlow's* Felix Turner?" Kayda asked, somehow more shocked by this news than the arrival of the gigantic cranes.

Marisol reddened further. "Oh my Goddess. That actually makes a weird kind of sense. I didn't know. He hinted but didn't actually say that outright." She whimpered again. "*Why* can't I shut up?"

"*Awwwkward*," Cathy sing-songed.

"I wish I had popcorn," Quaid said.

Gagan didn't seem fazed, or interested, in the romantic squabbles of mundanes. "Kayda Verdan, it is your dragon ancestry that aids you now. Your ancestors and mine are closely linked, and I trust that you are a woman of your word because of this. As long as young Alyssa remains by your side during your time in Navolt, no harm will befall her. Should her vampiric nature manifest in a manner threatening to Navoltan citizens in any way, she will be thrown into the hunting fields."

Alyssa issued an involuntary squeak of terror before hooking her hand under Kayda's belt and holding on tight.

"You have my word," Kayda said.

"Very well," Gagan said. "I will escort you to the Colony Lodge while Fiza flies ahead to warn them of your arrival. We aves are a proud people, but we are also sensitive. We know you use other terms in the hubs … griffels is the most common, I believe? It's limiting and offensive. We are avians or aves. Do not gawk. Do not stare. Do not refuse food."

Fiza screeched and took to the air. Her loud departure was so abrupt, everyone flinched, including the unflappable Gagan. Will cursed a blue streak.

A small, affectionate smile graced Gagan's unusual face. "I do believe she did that on purpose."

Without further comment, Gagan strode for the shack and, with a few hard tugs, pulled the door open. Inside was a short hallway that gave way to a slope that was swallowed by darkness after only a few feet. On realizing she'd have to go inside, Kayda's only consolation was that the doorway was tall enough that she'd only have to stoop a few inches to clear the jamb.

"You first, Kayda Verdan. Your ancestral instincts will guide your way."

Tamping down her usual impulse to say something along the lines of "the hells they will," she, with her tiny vampire holding fast to her belt, stepped into the dark shack, praying to the Goddess that her entire team wasn't about to become bird chow.

CHAPTER TWENTY-SIX

KAYDA

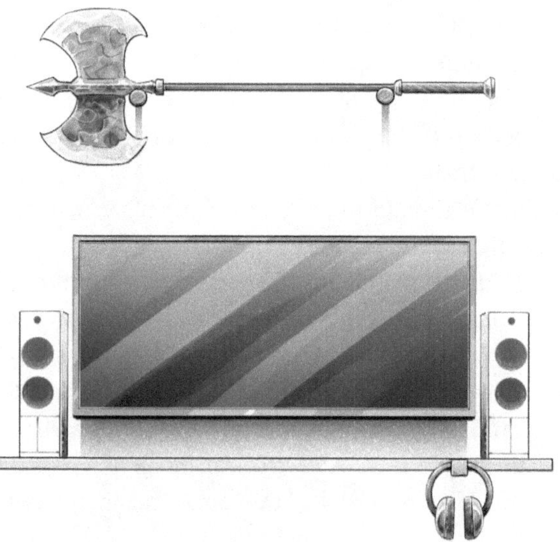

Kayda adjusted the dials on her sight to help better navigate in the dark. She didn't quite have night vision, but she could see in the dark far better than her human companions, who were all muttering under their breath about not being able to tell the difference between having their eyes open or closed. Alyssa, however, had relaxed considerably. The young vampire's ancestry likely would guide them even better than Kayda's.

Kayda still didn't know the details of how the girl had been turned in the first place. She didn't act like any vampire Kayda knew—though Kayda's experience was exceedingly limited. Other than the pronounced fangs and the decidedly traumatic childhood, the girl seemed like any other eight-year-old.

Kayda winced as she realized something. Alyssa hadn't expressed hunger yet, and all the chilled blood bags they'd pilfered from the hamlet were in a cooler in the back of the SUV. Gagan had said that refusing food in Navolt was a social faux pas. What if their food didn't mesh well with Alyssa's vampire constitution? Vomiting up bird food had to be more offensive than politely declining it.

Kayda rounded another bend in the seemingly never-ending tunnel system and softly called out the direction shift to her companions. She didn't know what to expect from Navolt, or what they were supposed to say to whoever was in the Colony Lodge, and yet somehow they had to convince these proud, sensitive, reclusive avians to help them. Kayda didn't have the first clue how to convince the avians to fly them to Elsher. Fiza had been horrified by Alyssa's mere presence; how would an avian feel about a vampire riding on their back?

Their plan might have been doomed the moment they picked up the little girl. Kayda bristled at the idea of Cathy being right yet again.

When Kayda finally reached what looked like a mundane door, a muffled commotion sounded behind her. Gagan, who had been bringing up the rear of their single-file procession, was making his way to the front now. Kayda placed a protective arm over Alyssa, like a crossbody seatbelt, and pressed Alyssa to her side. Alyssa shivered a little as Gagan walked past them and stood before the door. The door was ordinary enough, save for missing any kind of knob or handle.

As Gagan placed a palm against the metal door, a rune circle flared to life in bright blue below his hand. In a terrifying display of control, Gagan shifted only his head to that of his bird persona. He screeched a rapid-fire series of chirps, barks, and trumpet calls that were damn-near deafening in the narrow space.

A mechanism in the door unlocked with a reverberating *thunk*. As Gagan pulled his hand away and shifted back into a human, the thick metal door swung open. Warm sunlight poured into the tunnel and across the toes of Kayda's boots. She and Alyssa were still smushed against the wall. Their companions were clustered together in a tight knot behind Gagan.

No one moved.

Kayda considered throwing Alyssa over her shoulder and hot-footing it back to the car.

"Come," Gagan said, and stepped out into the sunshine.

Since none of her companions—not even the usually fearless Marisol—moved to follow him, Kayda gusted a heavy sigh and pushed away from the wall, pulling Alyssa along with her. A wide dirt-lined path sloped upward from the door—which she supposed made sense, seeing as they'd just emerged from a tunnel. The packed-mud walls on either side of her stretched up a good ten feet. They trudged up the incline. The temperature was cooler here, and the air smelled damp.

Once Kayda and the others reached flat land, they all turned in slow circles, mouths agape, as they took in their first full glimpse of Navolt. Kayda hoped gaping wasn't the same as gawking and that they weren't about to be struck down. She didn't understand what had kept her from seeing any of this while they'd been walking up the slope. Something like veil magic was at work in this place.

It felt like they'd just stepped into a rainforest. Wooden paths stretched in three directions from where they stood. Wide, vibrant-green palm fronds fanned out above moss-coated trunks, forming a canopy above each of the pathways. The greenery was so dense, darkness swallowed up the paths after a few feet. Around the base of the trees were leafy ferns and bushes dotted with bright red, pink, and purple flowers as big as Kayda's fist. Giant, vibrantly colored butterflies and iridescent beetles winged and buzzed by. All of the plants were dotted with beads of water, as if it had recently rained. There was a constant chittering of bird-song. The place felt alive in a way that couldn't even hold a candle to the hustle and bustle of Luma Proper in the early evening when the sidewalks were crowded and chatter and music spilled out of restaurants and bars.

Kayda pulled in a deep breath of fresh, clean air. Hells, if she was an avian, she wouldn't want to live anywhere else, either—and she'd only seen a fraction of it.

The all-green toucan-like bird that launched out of the canopy to snatch a butterfly the size of a mundane crow out of the air before zipping from sight again sort of killed the tranquility of the scene. The bird's massive beak had been at least two feet long. Kayda, even with her enhanced sight and hearing, hadn't sensed the bird until it was already in flight.

When she finally swung her gaze back toward Gagan, he at least looked a touch amused. Gaping in wonder was definitely different from gawking, then.

Gagan headed for the path straight ahead, rather than the ones that fanned to the left or right. That was fine by her; the all-green toucan had gone to the right. That didn't mean others weren't lurking in the lush green canopy above her head, though.

The rainforest stretched on for a while, populated by vibrant flowers, thick ropy vines covered in verdant leaves, and a handful of creatures Kayda had never seen before. Unseen animals added their song to those of the birds. Frogs croaked, snakes hissed, and insects buzzed. She wondered if the flying rodents with bat-like wings, the lizards with fans of scales along their backs as red as a sunrise, and the snail-like beings whose shells looked like roughly hewn rocks were from the fae realm or the product of magical manipulation. For all Kayda knew, creatures like this existed in mundane rainforests.

The rainforest slowly gave way to habitat similar to the one surrounding the hamlet where Kayda had found Alyssa. Pine became the dominant tree, the wooden path dotted occasionally with fallen needles. Some massive bird was screeching something fierce off in the distance. Kayda, remembering the massive dead Canada goose she'd seen lying on the rune array, feared that what she heard now was somehow larger.

When a break in the forest revealed packed earth dotted with mundane buildings, her brain couldn't reconcile what she heard with what she saw. She supposed she'd expected to see large nests in lieu of human-like dwellings.

Once they'd stepped off the walkway, it was clear they'd reached some kind of city or town center. The buildings didn't look like houses so much as restaurants or shops. Though, admittedly, Kayda couldn't see much beyond the backs of the buildings from here. Though the soft chatter of voices filtered to Kayda's ears, nature was still louder in Navolt.

"No gawking," Gagan reminded them, then started forward again.

The group walked in single file between two buildings made of stone and mud with thatched roofs. Gagan gave them another moment to get their bearings, standing impassively beside the group as if he were a patient teacher serving as chaperone to children on a field trip. Which wasn't that far off.

Humans and birds milled about in an area that reminded Kayda of a food court. Businesses arranged in a rough circle sat around an open courtyard dotted with tables and chairs. It appeared they were all made of wicker or bamboo. It wasn't a fountain that served as a focal point for the courtyard, but a pond. Two ducks whose size rivaled boats for children at an amusement park idly paddled around in water laden with lily pads. The ducks were beautiful—their bodies sporting blue, red, and yellow feathers, while their heads boasted striking sweeps of white along their cheeks and the base of their necks. Their orange beaks and bright-green caps made the ring of red around their eyes stand out even more.

Dotted among the benches were large circular troughs filled with a light pink substance frequently visited by hummingbirds the size of house cats. The continuous beating of their wings triggered Kayda's instinctual desire to swat away insects that buzzed too close to her ear. She supposed knocking a sapient hummingbird from the air would be an offense bad enough to land her in the hunting fields. Her gut told her that was where the horrific screeching had come from earlier. She imagined a bald eagle the size of a 747 and decided she didn't ever want confirmation of her theory.

No paved walkways snaked around the area, but there were a few signposts pointing out directions. A pole stood near a nectar trough with directional markers for The Bar, The Restaurant, The Cafe, and Snack Shack. Terribly creative names. The Orchards, Insect Farm, and Vegetable Garden were all to the right. Kayda glanced that way and easily spotted a four-story building—possibly the tallest building in the whole area—tucked among a copse of redwoods. It was easily a two to three-mile trek away.

Also to the right, but still within this town center, stood an onion dome–shaped building that reminded Kayda of the big top at a circus. It, too, was made of stone and mud and sported a thatched roof.

"That," Gagan said, pointing to the same building, "is the Colony Lodge. Kayda Verdan, you may choose one of your swarm to join us. The others are free to partake in a meal from The Restaurant. Breakfast is nearly upon us."

Kayda could only hope Cathy kept her grimace to herself. Goddess only knew what birds served for breakfast. "I choose Marisol Ortiz to join us. I assume it goes without question that Alyssa stays with me."

Gagan inclined his head. "You are essentially one entity."

Kayda turned to face her "swarm," and they huddled close together. They all eyed each other warily.

"I know I've been giving you a lot of grief, Kayda," Cathy muttered in a low voice, "but they seem to think of you as our bird-adjacent spokesperson. I'm a little worried about what's going to happen to the rest of us without your giant ass working as our shield."

"You're not very good at compliments," Alyssa said, and Kayda tamped down a smile.

"Just be polite—which I know is hard for you, Cathy, but your life might actually depend on it," Kayda said. "Don't refuse food."

Will piped up. "What if this meal isn't complimentary? Do they even use human currency?"

"I'm fresh out of bird seed," Quaid said.

Cathy snickered.

Kayda jabbed a finger at Quaid and Cathy in turn. "Get all that disrespectful shit out of your system now, 'cause if you get thrown in the hunting fields for being dicks, my giant ass isn't going in there to save you."

They both nodded tightly.

"It's just nerves," Will admitted, which was saying something, as the guy looked like a live-action GI Joe.

"Good luck," Kayda said, taking several steps back. "Let's go, Mari."

Marisol, uncharacteristically quiet, gave everyone a quick shoulder squeeze before heading Kayda's way. Will stared after Marisol a bit pensively, and Kayda figured Marisol was due for an uncomfortable conversation later.

Gagan's expression was still impassive, so it was hard to tell if he'd overheard any of that. "Come," he said once again, then turned on his heel and strolled toward the Colony Lodge.

Kayda easily fell into step beside him, keeping Alyssa on her other side. Marisol walked alongside Alyssa, still quiet. Perhaps Kayda's fearless friend was terrified of birds, too.

"Pardon my ineptitude," Kayda said in that seemingly uncontrollable affected tone that she took on when speaking to their avian guide, "but I'd rather stick my foot in my mouth with you, Gagan Darshelle, than in the Colony Lodge. Is it correct to assume we're meeting with the leaders of Navolt?"

Gagan's head tottered from side to side, and the slight breeze ruffled his feather hair. "Yes and no. We have elders. We make decisions based on community votes. The elders are our mouth-pieces when it comes to dealing with non-aves, as their decision-making stems from both knowing the will of the community and possessing the wisdom borne from age and experience. Two of our elders have been here since the so-called Glitch and had lived through many seasons before that. Some aves from the fae realm have life spans that rival those of dragons."

The small, knowing smile Gagan aimed at Kayda made her uneasy, if only because Gagan seemed to think Kayda had a stronger connection to her dragon ancestors than she actually had. If that imagined connection was supposed to sway the avians into helping Kayda and her companions get into Elsher, they were screwed.

The hustle and bustle of the town center hadn't dimmed much with their arrival, but Kayda felt eyes on her all the same. She wasn't sure if it was their otherness in general that made the avians keep a watchful eye, or if they'd sensed just how other Alyssa was. Kayda tightened her hold on the little girl's shoulder.

"Do the other aves know why we're here?" Kayda asked, hoping to distract herself from the death glare she and her companions were getting from an avian perched in a spindly tree they were going to have to walk past to get to the doors of the Colony Lodge. The avian wasn't that large, all things considered, but it was still larger than a sparrow should be. Despite being fully in bird form, its scowl was all human—and it was giving Kayda the heebies.

"The elders informed the populace that a member of the Food, Drug, and Magic Association had called in a personal favor and that those who were coming to speak to us had a topic of utmost importance to discuss," Gagan said, though his tone dripped with sarcasm. Clearly, he believed this whole thing was a waste of time. Perhaps the avians gave in to the whims of non-avians as much as they could stomach, if only to ensure the rest of the earthen realm otherwise left them alone. "The concerns of non-avians rarely affect us here. Our remote location is no accident."

Kayda thought of Elsher—also in a remote location—that had just been overrun. Alyssa was in Kayda's life because, not far from here, sorcerers were using yet another remote Canadian landscape to experiment with runework that could take down avians and use them as a food source for child ferals and hybrids like Alyssa. The "concerns of non-avians" might not have reached Navolt, but they were certainly creeping toward their doorstep. The idea of this beautiful place being sullied by monsters made Kayda's stomach turn.

So she smiled warmly at the basketball-sized grouchy sparrow in the tree as she passed it because she *wanted* that avian to continue living in exclusive, non-avian–hating Navolt. She wanted the sparrow to never have to worry about the world beyond this little haven if the avian didn't want to. She just had to hope that whatever she and Marisol came up with to tell the elders would be enough to convince them that this was the avians' fight, too, even if the only aid they provided was safe passage into Elsher.

Gagan stopped them just outside the entrance to the intimidatingly large Colony Lodge. The double doors were actually a curtain made of bamboo. The top of the jamb was several inches above Kayda's head. Chirps, whistles, screeches, and soft voices wafted out between the slats that gently swayed in the breeze like silent wind chimes.

Marisol spoke up for the first time in what felt like ages. "Are there rules about eye contact? Should we keep our heads bowed? Or use some kind of honorific to show our deference?"

In two graceful strides, Gagan had positioned himself between Marisol and the bamboo curtain. He crossed his arms and cocked his head in a very bird-like manner. His too-far-apart red eyes studied Marisol. "If I gave the impression that we seek deference over mutual respect, I apologize. As aves, we unsettle you. As humans, we repulse you. We've grown so accustomed to not fitting in anywhere in this realm that the majority of us have become bitter. But do not mistake our aloofness for an assumption of superiority."

Marisol nodded once. "Understood."

Gagan watched her a moment longer, clearly having expected an argument of some kind. When none came, he said, "Treat the elders—treat any of us—as you would anyone you respect, and you'll be fine." He turned toward the curtain and pushed a few pieces of hanging bamboo aside. Before he stepped through, he cast a glance over his shoulder. "Maiwenn Conure is our oldest elder. It is supremely disrespectful not to partake in her regurgitated offerings. If she lands upon your shoulder, open wide."

Kayda couldn't keep the grimace off her face. Marisol sucked in a gasp.

Alyssa yanked forcibly on Kayda's wrist, causing her to look down at the girl's horror-stricken face. "Does that mean we have to eat bird barf?"

Gagan's melodious chuckle faded as he slipped between the bamboo.

Kayda groaned. Just their luck to get an avian guide with a sense of humor. "Goddess help us," she muttered as stepped into the building, all but yanking a reluctant Marisol and Alyssa in after her.

CHAPTER TWENTY-SEVEN

RENATA

Renata hadn't been able to sleep. She'd tried, but nightmares about feral vampires had made that impossible. She'd trusted Paola and Joe—the two most experienced members of their group—when they'd said the group needed to rest, pack up supplies, and have some semblance of a plan. It was the smartest course of action, especially now that they seemed relatively safe in Dalton's apartment.

But Renata wanted *out* of Elsher. And she wanted out now.

She understood that there was nothing but endless stretches of wilderness outside the veil and that her terrible sense of direction would probably result in her accidentally walking off a cliff and into the ocean, but even that had to be better than staying trapped in the hub.

The four of them—Dalton, Paola, Joe, and herself—had gotten into Dalton's apartment yesterday with little fuss. Relatively speaking, anyway. They'd had a run-in with two more ferals who'd been prowling around like stray dogs. Joe had dispatched them with ruthless efficiency with that magical spear of his.

There'd been a handful of dead, picked-over, former residents in the lobby of Kensey Towers. One of them had been an elderly woman who worked as a cook at Cuisine Across the Realms. Her chest cavity had been torn open, most of the contents gone. Her eyes had been closed, which had somehow helped keep Renata's knees from buckling. No ferals had roamed the halls or loitered in the stairwells. Taking the stairs had been a necessity; the elevator didn't work. The power was out in the entire building—probably the entire hub. Which meant no access to the internet. No routers, no Wi-Fi. She couldn't even get her phone's hotspot to connect. Reception was always bad in this building, though, so she'd always had to rely on other methods to get in contact with her parents and sister.

She'd been dismayed that she and her companions had finally made it into the safety of Dalton's familiar apartment, only to still have no way to let anyone beyond Elsher know that they desperately needed help. Renata's own apartment was the next floor up. They'd wanted to get behind a locked door as soon as possible; hence, being crammed into Dalton's place.

There'd been a brief bout of panic when they reached Dalton's door only for Dalton to start frantically patting his pockets, realizing he'd left his house keys in his work desk drawer. Renata supposed it was lucky that, in addition to keys, most people used unlocking talismans for their doors. Since talismans could be crafted to look like a necklace, ring, or bracelet, people often wore their talismans daily as an accessory. He remembered soon enough that his unlocking ring was on his finger. Renata's own unlocking charm was around her neck.

With enough brute strength or lock picks, though, a door could still be forced open. Renata figured the talismans were more of a convenience than a safety measure—especially in a supposedly impenetrable place like Elsher.

They'd raided Dalton's dark, sparsely filled fridge, and his even emptier cabinets. Joe had nearly begged to take a shower after they ate, as the blood of one of the Bentley sisters still dotted his skin. Since he was experienced in stuff like this, Renata was unnerved by how twitchy he acted. Some part of her worried his sanity would give out and that Renata and her companions would end up the victims of friendly fire.

She couldn't blame the guy for wanting to shower, though. Renata planned to wash the dried, stinking feral blood off her own neck and face when it was time to venture up a floor to her place. She had to grab her travel talisman at the very least.

After Joe had showered, Renata, Dalton, and Paola had sat squished shoulder to shoulder on Dalton's small couch—with Dalton crammed in between the two ladies—while a freshly scrubbed Joe paced anxiously in front of the worn faux-leather ottoman that didn't match the sofa.

"*Joe,*" Paola had said, the quickly fired-off syllable like a gunshot.

Joe had flinched, halting abruptly. He'd hazarded a glance Paola's way, as if he feared he'd actually be staring down the barrel of a gun.

"What's this about Chancellor Thorpe *letting* these monsters in? And who in the hells is Lachlan Shade?" Paola had asked.

Joe had started talking a mile a minute. Thanks to his past involvement with the Vampire Hunters of America and his keeping abreast of the goings-on with the organization via VHoA's private forum, Joe was able to lay out a story that Renata would have dismissed out of hand for being ludicrous had she not seen the ferals with her own eyes. Hells, she was *still* having a hard time with it.

"The theory with the most legs," Joe had said, sucking in a lungful of air, "is that Lachlan has figured out how to get portals open to the fae realm, and he wants to have a monopoly on the magic. Once he can reliably open portals to the fae realm, he'll start opening them to other places, too." He shrugged hopelessly. "The idea of turning this realm into a waystation—like a magic-less bus stop—is insane. It'll throw everything into chaos. But he doesn't care about that. He's pissed about his thirty-year banishment and lost his mind along the way."

Paola had asked, "And he's in Elsher because we're the ones who know the most about opening portals? Seems like he knows a lot himself if he got himself back to the earthen realm."

Joe had looked nothing short of troubled. "I think, before he gets the portals open, he's going on a revenge tour. If he's got people like the chancellor helping him, whatever he's got planned is bigger than targeting the Collective in Luma. I'll eat my hat if Luma isn't one of the stops on his tour. The day he crawled out of exile, he reportedly said, 'Tell your Collective that Lachlan Shade has done the impossible. Tell them that I will do it again when they least expect it. They will pay for what they did to me.'"

The guy sounded looney tunes.

"If you work for the chancellor ..." Renata had said slowly, not sure where her own train of thought was headed, "and you found out she betrayed the entirety of the hub, how are you safe and sound here and not captured or worse?"

Joe had run a hand through his damp hair. "Luck." He'd swallowed hard before saying, "She's dead. The chancellor, I mean. There were half a dozen of us locked in her office when the attack started. Thankfully I got a call out to my VHoA contacts while

Thorpe was distracted, so I'm holding out hope that help is still coming.

"We went through lockdown procedures as if it was one of our monthly drills, and even though she instructed us to inform residents that we were being attacked by an unknown threat, once we finished with procedure, she told us what was actually happening. She said ferals and Lachlan Shade were in Elsher for a reason that was above our clearance level. She said if we cooperated, we'd be looped in.

"Once we were in full lockdown and the alarms went off, she made a phone call on her personal phone. Eventually she let Lachlan Shade himself into the office. He read a handful of names off a list, and when none of us were on it, he thanked us and said someone else would return in ten minutes to escort us to our new location. He told us not to be alarmed about what was going on outside the office, as it didn't concern us."

Renata had squeezed her hands into fists in anticipation of what was coming next—namely whatever had put that haunted look in the eye of a vampire hunter.

Joe had worried at his bottom lip while he'd stared into the middle distance, trapped in an image only he could see. When his eyes had refocused, he'd stared directly at Renata. His affect was flat—not manic like it had been earlier. "Chancellor Thorpe, without hesitation, opened the door at the sound of another knock. It was a hybrid that time. The hybrid stood in the doorway for a moment, sniffing the air like a damn dog. Thorpe asked where we were headed next, but the hybrid didn't answer. Then the hybrid made this weird barking sound, and two ferals barged into the room on either side of her. My coworkers started screaming. Chairs toppled over. People tripped over their own feet in their hurry to get away. Thorpe looked right at me when she realized we weren't, in fact, getting escorted anywhere. She mouthed that she was sorry. My stomach sank like a fucking stone. It was like she knew I was the only one in that room with any chance of surviving, given my history. I fully expected the hybrid to take

Thorpe by the arm, pull her out the door, and then leave the rest of us to die. But the hybrid went for Thorpe's throat instead.

"I keep my spear attached to the bottom of my desk. Holdover from my time as a hunter, I guess. By the time I'd pulled the spear free, Thorpe was already dead. The ferals were making quick work of the office staff, so once the hybrid was sated on sorcerer blood, she left the room, closing the door behind her so her mutants could feast in peace. I fought my way out. Killed both ferals and went out a window. Thorpe was right: I was the only one who made it out alive. I was the only one who knew how to kill them."

It was no wonder the guy had been desperate for a shower.

Dalton had awkwardly cleared his throat after several long tense seconds of silence. "Do you think Thorpe really believed this was some secret mission? Or was she telling you that to keep you calm?"

Joe had shrugged. "Some combination of the two. She ratted out the hub for her personal gain, I have no doubt. Whether she thought she'd successfully negotiated for the lives of her staff, I can't be sure. There was no mistaking how shocked she was that the hybrid turned on her, I can tell you that much. She didn't for a second believe she'd be added to the body count."

Paola's leg had been bouncing relentlessly in Renata's peripheral vision. "And you have no idea what Lachlan might have promised her?"

"No clue," Joe had said, running his hand through his hair again. "At this point, I don't really care. It doesn't matter. We just need to get out. Between you two," he said, waving a finger between Renata and Dalton, "we have two travel talismans, right? Mine's in my house. Why carry around car keys if you don't drive?"

The manic edge to the guy's voice had crept back in.

"I don't know how you two feel about breaking and entering, but I'm guessing the dead people in the lobby don't need their talismans anymore. I say we get some rest, then, early in the morning, if you know which units were theirs, I say we help ourselves. Same with their food."

"Shouldn't we go *now*?" Renata had asked.

Joe had shaken his head—hard. "It's too chaotic out there. The ferals are too hungry. We'll hunker down, get our strength back, and then see how things look in the morning." He'd hesitated then. "As far as I know, the telepad in the residential sector hasn't been blown up yet. If they're going to destroy it, it'll be soon. We don't want to get turned to mist on the wind in transit. We can cover more ground between here and home if we can use the pad to get out, but if it's compromised, we're going to need supplies to get us through the hike back to civilization. And for that hike, we can't be exhausted."

Renata had worried at her bottom lip, resisting the urge to point out that they didn't know how overrun with ferals the world was beyond the veil. Now that actually fleeing the hub was a possibility, she wanted nothing more than to scuttle under Dalton's bed and pray the Goddess sent the help Joe believed was coming. Getting out might solve one problem while creating a whole host of new ones.

They'd gone to bed after that—or at least tried to—each with a weapon nearby. Renata had taken a quick, frigid shower, then had to put her day-old undergarments back on. Dalton let her borrow one of his shirts to sleep in.

Renata had taken Dalton's bed while he slept on the floor. Paola and Joe attempted to share the pull-out couch. She was almost positive the occasional squeak of old springs coming from the living room was from one of them tossing and turning and not that they were hooking up out there.

The thought that kept plaguing Renata's sleepless mind all night—other than her wishing she had the guts to ask Dalton if he wanted to be the big spoon—was that she didn't fully trust Joe, though she couldn't say why. She didn't think he was up to anything fishy, per se. She didn't think he'd been sent into the residential sector by Chancellor Thorpe—who was still alive in this scenario—solely to look for her and Dalton.

His anxious vibe threw her off, though. So much so that it was hard to stay focused. Inability to maintain focus under pressure had always been Renata's downfall. It was a wonder she'd passed her exams at the academy, especially when so many of them had been a public affair.

When she heard either Paola or Joe creeping around the apartment in the morning, she gratefully flung off the comforter. Begrudgingly, she pulled yesterday's dirty and stained jeans back on, then tiptoed toward the door.

Dalton propped himself up on an elbow just as she made it to the threshold. His eyes were bloodshot. "Couldn't sleep, either?"

"Nope," she said, sighing.

When the four of them met up in the living room, Joe reiterated the same plan he'd suggested last night: raid apartments of fellow residents, collect their food, and find as many travel talismans as possible.

Renata said, "Mrs. Wiltshire was one of the people we saw in the lobby. She lived alone and had an apartment a few doors down from mine. Dalton and I can go up to my floor to get my talisman, and then we can look for hers. I need to change and pack fresh clothes, too. My fridge and pantry weren't well stocked, but I've at least got some snacks we can take. And a couple of sleeping bags."

Dalton's brows smashed together. His expression asked, *What are you talking about? Mrs. Wiltshire lived on the* first *floor.* When his expression leveled out to something more neutral a moment later, she knew he was going to roll with the lie, even if he didn't understand the reason for it. "Too bad we can't just drive out of here, huh? Would make this so much easier."

There *were* vehicles in the hub, but without functional vehicle telepads or vehicle-specific travel talismans, the veil magic—once a car crashed through it—would render the car inoperable. Or the people inside. Probably both.

"Seems like it would be safer to have me or Joe go with you, Ren," Paola said, her concern evident in every line of her face. "You both still look wrecked *and* you're the least experienced with dealing with ferals."

Dalton took a few steps toward Paola. Using a hand to cup near his mouth, he spoke to her in low tones. Renata could still hear him if she slowed her breathing. "She had nightmares all night. She's stressed. I can talk her off the ledge, but I need a little quiet time to do it. You know how she gets. This would be a lot for anyone, but she's … sensitive."

Paola offered a soft noise of agreement. Renata, who dutifully did her best to stare off into the middle distance with a haunted look in her eye, tried not to be offended.

"We'll be quick," Dalton said, still whispering. "Being in her own apartment will help too, I think."

"Fine. But don't dillydally," Paola said, whispering as well, but far louder than Dalton. "Life-and-death situations make people bolder; don't use this as your opportunity to finally make your move. Though I guess you should have done it last night. Either way, we can't spare the time."

Renata's cheeks heated. Dalton spluttered.

The sound startled Joe out of the muttered conversation he'd been having with himself.

Paola wouldn't let the pair leave until Renata took a weapon from Dalton's knife block. Renata had grown too fond of her blood-splattered and gore-encrusted broom to give it up, so she merely added the knife to her arsenal.

The last thing Paola handed them was a pair of empty pillowcases so they could load them with supplies.

"Meet back here in two hours," Paola said as the pair stood outside Dalton's apartment in the quiet hallway. No new bodies—feral or otherwise—had materialized overnight. Joe passed behind her periodically, scouring the small apartment again for more makeshift weapons. Clearly, sleep hadn't calmed the guy down.

After setting timers on their phones, Renata and Dalton headed for the stairs.

"Please don't die!" Paola called after them.

The journey down the hallway, up one flight of stairs, and to her own apartment was uneventful, but Renata's pulse still hammered in her ears, even after she and Dalton were safely inside. The recently used unlocking talisman under her shirt radiated a faint warmth against her skin.

"Thanks for coming up here with me," Renata finally said from where she stood with her back against her door.

She figured if she sensed movement in her tiny apartment, being as close to the door as possible was the safest option. Dalton, however, had immediately started prowling the space, checking under her bed, behind her love seat, and in the bathroom.

He came to a stop in front of her, arms crossed. "Of course. What's up?"

"We might be in bigger trouble than the obvious," she said. "I think it *might* be safe to tell Paola this, but not Joe. Something about the guy makes me nervous." Then she told him about her suspicions regarding Joan Calder and that Renata and Dalton might be on the master list. She hadn't had a quiet moment with him until now to unload that. "If someone comes for us, they could take you and me and turn the ferals on Paola. I can't stand the thought of it. Joe already went through that once, and I think it broke him. Who knows what he'd say or do to avoid dealing with it again? Maybe he'd rat us out to save him himself."

"Doesn't sound like that plan worked out too well for Chancellor Thorpe," Dalton said, having remained quiet for the entirety of Renata's monologue. His eyes had widened at opportune times, but otherwise he'd let her ramble, knowing she'd need to purge everything before she could relax. If she'd been able to say all this last night, maybe she would have slept better. "I can't believe Joan Calder is potentially a jerk."

Renata heaved a breath of relief, realizing she'd been worried

Dalton would admonish her for being foolish enough to divulge so much personal information to Calder.

"Survival-wise, I think we'd be safer if we stick with Joe and Paola. They're better suited to this than we are," Renata said. "But if we get caught before we can get out, we're all screwed, just in different ways."

Dalton considered this. "You think we should ditch them? We could try to get out instead of meeting them in a couple of hours. We can find some more travel talismans in the other apartments, then leave them outside your door with a note on the door telling them not to look for us. Joe might be squirrelly, but he can hold his own in a fight. Paola would be safe with him." He reached into his pocket and pulled out the travel talisman he must have grabbed from his own apartment. "Go take care of what you need to and pack and all that. I'll get the food. After we find some more supplies, we'll get out of here, okay?"

She couldn't decide if she wanted to cry or kiss him, so she just nodded and hurried to the bathroom.

Within twenty minutes, she was clean, changed, and packed. They discussed which apartments to search, then crept back into the hallway. Three of the fifteen doors they checked were unlocked. They loaded their pillowcases with food and found two more travel talismans after poking around in people's drawers. It felt creepy doing this, but Renata kept telling herself Joe had been right about this part—if the residents of these apartments were dead, they didn't need this stuff.

By the time they got back to Renata's place, they were loaded down with supplies, which made her feel a little less guilty about ditching Paola, if only because they were helping give the woman a better chance at surviving.

Even still, as she and Dalton did a final assessment of their haul, Renata was so anxious about this being an epically terrible mistake, she felt vaguely ill. They were just grabbing the handles of their duffel bags when someone knocked on the door with three rapid taps.

Dalton stilled. Renata whirled toward the door. It couldn't be Paola. Renata hadn't told her which apartment was hers. Unless Paola was knocking on every door up here in a desperate attempt to find them because something in the plan had gone awry. Maybe they'd been ambushed.

"Renata?" came a muffled, semi-familiar voice. "Renata, it's Megan. Are you here? Please tell me you're here …"

Megan! She was alive! Megan was Renata's friend from Lab 4. Renata had seen the broken-down door to her friend's lab and had feared the worst.

Renata turned to Dalton, brows raised. He knew Meg, too. They'd been frequent lunch companions, and the trio had met with other residents around their age for occasional game nights or group events at the bowling alley and arcade. Renata had actually feared for a while that Dalton had a crush on Megan.

Dalton said, "Let's let her in. She might have information about the residential sector telepad."

"Ren?" A series of frantic knocks. "Renata?"

Nodding, Renata hurried to the door and pulled it open.

It was in fact her friend who stood there, but the expression on her sweet, heart-shaped face made Renata take a step back. Her cheeks and nose were splotched; she'd been crying. One eye was swollen shut. Her bottom lip was split.

"*Megan*?" Renata asked cautiously when her friend didn't rush inside. Instead, she seemed to sway on her feet, as if she were moments from collapsing. Renata somehow knew it wasn't exhaustion that weakened her friend's knees, but something else.

"What the hells is *that*?" Dalton asked from behind her.

Renata tore her gaze away from her friend's face.

A cloud of black darkened the doorjamb. At first Renata thought it was a swarm of flies—conjuring images of Lab 4's lobby and the bodies covered in buzzing insects. But the cloud was … *solid*. Like ink—ink that seemed to have a mind of its own as it crept along the edges of the doorway and then oozed up the walls, over the floor, and across the ceiling. Renata took small steps backward as the black mass seeped into her apartment. She eventually crashed, albeit very gently, into Dalton. She issued a peep of alarm.

The jolt made her focus shift, and her gaze slid to Megan, still swaying just beyond the door. The inky black coursed around her, like she was an immovable boulder in a river.

"The theatrics are hardly necessary, Teo," a man's voice said, though Renata couldn't have pinpointed the direction it had come from. "We need her to help, after all."

A sigh gusted out of an unseen mouth—the breath warming Renata's ear. She flinched hard. Dalton clasped his hands around her hips, whether to be a grounding force or to still his own trembling, she couldn't be sure. Her head whipped toward the left, fully expecting to see someone standing there.

For a moment, she saw nothing out of the ordinary. Same short stretch of tiled floor that went from dining room to kitchenette. Fridge, wooden cabinets, faux marble counters, and the hand-me-down toaster oven whose handle had fallen off a month ago. A blink later, a column of black ink rose from the puddle that was quickly engulfing her apartment's floor. The column went from a gelatinous blob to something man-shaped, and then the black slipped off entirely, as if someone had dumped a bucket of water over the man's head, washing away the clinging black.

Dalton's fingertips dug into Renata's hips—an instinctive reaction, she guessed. Her teeth hurt from how hard she clenched them.

Renata never paid much attention to a person's eyes unless they were a striking, unusual color—like bright blue or green paired with a dark complexion. Otherwise, eyes were eyes. This guy's, though … they were hard to miss. Swirling black—much like the ink he'd just materialized out of—danced in the whites of his eyes. Wrongness wafted off him. The kind of wrongness that made the hair on your arms rise and your heart rate take off at a gallop.

He sniffed the air, his nose bobbing gently, like a bunny. "They're *both* magic-touched. Can I eat one?"

"No, Teo," the second voice said, sounding a touch annoyed. "We have food for you back at the town center. It's only been a few hours since you ate. You'll survive."

Teo's mouth had parted as he stared at Renata and Dalton. Saliva beaded on the end of one fang. Renata pushed a little harder against Dalton's chest. The look in Teo's bizarre eyes said he was unlikely to listen to the disembodied voice.

Several things happened in a matter of seconds. Teo hissed like a possessed cat. A second figure winked into existence to Renata's right, a rune array already being cast. The moment Teo lunged for Renata, the second man hurled the array. The glowing gold disc of magic slammed into Teo center mass, flinging him backward and into the kitchenette. The broken handle was the least of the toaster oven's problems now. Teo rolled off the counter and onto the floor. It took him several moments to get back to his feet.

Renata hazarded a glance at her "savior." It was the same elf from the town center—the one who was missing half of his left arm. The elf who commanded ferals. The elf who seemed to be the mastermind of Elsher's ambush. The elf who had a list of residents, courtesy of the now-dead Chancellor Thorpe.

Lachlan Shade was *in* her apartment.

Dalton was holding her so tightly now, she was sure she'd be bruised.

"Megan?" Lachlan called out. "Are these Renata Bernard and Dalton Edwards from Lab 9?"

Renata's gaze snapped to her friend still swaying listlessly in the hallway.

Lucidity overtook Megan for a few seconds as her focus skated over Renata and then Dalton behind her. "Yes, sir," she said, and then the lucidity leached right back out.

"Excellent." Lachlan waved a dismissive hand toward the still-open door. "Teo, *that* one you can eat."

Renata barely had the chance to scream a protest before Teo

was on Megan like a lion taking down a wounded gazelle. In what felt like moments, Megan, as pale as a ghost, hit the floor with a meaty thud. Teo, grinning a bloody smile, turned to face them. Blood trickled down his chin, and he wiped it away with the underside of his wrist.

"That was an unexpected treat," Teo said. "She had sorcerer blood—not much, but enough to give an added kick. Maybe her grandparents?"

Lachlan didn't seem interested in Megan's family tree. He smiled down at Renata. "It's nice to finally meet you, Miss Bernard. Mr. Edwards. I was worried you'd managed to escape. And given the packed bags, it looks like I caught you just in time. I need your help. Cooperate, and you'll both live. I have associates waiting in the wings in both Fredericksburg and Ione to help further dissuade you from being combative if necessary."

Saliva flooded Renata's mouth. How in the hells did he know where their families lived? Had he gotten that information out of Megan, too? Goddess knew what he'd done to her to turn her into that zombie-like version of herself.

"After you," Lachlan said, gesturing dramatically to the doorway no longer overrun with living black ink.

"We have no choice," Dalton whispered in her ear, confirming what her gut had already told her.

Leaving behind her belongings, all of their collected supplies, and her home for the last year, she stiffly walked forward. Her only comfort was Dalton's presence behind her.

As she stepped over the exsanguinated body of her friend in the hallway, her heart hammering so hard she was half convinced it would shatter her rib cage, she hoped Paola and Joe were still safe and that Teo had not drained them, too.

She mentally shook her head. Hope couldn't help her now—not with beings as unholy as ferals, Teo, and Lachlan Shade running around Elsher.

No, hope had died in the hallway with Megan.

CHAPTER TWENTY-EIGHT

FELIX

The continued lack of an update from Harlow was stressing Felix out. He sat in his car in the parking lot of the Ghost Lily, staring at the brick wall across from him. Spike had finished her cigarette and ambled back inside.

He debated, once again, going to the Tower today, just to check things out. Then he thought of the new information he'd gotten from Spike, and the itch to start researching reignited. He drove to his private office, where he could remotely access his Tower computer.

He'd just pulled into the small communal lot for the office park when his phone propped on the dash rang. His hope that it was Harlow checking in quickly morphed into surprise when he saw who was calling.

"Hi, Laurel."

"Oh. Hi, Officer Turner. I, um, is this an okay time? Oh gosh, I just realized how early it is."

"No worries. This is great," Felix said, glad she couldn't see the instinctive wince that had overtaken his face at the sound of her gravelly voice. "What can I help you with?"

"I remembered something. I wanted to tell you about it while it was fresh in my mind."

"Oh, that's great. Hit me," he said, scrambling for his glove box and the notebook he kept inside.

"Well, remember how I told you I donated venom for a while when I was younger?"

"Yeah, to help you make some extra cash, right?"

"Right. There was a venom donation center in Fresno. It was run out of a legit clinic in a shopping center. The name of the clinic was Blissful Bounty. When vamps went in to donate venom, they'd tell the receptionist they were there for their weekly checkup. One of my jobs was to pick up the venom donations every two weeks or so and deliver them. I had one of those ride-share stickers on my window, and I had one of those refrigerated bags in my car like food delivery people have."

Felix scribbled in his notebook. "How much venom would you pick up at once?"

"It would depend. But there were usually at least thirty vials. A vamp can donate one to three milliliters of venom in one sitting. I don't know the details of how Bliss is made, but thirty vials would go a long way in making the stuff." Laurel cleared her throat, and it sounded like it hurt. "Sorry, one sec. I need some water."

Felix made a few more notes while he waited for her to continue.

"Okay, I'm back. The clinic isn't even the part I wanted to tell you about," she said, sounding genuinely excited. "I would take the vials from Blissful Bounty and then drive them fifteen to twenty minutes into a residential neighborhood. I dropped them off at the same house every time. The details on the house are still fuzzy—I'm not even sure what color it was or if there was grass out front. But I do remember that the address was printed on this plastic box thing that was stuck on the side of the house. It almost looked like a butter dish—rectangular-shaped and made out of white plastic. The numbers were printed black and bold so you could really see them from the street. At night, the box lit up. Two-six-seven. I can see that in my head as clear as day. All the houses looked pretty similar, I think, so the numbers standing out like that really helped me find the right house."

Felix wrote down "267" and underlined it. "Any chance you remember the street name?"

"Started with an S-T. Strommel. Strovel. Sorry, that's all I've got."

"Don't sweat it. This is really great," Felix said, hoping someone familiar with the Fresno area had flagged a house with a similar address as one to watch.

"I can tell you who lived there, though," Laurel said.

Felix's brows hiked. "Really?"

"Darius Morton."

He stilled. "As in the vamp who got you hooked on fae blood in the first place?"

"Yes," Laurel said sharply. "Him."

It would seem that with her memories came strong emotions.

Laurel continued. "He wasn't the only manufacturer of Bliss in that area, but he had a pretty big operation. The front rooms of his house had windows facing the street and were decorated to look quote-unquote normal. He kept the blinds at half-mast and watched TV in there during prime-time hours to keep up the illusion for the neighbors that he was just as normal as they were. He even got a cat who sat in the windows overlooking the street. The rest of the house, though? Gutted and turned into a Bliss lab."

Felix whistled. "This is incredibly helpful, Laurel." He chewed on his bottom lip. Even though he wouldn't sit on this information regardless of how Laurel responded, he still said, "I know Darius meant something to you once—like the father you wished you'd had. But I need you to understand that if we investigate this, and the tip proves good, Darius could end up—"

Laurel barreled over Felix. "As much as Darius opened my eyes to what my mother had been hiding about who I was, I know now that he exploited that naivete. I'm grateful to him, but I despise him ten times as much. I want to help stop him from doing this to more young vamp kids. Not to mention all the fae kids … the kids I …" She paused. "I knew deep down what was happening to those kids. I was in a fog I couldn't find my way out of, but I wasn't stupid.

"I picked those kids up and dropped them off to Darius, even though I knew what would happen to them, because my addiction had such a chokehold on me. But it's no excuse. I can spend the rest of my life trying to make up for all the pain I caused, and it'll never be enough. I know that." She sniffled. "The guilt would have killed me by now if it wasn't for this baby. Getting Darius caught and his lab destroyed will be a start toward lessening that guilt a little. So I'm going to keep telling you everything I can remember, Mr. Turner, and I'm going to do as right by this baby in my belly as I can, because it's all I've got. I don't owe Darius Morton shit. Not anymore."

Felix smiled softly to himself. "Glad to hear it. I'll start researching this. And I'm still waiting on word from my sorcerer buddies about those runes, but know I'm working on it."

"I appreciate you, Mr. Turner. Thank you for trying."

He said his goodbyes to Laurel.

All the women in his life—no matter the strength of their

connection—were either stressing him out or giving him too much to think about lately.

By the time he arrived at his office, Harlow still hadn't replied. He *did* have a message from Marisol, though. Seeing her name on his screen made him smile for all of a second before he saw what her message said.

> **Marisol**
> I don't know how long my reception will last, but I'm in Canada. I might get murdered by bird people. In case I meet my end via talon, I just wanted to tell you I like you—a lot. (I can't believe you didn't tell me you dated Harlow!)

Shit.

> **Felix**
> Mari, what the hells do you mean you might get murdered by BIRD PEOPLE? Is that code? (I like you a lot, too.) (And I was going to tell you, I swear.)

A "delivered" notification didn't pop up under the text bubble. Then the bubble changed colors, a clear sign Marisol didn't have reception. Great.

"This is not a good omen for the day," he muttered to himself.

Felix wasn't one for superstitions, but his partner, Deever, was the department's black cloud. Bad luck followed that guy around like a stray puppy. Deever—the pain in the ass—was on vacation for the next two weeks. But now Felix was starting to think that the pall of the black cloud curse had settled over him in Deever's absence.

Now he was worried about Marisol, too.

And Harlow *still* hadn't replied.

> **Felix**
> Harlow, please answer me.

After letting himself into his office, he made coffee, booted up his computer, and warmed up a leftover burrito in the ancient microwave his mother had given him when his parents bought a new one a couple of years ago.

When he sat down at his desk with his food and extra-strong coffee, he checked his phone again.

> **Felix**
> Can you at least let me know if you're ghosting me on purpose?

Nothing.

Groaning, he tossed his phone into a drawer and slid it closed, telling himself he had to get at least an hour of work done before he really started to panic about the fate of the Fletchers. It was still early. She could be asleep. Granted, that wouldn't explain yesterday's complete radio silence …

Felix wanted to discuss his newly acquired information from Laurel with a Fresno-based cop buddy of his, but he wasn't in the right headspace for that call yet. So instead, Felix got to work on the Naomi West case.

Luckily, Yuri Bruin was a much less common name than Tatton Fairchild. The guy had gotten arrested nearly a dozen times for starting drunken bar brawls. Most of his victims were mundanes who'd ended up on the wrong side of the pit-fighter's fists. Spike's assessment of the guy might hold some weight—his life's path seemed to mirror that of Tatton's. He'd fought for cash in largely illegal pit fights against other shifters when he was younger, got into security work in his twenties, and then somehow wound up at the Ghost Lily. Felix wondered if Yuri had a personal connection to Tatton or if he just idolized the shifter.

According to Yuri's file, Tatton wasn't an immediate relative.

After another twenty minutes of digging around, Felix found a heavily redacted transfer request for a Tatton Fairchild dated eight years ago. From what little Felix could glean, this was the shifter in question, and he'd, in fact, been sent to Lideg, the Antarctic hub. Everything Felix could find pointed to the shifter still being locked up there.

He searched for Ella Sellers next—the name of the waitress who had most likely put the name Tatton into Denise West's head. Felix included first names like Ellen, Eleanor, Elizabeth, Arabella, and Gabriella in his search, in case "Ella" had been a nickname. A search of the Tower's archives proved fruitless. Either Ella Sellers hadn't had any run-ins with the law while she'd been in Luma, or Felix didn't have the right name.

He turned his search to social media on Forage and mundane sites. The waitstaff at the Ghost Lily seemed to be evenly split between fae and mundane. Spike had said Ella's sudden disappearance wasn't completely out of the ordinary, given the woman's history—whatever that might mean. It was possible she'd gotten spooked or found another job opportunity and slipped out into the vast mundane world.

But the timeline of Ella talking to Denise four years ago and disappearing around that same time worried Felix. After all, four years ago was when Denise herself had been followed home by a bear shifter who then beat her senseless, after telling her to stop harassing Oliver Randal. It was possible that same brute had seen Ella and Denise talking and had gone after the waitress.

Spike's theory was that the same fate that had befallen Naomi.

Sent into Luma at Camila's request to keep tabs on her daughter, Naomi had also been nosing around the Ghost Lily in search of what might be happening to fae teens who'd last been seen at the bar. Felix suspected that Naomi had originally joined the Fletchers in their on-going investigation of Bliss and fae trafficking because Naomi was still looking for her brother, Charlie.

When Felix had bumped into Camila on a job a little over half a year ago, it was the first time they'd seen each other in six years. Camila hadn't known Felix had joined the bounty hunters until then. He'd wanted to interrogate her about that fateful night that had resulted in her exile and Nelson's death, but Camila only wanted to talk about Harlow. That was the day he'd learned that, not only was Camila alive, but Naomi had been sent by Camila to spy on Harlow.

And Felix hadn't been able to tell Harlow any of it. He'd been in the mundane world chasing down a bounty who'd fled the hub system. Since he'd technically been working for the Collective at the time, most of what he'd learned on that trip had gotten locked behind the stupid Soul NDA.

Mere speculation told Felix that it was just as likely that Naomi's side mission at the Ghost Lily was something the two women had concocted together as it was that Naomi had been acting on her own. In either case, she'd asked too many questions of the wrong people, and they'd shut her up for good.

On Forage, he finally hit pay dirt.

A social media page had been set up for an Elizabeth Sellers. She was mundane, thirty-two at the time of her disappearance, and was last seen by her coworkers at the Ghost Lily. When she didn't call her mother for over two days, whom she spoke to daily, her mother had called the Luma PD and requested a wellness check. Elizabeth wasn't inside her apartment, but her beloved dog was. The apartment wasn't ransacked, her empty suitcases were still in the closet, and her dog—a black lab—had done its business on the carpet in a few places since it hadn't been let out.

At the end of the pinned post at the top of the page was a quote from Ella's mother. "I know something awful happened to my girl. She'd been doing so good. Got herself clean, was going to meetings, and was holding down her job. If she decided to leave town, she would have told me. And she never would have left Smokey behind—never. That dog was her whole heart."

Felix was pissed all over again that the Ghost Lily was allowed to keep operating despite everything.

Naomi West: Dead.
Elizabeth Sellers: Dead.
Denise West: Beaten and scared out of town.

Then there were the countless teens who had been trafficked in and out of there. The girls Harlow had helped find were an exception to what usually happened to anyone caught in the Ghost Lily's web.

Then there was Felix himself. It was looking more and more likely that the goons who ran the cleanup crew for Jalen Graves and his allies had come *this close* to taking out him and Harlow, too.

If Felix could prove which Collective sorcerer—or sorcerers—was in bed with Graves, he could take that proof to Sorceress Rhiannon. He had doubts about the breadth of her loyalties, but he knew the nonsense going on at the Ghost Lily was of personal interest to her. A few idle comments here and there suggested she thought one of her own was running the place, too. Felix wasn't under any delusions that the sorceress's main concern was that of the young lives irreparably harmed, if not wholly snuffed out. She was more concerned with the bigger picture—and her colleagues' role in it.

She'd been the one who'd put the viper metaphor in his head —the same one he'd told Harlow, hoping it would help make her understand that he wasn't just a mindless Collective hired hand.

If you're in the pit of vipers, you're in a better position to chop off their heads.

A muted buzz issued from the top drawer of his desk and Felix hastily pulled it open, hoping a message from Marisol or Harlow would be waiting for him.

Instead, it was an alert that one of the alarm talismans had just been triggered outside his house.

Movement on his computer screen pulled his attention away from his phone. Another alert. This one was triggered *here.*

Though his clients met him at his office on occasion, and this address was listed as a business on legal paperwork, he hadn't hung a shingle out front welcoming randos to waltz in looking for a PI. He kept the blinds shuttered and the door locked.

He'd buried and carefully hidden a good number of ward,

alarm, and protection talismans around the front porch, the windows, and the only door. The alarm talismans were tailored to alert him about certain fae lurking closer to the office than a random passerby strolling down the sidewalk. He had one set to detect pixies in particular, lesser fae in general, feline shifters, large animal shifters, and one specifically for badger shifters, as good things rarely happened when one of those unhinged loons showed up.

The alarm going off now was from a window at the back of the office—one not facing the street, and one rarely visited by anyone other than the occasional maintenance worker doing basic upkeep on the building.

A non-feline shifter had triggered it. The windows were all warded with anti-tampering spells that he'd had installed by a witch the day he moved into this office two years ago. The spells had to be topped off every three months. The wards were Level 3 —enough to knock fae on their ass without any potential magical shrapnel killing Felix if he was standing too close to a breached window. If an intruder was determined and strong enough, though, the ward might not accomplish anything other than giving Felix a few extra seconds to flee. He eyed his front entrance, searching for any hulking shadows beyond the covered windows.

The ward on the door was only a Level 2, if only because door wards were more expensive, and Felix had blown most of his security budget on the windows. Maintaining them all cut a hefty chunk out of his monthly budget, but between being a bounty hunter and a PI and having the ever-loving shit beaten out of him with tire irons five years ago, he was of the opinion that what he spent to protect himself wasn't nearly enough. Not for a mundane in Luma.

He pulled up his text threads.

> **Felix**
> Barth, I might be in trouble. I'm at my office

A timestamp almost immediately appeared below his message. No dots popped up to indicate his friend was typing.

"Asshole," Felix muttered.

Bartholomew had left Felix on read.

But Felix also knew the cat was probably already halfway here or was calling for reinforcements. Probably both.

Annoying as he was loyal, that was Bartholomew Scratch.

Another alert popped up on his computer screen. Non-feline shifter near the hedges on the west side of the building.

Felix really hoped it wasn't Spike who had sold him out. He liked her.

Hastily dropping his phone on the desk, he reached underneath it and pressed a thumb to the button embedded in the side of the left drawer pedestal. He winced at the sharp bite of pain. Blood welled in a perfect bead on the pad of his thumb. He quickly swiveled in his chair and bent over double before swiping the blood on the linoleum floor.

One second. Two.

Felix swiveled back to his desk, attempting to look the picture of calm.

Just as the front door was forcibly slammed open—the ward on the door giving off sparks of red lightning as the spell zapped the intruder before fizzling out a moment later—three nested circles of an elaborate rune array flared to life in a sea of brilliant blue. Felix's desk was positioned directly in the middle of the protective circle.

This one had cost more than all the other wards and talismans combined.

The yoked-out guy heaving in the doorway was cursing something fierce as he slapped at his clothes with his baseball mitt–sized hands. A faint aroma of burnt hair wafted through the room.

The man stalked into the office and kicked the door shut behind him. The doorjamb was charred in places, and the door didn't fully shut now. It would be a pain in the ass to get it replaced, but at least Felix wasn't currently dead.

Felix, feeling reasonably safe in his magical bubble, sighed. "You could have knocked, Yuri."

He'd seen the bear shifter's picture enough times in the last hour or two to recognize him instantly.

Yuri only let the surprise register in his dark eyes for a moment before he stalked to the edge of the rune array. He folded his large arms over his large chest. "I ain't got nowhere else to be, FT97. I'll just wait here till your bitch-ass spell runs out."

The guy's voice didn't match his face. It wasn't nasally so much as high and raspy.

Goose bumps broke out along Felix's arms the moment he heard it. It was confirmation he never thought he'd get. Yuri was one of the assholes who had come at him with tire irons all those years ago. He'd recognize that voice anywhere.

Which also meant this was one of the fuckers who had been stalking Harlow and had thrown pictures of her at Felix's feet as he lay bleeding and half-conscious on a bathroom floor.

Yuri grinned then, as if he saw the recognition flash across Felix's face and was pleased by it.

Another alert popped up on Felix's phone. He glanced away from Yuri's smug face for a moment to get confirmation of what he already feared. The front door of his house had been breached.

Yuri's partner in crime was *in* Felix's house. Thankfully, no one lived there other than him—not anymore anyway. He didn't even have a pet these brutes could torture.

Felix tried to sound nonchalant as he glanced back up at Yuri. "A lot of people are going to come looking for me if I disappear, Yuri. You won't be able to cover up my death as easily as you covered up Naomi West's or Ella Sellers's."

Yuri merely tapped the face of his nonexistent wristwatch, unfazed. It wasn't an admission that he'd killed them, but it wasn't a denial, either.

"I was just a guy trying to figure out what happened to a friend the last time you and I hung out," Felix said casually, silently begging Bartholomew to hurry the fuck up. There was maybe a minute left on the protection circle before the magic winked out. "I work for the Collective now. Guessing you know that, though. They sink too many resources into their bounty hunters to just shrug their shoulders at the mysterious disappearance of one of their assets. I suggest you rethink this—or you're going to end up in Lideg just like the disgraced Tatton Fairchild."

Yuri's face pinched minutely, but he otherwise didn't give in to the bait. Instead, he said, "It was fortuminous you decided to stick your nose in the wrong place again, today of all days."

Felix was so instantly on alert over that, he hardly registered Yuri's botched attempt at trying out words with more than three syllables.

"Oh ho!" Yuri said, chuckling. He sounded like a quickly deflating balloon when he laughed. "Maybe you don't know. That broad you dropped like a hot potato is at the Tower right now. She can't keep her nose outta stuff that ain't none of her business neither. I was told if you started in on your nosy bullshit—'specially today—I get to stop you by any meats necessary. Your bosses ain't gonna come looking for you if they's the ones who told me to come after you in the first place, are they?"

Going out on a limb, Felix said, "Jeffries is going through a hells of a lot of trouble just to keep his hybrid friends and hired thugs happy."

Yuri shrugged. "Rich dude thinking, you feel me? Got too much cash and not enough drama in his life, so he's gotta go find it for himself. Likes to be part of the party, even if no one wants his square ass there. He's good at bullshitting—claiming he's scarier than he is. Talks big, even though he doesn't really know what's going on most of the time. Kinda like you."

Buzz!

Buzz!

Buzz!

Three new alerts popped up on his laptop screen in rapid succession. Followed by at least half a dozen more.

The rune array surrounding Felix's desk flickered. Only seconds left now.

Slowly, he pulled a charmed machete free from its mounting hooks on the pedestal opposite the array-activating button. If Yuri noticed, he didn't show it. He was too busy grinning like a loon and cracking his knuckles. Keeping his arms below the desk, Felix pulled the machete from its magic-dampening scabbard.

Two seconds before the array gave up the ghost and timed out, something crashed into the front door. "Crash" was generous.

It wasn't a thud so much as the faint creak of hinges.

The array went dark.

Felix sprang to his feet—sending the rolling chair slamming into the wall behind him—and held the machete firmly in one fist. Green magic coursed along the blade like mist.

"Gonna need more than that little toothpick to—ahh! *Fuck!*" Yuri yelped, his charge toward Felix disrupted as he started frantically swatting at his own head.

Another creak of hinges was followed by a muted metal tap. Felix's gaze flicked to the mail slot in the middle of the door. It opened and closed as if the door were flapping its gums.

Pixie after pixie shot in through the mail slot and went after the shifter, apparently biting and stabbing him all over his massive body. At least one of them might have literally been *in* his ear.

Felix had been tipped off to that last one by Yuri furiously screaming, "Get the fucking fuck out of my fucking ear, you fucking bitch-ass mosquito!"

A wordsmith Yuri was not.

Felix cocked his head and slowly lowered his machete, watching in fascination as Yuri went absolutely berserk trying to rid himself of his tiny, lightning-fast attackers. The man clearly had never skipped arm or leg day in his life, but he was not a flexible man. Several of the pixies—who were armed with what looked like *actual* needles—were stabbing the man repeatedly in the back in spots that he simply couldn't reach thanks to his bulk.

They stabbed him in the calves and the backs of his knees. Goddess only knew what the one in his ear was doing.

After a solid thirty seconds of mind-melting panic, Yuri finally had the good sense to try to get the pixies off him by using his environment. He ran to a wall and slammed his back against it, clearly hoping to smush the pixies to death. He rubbed his back against the wall as his bear counterpart would a tree. The pixies stabbed him in the arms, neck, and legs instead. He bellowed and flung himself to the floor, bumping into the coffee table and sending magazines sliding to the floor as he rolled around as if he were on fire.

His continued screams suggested this method wasn't working, either.

Yuri still had at least one pixie who was screaming into his ear. He kept jabbing one of his sausage fingers into it, clearly trying to smash the pest. Felix thought it unlikely one of them had actually burrowed into his ear canal, but who knew at this point.

Felix idly wiggled a finger in his own ear in sympathy.

"Whirling dervish formation!" came Aster's tiny voice.

Half a dozen of the pixies started frantically flying around Yuri's head like a miniature pixie tornado. He slapped himself repeatedly as he tried to swat the pests away. The pixies were shriek-cackling as they spun and spun. Yuri was clearly growing dizzy now on top of causing minor damage to himself.

With a final bellowing roar, he said "Fuck this!" and ran for the door. Felix was surprised Yuri hadn't shifted into his bear to bodily slam his way out of the office. Then again, the guy was clearly out of sorts.

The shifter was only a foot from escape when the door smashed in and clocked him full in the face. The top hinge on the door tore free from the force of the collision.

Yuri pitched over backward like a board. Felix felt the reverberation of Yuri's large body hitting the floor through the soles of his feet. The pixies flew into the air with a tiny, uproarious cheer.

Bartholomew, with a few colleagues behind him, panted in his cat form in the doorway, partially blocked by the leaning door. He shifted seamlessly back into a human and got the door to stay propped up in the doorjamb. Since it was his day off, he wasn't in uniform. The strap of a messenger bag rested across his plain white T-shirt. With his dark-washed jeans, brown boat shoes, and slicked-back blond hair, he looked like he was ready for a relaxing bougie day.

The cat looked from the fallen Yuri to the small cloud of delighted pixies, to a bewildered Felix, and back again. "Honestly, Turner. It's your day off. Normal people watch TV or do yard work or something."

Felix let out a shuddering breath as the adrenaline ebbed. He waved vaguely at the unconscious shifter. "You gonna help me or what?"

Bartholomew dug around in his messenger bag and pulled out two leather-bound disc-shaped bundles—magic-dampening cuffs. The green-sleeved one would block fae magic, while the blue one would prevent a shifter from going furry. "Obviously. What kind of friend would I be if I didn't show up prepared to move a body?"

CHAPTER TWENTY-NINE

HARLOW

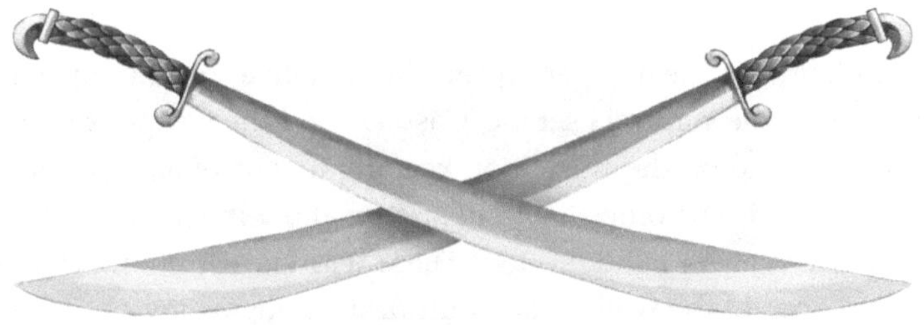

Yesterday afternoon, after getting the news that Sorceress Rhiannon had been killed and my mom and Soren had been arrested in connection to it, an argument about whether the sentient weapons should be allowed to attend the Very Important Sorcerer Meeting waged had hot and fierce. When Sorcerer Avery suggested my sword could come, but that the sickle and Tim should be sequestered in the alloy-lined box, the sickle's curved blade went beet red. It issued a grating, metallic battle cry and hurled itself at the sorcerer's neck.

Macrae had cast a rune array in a matter of one breath and flung it in the next. A concussive air blast that made all of Caspian's previous spells seem like a gentle breeze in comparison slammed into the sickle with such force, the sickle hit the glass of one of the cases, shattered it, and then slammed blade first into the wall. It wobbled in place, like a recently struck tuning fork. The blast was strong enough that it blew my curls away from my face and made Avery's cardigan flap around his waist, and yet only the sickle bore the brunt of the localized tornado—other than the obliterated, once-impenetrable, glass case, that is.

Perhaps *that* was what Caspian could have been capable of had he completed his schooling.

We finally agreed that my sword could float around on its own, but the sickle could only go if it was strapped to my person. Tim had shown himself to be so well behaved, the sorcerers agreed it could float around, too. I recalled how easily my sword had broken through any restraints I put it in but kept my mouth shut. I had to pray my sword would help me keep the crazy sickle in line.

Rhiannon's death *had* upset the timeline of the meeting, though, so the sorcerers set me, Caspian, and the weapons up in a swanky office on the fifth floor, keeping us out of sight until we were needed. The office had a bathroom and a mini fridge, so our basic needs were handled, too. There was even a phone charger snaking out of the wall, which I utilized, seeing as my phone was dead.

After plugging it in, I laid down on the stiff leather couch while I waited for it to boot back up. Caspian parked himself behind the desk.

I suddenly awoke with a desperate need to pee.

Rubbing a fist against an eye, I levered myself into a seated position. My back ached from the stupid expensive couch. I'd also clearly slept hard, which meant I hadn't moved much—if at all— in what must have been hours. Sunlight filtered through the blinds on the window behind the couch, projecting bands of shadow across the floor.

It took a few long moments for the disorientation to clear. I was in a fancy office in the Tower, Caspian was passed out face down on a desk, and the three sentient weapons were in power-down mode on various pieces of furniture.

What the hell time was it?

My bladder issued another protest. I hustled across the office to take care of that—grabbing my backpack off the nearby coffee table on the way. I was grateful for my backpack now, and I used the contents of my toiletry bag to aid in wrangling my hair into a bun. I also had a tiny toothbrush and paste, which was great, seeing as the inside of my mouth felt like a family of mice had crawled in it and died.

By the time I emerged, everyone was awake—including my phone. Caspian was grumbling and rubbing his neck. He headed for the bathroom next, while the buzz of a text message sent me back toward the couch where I'd plugged my phone in.

I read through the group messages I'd missed earlier while I'd been trapped with the sickle. Seeing that Welsh was well enough to not only text, but to do so snarkily, helped me feel a little better about his situation.

There were a boatload of texts from Felix, too. They were all sent this morning.

Wait.

This morning?

Caspian stepped out of the bathroom, and I glanced up.

"Dude," I said. "It's after six in the morning. We were in here all night."

"No wonder my neck hurts so bad. Got any painkillers in your backpack?" Caspian asked, helping himself to my bag that was lying on the coffee table again. "And don't call me dude."

"Okay, dude."

He looked up long enough to grin smugly at me, as if he knew I'd say that. I squinted menacingly at him, but the way he was looking at me was making my stomach do something weird, so like the coward I am, I returned my focus to the messages from Felix.

Felix
Are you OK?

Felix
Harlow, please answer me.

Felix
Can you at least let me know if you're ghosting me on purpose?

As much as I hated not knowing what was going on, being locked in a warded office gave me a small sense of comfort. Seeing Felix's texts made me think about my mom. I switched to my thread with her, but the messages weren't even being delivered. Everything started to hit me then—Rhiannon's death, Mom and Soren arrested, us trapped here for far longer than planned. What if something had happened to Avery and Macrae overnight, and no one knew we were in here? It wasn't as bad as being buried alive, but it still felt like the walls were closing in on me. I didn't know if I wanted to cry or scream.

"Pace," Caspian said from his spot behind the desk. "Start bitching, dude."

"I don't need to bitch, dude."

Within five minutes, I was pacing up and down the room, ranting up a storm. He didn't offer much of his own commentary; he was more of an internal ranter. Once he had his thoughts in order, I knew he'd let them all out.

The sickle—who'd I'd named Sera—was wildly more controlled when the sorcerers weren't around. Sera and my sword were currently huddled together, buzzing and humming, while Tim hung silently in the air by me, keeping pace.

By the time I'd run out of steam, though, Tim had powered down and was lying on the coffee table next to my backpack, his hilt dark. Caspian switched from listening to me to researching goodness knew what on his phone. Apparently Kayda had sent another round of pictures to just him of the runes burned into the ground. He occasionally muttered things like "tourmalinic char" and "interlocking givna rings." There was no getting to him when he was like that, so I left him to it.

What felt like eons later, there was a rustling at the door. My phone told me it was seven thirty. It wasn't the sound of the locking and shielding arrays on the door being dismantled or the mundane lock being unlatched that woke Tim from his stupor, but Macrae's shout of alarm when Sera immediately went in for the kill.

Once again, my sword got there in time to fling Sera away. She spun like a chucked boomerang and crashed into the glass-fronted bookshelf lining the back wall. That was the sound that snapped Caspian out of his research-fugue state, and his attention whipped up from where it had been glued to his phone.

Given that I'd seen Sera stop her own momentum on a dime, I figured she'd smashed into the bookshelf just because she wanted to hear the glass break.

Sera was a chaos demon in a sickle's body.

"I have my reservations about that thing joining us," Macrae said, eyeing the sickle that was still wedged into the spine of a leather-bound book.

"It'll be fine. She just *really* hates you," I said, grabbing my backpack off the coffee table and strapping it on.

"She?" Macrae asked.

I shrugged. "She shared her memories with me. Her energy *felt* female, but it's not like inanimate objects can have a gender, so who knows. There are entirely too many dudes around me all the time, though. Needed to mix it up."

Macrae shot Avery a look that seemed to silently ask, *Can we just chuck her out a window and be done with this?*

Avery gusted a world-weary sigh. "We apologize for the delay. Things have been a bit … chaotic."

I started to ask a question, only to have Avery raise a hand to quiet me.

"All I can tell you is that Camila and Soren are both still alive and well, though they're locked in cells on Floor I in Block 3." Avery shot me a pointed look.

Which meant they *weren't* on Haskins's floor. Haskins was on the floor for people with hopes of being released—the floor for mundanes and lesser fae. Mom and Soren were clearly being treated as higher-level criminals than that.

My stomach pitched uncomfortably. Tears welled in my eyes, and my throat tightened. I knew deep in my bones that, even with three sentient weapons, I couldn't get to my mom and Soren. I needed magic and sorcerer-approved clearance, of which I had neither. Caspian only had one of those things. Having zero power —metaphorically *and* literally—made me feel so impossibly human in this situation. I couldn't do anything but trust Avery and Macrae. Trust didn't come easy for me on the best of days.

My chest constricted.

I was going to snap. I was going to fall apart right here in front of these sorcerers who were my only chance at rescuing my mom. There was only so much compartmentalizing a girl could do before the flimsy walls keeping everything separated started to erode.

Suddenly Caspian was by my side. He slipped his hand into mine. The warmth of his palm and the steadiness of him beside me settled me a bit. I squeezed his hand.

Caspian asked, "Has anything changed regarding our role in this?"

Macrae shook his head. "We need you two to stay well out of the way until we're ready for show and tell. Harlow will demonstrate how the weapons are controlled—"

Sera issued a buzzing war cry, burned her way out of the spine of *War and Peace,* and attempted to murder Macrae again. My sword flung her into the ceiling.

Lips pursed, Macrae continued casually enough, though there was a waver to his voice. "And Caspian will give a soliloquy on norvinic pairings and boranig chains."

Despite the situation, Caspian's chest puffed up a bit at

hearing some of his favorite words, like a dog who was just told they were going on a walk. A wave of affection for him washed over me, and I squeezed his hand again.

He smiled down at me.

The meeting was to take place in one of the upper floors of the Tower.

After Sera pulled herself from the ceiling, Caspian helped me secure her to my belt with a roll of heavy-duty wire Avery had brought with him for this very purpose. She was fairly agreeable, as long as Macrae wasn't the one making the suggestions. Caspian then helped me secure Tim to my other side before casting a camouflaging spell over him.

My sword, as usual, was raring to go.

We loaded into the elevator and trundled up two floors to Floor 7. The sorcerers escorted us into what was apparently a boardroom, at least according to the placard beside the sleek black door. To my untrained eye, it seemed more akin to a penthouse suite. Instead of the massive space being taken up by a long table circled by desk chairs, a ring of plush black leather love seats sat around an elegant oval coffee table already bedecked with refreshments. A few of the chairs were taken, their occupants holding small porcelain plates topped with decadent pastries, piles of fresh fruit, and stacks of finger sandwiches.

While the wall with the door we'd just stepped through was solid wood paneling from end to end, the one opposite was made entirely of glass. A few guests stood before the windows and gazed out on Luma from seven stories up. According to my hastily checked phone during the short elevator ride, it was just after eight in the morning now. Sunlight glinted off the city below.

I instantly felt out of place, which annoyed me. I didn't know these people, and they didn't know me. Most of them wore some version of business casual—pencil skirts, slacks, button-up shirts, blouses, loafers. Still, none of them were what I'd call polished. No impeccable makeup, no elaborate hairstyles, no flashy jewelry. I was further annoyed that I still felt underdressed in my skinny jeans, graphic tee, and scuffed combat boots. The lack of access to a shower and fresh clothes hadn't been my fault.

I shouldn't have cared what any of them thought. Yet it was hard to ignore that aside from the pair of women scurrying around laying out the rest of the plates, silverware, and a beverage service on a table at the back of the room, I was the only human. And these sorcerers weren't just any sorcerers—they were all elites. They were the most powerful people in the hub system —in both magic *and* political clout—in the nation, if not beyond.

I recalled how quickly Macrae had thrown that rune array at Sera yesterday, using so much force, Sera had slammed into the once-impenetrable glass case and shattered it. What would have happened to my much more breakable human body had that blast been directed at *me*? I was fully outmatched here. My mom was far more cut out for this kind of thing than I was, and *she'd* wound up in a jail cell within less than twelve hours of stepping foot into this place.

Sweat pooled at my lower back. I realized then that I'd forgotten my backpack in the office upstairs. It was ridiculous, but the loss of it felt like I'd just misplaced a security blanket. I also remembered just then that the car keys to the SUV in the parking garage were in the bag, too. It wasn't as if Mom could drive out of here anytime soon, but it made me feel like I'd failed her all over again somehow.

Caspian and I were left to our own devices by the beverage table while Avery and Macrae flitted off into the room in different directions, plastering on much friendlier expressions than they'd ever bestowed on us.

My sword floated along the ceiling until it reached the windows, then proceeded to tap various parts of itself against different glass panes. I assumed it was searching for weak points in case we needed to get out of here in a hurry, but who could say?

Caspian's fingers grazed the back of my hand, but when I glanced up at him, I found his gaze scouring the room. He was ever so slightly shifting his weight from one heel to the other—a twitchy rabbit ready to bolt at the first sign of trouble.

I lightly hip-checked him, snapping him free from his own mental spiral. His smile was small and a little strained. Sera had been squished between our hips for two seconds and buzzed her irritation.

"I can't say the goo-goo eyes aren't a potentially good strategy for why you two are less than informed about the unfortunate business with Rhiannon and Camila, but I need you two to pay attention."

I flinched hard at the sudden appearance of Avery's voice in my head. Caspian's nose merely wrinkled in distaste.

I scanned the room for Avery, finding him on the opposite side of the room, chatting up a woman whose back was to me. I resisted the urge to flip him the bird.

"The man walking in now is from Mulgrew."

Even though I wouldn't have known this guy from Adam, the way the group at large reacted to his arrival would have tipped me off. He wasn't greeted with applause, nor was he tackled by hugs, as flashy shows of emotion weren't the sorcerers' way. But he was met with solemn head bows and even a gratuitous squeeze of the shoulder. The portly man in his mid to late fifties looked haggard. He offered people small polite smiles, then eased himself onto one of the love seats. His attendant was a gangly teenage boy who looked even more out of place than I felt. The boy filled a plate of food for the man, handed it to him, and then inexplicably headed straight for Caspian and me. I stiffened. My sword reached me just as the boy did.

"This where the minders are waiting?" the boy asked hurriedly with a hint of a Midwestern accent. "I'm Ethan. I don't remember you two from the last meeting." He thrust out a hand.

We each shook his offered palm and supplied him with our names.

Introductions done, Ethan shoved his hands into the pockets of his khakis. "I wasn't sure if we were going to be in an adjoining room. The meeting in Kensey a few days ago got so rowdy, maybe they thought it better to keep the minders nearby."

I blinked dumbly at him.

Ethan startled suddenly and whipped his head to the side at the sound of my sword issuing an irate buzz over being ignored.

"Ope!" the boy exclaimed, stumbling back a step. Then he swung his wide gaze back to me. His eyes were a vibrant blue that seemed to grow even brighter the redder his pale cheeks became. "I'm so sorry. You must be a … witch?" I guessed tales of the charm collector and her werecat-murdering sentient sword hadn't made it to Mulgrew, Iowa. He eyed Caspian. "You're a sorcerer. You must be. Ope, I'm in the wrong place. Again. Oh heavens. Please excuse my rudeness."

"We're not minders," Caspian said, halting Ethan's awkward attempt to back away, "but the level of authority we hold is no more than your own. We've been ordered to stand by the wall and not speak unless spoken to. And even then, we must be positive that our voices would add something of significance to the conversation."

Ethan's shoulders sagged in relief. "Oh, phew. I thought I put my foot in it again." Jabbing a thumb behind him, he added, "Walter Humphries is my uncle. His former right-hand man—and his *whole* family—was killed during the attack. I've had to fill in. I feel like I'm taking a final exam in a class I've never taken, to be honest."

Upon closer inspection, I guessed Ethan was probably around eighteen—a very *young* eighteen. His cheeks were dotted with the red bumps of acne scars.

"What happened at the meeting in Kensey that got things so heated?" I asked.

"*Well,*" Ethan said, his eyes widening and his brows hiking in the universal sign of *I've got the tea and I'm ready to spill it*. He leaned in, so Caspian and I did, too. My sword hummed anxiously near my head. "The meeting took place mere *hours* after the attack in Mulgrew. It started off as if they just wanted to hear the details from us and offer us aid or condolences or whatever, but isn't that what phone calls are for? And honestly, it was rude to make *us* travel to tell *them* about *our* trauma so soon after it happened, but no one asked for my opinion, did they?"

I tamped down a smile.

Caspian, either missing the sarcasm or ignoring it, said, "I'm assuming they did nothing of the sort."

Ethan shot him an *oh, well, bless your heart* smile and then refocused on me. "So there was a moment of silence and all that, which was nice, and a few people gave my uncle some mood-soothing talismans and other inane things that I swear are worse than mundane flowers. Anyway. After all the pleasantries and whatnot, they all sit down, and the minders are sent off to another room to be called upon when needed." He rolled his eyes. "I got to talking to some of the other minders, and it turns out that the hub in Colorado … you know … uhhh …" He snapped his fingers as if that would help kickstart his memory.

"Sedmak," Caspian supplied.

Ethan shot him a finger gun. "Right. Sedmak. They, just two days before Mulgrew, *stopped* an attack. Ever since the madness that happened over here with you guys, a lot of the hubs have started werecat patrols outside the hubs at night. A whole group of ferals came charging toward the eastern end of Sedmak, but the patrol was heavier in that spot because the Collective knew the veils were weaker there. A few ferals got in, but the werecats were ready for them and tore them down." He offered swipes of his pretend claws in the air. "But, supposedly, one werecat said when she had a feral pinned to the ground, the feral … *oh.* Sorry. I forget myself sometimes. I just get so excited. Is this an inappropriate story?"

I arched my brows. Caspian sighed. Ethan grinned. Clearly he knew he had a sucker on the hook—*me.*

"If you don't continue, I will strangle you," I said, unable to help myself.

"The feral … *spoke*!" Ethan uttered the last word in a dramatic whisper. "It begged the werecat to kill him and put him out of his misery."

This mutating feral thing was really starting to freak me out.

"Turns out that in the main room, the same story was going around," Ethan said. "Half the Collective thinks it's all made up—that the werecat was telling tall tales to impress her friends. Then someone else chimed in about rumors of vampires wielding magic like witches do. No one knows which stories are true and which ones are urban legends. Emotions were already so high over the Mulgrew attack that the meeting devolved almost immediately. There was even name calling!"

I eyed the smug young man. Even if he felt out of his depth in these political situations, he found the whole thing thrilling. He looked like a proud peacock now, clearly enjoying being the one with juicy intel to share.

I knew if I told the kid that the rumors about magic-wielding vamps were truth, not fiction, and that we knew of at least two fae who had turned shadow vamp, all of Iowa would know about it by morning. I opted not to utter Welsh's *or* Kessler's names.

"Do you know which sorcerers here thought the werecat was making things up about talking ferals?" I asked.

Ethan cocked his head, his brows smashing together.

"I'm just wondering if it's a regional thing," I said quickly. "Maybe most of the skeptical ones are all from the same general area. Certain states or regions might be safer than others from feral attacks. I don't have any plans to leave California, but shit, if ferals want nothing to do with certain states, my ass could be convinced to move."

Ethan chuckled at that. "Right? If they hate Florida ... oh no, guess I need to relocate and park myself on one of their feral-free beaches." He turned around for a moment, presumably eyeing the crowd. I glanced up at Caspian who shrugged helplessly at me. "Okay!" Ethan said, whirling back around. "There are three I know of who've been the most vocal at these things. I heard these same names come up from other minders. There's Sorceress

Brianna from Montana, Sorcerer Paulson from North Dakota, and Sorcerer Timms from Minnesota."

The sorcerer naming convention made no sense. Some were referred to by first names, others by last names. Surely there had to be more than one "Brianna" during the hub-wide roll call.

Ethan said, "I haven't seen the Montana lady yet, but I assume she'll be here."

Caspian hmm'ed. "All states that border Canada."

Ethan arched a questioning look, but I understood what Caspian meant. There was some pretty significant shit going down in Canada right now. Did these three sorcerers *also* know about the significant shit going on in Canada, or had they all been spared the onslaught of feral activity as of late and therefore thought everyone else was erroneously wailing about the falling sky?

The boardroom door opened a few seconds later, and in walked two people: a middle-aged woman and a man who kept his eyes on the floor. Another minder, perhaps? Something about his posture spoke to someone beaten down more than being shy, like our new friend Ethan had initially been.

After taking a few steps into the room, the man lifted his head to better hear what his companion whispered to him.

Avery muttered, *"Well, shit,"* in my head at the same time that Caspian, seemingly out of instinct, latched onto my forearm.

Ethan turned at the sound of the door opening. "Speak of the devil," he said, turning back to face me. *"There's* the Montanan sorceress."

I was considerably more focused on the fact that Albert-fuck-ing-Sweeney had just joined the chat. We hadn't seen him since Washington. Sweeney had been in cahoots with Domino the orc mob boss; we'd run into him at the auction that resulted in us buying the treasure chest that had once belonged to Margaret Fengast.

I'd had no idea what fate had befallen the guy after Caspian, my sword, and I left him knocked out in a motel room as we fled from a very angry troll. Collective werecats *and* mundane police had been swarming to the motel just as my mom had shown up in time to whisk us away. My stomach pitched again at the thought of my mom.

I gave my head a quick, clearing shake. I knew the odds of Sweeney escaping capture were slim. So how the hell was he here?

"We know all about your altercation with Sweeney in Washington," Avery said in our heads, refocusing me. *"As punishment for his numerous indiscretions, he's been locked into magic-suppressing shackles and was sent to another hub to be an errand boy for a minimum of a year before we revisited the possibility of him resuming his role in the Luma Collective."*

Seeing as the Washington fiasco had happened less than a month ago, Sweeney shouldn't have been here.

Sweeney's gaze shifted and landed squarely on me. To his credit, his brows lifted in the barest hint of surprise. When his attention slid to Caspian, his eyes widened.

A band of blazing red flared in my peripheral vision. I shouted an apology to Ethan in one breath and lunged forward in the next, somehow catching my sword by the hilt with both hands before it finished what it had started back in that motel room. While Caspian and I had been frantically packing up, I'd lifted my sword's maim ban. Sometimes I could still hear Sweeney's pained protests echoing in my head.

Ethan landed on his backside with an "Ope!"

There were no visible scars on Sweeney's face, neck, or fore-arms, but that didn't mean there weren't any hidden beneath his clothes. I was pulled forward several inches on the plush carpet as I pulled back on the sword that was desperate to get to Sweeney.

The sickle issued a discordant note that somehow gave off the impression of asking *Is it okay if I help my sibling fuck up this stranger?*

"No!" I hissed in the general direction of my left hip.

The sickle offered a disappointed hum. Tim had powered

down on the elevator ride up here and was seemingly still asleep.

Caspian darted around in front of me and was taking slow steps back that matched the pace of me being pulled across the carpet. Hopefully the friction between my boots' soles and the carpet fibers didn't set the room on fire. My arms and shoulders were already sore.

Hands out, Caspian said, "Now is not the time, cutlass. We don't have any facts yet."

My sword's blade glowed even brighter.

"This," I ground out. "Is not. Being. Incognito. You fool sword."

It vibrated indignantly in my hands.

"I'll stop calling you a fool," I said, "when you stop. Acting like one."

In a matter of moments, my sword stilled, inverted itself, and then shot straight for the ceiling, yanking itself out of my hands. My palms were left unscathed, but the abrupt shift in momentum sent me careening into Caspian. We went down in a heap. The greatest miracle of all was that the weapons strapped to my waist didn't gut us both.

Scratch that. One weapon. I couldn't sense Tim anymore.

He'd presumably detached himself, but he was still cloaked, so I had no idea where he was. And, for once, he wasn't constantly asking for mission instructions.

Shortly after my tumble, the sickle broke free from its bindings and went shooting into the air to cavort with my sword, if the shouts of alarm echoing around the room were anything to go by.

I sighed dramatically into Caspian's shirt. We didn't fall perfectly on top of one another, chest to chest, like in a romantic comedy. No, I accidentally elbowed him in the chin while his knee gut-checked me. By the time we'd come to rest on the plush carpet, my nose was wedged perfectly into his armpit. Luckily for me, his deodorant hadn't failed him yet.

I pried my face free. He was flat on his back, gaze fixed on the aggrieved weapons above us. Hopefully he wouldn't have a bruised chin to go with his bruised cheek from our altercation with O'Neill in the lobby yesterday.

Chatter filled the room, the sorcerers' voices growing louder over the ringing in my ears as more people inched toward us.

"Are those the sentient weapons I keep hearing about?"

"Isn't that the Fletcher girl? I don't understand how she's not in prison for multiple counts of homicide."

"The rumors about Luma's leadership letting the inmates run the asylum might not be rumors after all."

"I'm not sure if I'm proud or horrified that you two managed to turn this meeting into a circus before it even officially began."

That last one had been *in* my head. Avery sounded a touch amused, at least.

Caspian and I scrambled to our feet at the same time, clunking foreheads as we did so. I slapped a palm above my right eye and moaned pitifully.

"Definitely horrified," Avery said.

I hazarded a glance up, semi-relieved to find that the weapons —the visible ones, anyway—were more focused on each other than spilling blood all over the carpet. When I lowered my gaze, I winced. The sorcerers had formed a loose semicircle around us, their gazes flitting between me, Caspian, and the weapons. Most of the sorcerers wore impassive expressions, but I'd spent enough time around Caspian to know that the impassivity often meant big feelings hiding behind the mask.

I felt Tim behind me now, by my right shoulder. None of the sorcerers glanced in that direction, so I assumed Tim hadn't lost the camouflage yet.

I will shower the plush carpet with their life fluids at your first command.

Uhh, I thought at Tim. *Thank you?*

"Avery? Macrae?" a man called out, turning to face the main part of the room. "Rhiannon has an excellent excuse to not be here to lead the proceedings, but surely you're not so ill-equipped that you cannot fill her shoes in light of her unexpected absence. Are you two even still in here, or did you slink out the door? I pray these children are your hired jesters meant to provide a bit of slapstick comedy before the task at hand. Otherwise, I do fear you two may have lost the plot."

Jeez! It was like being insufferable assholes was baked into their DNA.

The crowd parted a bit to reveal Macrae. He pushed his glasses up his nose. He stopped a few feet from us but addressed the group at large. "The jesters—Caspian Blackthorn and Harlow Fletcher—are the ones our Collective spent countless resources to apprehend. As you can see, they're far from criminal masterminds, and the weapons, while bonded to Harlow, are capable of independent action and thought."

I squinted at Macrae, trying to ascertain whether or not I'd just been insulted. He might have also just insulted the Collective. I couldn't figure the guy out.

A dozen heads tipped back to warily observe the weapons. The sickle was currently spinning a zillion RPM a foot from the ceiling while my sword, in the inverted position, buzzed angrily while jabbing itself upward repeatedly like an upside-down jackhammer. It was disconcerting that they both kept getting weirder.

After extolling Caspian's numerous skills with runework, much like a proud parent, Macrae added, "Jesters or no, they both possess an advantage that we don't. And we need all the help we can get to first, stand a chance against the growing feral hordes that threaten our veils, and second, stop Lachlan Shade."

I shifted uncomfortably from foot to foot. If there *were* Shades among Luma's Collective, surely at least a couple stood within these walls. Was Macrae hoping that those who protested too much about the threat Lachlan posed would reveal themselves as Shades?

"Those *are* the topics at hand, are they not?" the asshat from earlier asked.

Avery's voice boomed from somewhere beyond the semicircle. "If you would resume your seats, we can get started."

The group at large cast a few more apprehensive glances at us, then made their way to the ring of plush chairs. Of the last few to move were the woman from the Montanan hub and her minder, Sweeney. I'd almost forgotten about him. Sorceress Brianna angled her head toward Sweeney's ear. He listened intently, nodding on occasion as he kept his eyes focused on the floor. With a final nod, Brianna left his side so she could join the others.

The room was so cavernous, it felt like the sorcerers were in the next state.

Sweeney lifted his head and watched us for a moment before blowing out a fortifying breath. He marched toward us.

Actually, "marched" was generous—he shuffle-stepped. My gaze snapped to his feet. He wasn't wearing anything as obvious as manacles, but there was a faint tendril of blue that stretched from ankle to ankle, and it sparked with every step. His wrists weren't bound together, but a tight bracelet ringed each one. The bracelets were a soft green—like jade—and didn't strike me as the kind of accessory the guy would wear by choice.

Once he finally reached us, I wasn't sure if he was annoyed or embarrassed. "Nice to see you again," he said in a clipped tone, as he eyed me and Caspian in turn. He nodded once to Ethan who had wedged himself between me and the beverage table. "Ethan," he said in acknowledgment.

Ethan audibly swallowed next to me. "Hello ... Bert."

Bert?

Caspian and Sweeney attempted polite conversation that was as awkward as it was stilted, topped with an edge of tension.

In what I'm sure Ethan thought was a whisper only I could hear, he leaned in close to my ear and said, "Bert used to be a Collective sorcerer *here*. He sold government secrets on the black market and got caught, so now he's a lowly minder like us. Well, uh, me. I'm still not sure what *you* are."

That should have sounded more offensive, but Ethan had an easy charm about him that was wholly accidental. A golden retriever puppy in human form.

Offering Ethan a silent apology for playing dumb as long as I had, I turned to Sweeney. "So, Sweens, they shipped you off to do grunt work, and yet you're back in Luma in under a month. Not sure if I'm more concerned about what *you're* up to or your boss over there is."

The elite sorcerers were deep in conversation across the room. A few other so-called minders were doing the wallflower thing, too, but farther down. Perhaps they were trying to keep their distance from the sentient weapons that were now hovering several feet above the sorcerers, deathly still.

Tim hovered, still invisible, somewhere above my head.

Sweeney appeared grateful to no longer need to make painfully awkward chit chat with Caspian. He held up his unbound wrists. The jade-like bracelets were so tight, they almost looked tattooed on. Each was etched with runes. "I currently possess no more magical prowess than you do. Sorceress Brianna, I suspect, was asked specifically by one of my former colleagues to make this experience as demeaning as possible to further drive home how far from grace I've fallen."

Caspian eyed Sweeney's cuffs warily, as if imagining what it would be like to have his own magic hamstrung in such a way.

I crossed my arms. "Those cuffs and that magical ball and chain on your ankles didn't do anything to the knowledge you've got kicking around in that skull of yours, though. Did they lock you into a Soul NDA to make sure you didn't go around blabbing any more government secrets?"

Sweeney pursed his lips. "One cuff for severing my magical abilities, the other to make it nearly impossible to have anything other than asinine conversations with anyone new beyond the state of the weather and whatever silly TV show is popular."

Ethan made a soft noise like a slowly deflating balloon. "I thought you actually liked *Faet of the Heart* ..."

Sweeney offered him a conspiratorial smile and whispered, "I gasped so loudly when Greta walked in on Kendrick, I startled my cat."

Ethan grinned at him. "*Right?*"

My lip curled. What alternate universe was I in that "Bert" had a cat and watched soap operas?

A chill raced down my spine, and I froze.

My heart rate ticked up.

I quickly scanned the room, wondering what had triggered my sixth sense. All of the sorcerers were focused on an elderly man, his hands gesticulating wildly as he spoke. I couldn't hear what he said.

"*What is it, Harlow?*" came Avery's voice in my head.

The very air in the room felt off, like it was charged with electricity. I lifted an arm, expecting to find the fine dark hairs standing on end, as if I'd just run a balloon over my skin. My gaze shifted to the ring of sorcerers, and I locked eyes with Avery, the only sorcerer who seemed to notice something had changed.

I shrugged and shook my head.

Five long seconds later, the feeling had ratcheted up enough that the weapons had harpooned back to me. Sera spun in a slow, lazy circle a foot away, while my sword buzzed in agitation in my face, its blade beet red.

A*waiting instructions*, Tim intoned.

Two seconds after that, the other sorcerers noticed it, too. Several sprang to their feet. The minders farther down the wall scurried over to their bosses—though Sweeney and Ethan stayed standing with us.

I leaned toward Caspian. "Any ideas?"

He shook his head, not looking at me since he was scanning the room. "You noticed it sooner than anyone else. Do *you* have any idea what it is?"

Sweeney cursed softly. Caspian had to dart out of his way as the man moved *away* from the apparent threat and shoved himself between us. He pressed his back to the wall. "Portal."

I swallowed. "Excuse me, what?"

"Someone," Sweeney said slowly, voice tight, "is opening a portal."

CHAPTER THIRTY

FELIX

Yuri was still bound in Felix's private office. The guy had come-to only twenty minutes after he'd been knocked out. He woke up bellowing like a ticked-off bear—which was appropriate—and only grew more and more agitated as he realized he was cuffed and unable to shift. The cuffs dampened some of his strength, too, but he was still a massive dude. It had taken Felix,

Bartholomew, Masters, and Silvia to tackle the guy back to the couch.

"I ain't telling you fuckers shit!" he'd screamed when he was first knocked down.

He tried to escape four more times in the next half an hour, but he'd since lost steam. Yuri's partner in crime had already been apprehended. Goddess knew what he'd done to Felix's house before then. Probably ate all his food and pissed on the furniture.

Masters left to grab food for the group. When the small office filled with the scents of breakfast burritos, pancakes, and bacon, Yuri started cussing a whole lot less. Felix and his companions sat around the now-lopsided coffee table and ate in front of Yuri while he remained on the couch with his hands cuffed behind his back, practically drooling.

Felix glanced up to find Yuri having a staring contest with the bag of food still sitting on the coffee table. Bartholomew had written a note on the bag in black Sharpie and had angled it so the message faced the bear shifter's position on the couch.

Only nice bears get brekky 😊

Obnoxious.

But the message was clearly working.

"What continuants nice?" Yuri finally asked.

Bartholomew knew better than to make fun of the guy's terrible vocabulary. If they wanted the guy to talk, they had to be nice, too. "We ask questions, you get food. That simple, Jack."

"My name's Yuri, dumbass."

Silvia nearly choked on a bite of her burrito.

"My apologies," Bartholomew said, sweet as pie.

"What you wanna know?" Yuri asked, gaze focused squarely on the white bag on the table.

Bartholomew, who had been sitting on the floor, leaned back on one hand and gestured at Felix with the other. His feet were crossed casually at the ankles.

Yuri glanced up at Felix, who was seated across from him. "What, you wanna know if I'm the one who took out your little friend? Natalie?"

"Naomi," Felix corrected.

"Whatever. Yeah, it was me. And it was me who beat your ass half to death with tire irons, too," Yuri said, grinning at Felix as if he had the upper hand, despite him being cuffed and surrounded by bounty hunters and werecats. "I know my rights, though. You can't use none of what I say against me because you didn't magnetize me."

Silvia almost choked on her sip of coffee that time.

"Woof," Bartholomew breathed. "Look, Jack, Mirandizing is a mundane world thing. We're just having a chat. You're already screwed because you attacked a Collective bounty hunter—unprovoked and in his private office, I'll add. Those wards you set off were logged on his computer and his phone. We'll all corroborate his story that we showed up here today because he asked for help. There's a log of that, too. Our bosses up the food chain will decide if you need to get officially interrogated by a sorcerer. If they think you're lying, you'll get truth-serumed, and then you'll tell them *everything*, whether you want to or not. If you're honest with us and give us what we need, this will go better for you. But, I reiterate, you were screwed the moment you busted in that door."

Yuri swallowed.

Silvia, a fellow bounty hunter, held up a tablet. "See this? I've been doing some research on you. You've had a low-level bounty out on you for years. You punched a *kid*, Yuri?"

A reddish-purple hue crawled up the bear shifter's neck. "That was ages ago at my kid sister's birthday party. That little shit had it coming."

"According to this, it was your sixteen-year-old cousin," Silvia said. "You failed to finish your anger management courses to complete the terms of your sentencing."

Yuri grumbled to himself. "I only had one class left. Waste of time."

There were tons of crap bounties like that in the system—people who hadn't completed this course or that. If the officers running the courses felt like an offender who didn't complete their sentencing was going to be a problem to society, they got punted to Bounties. Low level meant they were problematic but not an immediate danger. The payout bonus for bringing in a low-level offender was rarely worth the effort. Medium meant they were likely to re-offend. The nature of the offense determined how quickly hunters snagged the perp.

High meant all hands on deck, track the deserter down *now*.

A low-level designation was kept for exactly this reason: The next time they offended the terms of their sentencing—in this case, unnecessary violence—then the pending bounty meant the perp could be hauled in for nearly any reason and forced back into the program, this time under closer Collective supervision.

It was a loophole in the system that was exploited often.

Silvia shrugged. "You're going back into the anger management either way. Might as well cooperate. After all, if the sorcerers running the program don't like your attitude, you'll be in far more hot water with them than you'll ever be with us."

Felix knew from his perusal of Yuri's files that he'd been on the suspect list of at least four murder investigations, including Elizabeth Sellers. The werecat guards weren't going to go easy on a shifter with a rap sheet like Yuri's. Confessing was honestly the best thing Yuri could do for himself.

"Why'd you kill Naomi?" Felix asked.

Yuri only thought about it for a few more seconds before he started talking. "There was something off about that girl from the day she started working at the Lily. No one saw it but me. I got a sixth sensation, you know? I can tell things about people. And that girl wasn't right. She wore glamoured eye contacts. Did you know that? Hid her freaky goat eyes."

Felix *hadn't* known that. She'd been more fae than he or Harlow had known.

"She used her weird goat powers on Graves, too. Them fauns can make you feel things. Make you feel safe if you're actually scared or whatever. She did that to Grover all the time. He'd call her into his office 'cause she scared off a young girl one of the top guests wanted. Graves would be *spitting* mad. I'd wait outside, sure she'd get canned, and then she'd walk out to finish her shift, and Graves would be in his office smiling like a damn Chester cat, talking about how glad he is he hired Naomi."

Bartholomew cocked his head in a very catlike way. "Graves couldn't tell?"

"Nah. Not for a long time. And I didn't say nothing, 'cause I knew my place. But after it happened enough times, I used my own money to buy a talisman. It wouldn't stop nobody from charming you, but it would flash blue if someone was using a cloud-charm spell. Wouldn't work if it was a mind-charm spell— like the one-on-one spells vamps or sirens or some of the sorcerers can do."

Most fauns who Felix had interacted with didn't have strong magic. But he knew with cloud spells, the wielder could cast one that affected everyone in an area indiscriminately. Cloud spells were apparently easier to cast, as far as magical expenditure went, depending on the size of the crowd. A spell used to affect the mind of a single person required more magical output, more training, and more concentration. Felix thought of a cloud spell more like a defensive one—like a skunk spraying a foul odor to distract predators.

"Anyway," Yuri said. "The talisman was expensive as hells, and I had to save up for months to get it. It only had three charges, too. I gave it to Graves and said, 'Just keep this on your desk and if it goes off when she's talking to you, she's pulling a quick one.'"

Felix sighed. "And when it went off during one of their talks, instead of Graves firing her, he sent *you* after her?"

Yuri shrugged. "She was a threat to his business and Graves pays good."

Felix resisted the urge to slam his fist down on the bag of food until Yuri's burrito was nothing but lukewarm paste. "Why Ella Sellers?"

"She actually *was* a spy," Yuri said. "Graves found proof that Ella was a runner for a rival dealer. She was trying to inflagrate the Lily and take back secrets on how we do things. He told me to keep an eye on her. Then one day I sees her talking to Naomi's mother. Graves said he saw that, too. We never actually got super clear proof that Naomi was a spy, but she was using those goat powers on Graves, so she was clearly hiding something. That was good enough reason to kill her far as I was concerned."

Another frustrated sigh eased out of Felix's nose. It sounded like once Yuri had willingly killed Naomi for the cause—and possibly others before her—Graves knew he could rely on Yuri to dispose of anyone deemed a threat. Graves fed Yuri a bullshit story about Ella, tapping into Yuri's natural paranoid tendencies, simply because Graves didn't like the implications that stemmed from Ella talking to Denise. The saddest part about Ella's situation was that she'd done what she was supposed to do. She gave Denise a code name that would lead Denise exactly nowhere. They'd killed the woman for even less of a reason than Naomi.

In the corner of his eye, Felix clocked Bartholomew languidly getting to his feet. He shot Felix a "cool your jets" look, then snatched the bag of food off the coffee table. The cat plopped down next to Yuri.

"Since you're still bound, you and I are gonna have to get real comfortable with each other, Jack," Bartholomew said.

"The fuck?" Yuri asked, jerking away from Bartholomew as if he'd cattle prodded him.

Bartholomew pulled the burrito from the bag and folded down the foil. "You need to eat, and we're not uncuffing you." He made airplane noises as he made the burrito slowly glide toward Yuri's face. "Is the big teddy hungry?"

Yuri blanched. "I'd rather the dame feed me," he said, jutting his chin at Silvia.

Without looking up from her tablet, Silvia said, "This dame would rather stick poisoned needles in her eyes."

"Bitch."

Bartholomew, without missing a beat went, "Oh, no, Captain! Mayday! Mayday!" and rerouted the burrito from a course toward Yuri to his own face instead. "Coming in for a crash landing unless Yuri the fuck-weasel apologizes to Silvia!" He made an absolutely ridiculous series of battle noises as the burrito wove through the air. A chunk of scrambled egg that hadn't made it into the tortilla slipped free and splattered onto Felix's otherwise pristine couch.

When Yuri did nothing other than scowl, the pixies—who had been lounging in various parts of the office—started making their own airplane noises. They quickly formed a cloud a few feet above Yuri's head, their wings glowing bright red, all screaming about how much damage they could do to him while he was bound.

"*Ahh, fuck!* Okay, sorry! Sorry, Miss Silvia. I didn't mean nothing by it. I'm just so hungry," Yuri blubbered.

A smattering of what looked like syrup splattered on the knee of Felix's jeans. It had come from high above his head.

He lifted a hand in the air. "Stand down, pixies."

"You never let us have any fun," Aster complained.

The pixies dispersed. Masters had bought them food, too. Felix was almost positive that the cups of salsa, butter, and syrup that had been included with the food were now doubling as small, sticky hot tubs for some of the pixies. He could only imagine the disaster they were leaving on his desk. The tiny pancakes had been damn cute, at least.

Bartholomew shot a look at Silvia, who shrugged. "Course rerouted. Coming in for a landing at Bruin International!"

The next couple of minutes were just ... weird. Bartholomew fed the shifter, who moaned occasionally in satisfaction.

Bartholomew wiped Yuri's mouth when salsa dripped down the shifter's chin.

"This from Mercado Grill?" Yuri asked after swallowing a mouthful of country potatoes. "I ain't been there in a while. This is some good shit."

Masters, who was seated beside Silvia, lifted a bag sitting by his hip. "There's a stack of pancakes in here. The plastic lid is fogged up, so they're probably still warm."

Yuri smacked his lips, then cast his gaze at Felix and lifted his brows in question.

"Why did you leave Denise West alive?" Felix asked. When Yuri's head tipped to the side in confusion, Felix clarified, "Naomi's mom."

"Ohh. Her. The first time I roughed her up, it wasn't Graves who told me to do it. There's a bunch of VIP guests at the Lily, and Graves says if they need help taking care of people, we're supposed to help out. Part of the service or whatever, you know? Anyway, it was that caracal guy who asked me to do it—Randal. The guy who got sliced up by your ex-girl's crazy sword." Yuri shuddered a bit. "Randal didn't tell me to kill her—just scare her real bad. It kinda sucked. She cried a lot. Like *a lot*, a lot. And she kinda looked like my Aunt Shirley.

"When she showed up weeks later and was talking to Ella, Graves told me to take them *both* out. I went after Ella, and Frankie went after Denise. Frankie was in the middle of fucking up Denise's house in preparation for her showing up, but he got a call from Graves saying there was some emergency with a run on the mundane side. You don't make Graves wait when he calls with an emergency. So Frankie left a note on the wall telling Denise to fuck off or die, so she did the smart thing and bounced. That phone call from Graves saved her life, I guess."

Silvia asked, "Frankie Gallagher?"

"Yeah, that's ..." Yuri said, then cursed. "Shit. Low-level bounty on him, too, right?"

"Bingo," Silvia said, still tapping away on her tablet.

She and Masters had been busy on their tablets for the past half hour. Once they'd secured Yuri on the couch, Masters had called in the break-in at Felix's house. Within twenty minutes of the call, an arrest had been made—a gorilla shifter named Franklin Gallagher. Hopefully he was currently rolling over on his buddy Yuri.

Silvia would call in the break-in at Felix's office as soon as they were done talking to him. Once Yuri was in werecat custody, Felix was unlikely to ever see the guy again, so he wanted to ask him everything he could think of while he had the chance.

Felix's next line of questioning was sure to shock his colleagues. But Naomi's file was redacted for a reason. He wanted to learn the reason for that almost more than the identity of Naomi's killer. "How many sorcerers are working with Graves, other than Jeffries?"

In his periphery, both Masters's and Silvia's gazes swung toward him.

Bartholomew whistled. "Fucking hell. Really? *Jeffries?* That's like finding out your nerdy accountant runs a BDSM club on the weekends."

"That boy is a *freeeeak,*" Yuri said, seemingly delighted that he knew more than his captors.

Bartholomew gagged, like a cat coughing up a hairball, and pressed a fist to his mouth.

"I don't know all their names, but there're probably four total who I've seen with Graves," Yuri said. "I can tell which ones they are because they aren't dressed like people who go to the Lily, you know what I mean? But they feel magical. It's creepy. They stick out like sore toes 'cause they don't look like they fit, but they act like *everybody else* is the ones who ain't supposed to be there."

Yeah, that summed up Collective sorcerers all right.

"Two dudes and two chicks—Jeffries, Timms, and Brianna are the names I know. I think one or two of them ain't even from Luma. One's from the Montana hub, maybe? The other chick is younger than the other ones. Thirty, maybe? She's real skinny and a stuck-up bi—" He cast a look at Silvia. He cleared his throat. "She's snobbier than all of them. Don't know her first name, but I think her last name is Shade?"

Felix stiffened. "Why do you think that?"

Yuri shrugged. "Graves calls her *a Shade,* so I figured that's some rich asshole family name. Talks about her like her shit don't stink. He kisses all the sorcerers' asses anyway, but when the Shade chick comes in, he acts like she's the fuckin' queen of France. Shuts everyone out of his office when she shows up. I don't know what she comes in for. Doesn't use Bliss, doesn't want any of the boys *or* girls Graves offers, doesn't ever use runners or ask for favors. She creeps us out."

Even if the general public in Luma didn't know the name Lachlan Shade, his name was well known among the Tower's employees by now. Felix knew that keeping the truth about Lachlan's escape from exile through a Goddess-damned portal powered by the life force of over a dozen elf teens was being kept out of public discourse to prevent the average citizen from panicking, but the guy would become a household name sooner rather than later.

It shouldn't have surprised him that a Shade was tied to the Ghost Lily, but it still did. The speculation among his colleagues was that the Bliss cartel was helping fund the Shades' efforts. What in the hells the hybrids were getting out of this arrangement was beyond Felix.

While Felix mulled this over, Bartholomew fed Yuri his stack of pancakes. He cut the stack into triangles and fed them to the shifter, syrup and melted butter ending up splattered on his shirt. The sight wasn't something Felix needed in his life.

Once done, Yuri sat back, glutted. "Thanks, man. That really hit the spot."

"Last question," Felix said. "When you first busted in here, you said that my ex being in the Tower today—of all days—was significant. Why?"

Yuri chuckled, and the sound made the hair on Felix's arms raise. "Finally you ask the only question that matters."

"What the hell does that mean?" Felix asked, trying to sound relaxed despite the fact that his colleagues were all on alert now. The pixies were growing agitated, too.

"You were pals with that Sorceress Rhiannon lady, yeah? Too bad she's dead. Your ex's mom finally got her revenge, and that little sorcerer got shredded by ferals in front of an audience, my guy." He cackled. "Fuckin' *bruuutal.*"

While Silvia and Masters furiously tapped at their tablets seeking confirmation and Bartholomew pummeled Yuri with questions, Felix sprang to his feet to grab his phone. He'd left it on his desk. While his desk was an absolute sticky disaster thanks to whatever in the hells the pixies had been doing, his phone was untouched.

He hurriedly pulled up his text thread with Harlow.

> **Felix**
> If you don't reply to me soon, I'm going to have a heart attack, Low.

> **Felix**
> I KNOW there's no way your mom was the mastermind of an assassination plot. Are you also hearing that Rhiannon is dead? Low, what in the FUCK IS GOING ON?!

> **Felix**
> Shit. Not even all caps worked

He was two seconds from chucking the phone across the room when it buzzed in his hand.

> **Harlow**
> Mom and Soren have been arrested. And, yes, Sorceress Rhiannon is dead

> **Felix**
> Finally you reply!

> **Felix**
> Are you still in the Tower?

Harlow
Yes. The sorcerer meeting didn't start until this morning

Three buzzes sounded from yet another device. The sound was echoed around the room. It was a very familiar sound to bounty hunters. Quick, quick, slow.

He snatched his bounty mirror off his belt and flipped open the lid, reading the message etched across the glass.

Tower compromised
Evacuation mandatory for NEP

He cursed, snapping the lid closed again. Sticking the mirror back into the holder on his belt, he returned to his text thread with Harlow.

> **Felix**
> We just got alerts that nonessential personnel have to evacuate the Tower. Is this because of Rhiannon?

Harlow
Um. Kinda?

> **Felix**
> Elaborate!

Harlow
Don't freak out, but a portal is opening. Avery, Macrae, and several sorcerers from other hubs are in here. Get somewhere safe

Felix
Fuck

He stalked back over to his friends and Yuri.

"What'd you hear, Felix?" Silvia asked, her voice uncharacteristically shaky. "Is it true?"

Without looking away from the cuffed bear shifter on his couch, Felix said, "It's true. Rhiannon's dead." He did his best to ignore his friends as they cursed and paced the room. "I'm asking you one more fucking time, and you'd better give me a straight fucking answer, Yuri. You said my ex being in the Tower today—*of all days*—was significant. Why?"

Yuri flashed a shit-eating grin. "Why else do you think I tripped your wards? Why do you think I've been chatting you losers up? The main part of my assignment wasn't to kill your scrawny ass. It was to keep you away from the Tower, dumbass. Jeffries used his clairboyence and saw that if you got there too soon you could mess up the plan."

Felix worked his jaw. "What plan?"

As if it were obvious, Yuri said, "Today is the day of the coup."

CHAPTER THIRTY-ONE

HARLOW

"Someone," Sweeney said slowly, voice tight, "is opening a portal. Domino had a few elves he worked with who could semi-open inter-dimensional portals. It's what telepads do, but more freeform. Open a door here, open a door where you want to go, step through, and … poof. I've only seen one open successfully once. Everyone else died in some horrific way in transit. It always felt like this—like the air was charged with electricity."

A few feet from the outer edge of the chair circle, a vaguely oval-shaped mass formed in the air. My sword and the sickle issued off-kilter hums. That wasn't a good sign.

Even Tim hummed softly.

Avery beelined for a landline phone—or maybe it was part of

an intercom system—on the wall opposite where we stood. Was he calling down to the Portal Relations department?

I tugged on Caspian's sleeve. "Wanna get out of here?"

Before he could answer, Sorcerer Humphries called out, "Ethan! Come, boy. We can't risk whatever this is."

Ethan offered us a weak smile and jogged after his uncle, who was currently hauling tail for the door. Several others followed suit. Avery watched them as he hurriedly spoke into the phone.

My gaze flicked to the swirling mass where it hovered in the space between the farthest edge of the ring of chairs and where Avery stood talking into the phone. I was alarmed that the thing seemed to be growing so rapidly. All I knew about portals came from my mom, who'd had a front-row seat to Lachlan's exile. She'd told me that the portal opened slowly, that even an experienced sorcerer from the Portal Relations department couldn't wave his hand or snap his fingers to get the portal to reverse course, and that the only way to close it was to offer it a sacrifice.

Yet another runaway train that was potentially impossible to stop. It had gone from the size of a basketball to a vanity mirror in the matter of a minute.

What if this wasn't a portal meant to let someone through but was actually like a black hole that sucked everything *in*?

Humphries flung one of the double doors open, only to stumble back several steps, crashing into Ethan, who then crashed into someone behind him. The half dozen people didn't go down like bowling pins, but it was close. The second door opened then, giving a wide view of the hallway. Standing there were two sorcerers with rune arrays already primed and glowing. The arrays' bright golden haze took up the entire doorway. At the sorcerers' feet, on either side of them, stood four werecats in snarling cat form.

Macrae marched toward them. "What's the meaning of this?"

"Both of those are fire arrays," Caspian said close to my ear, his voice carrying a shake that I didn't like one bit. "There's no way we're getting past those unless someone in here attacks first."

I couldn't imagine the Tower's neutrality laws mattered much in a situation like this, but I figured Caspian meant that if we tried to get out the doors, we'd be hit with the arrays and burned to a crisp. I figured as soon as someone made the decision to start throwing magic around, all hell would break loose. Every sorcerer in here except for Sweeney was an elite. I assumed the two in the doorway were, too. Those fire spells wouldn't be mere fireballs like Alice Winchell had thrown at Domino—even though her power had been enough to roast an orc to death. Just one of these arrays would be equivalent to a flamethrower, a conflagration, an inferno. And depending on who the two fire-wielders ultimately worked for, they might not care if they died in the name of the cause, as long as everyone in the room died, too. Hells, maybe that was the plan.

My phone buzzed in my back pocket. It scared me so badly, I yelped. Pulling it free, my heart lurched at the sight of Felix's name. Maybe he had news about my mom!

Felix
We just got alerts that nonessential personnel have to evacuate the Tower. Is this because of Rhiannon?

Harlow
Um. Kinda?

Felix
Elaborate!

Harlow
Don't freak out, but a portal is opening. Avery, Macrae, and several sorcerers from other hubs are in here. Get somewhere safe

Felix
Fuck

I hemmed and hawed about how much information to give him. I didn't want to trigger his savior complex.

> **Harlow**
> The exit is blocked by two sorcerers and at least four cats. Collective has Shade spies. Stay away from the Tower

Dots appeared and disappeared several times. I was about to give up waiting on him so I could focus on whatever Caspian and Sweeney were furiously whispering about when Felix's reply finally came in.

> **Felix**
> On my way

Really? *Really?* What the hell did he think he could do against the small army standing in the doorway? I was about to tap that out as a response when the two fire-wielders at the door parted long enough to allow another person into the room.

It wasn't anyone I recognized, but her presence caused a ripple to go through the crowd. The woman was tall and thin—possibly too thin. She was younger than a lot of the sorcerers were—maybe in her early thirties. She had more of a fresh-faced energy to her than the world-weary expression the older ones wore. I supposed the spark in her eye could be from her being a lunatic who was excited about impending bloodshed more so than from youthful exuberance. Dressed in leggings, an oversized sweater, and ballet flats, she looked like she belonged behind a counter at a clothing boutique, not strolling into a room full of sorcerers. Two of the werecats—a pair of pumas, which at least let me know neither of them was O'Neill—padded into the room on giant silent paws before sitting on their haunches on either side of her.

I hazarded a glance at the portal everyone else was largely ignoring now. It was a good five feet tall and growing by the second.

"Hello, esteemed colleagues," the young woman said. "As you might have guessed, we needed you all here in one location to help streamline things. Shades, please join me on this side of the room."

No one moved at first. One beat, two. And then a trio of sorcerers joined her, turning their backs on the fire-wielders still standing in the doorway. All three were the ones Ethan had mentioned earlier—the ones whose home states bordered Canada. A few moments later, Humphries joined them.

"Uncle!" Ethan said, trotting after his uncle as if pulled by an invisible rope, only to stop a few feet in front of the werecats. One growled at Ethan, and he stumbled a step back. "What ... but Mulgrew ... how ... did you ..."

Humphries looked no less exhausted than he had earlier. "The path to a brighter future isn't lined with rainbows, dear boy. You'd do well to remember that. Join me on the right side of history."

Ethan inexplicably turned to look at *us*. His expression was pleading. I didn't know what to tell him. I didn't think the "right" side of history was standing with the Abercrombie & Fitch lady, but I also didn't think our side would keep Ethan from getting horribly murdered.

Sweeney, still pressed against the wall, made a shooing motion with both of his hands. Even from this distance, I could see the violent way Ethan's lower lip shook. Head drooping, Ethan shuffled past one of the snarling pumas to stand beside his uncle, who slung an arm around the boy's shoulders.

"Anyone else?" the young woman asked.

I scanned the room for Macrae and Avery. Macrae had collapsed into one of the love seats with a hand clutching at the fabric of his shirt over his heart. A young woman was squatting before him, periodically wiping at his sweaty brow with a napkin. Avery still stood near the landline at the back of the room, though he'd hung up by now, and alternated between glaring at Abercrombie & Fitch and the portal.

"Portal Relations will shut this down by any means necessary," Avery called out. "Do you really want to follow in the footsteps of your deluded savior and wind up in a random world with no way home?"

"My deluded savior can reopen the pathways between worlds," the young woman said. "Pathways you and your so-called Portals Relations were supposed to open yourselves. But you are old and tired," she said, gesturing to Macrae, who very much looked like he was on the verge of a fatal heart attack. "Luckily for you, Lachlan Shade is reasonable. He would not punish you for joining the party late. You *do* remember what parties are, don't you, old man?"

Avery fished a peppermint out of his pocket, unwrapped it, and popped it into his mouth.

"Shade grants us all a choice. He values choices—something the antiquated Collective does not," the woman continued, addressing us all now. "The portal will be fully open in roughly one minute. Portal Relations will not get here in time. The stairwells and elevators are guarded. Those not standing with me will have made their choice, and what comes through the portal will eliminate the rest."

Two more sorcerers joined the Shades.

I whirled toward Sweeney. He hadn't moved an inch since this started. I knew my tone dripped with nothing but suspicion when I slowly asked, "Why aren't *you* standing on the right side of history?"

Sweeney, lips pursed, slid his wide gaze to me. "You two have seen and faced off against what's out there in the mundane world, not just talked about it from the safety of a fortified tower decorated with high-end furniture. Say what you want about Domino, but he was smart enough to be scared. He supplied people on the outside with the weapons they needed to survive. None of these people," he said, waving a shaking finger at the remaining sorcerers who hadn't yet moved, "know how to survive. Not really. If I have to be on the wrong side of history, I at least want to stand with those who have a fighting chance."

Couldn't say I liked any of *that*.

I hurriedly pulled out my cell again and opened my text thread with Felix.

> **Harlow**
> Seriously. Don't come to the Tower

No dots.

> **Harlow**
> Felix! You have nothing to prove to me, okay?

> **Harlow**
> If I say I forgive you, will you stop?

> **Harlow**
> Are YOU ghosting me on purpose?

> **Harlow**
> The portal will be open in less than a minute. DON'T COME TO THE GODDESS DAMNED TOWER

> **Harlow**
> You're right. It's twice as disappointing when all caps don't work

> **Felix**
> lol

That was it. That was his entire response.

I hoped we both lived through this so I could kill him. I angrily shoved my phone back in my pocket.

"Don't react," Avery said in my mind, and I flailed. He sighed dramatically. *"The sickle is acting on my request."*

Startled, I glanced to my right, where Sera had been slowly

spinning earlier. She wasn't there. My sword still hovered near my shoulder, humming nervously. Tim had gone silent again.

I soon found Sera near the ceiling, slowly gliding below the smooth cement. I wondered just how voluntarily the sickle was acting on this request.

The Abercrombie & Fitch lady made a dramatic show of checking her watch. "Thirty more seconds until you meet your fate beyond the portal."

One more sorcerer chose Shade.

"Get ready," Avery said.

The sickle had just passed over the woman and her group of traitors when it harpooned from the ceiling and shot straight for one of the fire-wielding sorcerers at the door. The man released his array in surprise, and he went sailing out the doorway as the sickle slammed into him. They crashed into the wall of the hallway. His blast of fire had shot upward at a diagonal angle, scorching part of the ceiling and igniting the back of a traitor's jacket, but otherwise avoided roasting half a dozen people to death.

Pandemonium erupted.

The young woman and her traitors hit the floor just as the second fire-wielder cast his full array into the room. My vision lit up red, as if the entire room had instantly gone up in flames.

A breath later, feeble Macrae launched out of his chair like someone had just zapped him, and he flung a fully formed array at the door. My first thought was that it was a wind array—some great gust of air to blast the fire back out of the room. I briefly feared that so much oxygen would ignite the fire that much faster, turning the room into a localized bomb that would blow out the seventh floor before the entire tower went down with it. Perhaps Avery and Macrae had reasoned that the best way to stop whatever horror from coming out of the portal was to just blow the Tower sky high.

I sucked in a breath, my lungs seizing. I grabbed at my chest much the same way Macrae had been earlier. It felt like there was no oxygen left in the room to inhale. My chest felt like it was contracting in on itself—imploding instead of exploding.

I sank to one knee, hand on my throat.

Sweeney slid down the wall. Caspian staggered, hands on his knees. Someone in my peripheral vision collapsed.

My ears rang, popped, and then sound went out altogether.

All at once, sound and oxygen rushed back in. I gasped and coughed, hands on the floor. My chest burned.

I lifted my head, stumbled onto one foot, then got my weight centered and stood. I swayed. My ears still rang. The second fire-wielder was gone, and Macrae was collapsed on the floor, flat on his back. I honestly wasn't sure if he was dead or not.

Werecats sprang for sorcerers, sailing incredible distances through the air, only for sorcerers to fling arrays that knocked the animals off course with blasts of wind, an airborne chair, or gouts of fire. But no sooner had my senses come back online than the first feral came scuttling out of the portal like a giant, misshapen spider crawling out of a tear in the underworld.

A sorcerer knocked a werecat aside with a blast of air that hit the cat so hard its skull audibly cracked against the cement wall, only to have a feral leap onto the sorcerer's back and tear out her throat.

Three more ferals slipped free from the swirling black abyss.

Pandemonium really set in then.

The ferals didn't know who in the room was friend or foe, so they attacked indiscriminately. The sickle had turned into a whirling dervish of destruction, cutting down a pair of ferals just as they launched out of the portal.

Tim! Kill the ferals!

A silver torpedo winked into existence as Tim went streaking toward his first target, his camouflage falling away. *FINALLY! MAY THEIR ENTRAILS DECORATE THESE BLAND WALLS!*

Go nuts, buddy.

I watched, horrified, as a werecat was decapitated by a feral, its head spraying blood across the plush carpet in vivid streaks of red. The Montanan sorceress bolted for the door, but a feral stopped her in her tracks with a vicious slice of its necrotic claws down her back. She stumbled into the hallway, hit the floor, and screamed as she flipped onto her ruined back. Her very human fear overrode her ability to throw even the smallest of arrays when faced with a monster who she'd clearly thought she'd be protected from. Hands out, she begged the feral to leave her be, that she was a Shade like itself. She scooted on her backside, the soles of her shoes squeaking on the tile as she scooted away. The feral tore her torso open from navel to chin.

Everything—from the sickle's attack on the fire-wielder to the death of the Montanan sorceress—had happened in a matter of ten seconds. I blinked, and five more ferals leaped into the room.

Blowing a long, shaky breath, I glanced at my humming sword. "Ready?"

It let out a high-pitched note that I took to mean, *When am I not ready?*

I held out my hand, and the sword slammed its hilt into it.

"Sera!" I bellowed.

I yelped when the blood-coated sickle was in my face a second later.

"Keep Caspian alive, okay?"

The sickle dropped to the floor and gave the carpet an unsatisfyingly quiet tap. It buzzed angrily as it rose to Caspian's eye level again.

"If you can help keep the ferals at bay ... I should ... be able to get ... the portal closed," Avery said in my head. *"Try and keep the beasts away from Macrae, too ... if you're able. He's going to be ... out cold for at least an hour."*

I got on my tiptoes, scanning the area near the tables for the old man. The coffee table piled with snacks had tipped over—cheeses, caviar, and fruits were mashed into the carpet. I could make out the top of Macrae's head from where he lay supine on the floor between the fallen table and an overturned chair.

Tim. New mission: Keep Macrae alive.

A feral landed on said chair on all fours, chittered, and glanced down at Macrae's unconscious body, its head cocked curiously. Blood coated the feral's face. Without thinking, I chucked my sword at the feral, knowing there was no chance in hell I would have been able to hit the broadside of a barn had this been a normal sword. But my sword course-corrected, sped up, and slammed so hard into the feral's trunk that it was airborne for a solid three seconds before it hit the floor with a mighty thud.

My sword was back in my hand a few seconds later, coated in blackish blood.

A bloody Tim arrived near Macrae just in time to dispatch another feral.

Caspian gave the sickle a few test swings. He nodded at me.

The sword's magic flooded my system. My senses sharpened. My heart rate slowed.

We charged into the fray.

CHAPTER THIRTY-TWO

HARLOW

y sword and I cut down feral after feral, but they kept crawling out of the portal like baby spiders pouring forth from an egg sack.

I was having a hard time letting go of the spider analogies.

If a feral slipped past us and went charging after a werecat or sorcerer, my sword would shout demands at me, and its magic would force my limbs to react before my brain knew what was happening. Which seemed backward, but magic was weird.

Some unknown time later, my sword issued a *Prepare yourself!* as my only warning before it yanked itself out of my hands. I swayed on my feet and my stomach churned, but I somehow didn't collapse to my knees and retch. I had a feeling my sword could tell I'd been teetering on the edge and had extricated its magic from my feeble human body before I got flattened. It took me a few long seconds to get oriented and regain my bearings.

My sword had deposited me by the windows, well away from the battle still being waged in the room. New faces had joined us, but I didn't recognize any of them. My excellent deductive reasoning skills told me the people were sorcerers from Portal Relations, if only because four of them had huddled around the portal with Avery, and several open containers stood at their feet. The boxes looked like some cross between a toolbox and a treasure chest, and all manner of flotsam spilled out of them and dotted the floor. There were metal boxy contraptions like old-school walkie-talkies, large clear flasks filled with pearlescent liquids, large pieces of paper that reminded me of accordion-folded maps, and foot-tall tripods topped with a single spire that sparked with blue electricity. The last one reminded me of the tendril of energy that ran between Sweeney's ankles.

I quickly scanned the room for Caspian, finding both him and Sweeney squaring off against a werecat in cheetah form. Caspian swiped at the lightning-fast cheetah with the sickle, while magic-less Sweeney chucked items from the beverage table at the cat. Sweeney hurled a round serving tray like a frisbee, clocked the cat hard enough to distract it, and in the next moment, the sickle and Caspian divested the cat of its head. My stomach roiled again.

Tim was still dutifully watching over the still-unconscious Macrae. Based on the nearby pile of bodies, he'd killed at least three ferals.

Four! he happily corrected in my head.

Giving my head a clearing shake, I refocused on Avery. Ferals weren't streaming out of the portal with the same frequency as before, but they were still coming. The sorcerers on our side numbered around ten. I didn't know if they were from Portal Relations or if they were elite allies who had come to our aid while I was lost in my sword's magic-fueled blood fever. All I knew was that the good guys were still in the fight, but they were flagging. My sword appeared to have tasked itself with keeping ferals away from whatever Avery and the Portal Relations sorcerers were doing. They'd placed the tripods in a circle around the portal and would begin a spell of some kind, only to have a feral or werecat charge at them and break the incantation.

"Are you quite done frittering away over there? Would you like someone to bring you a bathrobe and cold compress for your forehead? I wouldn't want to inconvenience you, but your sword is strangely more efficient when it's paired with you. A fact so bizarre, it's sure to haunt me till my dying day."

You insufferable ass, I mentally replied, willing Avery to hear it.

I flipped him off, even though his back was to me. I was about to call out for my sword, but it was currently very busy warding off ferals. I crept along the windows, waiting for a lull in activity from the portal.

A pair of unfortunate people had been tasked with pulling the dead feral bodies away from the portal and the tripod devices ringing it. Every time Avery and Company really got going on the spell, a feral would come through, my sword would kill it, and then it was a crap shoot whether the body would land in such a way that it severed the sparking tendril of energy running between two of the small tripods. If that happened, the group had to start over again. My sword was clearly trying to lure the ferals farther into the room to prevent this, but the living ferals also managed to disrupt the setup as they came charging out of the portal. It was like trying to stack a house of cards on the deck of a ship caught in a windstorm.

I banked left, jogging slowly toward the portal, praying none of the ferals or werecats would spot me and realize I was an easy, unarmed target.

"Any day now, Harlow!" Avery snapped in frustration.

Another pair of ferals had just wiggled out of the portal at the same time, gotten into a tussle with each other, and knocked over two of the tripods. The tendril of energy between the two tripods, before it winked out, sliced a feral across the ankle, severing its foot clean off. It howled in agony and crashed into one of the Portal Relations sorcerers. The two went down in a heap of limbs and snapping teeth. My sword zipped downward and stabbed the feral in the back, somehow managing not to skewer the sorcerer below.

A roar sounded, and my gaze whipped in the direction of the doors just as three more werecats charged into the room. A feral leaped over them and disappeared into the hallway. A distant scream echoed a moment later.

Oh, we were all so screwed.

I hoped Felix was okay.

A series of agitated buzzes came from my sword several feet ahead of me, and I instinctively lifted my hand. The sword slammed into my open palm a moment later.

Behind you!

I whirled and thrust upward, catching a feral in the throat just in the nick of time. Its claws had raked down my arm but somehow only left a torn shirt sleeve and superficial cuts to my skin.

Between my sword's magic and Avery's mental instructions, I ended up positioned a few feet from the portal where the sword and I hacked and slashed at the ferals efficiently enough that the Portal Relations team could set up their tripods again. I couldn't glean much when the sword's magic overrode my system, but I still managed to figure out that the tripods were portal stabilization devices. Once the portal was stabilized, regardless of who had created it, it could then be turned off. But it was an involved process that required several sorcerers and no interruptions.

In my periphery, bodies of ferals were lifted via magic and hurled away from the portal. Avery circled the group like a mother hen, aiding in keeping the chanting sorcerers from being thwarted in their task of closing the portal before the Tower was flooded with monsters. Even with elite sorcerers on the good team, I knew we couldn't hold out forever.

We needed the portal closed so the sorcerers could focus on wiping out the traitors. Which would be difficult in its own right, as everyone was going to be exhausted.

An untold number of ferals were also running loose in the Tower.

After what felt like a millennium, the lull between ferals lasted long enough that my sword slowly pulled back on its magic even while remaining physically in my hand. As the magic receded, the ache in my sore muscles increased. I wanted to sink to my knees and take a nap. The battle still waged behind me. Werecats roared, a feral or two snarled, and sorcerers hurled their rune arrays. Scorch marks and deep gouges marred the plaster of the wall across from me. I dared not turn my head, just in case another of the necrotic monsters came through the portal. I held my sword's hilt in both hands, my feet firmly planted on the soggy carpet, and my knees slightly bent in case I should need to spring back into action.

The monotonous chanting suddenly quieted, and my gaze jerked away from the portal. The Portal Relations sorcerers dropped the hands of their neighbors. Lucidity crept back into their eyes.

"The portal is stable," Avery said.

I eyed the swirling black before me, noting that the wafting blue energy around the black oval had solidified somewhat. Instead of resembling crackling blue fire, the energy softly undulated like water. It was sort of pretty.

A feral launched out of the portal, and my sword's magic slammed back into me with so much force I almost pitched backward. We made quick work of the monster.

"How can there still be more of them?" I asked, breath ragged. "What if it's like a coliseum full of them and that was only the first wave?"

A werecat whizzed overhead, its long, whip-like tail

thwacking me in the back of the skull. The cat crashed into the wall along with a spray of fist-sized boulders that I guessed were the result of a successfully cast earth array.

"An excellent question," Avery said in my head. *"This may hurt."*

All sense of self-preservation flew out the window as I whirled toward Avery, putting my back to the portal. My sixth sense had shrieked an alarm before I even locked eyes on the rune array Avery cast. I managed to find Caspian in the crowd for only a breath, his wide gaze fixed on me just as Avery's wind spell hit me square in the chest, sending me hurtling backward directly onto the portal.

"You fucking bastard!" was the last thing I heard Caspian say before my sword and I were swallowed by total darkness.

Sweeney had made it sound like portal travel was as instant as using a telepad. Step into a doorway one moment and stroll out another in the next. Maybe it was that fast in reality, but it felt like I was suddenly lost to time and space. The air was so cold, it felt wet, as if I was walking through a rainstorm. My teeth would have been chattering if I had any. In fact, I no longer had a body at all. I was a floating, sentient cloud. I had both the sensation of flipping end over end—doing cartwheels through an endless void— and complete stillness.

Maybe I'd died.

If this was eternity, this place sucked.

I crashed knees first on hard-packed earth. The pain was so sudden and all consuming, my stomach heaved. The onslaught of light shot daggers of pain through my temples, and I squeezed my eyes shut.

My sword jabbed its hilt into my side incessantly, like a little kid trying to get my attention. It buzzed furiously.

The details of what had just happened came back to me in a rush. I staggered to my feet.

The thing I noticed first was that I was not, in fact, in a coliseum swarming with feral vampires. Currently, I didn't hear or see any ferals at all—not living ones, anyway.

The second thing was that I didn't have the first clue where I was. While the portal I'd been unceremoniously pushed through had been indoors, now I was outside. This portal, like the previous one, was surrounded by a ring of people holding hands. These people, however, were elves. Though my heartbeat thundered in my ears, I felt a shred of relief that these elves didn't look like teenagers. If these weirdos were going to be sacrificed, at least it was adults making the decision to throw their lives away in the name of Lachlan's grand plan.

My anxiety that I'd just landed in the middle of a school of hungry sharks lessened a smidge more when it was clear the elves were oblivious to my sudden arrival; they weren't snapping out of the trance like the Portal Relations sorcerers had once the portal stabilized. I didn't know if that meant their task was still incomplete, or if they were stuck like this until someone intervened and broke the spell.

That someone would *not* be me.

A quick scan of the portal's base told me there were no portal-stabilizing tripods here. The blue energy surrounding the pitch-black, six-foot-tall swirling portal waved wildly, like crackling flames. Which pissed me off all over again. It was one thing for Avery to kick me through a stable portal that opened to locations unknown, but anything could have happened to me when the *exit* was unstable. The instability was the main reason I didn't just jump right back through so I could slap Avery's ass into next Tuesday. Plus, for all I knew, the portal on that side was closed already.

I eyed the ring of elves again. They all had their faces turned toward the sky, their eyes closed, and their mouths a little slack. Although chanting in unison would have been creepy as shit, them being totally silent wasn't all that great, either. Hopefully that didn't mean they were on the verge of waking up and skewering me to death with thorn-laden vines or whatever fucked-up nature magic evil elves wielded.

My sword was currently nowhere to be seen, which I hoped

meant it hadn't sensed any immediate danger and therefore it was safe to leave me unattended.

I wondered if my command to Tim to stay with Macrae had been negated once I'd gone through the portal. I willed him to stick close to Caspian and not go off on his own, searching for a worthy owner.

I pulled out my cell phone, relieved it had survived the portal. I only had one bar, though. It watched it disappear and be replaced with a box that said No SERVICE. A few seconds later, the single bar was back.

I quickly typed out a message to Caspian.

> **Harlow**
> I'm okay for now, but I have no idea where I am. I'll update you as soon as I do. Kick Avery in the balls for me when you get a chance

I hit send. After thirty seconds, a red exclamation point appeared, marking it as undelivered. The no-service box was back.

I shoved the phone back in my pocket and glared at the portal. As long as the ring of elves was unbroken, there was a good—decent?—chance I could get back to the Tower, right?

A voice in the back of my head reminded me of what I'd *just* told myself about the danger of unstable portal travel. Feeling completely disconnected from everything worked great at over-riding rationality.

A snarl sounded, and I whirled around. I was forced to really take in the hellscape I'd landed in. It appeared to be a courtyard of some kind. A large fountain—thankfully *not* topped by a statue of Vincent Roch—stood in the middle of an area circled by shops and restaurants. Tables and chairs that had probably once dotted the space were tipped over, mangled, and splattered with blood from the slain people and ferals who were heaped everywhere. There were far fewer dead ferals than I would have liked. Was I in Mulgrew?

I shook my head. That attack had been days ago.

I refused to even entertain the possibility that portals could double for time machines.

So I had to be in the middle of yet another town that had been ravaged by ferals. It had been an absolute bloodbath.

The snarl sounded again, and I got on tiptoe to better scan the courtyard. I wondered if I could use one of the elves as a meat shield. It would probably break the spell if one of the elves were killed, and then I'd have a whole new host of problems.

Where the hell was my damn sword?

Two ferals on all fours were loping in my general direction, but they were slightly slowed by the bodies and debris they had to skirt around and jump over. They didn't seem to be in a hurry. They were presumably heading for the portal and not me specifically, but seeing as how I was standing in front of their likely destination, I needed to get my ass somewhere else.

I hot-footed it around the back of the portal—and came up short. What looked like a telepad station had been blown to bits. While not much of the station was left, the base of the telepad was still there, instantly recognizable, even though it was charred and dormant.

I whirled toward the backside of the portal. The pitch-black mass was flat, confirming one could only enter a portal through one side. Confident I was hidden from view, I let out a slow, calming breath and tried to *think*.

All at once, the portal winked out of existence. My eyes damn near bugged out of my head.

The ferals, who had been a few feet from the ring of elves, hit the brakes and skidded to a stop, their gore-covered chests heaving. Their wall-to-wall black eyes were unblinking and fixed squarely on me.

"Sword!"

The elves woke up.

I was relatively certain the vanishing portal was what woke the pointy-eared cult members, but some part of me worried they'd still be in that trance had I not panic-screamed for my sword.

The elves dropped their clasped hands, blinked unfocused eyes, and rolled their heads on stiff necks.

Before any of the dazed elves moved, something out of the corner of my eye came hurtling through the air and slammed into the head of one of the ferals—and then *lifted* the monster into the air.

"Turn to your six!" a voice shouted in my head.

My brain was short-circuiting so badly, I blindly obeyed the unfamiliar voice, spinning one-eighty degrees.

Could Stabby talk to me telepathically now, too? I'd need to start buying OTC painkillers in bulk.

My sword was harpooning toward me, and I thrust out a hand. Its hilt collided with my palm. I was considering saying something like, "Maybe these elves are just misunderstood, and they want to be freed from the pressure of Lachlan Shade's thumb. Let's work together!" when one of the elves shouted, "This must be the unfortunate spawn of Camila Fletcher—the one who wields living weapons! We must slay her! An enemy of our savior is an enemy of us all!"

Yeah, fuck these guys.

Also, dramatic much?

My sword and I went into battle mode. I had my doubts we would survive one on six—uhh … seven?—but the creature that had launched itself at one of the ferals was still in the mix. And as I spun, parried, thrust, dodged, and sliced, additional movement flared in my peripheral vision. Sparkling green magic. The glint of sunlight on metal.

We had allies.

Had my sword been gathering friends while I'd been trying to get my bearings?

Things were going relatively smoothly as far as murdering a group of elfin cult members went when a mind-numbing pain shot through my sword arm with such ferocity my grip slackened.

Then my sword was unceremoniously yanked from my hand, abruptly taking its magic with it.

My legs went out from under me, and my knees once again hit the hard earth. Bright-green vines covered in inch-long thorns shot out of the dry ground, waving around like cobras poised for a strike. I was so weak, I could only watch as the vines lashed out and wrapped around me like boa constrictors. I did possess enough energy to scream, however, and howled in agony as the thorns sank in deep. Blood trickled down my arms and sides, soaking into my T-shirt.

I caught a whiff of something burning before charred bits of plant matter rained down on my head and around my knees. A severed elf head landed on the ground in front of me with a meaty thunk a moment later. Blue blood oozed out the neck hole and soaked into the hard, dry ground. My vision went a little fuzzy at the edges. I hastily looked away from the glassy green eyes of the elf.

The vines encircling me slackened, but unfortunately for me, the thorns stayed where they were. I hoped they weren't poisonous.

Just when I was sure my exhausted, overstimulated brain couldn't take anymore, an enormous eagle alighted on the elf's head, as if the elf's pointed ear were a branch to perch on. Another spray of blue blood pumped onto the ground. Bile clawed up my throat.

"Fancy meeting you here," a semi-familiar voice said in my head. *"I've been trying to contact Caspian, but I don't think he can hear me. It's unclear if distance is the hindrance, or this place specifically."*

Dawning understanding finally hit me. This was the creature who had dive-bombed the feral earlier. "Rory!" I slurred, remembering that Henri had been sent to Caspian's house to get a message to Julip. The pixie had done her job; Rory had been recruited to scout out the goings-on in Elsher. It sounded like the aeorci had been here ever since. "Hi! You're talking to me. I'm going to rub it in dumb Welsh's face. Lookit me! Talking to an eagle!" My vision went fuzzier still.

Rory's feathers puffed up in what appeared to be indignation. His talons dug into the smooth, blemish-free skin of the elf's severed head. *"How dare you, madam! I am a falcon!"*

"Pretty birdie," I muttered before pitching headfirst into unconsciousness.

CHAPTER THIRTY-THREE

FELIX

Felix stood in the sixth-floor stairwell of the Collective's Tower with a handful of fellow bounty hunters and a trio of werecats—all of them in cat form. Information on what in the hells was going on was inconsistent at best. There seemed to be two nefarious factions running around—Shades, and the contingent of Collective sorcerers who'd had Sorceress Rhiannon assassinated and Camila arrested. Whether those two factions were working in tandem or counter to each other was still a mystery. All Felix knew was that Harlow was on the seventh floor, and a portal was letting in ferals. Once he got her far away from here, he could figure out the rest.

He cursed Yuri all over again. Felix and his colleagues had lost precious minutes hauling the completely uncooperative bear to a nearby mundane police station that was outfitted with a few temporary rune-reinforced cells. Given everything happening in Luma today, though, Felix figured one of Yuri's Collective sorcerer buddies would get the guy out of jail sooner rather than later, but Felix couldn't worry about that now. He bristled at the idea that Sorcerer Jeffries had seen this time-eating inconvenience in one of his brief glimpses into the future and had made plans to ensure it happened.

He made himself focus on the task at hand.

There'd been anecdotal stories over the past half hour about ferals running amok on other floors, but at least the ferals that had been spotted—and cut down—were in ones and twos. The monsters weren't flooding out the doors of the Tower in droves. Not yet, anyway.

Felix had seen the footage from Mulgrew. He'd rather die than let anything like that happen here. He knew the others felt the same.

"Any word from your girl?" Bartholomew asked.

Felix resisted the instinctual urge to say "She's not my girl anymore," because, regardless of the truth of that statement, it also didn't matter. "Nothing in the past ten minutes. Her battery might have died or something, though. I called her a few minutes ago, and it went straight to voicemail."

Felix's actual worry was that they were too late—that the ferals had overpowered everyone on the seventh floor, and Harlow's phone *and* body were in pieces.

Masters shifted from caracal to human and pressed his ear to the door. They'd gotten a routine going since the first floor: check the entire floor for ferals, dispatch them, then pile into the stairwell up to the next floor before repeating the process. The elevator felt unsafe.

Bounty hunters technically weren't supposed to be in the building. Everyone's bounty mirrors had again buzzed at the same time, back when they were still in Felix's private office. The message etched on the glass had been simple:

Tower compromised.
Evacuation mandatory.

Felix was a little disappointed in his coworkers; aside from the four of them in the stairwell now, he hadn't seen any other hunters during their sweeps of each floor. Sure, evacuation had been an outright demand, and sure, no smart mundane wanted to piss off their elite sorcerer bosses.

But he was disappointed all the same.

Felix refocused on Masters at the door. He reared back from the metal and shot a glance over his shoulder. "There are at least four of them in the hallway. They sound like they're … eating."

Felix clenched his jaw and got a better grip on his magic-enhanced machete. Masters yanked the door open. Bartholomew shifted into a puma and shot down the hallway. Felix grabbed hold of the door so Masters could shift and take off after him.

Silvia, the only other bounty hunter, bolted past Felix—magic crackling off her battle-ax in brilliant blue. They all had their standard-issue nine-millimeters, too, but guns didn't down a feral as quickly as one would think. Even a point-blank shot to the dome didn't always take the bastards out. A blade used to sever the head, though? That worked every time.

The ferals had been so engrossed in their meal of two sorcerers that they didn't realize they had company until Bartholomew was already airborne. Black blood sprayed across the walls and soaked into the floor as claws tore open throats and ripped off limbs.

Felix had been about to make a joke about the werecats never leaving any fun for the mundanes when a snarl raised the hair on his arms. He whirled, thrusting his machete at the same time, and skewered a feral in the chest. The magic sizzling along the blade ignited once it had made contact with flesh. The feral's ragged clothing went up in green flames. Felix held fast to his machete's handle, keeping the feral in place—it was a bit like holding on to a kite's string during a hurricane. Silvia was at Felix's side a moment later to sever the feral's head. When Felix yanked his weapon free, the body fell with a muted thud. The flames went out in a puff of acrid green smoke.

Felix's team crept as a unit down the hallway, the cats prowling ahead, as their hearing was miles better. When they determined the sixth floor was clear, they piled back into the stairwell and inched up to the next floor.

It was instantly apparent that this floor would be different. Beyond the metal door, magic crashed, people yelled, and bodies hit the floor and walls.

"Ferals?" Felix whispered, eyeing Bartholomew, who had his human ear angled toward the door again.

"I can definitely hear them, but they aren't in the hallway," Bartholomew said. "Not yet anyway."

"The portal is in the boardroom," Felix said.

Like on the last floor, they yanked the door open, the cats filed through, and the bounty hunters brought up the rear. The boardroom was in the middle of this stretch of hallway. Even if Felix hadn't already known this was where the chaos was going down, the double door being blown to hell, the scorch marks on the walls, and the bodies littering the floor would have tipped him off.

"Goddess above," someone muttered.

They were a few feet from the door when a feral and a werecat tumbled out into the hallway in a tangle of claws and limbs. Felix hated that so many of the cats looked the same. He had no idea if that cat was friend or foe.

Bartholomew, already back in cat form, immediately galloped forward, hissing furiously. Masters sprinted after him.

The infighting among the werecats employed in the Tower seemed even more complicated than whatever was going on with the sorcerers. But regardless of whatever animosity was happening with the cats, instinct overrode it when one saw another cat in danger.

Sighing, Felix crept toward the doorway, using one of the mangled doors hanging by one hinge as a shield. The boardroom was in total chaos. There was a veritable mountain of slain ferals in the middle of the room. Sorcerers flung arrays—though one of them seemed to be throwing anything he could get his hands on. The guy winged a love seat cushion with impressive accuracy, stunning a werecat long enough that a dude with a sickle could lop off its head. A few more moments of watching made Felix whirl around. And just in time, too. Bartholomew, his muzzle covered in gore, was charging toward the door.

Felix ran into his path, hands up. "Don't go in as a cat! No one in there will be able to tell which side you're on."

Bartholomew shifted seamlessly into his human form and sprinted past Felix, his artfully gelled blond hair speckled with black blood. Masters did the same.

Felix ducked back behind the ruined door, needing a semi-safe place to stand while he scanned the room for Harlow.

Silvia sidled up next to him. "You see her?"

Felix tightly shook his head.

There were half a dozen living ferals in the room, eight sorcerers, the guy with the sickle, a dozen cats, and Felix's crew. All the cats were going after the sorcerers, so he figured all of them had joined the dark side.

"Doesn't look like ferals are coming out of the portal anymore," Silvia said.

She was right. Notably, the only people who seemed to be paying the portal any attention at all were a pair of ladies from Portal Relations. Felix had no idea what they were doing, but he knew they were the Tower's best line of defense right now.

Felix's gaze shifted toward a back corner, where Sorcerer

Avery squared off against two werecats. "With me," he told his friend.

Felix and Silvia rounded the mangled door and jogged into the room, hugging the perimeter as they headed toward the old man. Avery was casting low-level arrays—spells strong enough to knock the cats back or discombobulate them but not enough to do any lasting damage. The closer Felix got, the more signs of Avery's exhaustion were evident. His skin was sallow, sweat beaded at his hairline, and he was breathing hard, like he'd just run a marathon. The cats didn't seem to be doing much more than threatening the man enough to force him to use his magic. They were toying with him—wearing him down so they could strike once he was spent.

"If you can take down one, I can take the other," a voice said in Felix's head.

He didn't break stride. Felix was used to Sorcerer Avery's preferred method of conversation—one-sided and invasive. Avery was certainly not on Felix's Favorite Sorcerer List, but Rhiannon had respected him. That was good enough for Felix.

"Gnomish backhand in five!" Felix called over his shoulder.

"Jaguar or leopard?" Silvia called back.

Luckily they were well all versed in types of big cats, so telling the difference between the two massive spotted felines came easy.

"Leopard," Felix said. "Three, two … one!" He ducked, running in a crouch, just as Silvia's one-handed battle-ax went whizzing around Felix's head like a boomerang, spinning horizontally like a murderous top.

Gnomes had a favorite move in battle that involved whacking an opponent with the flat side of their weapons—often in the face —to stun them before doing worse damage. The move looked like a backhand swing in tennis.

The flat of the ax thwacked perfectly into the leopard's back haunch, where it then issued a pulse of freezing magic so strong, a wide patch of ice fanned out across the cat's rump.

The leopard yowled and whirled around, but Felix hadn't

slowed his pace, still crouched, so the cat only had a moment for surprise to register in its golden eyes before it had a machete buried hilt-deep in its chest.

A breath later, Silvia scooped her ax off the floor and divested the leopard of its head. The magic still skittering along the blade froze the skin on contact, preventing an otherwise messy spray of blood and gore.

Felix yanked his machete free and focused on the jaguar, only to come up short. The jaguar was already dead at Avery's feet. The sickle that had been the weapon of choice for the sorcerer on the other side of the room now floated freely above the spotted cat's body. The weapon was slick with blood and viscera. A hum that somehow reminded Felix of an upbeat sea shanty wafted from the blade.

"I thank you for your assistance, sickle," Avery said slowly, backside resting against the wall and hands on his hips. He breathed heavily. "You may return to Mr. Blackthorn."

The sickle took off like a shot.

Blackthorn? As in Caspian *Blackthorn?*

Felix spun to watch the sentient weapon beeline for the same guy who'd been wielding the thing earlier. The sickle, much like Harlow's sword, flitted about the guy. Felix couldn't know for sure, but it seemed like Blackthorn was arguing with the sickle—Blackthorn seemed to want to leave the room, while the sickle was doing its best to keep Blackthorn where he was.

While the argument seemed heated, it lacked the level of urgency Felix thought appropriate for the life-and-death fight being waged. He cast a quick look around the room, noting that the only people left standing were five elite sorcerers, his own team, and Blackthorn. The werecats and ferals were all either dead or had fled.

Felix still didn't see Harlow or her sword anywhere, and now that the immediate danger of the situation had subsided, he found himself scared to ask anyone where she was. Instead, he pulled out his phone. His last text message to her remained undelivered.

"Hold your horses. We've almost got it!" one of the Portal Relations ladies yelled, apropos of nothing, abruptly pulling Felix's attention away from his phone.

Felix supposed the lady was replying out loud to Avery's mental prodding.

Blackthorn's argument with the sickle grew louder. He was saying something about there still "being time" and that it wasn't "too late." The sickle's own irritated buzzing was loud enough that it occasionally drowned Blackthorn out.

"Need us for anything else, boss?" Felix asked, turning toward Avery, working himself up to asking about Harlow's whereabouts. What if she'd been arrested, too, somehow, and was holed up in a Collective jail cell on a floor Felix didn't have clearance for? At least that would explain why messages weren't getting through. "Need me to cart you down to the infirmary? You don't look too good."

Silvia had her focus pointed elsewhere. "He doesn't look as bad as Macrae. Hey, Barth! Is the old man breathing?"

Bartholomew mumbled something unintelligible. Probably his oft-employed complaint about being called Barth. "He's breathing. Just unconscious."

"No, *Mr. Turner*," Avery said a bit louder than necessary. "We don't require more assistance. Especially since all mundane employees were *explicitly* told to leave the premises."

"And if we had listened, there's a good chance you wouldn't be well enough to bitch about us saving you," Felix said.

Avery sniffed and waved a dismissive hand. "Yes, well … thank you for defying orders."

"I do it as often as I can."

Blackthorn shouted, "We don't even know where she is!" Louder, he added, "Are you going to tell him what you did to Harlow, Avery? I'm guessing Felix wouldn't be playfully bantering with you if he knew."

Felix's gaze snapped to Avery, who looked the picture of innocence. His liver-spotted hands trembled slightly as he fussed with the wrapper of one of his beloved peppermints. "What's he talking about?"

"Got it!" called one the Portal Relations ladies.

With a sick feeling of dread in his gut, Felix turned toward the portal just as it popped out of existence.

"Harlow, I'm afraid," Avery said, "is wherever that portal opened up to." He let out a triumphant, "Ah!" as he freed his candy from the wrapper and popped it in his mouth.

"Excuse me, what?" Felix asked, pulse thumping in his ears.

Blackthorn was by his side a second later, with Harlow's sword floating beside him. The sickle was hovering by Avery's shoulder. Was the sickle Avery's new pet? Maybe Harlow was starting to give the things out like party favors.

Harlow's sword was acting strange, relatively speaking. The sword usually had an almost doglike personality, and currently it was just floating there, silent and still. Was it forlorn that it didn't know where Harlow was?

Felix gave Blackthorn a quick once-over. There was nothing immediately noteworthy about him—average height, average build, hazel eyes, brown hair, brown wardrobe. It was a little disappointing, honestly. Blackthorn had eluded all branches of law enforcement for years, including when the whole city had been looking for him and Harlow. Felix would have figured he would have an otherworldly charm that flew in the face of his sorcery training or something, what with him being a rogue. But he just looked like a normal dude—a normal dude whose jaw subtly ticked as he stared down an elite sorcerer. Felix kind of liked Blackthorn on principle.

"Get your mental hooks out of the sickle's consciousness," Blackthorn ground out.

"The hooks are wedged in there so tightly, I worry the sickle would be so furious once I released them that it would kill me immediately," Avery said, sounding completely nonchalant about his own possible demise. His peppermint clicked against his teeth.

"You say that as if I give a shit," Blackthorn said.

"My, you're even more fond of the girl than I realized," Avery said, head cocked. "I've never heard such filth pour from your mouth. Not since the day of your final exam, anyway."

Felix put up his hands. "Look, I have no idea what the fuck either of you are talking about, but I need one of you to explain where in the hells Harlow is. None of your circular conversation bullshit, either. Where is she?"

Blackthorn crossed his arms and cocked a brow at Avery, silently asking, *Are you going to tell him, or shall I do the honors?*

"Wait, wait," Bartholomew said.

Felix glanced around to find his team huddled up behind him. Beyond them, a pair of elite sorcerers were still in the blood-and-gore-soaked boardroom, both of whom seemed to be tending to a still-unconscious Macrae. When the hells had the others snuck out of here? When Felix caught the faint, persistent hum of buzzing flies, he looked back at Avery who, infuriatingly, didn't look the least bit ruffled by the ire aimed his way.

Bartholomew wrapped an arm around Felix's neck from behind. He was a good four inches taller than Felix. "I figure whatever you're gonna say is gonna piss this guy off," he said, giving Felix's shoulder a pat, "so I'm preemptively holding him back."

Avery gestured at Blackthorn.

"Coward," Blackthorn muttered, then turned toward Felix.

In an even cadence, Blackthorn explained in exacting detail how Avery had aided the Portal Relations team in stabilizing the portal, had lured Harlow in front of it, and then had shoved her and her sword through.

Bartholomew's hold on Felix tightened considerably.

It was possible that Harlow's messages weren't being delivered because there was no reception in other realms or in the space-time continuum or wherever fucking unknown place Avery had sent her. He was currently so angry and so worried, he couldn't even form a cohesive thought.

"Furthermore," Blackthorn offered in that same bland tone,

"Harlow managed—in the same way she had with the cutlass—to win the sickle's loyalty through mutual respect. She entrusted the sickle to me while in combat. Even while using the sickle, I could feel how much it would have rather been by *her* side, but it adhered to Harlow's request to help keep me safe.

"At some point after Harlow was banished to locations unknown, Avery began using his manipulation skills on the sickle. I could sense the change in its magic, though I hadn't been able to pinpoint it until now. The sickle turned on me, in a way, to prevent me from jumping into that portal after Harlow. And now it floats beside a man who the sickle loathes—not as much as it despises Macrae, but its hatred is still … potent. The sickle, like the cutlass, if it belongs with anyone, it's Harlow. Before I figure out how to get to her, I want the sickle released from whatever mental prison it's now trapped in." Blackthorn focused squarely on Avery. "Release your hooks, or I will do it for you."

Felix normally would have his doubts about threats leveled against the elite sorcerer that came from anyone other than his own kind, but Blackthorn was pissed, and Avery was gassed out.

As if he hadn't heard a word of Blackthorn's monologue, Avery said, "Rhiannon's allies are making their way to the top of the Tower and are going to seal it off to the best of their ability. Portal Relations is working to establish a portal barrier as well."

Blackthorn offered a grunt of frustration. "What does that have to do—"

"The Tower," Felix said, catching on to Avery's meaning faster than Blackthorn, "is the central pole that supports the tent that holds up the veil over Luma. If the central pole goes down, so does the rest of it."

Felix wasn't sure which was worse: Luma civilians being ambushed by ferals, or the entire veil falling and exposing the hidden city to the world.

Blackthorn's rage subsided a bit as he caught on. "And you think that was the plan here? To destabilize the Tower so Shades can knock out the veil?"

Avery shrugged one shoulder. "It's one theory among many. In any case, we can't leave the Tower unprotected. During the past few years, any time there were high-profile meetings in the Tower, Rhiannon—in her infinite wisdom—stocked the command room with a core of her allies skilled in defensive arrays. If anyone managed to get into the command room, they'd have half a dozen sorcerers on hand willing to violate the neutrality law."

Blackthorn said, "There were two women on the top floor of the Tower when we first arrived to meet with you, Macrae, and Rhiannon. They were watching us. Were they Rhiannon's?"

"Yes," Avery said. "There were several others keeping a close watch as well, just in case Harlow and her band of misfits came with ill intent."

Blackthorn scoffed.

"When the portal first appeared, I mentally warned those in the command room that an attack had been waged and that they were to begin lockdown procedures immediately," Avery said. "My first call to Portal Relations was to send one team to the command room and a second team here. The command room is currently secure, but the rest of the Tower is anyone's guess. Even with her trusty sword by her side, how well do you think Harlow would fare getting out of this Tower?"

"Wait," Felix said, pointing at the silent sword hovering by Blackthorn. "Her sword is *with* her? Then what's that?"

"That's Tim," Blackthorn said, as if that explained a damn thing.

Undeterred by the interruption, Avery continued. "How well do you think Harlow would survive in Luma when the werecats at large have it out for her? Not to mention that neither of you men would be able to convince her to leave this Tower without at least attempting to free her mother. If she were determined enough, that sword would cut either of you down if you stood in her way. As would the sickle and … Tim. I might not know where I've sent her, but I'd wager that she's safer there than she is here.

And that diabolical sword is with her to keep her out of harm's way."

Felix honestly didn't know how to respond. Avery's logic was faulty as fuck; there was no way to know if Harlow was safer. All they knew was that this other location had ferals, which would imply it was a place in *this* realm, but there was also no guarantee Harlow had even made it there.

Suddenly, a voice piped in from unseen speakers. "This is a reminder that all mundane staff are mandated to leave the premises. Any mundane remaining in the building—aside from those in the holding cells—after the next five minutes will be deemed a dissenter and will be punished accordingly.

"Today, one of our own let her misguided trust of mundanes allow for dangerous individuals to infiltrate our sacred neutral space. That mistrust not only led to her own death, but it also gave the Shades a perfect window of opportunity to exploit a gaping hole in our defenses while we reeled from the horrific death of Sorceress Rhiannon Crenshaw. Goddess rest her soul.

"Mundanes might not possess literal power the way the magic-touched do, but they know the ways of this realm better than we ever will. They manipulate. They deceive. They convince the softer-hearted of us, like Sorceress Rhiannon, that they want the same things as we do. But the truth is, the hubs were doomed to fail the moment mundanes were included. They drove the ancient beasts to extinction with their greed and superiority complexes. Their hubris leads humans like Harlow Fletcher to believe they can wield magic, when all it does is warp them into something evil, something unmanageable. We've lost countless good, hardworking werecats to the dragon blade that turned Harlow mad.

"And even when mundanes are given magic-born constraints like Soul NDAs to keep their conniving instincts in a vise grip, they still manage to break free. Now our beloved sanctuary, from which we lead with an iron yet gentle fist, is overrun with monsters. Camila Fletcher might not have opened the portal herself, but she *did* allow her very human emotions to lead her. Despite giving her and her late husband a life no average mundane could ever hope to live, she blames the Collective for her lot in life. Clearly, she passed on her rotten nature to her daughter.

"Camila's unyielding quest for revenge—one that she'd clearly been planning while AWOL … a circumstance not unlike Lachlan Shade's—set off today's series of truly unfortunate events. It's no coincidence that the worst attack on Tower grounds occurred once the two Fletcher women and the rogue Caspian Blackthorn arrived. I am not one to disparage the dead, but I do wonder how differently today would have gone had Rhiannon not trusted mundanes so freely."

Felix, his jaw so tight it hurt, shot a furious glance at Avery. "Who the hell is this blowhard?"

Almost in unison, Blackthorn, Avery, Masters, and Bartholomew all said, "Jeffries."

Blackthorn somehow looked even more pissed. "I'd know that voice anywhere."

"You'll be shocked to hear that Jeffries has been one of Rhiannon's most vocal opponents," Avery said, then pursed his lips so tightly they went white.

Jeffries continued, his voice ringing out crisp and clear through the ceiling's speakers. "The Collective's Tower is the heart of Luma. We, the Tower's keepers, keep that heart beating. Without us, Luma would die. Without us, the veil would fall, and magic-touched of all stripes would be subjected to the rules of this realm that are not made in our best interests, but those of the mundanes. Don't forget that a beast as powerful and as mighty as a dragon can be felled by something as tiny as a microscopic organism. Don't mistake the mundanes' obvious shortcomings as weaknesses.

"We know now that we need to tighten the reins on what we value, not loosen them in the name of inclusivity. We must band together—sorcerer and werecat—to fight our immediate threat:

the Shades. Those in this Tower are either with us or with him. There is no middle ground. We grant you a choice, just as Shade has, to choose a side. Those not with us in the lobby in the next half hour are with Shade, and you will be punished for treason. Once we have rid ourselves of the psychopathic elf, we will work —together—to strengthen our Collective. Luma will be the shining example of what a true collective should be. Join us."

Stunned silence hung in the boardroom for several long seconds after that. The mundane staff's five-minute warning to get the hell out of the building was already up. It made Felix queasy to think that maybe Avery had been right after all: Harlow had to be safer wherever she was—even if that was caught in some endless pocket of time—than in this Tower.

"How are we supposed to get out if the only exit is swarming with Jeffries and his goons?" Bartholomew asked, his arm still draped around Felix's shoulder. Felix wondered if his friend hadn't let go simply because Bartholomew needed something solid to hold on to.

Silvia said, "At least the cats can pretend to join Jeffries and then sneak away when no one is looking."

Bartholmew had a distinctive hiss-like laugh even when in human form. "Ignoring how many times you managed to insult my kind in one sentence, there's no way we're leaving you pathetic sacks of meat on your own."

"We can't leave Camila in here," Blackthorn muttered to himself, as if he hadn't heard Silvia or Bartholomew. "I thought they were just going to ship her and Soren off to the Antarctica hub, forced to do manual labor until it killed them. But Jeffries and his followers won't let them off easy. They might assassinate them in a public square as an example to other mundanes about what happens when they disobey."

Felix's queasiness intensified. Regardless of Camila's relationship to Harlow, the Fletchers had been like second parents to him. Nelson's death had rocked Felix so badly, his unrelenting desire to figure out what happened to the man had indirectly led to

Naomi's death. He'd never forgive himself if he left Camila behind—assuming he could get himself and his team out of the Tower at all.

"Your chances of getting Camila out of confinement go up considerably with the sickle," Avery said, drawing everyone's attention to him, "but you're not getting beyond the parking lot levels without an escort with appropriate clearance."

Felix's gaze momentarily shifted to one of Avery's oversized cardigan pockets.

Avery must have noticed, because he patted said crinkly pocket. "You could attempt to overpower me and steal my key card. But you'll require handprints and/or array activation to get to the lower levels. Assuming, of course, that you could gain entrance to an elevator in the first place." His gaze flicked to some spot behind Felix. "*Your* handprints were added to the no-access list. If you attempted to get your pals to the jail, an alarm would go off, and the elevators would lock until someone arrived to escort you out—likely in zippered black bags."

Felix turned to suss out who Avery spoke to. It was the sorcerer who had been chucking everyday items at werecats and ferals instead of using magic. Jade bracelets ringed both wrists, and a faint tendril of blue crackled between his ankles. Felix had heard a rumor about a sorcerer falling from grace and getting shipped off to another hub, but he couldn't remember his name. Swanson?

To Avery, Blackthorn said, "We could cut off your hand and use *that* to gain access."

Avery remained unfazed. "Would you believe there's a failsafe built into the arrays to account for that?"

Sorcerers were nothing if not thorough. But Avery also purposefully presented that as a mere possibility rather than stating it as a fact, leaving everyone on unsure footing. Dismemberment wasn't the kind of thing one wanted to do for the wrong reasons.

Felix noted that sweat beaded Avery's forehead anew. If Felix didn't know any better, he would have thought the sorcerer was nervous.

Avery said, "You'll also need someone with knowledge of the secret passageways. There's no way you're making it to the lower levels through the most obvious routes. It's a maze down there."

In Felix's periphery, Blackthorn cocked his head curiously. After a few beats, Blackthorn let out a disbelieving chuckle. "You *need* us low-level sorcerers and mundanes, don't you? If Jeffries's lackeys start sweeping the floors for so-called dissenters, you're as good as dead. You need bodyguards to help you out of here until you're back to full strength."

Felix's brows arched when Avery did nothing more than work his jaw.

"Unshackle me," Maybe-Swanson said to Avery. "I'll be at full power. In exchange, if I help get everyone out of here in one piece, I get reinstated."

In a stage whisper, Masters asked, "Isn't that like begging for your job back at a company that just got liquidated?"

"I can free him," one of the remaining elite sorcerers said. "If *you* do it, Avery, you'll lose your already dubious hold on the sickle."

Felix's attention slid to the floating weapon, which had hardly moved since taking up residence at Avery's side. Though he admittedly knew little about sentient weapons, its placid behavior *did* seem odd. Even odder than "Tim" floating beside Blackthorn.

Avery huffed a sigh that seemed to weaken him even further. His gaze roved over the small assembled group of five elite sorcerers—one of whom was still unconscious—two werecats, two mundane bounty hunters, a rogue sorcerer, a sentient sickle, and a Tim. "Unshackle Sweeney. The rest of you, put your thinking caps on. We have a prison break to plan."

CHAPTER THIRTY-FOUR

KAYDA

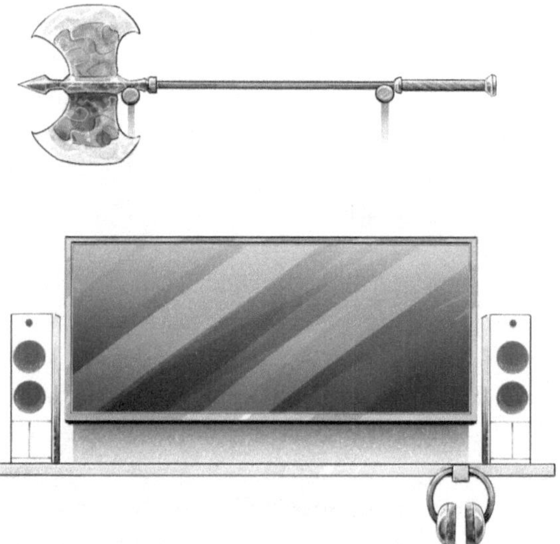

The Colony Lodge was positively alive with activity. While a few of the avians glanced their way, no one seemed particularly concerned with the three non-avians gracing their doorway. Kayda had no idea where Gagan had disappeared to. She supposed he was rounding up the elders.

The lodge's interior was some odd combination of a circus tent and the world's largest birdcage. Rafters crisscrossed the ceiling in a confusing conglomeration of wooden and metal beams as well as rope, thick wire, and rubber tubing of varying lengths snaking around with all the uniformity of a bramble bush left to grow wild. Birds of all sizes, shapes, and colors were perched above. Strategically strung tarps caught the various, and near-constant, droppings from the avians, preventing most of it from hitting the packed-earth floor below. Not all of it, though. Kayda, Marisol, and Alyssa had only been standing in the entrance for a minute and there'd already been two audible wet slaps. A human maintenance worker came bustling out armed with a small rake and pan to scrape the mess up before hustling out of view again.

Along the walls on either side of the entrance were a few benches vaguely reminiscent of bleachers. Avians in their bird forms, as well as a few mundanes, took up a few spots there, most of them engaged in quiet conversation in groups of two or three. Scattered in a haphazard array were wooden structures that seemed more akin to playground equipment than furniture. There were handcrafted trees that boasted flat platforms at the Y junction of branches—almost like a cat tree, but massive in scale. Rope ladders, hoops, and giant baskets hung from the rafters. Perhaps strangest of all was the ten-foot-diameter circle of wood mounted on the back wall. Six long pegs the length of broom handles stuck out at even intervals around the outside edge. Two vibrantly red cardinals, a snow-white owl, and three birds that looked like the love children of an ostrich and a flamingo were perched on the pegs. Round and round the circle went. An avian Ferris wheel. The chirps and shrieks from the birds said they were having a grand time. A short line of other birds on a nearby platform patiently waited their turn.

In three places on the ground stood giant round bowls filled to the brim with what appeared to be snacks. Kayda got on her tiptoes, trying to figure out what lay inside each. Avians were perched on the lip or standing around each of the bowls, chowing down on whatever was on offer. Her best guesses were worms in one, sunflower seeds in another, and nectar in the third.

The only area in the Colony Lodge that *wasn't* crowded was the six-foot-wide circular platform—similar to a ringmaster's stage—in the dead center of the room. Light poured onto it, like a spotlight, thanks to the oculus cut into the top of the dome. Through it, Kayda watched clouds scudding across a clear blue sky.

Marisol leaned toward her. "Are we just supposed to wait? What if Gagan abandoned us?"

"He'll let us know when it's time," Kayda said, turning her attention to her friend.

Marisol was quiet for a few beats. "I'm glad you're here. What was it you said to me in the car? *'Obviously someone out there thinks you're capable of getting the avians to help. I can guarantee you no one thinks that of me.'* I might have gotten us in here, but I have a feeling you're the one who's going to get us out."

"She said the birds make her want to pee her pants," Alyssa whispered.

Marisol laughed. "They make *me* want to pee my pants, too."

"Yeah, same," Alyssa admitted.

"Does this mean, when it's time to plead our case, you want *me* to do all the talking?" Kayda asked.

"One hundred percent," Marisol said, nodding vigorously. "I'll help where I can, but this one is all you, girl."

"Ugh. It's not like I'm the public-speaking type. You're the one who runs classes and hosts recruitment seminars," Kayda said.

A cacophony of tingling bells went off, and Kayda flinched, glancing up. The edges of the walls, where wall met roof, were lined with a string of bells Kayda hadn't seen before. They were all jangling now, and she suspected someone—perhaps one of the maintenance workers—was yanking a cord somewhere. She wondered if one such worker was related to Nial Douglas—the man from the FDMA who was worried about his radio-silent nephew.

The chitter and chatter in the lodge quieted quickly. The Ferris wheel in the back of the room stilled as all of its riders hopped off and found a steady place to perch.

From the far side of the bleachers on the right side of the room came a procession of avians in a single-file line. The way the other avians in that vicinity of the room, either perched on the ground or in the rafters, bowed their heads and spread their wings suggested that the elders made up the procession. Like a slow-moving wave, avians bowed as the elders passed by.

When the foursome hopped or flew onto the platform in the middle of the room, Kayda hastily bowed as well, arms out to her sides as if mimicking wings. Marisol and Alyssa quickly followed suit. Kayda stared at the ground. She could only hope the gesture was seen as respectful and not mocking.

"We welcome Kayda Verdan and her swarm to approach the stump and share her news from the outside world," a female voice boomed.

Kayda stood to full height and eyed the four avians on the platform. If she had to slap a label on them, she would have said they were all parrots of some kind. But while one was as tall as herself, another was closer to the size of a mundane eagle. It sat upon the outstretched arm of a man who Kayda could tell at first glance was an avian in human form. All four of the elder avians bore striking color patterns. Many of the colors were in-between shades she couldn't identify. Labels like cerulean, chartreuse, heliotrope, and vermilion didn't feel descriptive enough. Perhaps some of these colors didn't even exist in this realm. Kayda feared she was dangerously close to gawking.

"I think that's our cue," Marisol hissed close to Kayda's ear.

That jerked her into action, like getting goosed by, say, a ten-ton goose. She scurried toward the platform, pulling a quivering Alyssa along with her. Kayda sweated under the weighty gaze of so many creatures—around *and* above her. She imagined saying the wrong thing and getting covered head to toe in bird shit before being cast into whatever hells lurked in the hunting fields.

Gagan stood near the platform, arms behind his back. He arched a brow at Kayda when she, Marisol, and Alyssa came to an awkward halt a few feet from the elders. She noted then that even his eyebrows seemed to be made of feathers. She chastised herself to stop staring. The look he sent her clearly said, *Don't embarrass me. If you do, I will not come to your aid.*

He didn't go running off now that he'd completed his task of rounding up the elders for her, though. She was grateful for that.

Marisol silently reached for Alyssa and gently pried her away from Kayda. Marisol draped her arms over the little girl's shoulders and gently hauled her to her, Alyssa's back against Marisol's stomach. Kayda nodded at them each in turn—an assurance to Alyssa, and a thank-you to Marisol—before she swung her gaze back to the collected elder avians.

"H-Hello," Kayda said, cheeks flaming. She cleared her throat. Being watched by this many birds was really doing a number on her. Sweat pooled in her armpits and dotted her upper lip. A bead of it even slid down her temple, as if she were under the roasting lights on a movie set. The oculus above her and the bamboo curtain for a door behind her actually assured that the dome got decent circulation. It was cool and comfortable—save for the mind-numbing anxiety, anyway.

Gagan chuckled politely. "Forgive Kayda, elders. She is simply in awe of your plumage."

"I've never seen hues such as the ones that grace your feathers," Kayda said, thankful that the instinctual affected tone still came out of her mouth, even if her comment was asinine.

Asinine or not, two of the elders ruffled those beautiful feathers, and a third gave its wings a proud flap, revealing a rose-colored chest shot through with shimmering silver feathers. The gargantuan parrot, however, merely turned its head to the side so it could better regard Kayda with its golden eye.

A moment later, that parrot morphed into a human. The woman looked to be in her seventies at the youngest. Her hair fell to her back in wide purple ringlets that were more hair than feathers. Like Gagan, she was dressed in a simple pair of gray linen pants and a tunic. The ties of her tunic were looped into a bow that rested against her pale, freckled chest. Her eyes were the same gold as in her avian form and were flecked in a hue of purple that matched her hair. Her serene face bore prominent laugh lines. Kayda idly wondered if birds used the term "crow's feet."

"Are you not the liaison sent from the FDMA, Kayda Verdan?" the woman asked.

So many of the avians had pleasant voices. This woman's, while a bit aged, was rich and full. Kayda imagined them all being beautiful singers in their human forms. Perhaps they all met here in the Colony Lodge in the evening, or in the town center, and sang as a group.

"Gagan," the woman said in an easily heard stage whisper, "is this human ill?"

A smattering of laughter and chirps filled the room.

"I … I apologize, Ms. …" Kayda said, brows raised.

"Isa Dialloctus," said the woman. "You may call me Isa, if that suits."

"Thank you, Isa." Kayda rolled her shoulders back and willed herself to focus. She'd been about to launch into what they needed —passage to Elsher—when she suddenly changed her mind. Reaching into her back pocket, she said, "May I show you something?"

Isa pursed her lips but nodded tightly once.

Kayda swiped through her pictures until she found one of the downed Canada goose they'd found near the hamlet. "This may be upsetting, but you need to see it." She swung the screen toward Isa.

Isa gasped softly, long, elegant fingers pressed to her lips. The other elders morphed into humans, too, and huddled together to stare in horror at the screen. Kayda showed them the other pictures, including the ones of the rune array devoid of a body.

One of the elders turned to Gagan and said, "Fetch Yetka."

Gagan nodded once, gave Kayda's arm an unexpected squeeze, and then hurried for the door—shifting into a crane on the way. He flew out the bamboo curtain with a soft clatter.

That same elder—a man who sported silver hair that shimmered like sunlight-dappled water—turned to address the others in the room. Arms wide, he said, "The outsider has brought us word of Luwin Bergerdensis! He has been slain by a sorcerer!"

Those in attendance issued an ear-splitting chorus of caws, trumpets, and screeches. Downy feathers rained from the rafters. One avian was so upset, it launched straight up and out through the oculus.

The male elder called for order—which was quickly granted—and then whirled toward Kayda. Gesturing at her phone, he asked, "How did you discover him?"

The four elders clustered together in front of Kayda while staying atop the platform. They were as intense in their human forms as they'd been as birds. Their piercing gazes made her anxiety ratchet up again.

Marisol's voice rang out behind her. "We had been in the Northwest Territories for our own assignment when we happened upon a small group of feral vampires."

"And is that where you picked up this one?" Isa asked, pointing a delicate finger at Alyssa.

"Yes, ma'am," Marisol said. "We believe a sorcerer was experimenting on children in the remote wilderness and created arrays to capture food for them. Luwin Bergerdensis fell victim to this sorcerer. If you've had other unexplained disappearances of Navoltan citizens, it's possible that they met the same fate as Luwin."

Another wave of agitation swept through the lodge.

Kayda chimed in. "We were on our way to Elsher, which is a research hub in this area."

"I know of it," Isa said. "We export foodstuffs from Navolt. We are a mostly self-sustaining community. We grow all our own food. We have robust orchards and farms. Because we still have needs beyond this to sustain our human halves, we require the ability to purchase such items with mundane currency. Elsher is one of the hubs we sell surplus goods to."

Kayda swallowed. "Have you done business with them recently?"

Isa frowned deeply. "We have a scheduled shipment to go out to them in two days. We have not been in contact with Chancellor Thorpe since last week."

Blowing out a slow breath, Kayda said, "Sometime yesterday, Elsher was overrun by ferals."

Isa gasped. The other elders lowered their heads.

With Marisol's help, Kayda explained who Lachlan Shade was and that he had an army of elves and hybrids—with their ferals in tow—working with him to carry out whatever mission he was on.

"Elsher is protected from anyone traveling into the hub without the proper talismans or security clearance," Kayda said. "Even more so than other hubs because of the secret research they do there. Communication has been cut off. Most, if not all, telepads have been destroyed, so even if we *could* get in that way, that method of travel isn't safe. Elsher is full of people who are not prepared to fight off ferals. We need to find a way in to see if there's anyone we can help."

Isa stared at Kayda for a long while. "It could very well be a suicide mission."

"I understand that, ma'am," Kayda said.

"And I suppose you're asking us to provide you safe passage?" Isa asked.

"Yes, ma'am."

Without a word, Isa turned her back to Kayda and huddled with her fellow elders. They shifted back into avians to discuss the matter further. There was squawking and flapping, and one elder viciously pecked at another's neck until it bent low at the bird's feet, wings cocked at half-mast. After a very awkward few minutes, Isa shifted back into her human form and addressed Kayda.

"What advancements has your home hub made in cloaking magic?" Isa asked.

It wasn't a question Kayda had anticipated, and she cocked her head. "I … don't know."

"Ah." Isa pulled a small pendant free from where it hung behind the bow of her tunic's strings. It was a simple circular pendant with a hollow in the middle—similar to a travel talisman. While the hollows of travel talismans swirled with small vortexes of energy, this talisman's hollow was empty. Isa held the pendant by the outer edges, as if it were a coin. With a few uttered words of a spell in a language Kayda didn't recognize, Isa … vanished.

"Whoa, cool," Alyssa said, speaking for the first time since this conversation began.

A few moments later, Isa popped back into view—*next* to Kayda. Kayda jumped and clapped a hand over her racing heart. Her senses hadn't picked up Isa's movement.

Isa said, "We use cloaking magic more than any other. We're all born with an aptitude for it. In the fae realm, aves were hunted for our feathers. Some of our species were driven to near extinction due to poaching. Cloaking magic was our best line of defense against predators—in that realm, many of our enemies were even better fliers than we are."

Kayda was mildly horrified. It was like people hunting other people for sport, in a way. No wonder avians wanted a place like this to themselves. They were safe here. Possibly safer than they'd ever been in their own realm.

"We've found ways to create talismans that hold the cloaking power," Isa said. "For our surplus drop-off locations, we place a cloaking talisman within the cache, activate it, and then inform our contact where the hidden cache is. Our Elsher contacts requested this. We didn't ask questions about what they did in their hub, and they didn't try to infiltrate ours. It was a good system; everyone got what they wanted, and we both maintained our secrecy." Isa had the pendant held between finger and thumb again and gazed down at it. "Cloaking magic allows passage through a veil."

Kayda's brows hiked. "Really?"

The elders on the stage were grumbling under their breath, clearly unhappy about Isa sharing Navoltan secrets.

"We can fly you in, as our animal forms will allow us through, and those on our backs will pass though as well. The cloaking magic will get you past the Elsher veil, but once you're in, you'll have to find your own way out. We will not gift you any cloaking talismans; they're too precious."

Kayda chewed on her bottom lip as she stared down at the woman. She was only a foot shorter than Kayda, but the woman was so slight, she seemed almost frail standing beside Kayda's bulk. Or maybe that was just Kayda's insecurities needling at her again. "Have any of you ever snuck in to spy on Elsher?"

Isa tsked. "What, because we're no better than teenage mundane boys whose first course of action should they develop invisibility would be to sneak into the girl's locker room?"

Kayda shrugged. "Well, yeah."

"Yes, many times."

Kayda snickered.

"No one, as far as I know, has spied on the hub in quite some time, though," Isa said. "We did so in the early days of our agreement, just to make sure we weren't supplying food to a criminal enterprise. It would be quite terrible if our supplies made it easier to craft weapons that could then be used to yank Navolt out from underneath us, no?"

Kayda couldn't argue with her there. "So no warheads or anything?"

Isa shook her head. "Nothing but mild-mannered scientists hoping to master the art of opening portals."

"Huh," Kayda said. "Isn't that a *little* like feeding a criminal enterprise, if the fae realm was such a harsh place for avians to live? Seems like you'd want that door shut for good."

Isa shrugged one elegant shoulder. "Just because the door is open doesn't mean we have to walk through. Besides, the younger generation who were born in this realm are deeply curious about where they came from. Knowing one's roots helps one understand oneself better, don't you think? If you were given an opportunity to learn from your dragon ancestors what it truly meant to be a draken, would you turn such an opportunity down?"

Kayda already knew she wouldn't.

Isa nodded knowingly. "Let us share a meal together and discuss our next steps. We'll need to make many promises to Knuckles—perhaps allow him to eat his avian bodyweight in mealworms instead of his human bodyweight, as is customary." Isa said this more to herself it seemed than to Kayda, seeing as the woman stared off into space and idly tapped her chin.

"I'm sorry," Kayda said. "Did you say *Knuckles*?"

"Oh, yes," Isa said, waving a hand dismissively. "He's ... well, Knuckles is a special soul. But he's the only flier we have who could support someone of your ... girth."

Kayda wrinkled her nose. There *had* to be a better word than that.

"He's also probably the only one who won't balk too hard at the idea of a vampire on his back," Isa said, turning briefly to eye Alyssa. The girl pushed herself further into Marisol, as if Marisol could absorb the girl into her body. Golden eyes swiveled back up at Kayda. "The little one is an anomaly, isn't she? Perhaps such a fact will appeal to Knuckles. That's not his real name, of course. He insists on the nickname. He's been a bit ... *off* since the accident. But a great heap of worms should be the ticket. I should perhaps sweeten the deal with a month's worth of crickets as well ..."

"I'm a little scared to ask this," Kayda said, "but what type of avian is Knuckles?"

"A swan," Isa said. "An unhinged swan, one could say, but he's *our* unhinged swan, you know? Come, let's get supper."

Isa took a few steps away from Kayda, seamlessly shifted into her gorgeous multicolored parrot form, and flew through the bamboo curtain.

When Kayda glanced around the lodge, she found that quite a few of the avians had left the lodge while Kayda and Isa had been in conversation. The other three elders had flown the coop, too.

Kayda's phone buzzed in her back pocket. A chime also issued from somewhere on Marisol's person.

Pulling her phone free, she found new texts in their VHoA group thread. One message had been sent by Quaid almost half an hour before. Kayda guessed she hadn't heard it during the hoopla.

Quaid
Oh my Goddess. Just leave me here to die

The most recent message was from Cathy.

Cathy
The meeting must be over because a bunch of birds just waddled into The Restaurant. You two survive?

Cathy
By the way, if you're forced to eat, avoid the mealworm sandwich at all costs. Quaid excused himself to use the bathroom (basically a porta potty) about twenty minutes ago. He's been barfing his guts up ever since

Quaid
There was a sauce on it that was somehow tacky, sour, *and* chunky. It was the color of egg yolk. I don't think those worms were actually dead. I think they were lying dormant until they were awoken by stomach acid. I swear I can feel them crawling around in there. Are they eating me from the inside?

Cathy
This was the first time I'd eaten a salad, found bugs in it, and didn't immediately send it back to the kitchen. I ate a beetle I thought was a crouton. Liquid shot out of it. Now I get to sit here and think about the various liquids that exist in a beetle

Quaid
Oh Goddess. Here comes the rest of it…

Kayda glanced up at Marisol, who was still holding onto Alyssa, so she hadn't read the messages yet.

"What's up?" Marisol asked.

Kayda shoved her phone back into her pocket, closed the distance between herself and her companions, and draped an arm around Marisol's shoulders. Alyssa untangled herself from Marisol's grasp and then slipped her palm into Kayda's free hand. Kayda guided the two across the lodge and toward the door. "It's probably best not to know."

CHAPTER THIRTY-FIVE

KAYDA

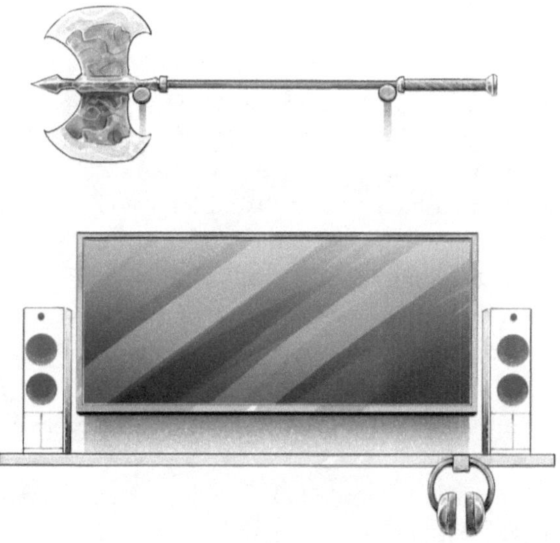

Knuckles the swan was the single most terrifying creature Kayda had ever had the misfortune of meeting. Somehow, he was less intimidating as a swan than as a man, but only by a small margin. As a swan, he stood fifteen feet tall, and as a man he topped out at nine. He was yoked out like a bodybuilder, his face and body were awash in scars, and his eyes were black, bottom-less pools.

Kayda had always heard that if you looked into the eyes of a psychotic serial killer you could feel the evil residing in them like a physical being.

That was what she saw when she looked into Knuckles's eyes: the soul of a murderer.

As a man, he only spoke in grunts. As a swan, he communicated with infrequent hissing.

When Knuckles had first been introduced to Alyssa, Kayda was sure the monstrous swan would take one look at the tiny vampire and gobble her down like he had the contents of the ten-gallon bucket of mealworms Isa had brought him as a bribe. Instead, he'd angled one of those depthless black avian eyes on the trembling girl, stared at her for five long seconds, and then issued a positively cheerful series of soft chirps. That was when he'd buried his scarred beak in the bucket of worms.

"Oh my," Isa had said, hand pressed to her chest. "He likes her. He will take you." The elderly woman had begun to walk away, then turned back to say, "We'll load you up with saddle-bags packed with mealworm patties and beetle crunch. As long as you keep him fed, he'll behave."

Kayda, who had been on the back of the giant swan now for the better part of half an hour, was well versed in how to feed a swan during flight without getting her arm bitten off. The sheer terror of it all was likely to leave Kayda as scarred as Knuckles's face.

Knuckles probably would have much preferred to have Alyssa feed him. But just before takeoff, the girl had wrapped her small arms around Kayda's waist and buried her face against Kayda's back, and she hadn't moved or spoken since.

Both of their bird fears were full-blown phobias now.

Kayda's companions rode on the backs of geese or swans, though Marisol somehow wound up on a gray harpy eagle. The eagle had something human-like about it, even while in avian form, which was decidedly upsetting. But her disposition was the polar opposite of Knuckles's. She'd looked at Marisol, shifted only her head to that of a human, happily declared, "I like her hair!" and that was that.

Even though all the avians in their current mismatched flock were aware of Elsher's location, Isa had joined them, sans rider. Knuckles maintained the front position in the V, the updraft off the gigantic bird's wingtips making the flight infinitely easier for the next two birds in formation.

Each avian wore three cloaking charms—one around their neck and one around either ankle, like identification leg bands typically placed on wild animals by scientists. Isa assured Kayda that the cloaking magic included anything on the bird's body, but Kayda still feared someone in the remote wilderness would look up and see six people zipping through the air, as if seated in an invisible plane.

When they finally got close to Elsher, it wasn't Knuckles or even Isa who tipped Kayda off, but Alyssa. "Did a bomb go off in that city? Why are there so many bodies?" She nuzzled her face against Kayda's back again.

No matter what Kayda did to adjust the dials on her sight, she couldn't see what had upset the girl. There was nothing but untouched wilderness as far as she could see in any direction.

A minute later, Knuckles finally began his descent, which was more of a plummet in a too-fast corkscrew dive that made Kayda feel like she was circling the world's largest drain. Her stomach pitched into her throat. The fact that she still couldn't see anything that even hinted at a city wasn't helping her nerves. Mostly because she didn't fully trust Isa's assurance that not only did cloaking magic encompass an avian's rider, but so did the ability to pass through veils. What if all six of Kayda's party tried to slip through the loophole in Elsher's veil magic, only to be shorn off their mounts' backs and wind up like insects splattered on a windshield?

"Ugh, it stinks!" Alyssa shifted behind Kayda. "Oh no. No, no, no. I changed my mind. Can we go back to the bird place? There are so many bodies! What if the monster that killed everyone is still in there!"

Again with the bodies!

Kayda was about to shout at the girl to calm the hells down—which would be hard to hear with the wind whipping in their ears—when an all-over buzzy feeling shot up her body from toes to head. A breath later, Kayda was *in* Elsher.

Knuckles didn't descend to the ground, though. Once they were through the veil, he just … stopped, like a hummingbird. A hummingbird the size of a school bus, but still.

Kayda gagged, quickly adjusting her sense of smell to block out the scent of bodies baking in the sun. It said a lot about the power of Elsher's veil that even odors could be trapped inside it.

Kayda cast a glance around, relieved that all her friends had made it. None of the other avians approached the ground, either; they all hovered several hundred feet above the city, wings pumping. She didn't think mundane avians other than a few birds of prey could do that.

Below them, what might have been a town center was littered with bodies of mundanes, ferals, and even a few elves. Kayda didn't sense any movement, but that didn't mean living ferals weren't lying in wait.

She craned her neck and eyed a massive swath of barren earth adjacent to the town center, populated only occasionally by boulders, training dummies, and wooden structures—most of them charred. Kayda pointed toward it. "Can you all land over there, and then we can assess what to do? If anything comes at us, at least we'll see it coming."

A few screeches and caws exchanged between the avians later, the birds complied.

Kayda and her companions slid off the birds' backs and onto shaky, tired legs. The avians were instantly fidgety. They flapped their wings, puffed out their feathers, and idly snapped their beaks.

The wind shifted, bringing with it the smell of rot. It hadn't been long enough for the human and elfin bodies to start decomposing, but there was something rotten about feral bodies, even while they were alive. The smell only seemed to agitate the avians further.

The only one to shift into human form was Isa, who looked deeply troubled. "I had not truly believed your claims about feral vampires being in this area until now. The reek is … unnatural. If Navolt were ever under siege, we have the advantage of flight to escape, but it would mean abandoning our home. We must prepare should this threat breach our veil as well."

Without warning, most of the birds took to the air and shot straight up and out of the veil. Marisol's harpy eagle nipped at Marisol's hair, then she was gone, too. The only ones left were Knuckles and Isa.

Knuckles shifted into his massive, scarred human form and glared menacingly down at Kayda and Alyssa. After a beat, he dropped to one knee and craned his neck to get a better view of the tiny vampire hiding behind Kayda. "You are welcome in Navolt any time. When I was an orphaned chick, it was a family of vampires who raised me. They showed me more kindness than I've ever known." He reached a hand into his pocket and pulled out a travel talisman. "If you ever find yourself without a home, know you have one with me."

The talisman looked positively tiny lying in the middle of the man's giant mitt. Kayda held very still and waited for Alyssa to gather the courage to pluck the talisman from his palm.

Alyssa, after taking the gift, waited until she was back behind Kayda before squeaking out a thanks.

With a nod, Knuckles stood to his full height again. His thick, feathery brows smashed together as he shot daggers into the top of Kayda's skull.

When long seconds ticked by without the man moving away from her, Kayda hazarded a glance up. His top lip lifted in an expression of apparent disgust, but then his bottom lip inched down, revealing his clenched teeth. If she didn't know any better, she would have thought he was trying to smile at her.

He reached into his pocket once more, but this time he pulled out a necklace that looked remarkably similar to the one Isa wore. "Luwin Bergerdensis was one of my best friends."

Kayda racked her brain for who in the hells that was. This guy scared the bejesus out of her, and her brain was mostly in panicked survival mode. Then she remembered. "The goose!"

Knuckles smile-snarled at her again. "I have been very sad since Luwin disappeared. He went out searching for his mate, who had disappeared months before. Her body was never found."

Kayda remembered that enclosed area full of giant bones and worried Luwin's mate had befallen the same fate as Luwin himself.

"You brought me great peace in knowing what happened to my friend." Knuckles thrust the necklace at Kayda, who reared back as the star-shaped pendant almost thunked her in the nose.

Kayda laid the delicate pendant against her palm. The star was made of a lightweight golden material, with a purple gemstone embedded in the middle. "It's very pretty."

Knuckles grunted. "If you activate it while holding hands with the little vampire girl, it will cloak you both. It is a thank you. From me." Kayda would have felt considerably better about this supposed offer of gratitude if the guy didn't sound like every word was painful, like he was being held at gunpoint. "I also … uhh … would like to throw my hat in the ring, as the mundanes say, to be in consideration for your mate."

A stifled series of coughs sounded behind her, and she figured either Marisol or Cathy had nearly choked on their own tongue. Kayda watched in utter dismay as the big man wrung his scarred hands. She made *him* nervous?

"Even though I know draken no longer shift into dragons," Knuckles continued, "the mere idea of you being able to turn into a beast even larger than myself causes a great tingle in my cloaca."

"Uhh …" Kayda tried but had nothing else to say. She was sure her skin had gone as green as grass.

"Feeling your girth upon my back brought me a greater sense of arousal than I anticipated," Knuckles said. "Are you mated?"

"Yes!" she said a bit too loudly, then cleared her throat. "Yes. His name is Henri, and he's also a draken."

Knuckles nodded solemnly. "He is a lucky male. Should he ever perish, know that I would be honored to take his place."

In the weirdest course of events so far, Knuckles produced a cell phone from one of his pockets. The forlorn look on his face was the only reason she swapped contact information with the guy.

"I will come to your aid whenever you may need it, my girthy maiden," Knuckles said, taking Kayda's hand and kissing the back of it. "I must depart. The air here is … wrong. I feel light-headed." His eyes had gone bloodshot, and sweat beaded at his hairline.

After giving her instructions on how to use the cloaking charm, he took several steps away from her, morphed into his nightmare swan form, and shot straight into the air, leaving a plume of dust in his wake.

Kayda turned to her companions, coughing and swatting away the dust cloud. Her friends were all either horrified or doubled over in laughter, so she ignored all of them and faced Isa. "Thank you for helping get us here."

"Be safe, Kayda Verdan," Isa said, her voice raspy and a bit labored. "I was going to ask for your contact information, but it seems I can get it from your new beau."

Kayda spluttered.

Isa smiled weakly. "Giving a woman a cloaking charm is close to giving someone a promise ring. It's not something that's done lightly, but it also isn't as serious as him proposing. It simply means he likes and respects you. I am pleased to see that your visit, no matter how brief, has brought our Knuckles closer to healing." She glanced behind her at the town center in the distance and gave a little shudder before turning back toward Kayda. "Please let us know if you discover anything here we should be aware of. I must be getting back. The unnatural aura of this place is making me a bit queasy, if I'm honest … as if the air itself is poisoned. We have much to do in Navolt."

With a screech, Isa, too, shifted into her avian form. She gave her vibrant, multicolored feathers a mighty flap before she took to the air.

Sighing deeply, Kayda focused on her friends again. Quaid and Will exploded into such wild hysterics, they had to hold each other up. Marisol's laughter was mostly silent, but she was near tears.

Cathy, grinning like a fool, spoke first. "Where to first, my girthy maiden?"

Kayda flipped her the bird, then stalked forward, Alyssa scurrying along behind her. Kayda clasped the star-shaped pendant around her neck as she walked, then tucked the delicate thing under her shirt. Her friends, snickering and muttering to themselves, scurried to catch up.

CHAPTER THIRTY-SIX

KAYDA

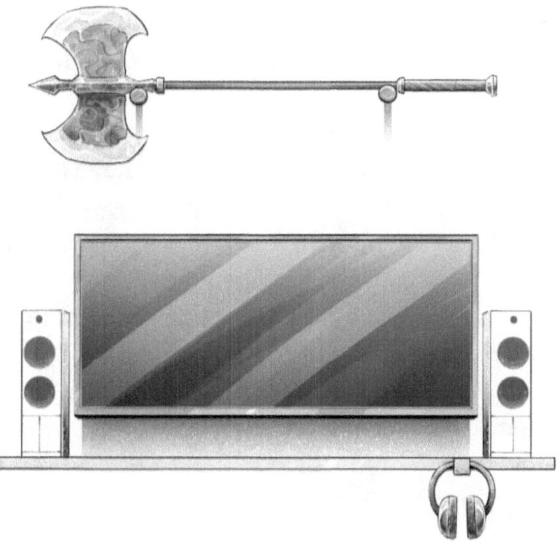

Kayda instructed Alyssa to climb onto her back, then Kayda unsheathed her battle-ax. The others readied their weapons, too, as they all quietly jogged toward the path that looped around the town center. Kayda adjusted the sensitivity on her hearing as she moved, but she still couldn't hear anything scurrying around. The closer she got, the more likely it was that ferals would come crawling out of the woodwork, able to sniff out the fae blood pumping through her veins.

Kayda eyed the dead man lying on his back on an otherwise pretty installation of flowers—a colorful mini garden that contrasted sharply with the desolate area she and her friends had originally landed in. The man's eyes had been plucked out of his ruined face.

Slipping between two buildings, Kayda crouched behind a knocked-over table. She heard the others shuffle into spots behind her, magic crackling faintly. She gave it thirty full seconds before she got up to crouch-walk behind a trash can.

After another thirty seconds without any noise other than buzzing flies, she was about to scuttle toward her next spot when something flashed in her peripheral vision. Her pulse thundered in her ears.

"Did you see that?" Kayda whispered to Alyssa. The little girl's arms were wrapped so tightly around Kayda's neck, it was borderline uncomfortable.

"See what?" Alyssa asked, voice trembling. "I don't like all these flies."

Kayda wasn't a fan, either. The closer her group got to the fountain in the center of the town—the water of which was a sickly brown color—the louder the buzzing got. There was a pit in Kayda's stomach as she realized she'd only been concerned about running into a horde of ferals; she'd already assumed everyone else was dead, and that Lachlan Shade was long gone. They were too late.

She couldn't imagine anyone had survived this.

She gave it a full minute before she moved again. She'd only taken a few steps when she heard the faint sound of a person running. The gait was a little uneven, but not that of a galloping feral. It was a human—she'd bet her life on it.

She angled her head toward the sound, closed her eyes for a

moment to settle on the direction, and then started running. Alyssa yelped as Kayda picked up speed. "Someone's alive!"

Two more sets of footfalls had joined the first one. There was a faint hum of voices, too. Kayda leaped over bodies, skirted fallen patio furniture, and headed toward the other end of the town center. Taller buildings and houses lay beyond this body-strewn area. Maybe people had been able to hole up in their homes while the monsters rampaged through the busiest part of the hub. As she ran, she adjusted the dials on her hearing to turn down the sounds of her friends running after her and turn up whoever was running toward them.

Kayda thought, belatedly, that these might be elves who were killing off anyone the ferals missed. Ferals weren't exactly civilized enough to use doorknobs and elevators to gain entrance to residences to check for stragglers. A magically reinforced door could probably keep the mindless beasts out.

The next time a voice reached her ears, the surprise of it almost made her lose her footing. She knew that voice. Was the potentially poisoned air of the hub making her hallucinate? She called out to the person all the same.

"Harlow?"

The approaching footsteps skidded to a stop for a moment and then resumed at double the pace.

"Kayda?"

Kayda saw her wildly bouncing curls first. Kayda's throat tightened at the sight of her. And it wasn't because she was filthy and her skin was covered in white dots. Hopefully being in Elsher for too long didn't result in a pox.

Kayda leaped over a few more bodies as Harlow barreled between two buildings and into the square. They reached each other in a matter of seconds and slammed into a hug—a hug that was easier for Harlow than Kayda, given that Kayda was carrying extra cargo. Alyssa jumped off Kayda's back soon afterward.

"How are you here?"

"What are you doing here?"

"Are you okay?"

"I'm not hallucinating, am I?"

The questions came so fast and were so muffled by the ladies' tight embrace, Kayda wasn't sure where her questions ended and Harlow's began.

A tiny voice asked, "Birds as big as a T-rex don't make you cry, but this lady does?"

Kayda pulled away from Harlow and quickly wiped at her face. By the Goddess, she *had* been crying! She sniffed. Harlow, for her part, was full-on blubbering. Her eyes were squeezed shut, her shoulders quaked, and thick tracks of tears ran down her face. Kayda pulled Harlow back to her, who wrapped her arms around Kayda's middle and rested her cheek on Kayda's shoulder. Softly, Kayda told Alyssa, "She's my best friend. Haven't seen her in a while."

At the slow approach of footsteps, Kayda remembered Harlow hadn't been alone. Her own group was coming up behind Kayda, the urgency of the situation dispelled by the tearful reunion. Kayda's gaze snapped up just as two people emerged from between the buildings ahead of her. She'd been about to call out a cautious greeting when Marisol went tearing past her.

"Joe!" Marisol cried.

"Goddess above! Mari?"

The guy, Joe, grabbed Marisol and swung her in a circle while she held fast to his neck. There was more blubbering as he set her down, but it was mostly all him. When he let out a sob that racked his whole body, Marisol pulled him into another tight hug.

"He's a bit old for her, isn't he?"

Kayda glanced to the side to find Will standing with a hand on Alyssa's shoulder, a scowl on his usually impassive face.

"I thought she was seeing Felix somebody," Quaid said, which resulted in Will's scowl being aimed at him instead.

Joe and Marisol were far enough away that they were probably out of earshot.

"Normally, Will," Cathy said, coming to a stop on Kayda's

other side, "I'd torture you by heavily implying Mari is whatever a reverse cougar is, but that's Joe Taylor. Their families go way back. He's like an uncle to her."

Quaid arched a brow at Cathy. "Why are you being pleasant?"

Kayda said, "Maybe eating bugs for lunch altered her brain chemistry."

Quaid groaned and placed his free hand on his stomach.

"Pro tip," Cathy said, "wait at least twelve hours to get on a goose after eating a beetle salad."

Kayda took a hard look at Cathy then, noting that there were bits of lettuce in her hair as well as a few mangled beetle carapaces stuck to her shirt. The woman looked more than a little pale.

Harlow sniffed again and unlatched herself from Kayda's side. She looked up at Kayda, her eyes watery and red. In a shaky, weak voice, she asked, "What in the ever-loving hell are you all talking about?"

"That's probably not even the weirdest thing that's happened today," Alyssa said.

Harlow turned to her, head cocked. "Oh yeah? How weird we talking?"

"This real big swan named Knuckles basically asked Kayda to marry him."

Harlow swiveled her bewildered expression back to Kayda. "You know I'm Team Henri all the way, but was Knuckles hot?"

It was such a ridiculous question, asked in a situation that didn't warrant it whatsoever, yet was such a Harlow thing to ask, that Kayda, inexplicably, burst into tears. She wailed as if everyone she'd ever loved had just perished a hundred times over and she'd been forced to watch.

Harlow whimpered. "Oh my Goddess! What'd I say?"

"I missed you so much!" Kayda blubbered.

"Oh, honey," Harlow said, half laughing, half crying. "I missed you, too."

"*Honey?*" Cathy whispered incredulously under her breath.

Only Harlow and Henri could get away with calling Kayda that without fear of getting popped in the mouth.

Harlow gave Kayda a minute to lose her shit. "We gotta pull ourselves together and get the fuck outta here. I haven't been here long, but we took out two ferals and several culty elves. Joe and Paola don't know if there are more. The portal's closed, but who knows if they have another one set up. Stabby and Rory are out scouting. Rory said your bird taxis left already, so I'm guessing we can't use them to get out. So we need talismans or a telepad."

Harlow, as usual, knew the fastest way to calm Kayda down. Harlow needed a hug, time to process her feelings on her own, and then a sympathetic ear when she needed to rant. Kayda, however, didn't need soothing words or excessive physical comfort. She needed information. Information gave her a direction to focus her emotions.

Kayda blew out a long slow breath, watching as Marisol, Joe, and presumably Paola—who had been standing off by herself looking incredibly uncomfortable—headed her way. Once the whole group was together, Kayda said, "The large vehicle telepad is down for the count. Any word on the smaller ones?"

Paola piped up. "We think the one in the residential district might still be up and running. We didn't hear it explode, anyway." She opened her mouth and closed it again several times, her forehead pinched. "Do you know who Lachlan Shade is?"

Most everyone grumbled in the affirmative.

"Well," Paola said, "he was here. We're pretty sure his people kidnapped two of our friends. When we didn't hear from them after two hours like we planned, we went looking for them. Their packed bags were still inside her apartment. Looks like there might have been a fight in the kitchen. One of Ren's friends was dead outside her apartment, but given the blood trail, someone dragged her over the threshold so her body could be used like a doorstop. There were two travel talismans by her body, and they'd been smashed to pieces. It was all very ... deliberate. Who knows why they didn't track us down and kill us. Mind games, probably."

Joe said, "Shade had a list of residents. If you're on the list, he takes you to Goddess knows where. If you aren't, well ..." He gestured vaguely to the dead bodies littering the town center. "We don't know why he wanted some people and not others. But given that this place is a research facility that specializes exclusively in portal magic—"

"*Ohhh*," Kayda and Harlow said in unison.

"We figure Chancellor Thorpe gave up the names of the most promising residents as far as talent and/or experience went in exchange for ... who knows what they promised her." Joe shrugged. "Doesn't matter. Once Lachlan got what he wanted, he had Thorpe killed."

"We haven't exactly scoured the whole hub for survivors, but we haven't come across anyone else in a while." Paola nodded at Harlow. "She came flying out of a portal when the chaos here was already winding down. Haven't seen much in the way of ferals, either."

Kayda gusted a sigh. "Do you think telepads or talismans are better as far as getting us out?"

Joe and Paola exchanged a shrug.

"They're both risky," Paola said. "Talismans guarantee we can get through the veil, but without transportation, it's a long-ass walk to civilization. We currently don't have enough talismans for everyone. There are a few cars here, but it's a matter of tracking down keys and vehicle talismans meant for cars. Maybe we could raid Thorpe's office?"

Joe shook his head. "There was so little use for cars here, I'm honestly not sure if she even had any vehicle talismans. Supply drivers used the pad."

"We have a rental," Kayda said, "but we left it in the middle of nowhere outside a hidden entrance to Navolt. We could hoof it if we can make it past the veil, but it would be a long-ass walk."

The group mulled that over.

"The problem with traveling by telepad is that we don't know if Lachlan has some way of shutting down the unit," Paola said. "Maybe it's rigged to malfunction as soon as someone fires it up. I don't know. But as far as getting us far away from here and closer to better resources? I vote telepad."

Kayda nodded once. "Lead the way."

They walked as a group through the town center and then across what Paola called Elsher's Loop. Paola and Joe—who kept an arm wrapped around Marisol's shoulders—walked in front of Kayda, Harlow, and Alyssa. Will, Cathy, and Quaid brought up the rear.

Their guides' body language seemed relaxed enough, but Kayda kept her senses primed all the same. Hopefully if something undead and bitey was nearby, Rory or the sword would give them enough warning.

"When you going to tell me about your new kid?" Harlow asked.

Alyssa, who was on Kayda's other side and was once again holding fast to her hand, leaned forward and hissed, revealing her tiny fangs.

Harlow didn't even flinch. "Eh. You can't scare me, kid. I practically have a high vampire as a stepdad. All the vamps in Tercla are way more terrifying."

Alyssa gasped, yanked her hand out of Kayda's grasp, and then was suddenly holding Harlow's hand. "You really went to Tercla? My kinda big sister told me that it's like Disneyland but for vampires. Is that true?"

Harlow and Alyssa chatted away about Tercla, the hamlet Alyssa had been living in for two weeks, and Luma. Kayda mostly tuned them out so she could scan for any sign of ferals. And she heard nothing—until they were a block away from the telepad station.

"Wait!" Kayda hissed, then stopped short.

Harlow and Alyssa quieted immediately. What seemed like a breath later, the sword was buzzing in Harlow's face.

"Holy poop!" Alyssa said, eyes wide. "You really *do* have a magic sword?"

"I don't know what's going on either, sword," Harlow said, clearly too distracted to answer Alyssa. "I think Kayda heard something."

Kayda cocked her head and closed her eyes. "I swear it only sounds like *one* feral, and it's ... pacing? I also hear the faint sounds of someone talking. If I had to guess, I'd say they were in the same room. Maybe it's an elf and a feral?" She opened her eyes and pulled her battle-ax from its loop on her belt, then quickly unsheathed it.

"Oh *shit*," Harlow said appreciatively. "Level 5? That thing really suits you."

"Right?" Kayda asked. "Favorite accessory so far. Even more than those Kingmeyer heels."

Harlow nodded. "The blue magic really makes your eyes pop."

Harlow's sword hovered near Alyssa, silent and menacing. Alyssa hissed at it. The sword buzzed angrily in response, its blade going red.

"Oooh, pretty," Alyssa said.

The blade instantly cooled, then dropped to the ground once to tap its hilt on the cement.

"It just said it agrees that it's beautiful," Harlow said.

The sword tapped on the cement again. Alyssa giggled.

Marisol cleared her throat. "Will, can you look after the kid?"

Before Alyssa could issue a protest at being left behind, Will ran up behind the girl, scooped her up, and tossed her over his shoulder in a fireman's carry. Will made airplane noises while he ran around in a circle, Alyssa laughing.

Cathy sighed deeply. "And I'll keep an eye on them, just in case their antics alert the dormant undead to our location." She trudged after the pair, Quaid on her heels.

"I bet she's fun at parties," Harlow muttered.

"As if anyone would invite her," Kayda said.

Cathy flipped them off without turning around.

Marisol sighed loudly, suggesting she didn't think Alyssa was the only child in the group. "Kayda … you, me, Joe, and Paola will go check out what's going on." She gave Harlow a quick elevator scan and then offered a smile that was probably supposed to look encouraging. "Harlow, uhh … are you and your sword up for tagging along?"

Harlow held out her arms covered in white dots. "I look worse than I feel. It's just dried baking soda to help pull out any potential poison injected into me from the cult elves' vines of death. I haven't keeled over yet, so I'm probably okay."

The sword tapped on the ground once.

That was all the encouragement anyone needed. Joe, Paola, and Marisol all pulled out weapons—though Paola's was nothing more than a mundane meat cleaver.

Paola must have seen Kayda's dubious expression, because she said, "If you think this is bad, you should have seen what we were fighting with before." Without waiting for a reply, the woman set off.

It took only a minute or two to reach the telepad station. The outside looked like a small one-room cottage, the wooden siding painted a baby blue. A wooden sign hung above the door, swinging gently in the breeze on silent hinges. Well-maintained hedges lined the small yard on three sides. The black gate in the middle of the front-facing hedge stood ajar.

The group crouched behind the bushes to stay out of view of whoever might pass by or peer out the windows on either side of the white door. Kayda felt four gazes and a blade angle her way, expectant. She closed her eyes.

"Nothing much has changed in there," Kayda said after a moment, her head cocked. "Still sounds like one feral and a second person who has the ability to speak. It's a … woman. Her speech is kind of slurred, but I think she's trying to reason with the feral?"

Harlow whimpered. "And you're sure the feral isn't talking

back?" When everyone except for the sword looked at her like maybe her brain was riddled with poison after all, she said, "There have been a lot of anecdotal stories lately about ferals mutating—including them being able to talk."

Paola said, "Renata—the friend of ours who was probably kidnapped—said something similar. There was a feral who looked more hybrid, even if it acted feral, and Renata said that, just before we killed it, the thing said 'Please,' as if it were self-aware enough to ask for death."

Joe shuddered. "This is even worse than the shift in zombie lore when they went from shambling to sprinting."

Harlow shivered, too. "Amen."

"All right," Marisol said. "Joe, Paola, and I will go around the back. Kayda, Harlow, and the sword go in through the front."

Keeping low, the group crept through the ajar gate. Joe, Marisol, and Paola inched along the hedges lining the yard and then disappeared around the side. Kayda didn't hear a change from the two inside, so she assumed the feral hadn't heard their approach.

The two steps that led to the small front porch were made of concrete, so no creaking floorboards gave away their presence. Kayda hunkered down below the sill on the right, while Harlow and the sword took the left.

The glass was a bit grimy, but Kayda could easily make out the meager interior of the tiny station. A telepad tube took up most of the room, standing resolutely in the center of the space. The feral paced around the telepad tube in a slow circle, very reminiscent of a caged animal. It didn't prowl on all fours, though. Its back was sharply hunched, there was a slight limp to its gait, and black blood was visible beneath its pallid skin—but it walked upright. It chittered periodically, as if talking to itself. On one of its loops around the front of the telepad, Kayda made out one raspy sentence. *"Do not kill her."*

It seemed to be repeating the phrase on a loop.

The screen of the control panel propped on a freestanding

pole beside the tube was dark. A very faint blue glow emanated from the base of the tube, indicating that the thing was operational, at least. Most notable, though, was the woman—her face bloody and bruised—chained to the pole. The feral hardly paid her any mind, either stepping over her slumped body or skirting around it, all the while repeating its mantra not to kill the woman.

The mechanism keeping the woman in place was similar to handcuffs, but yellow-tinged magic skittered along the cuffs, one fastened around the pole and the other around the woman's wrist, as well as along the short chain. Kayda guessed the woman had only recently regained consciousness after her beating.

Kayda didn't know much about the claims of mutating ferals Harlow mentioned, but the fact that this one could remain cooped up with a bleeding woman spoke volumes. Especially since her blood was blue, marking her as fae.

Doing her best to keep her voice low, Kayda glanced at Harlow and said, "When it's behind the tube, you open the door, and I'll run in to ambush it. Looks like it's guarding the woman, not that it plans to kill her, so I think she'll be safe. Sword, will you be my backup?"

It tapped once, very softly, on the porch.

Kayda and Harlow tiptoed into position, with Harlow keeping one hand on the doorknob while Kayda crouched by the same window Harlow had been peering into earlier.

"Now!" Kayda hissed.

Harlow yanked open the door, Kayda charged into the room, and the sword loudly crashed through the window. The feral was so startled, it came up short, allowing the sword to corral the monster against the back wall with its blade a mere inch from the feral's neck.

Kayda sighed, letting her battle-ax hang by her side. She wasn't sure why she thought the sword would adhere to her plan.

"*Oh shit!*" someone from outside yelled, followed by the snarls of several ferals.

Kayda debated running out there to help, but her heightened senses picked up Marisol's labored message.

"If you can … hear me, we're … okay, Kayda. There's only four, and Joe is … terrifying with a … spear."

Heaving a breath of relief, she focused on Harlow, who was squatting beside the bleeding woman. The woman looked decidedly more alert now, though her speech was still slurred.

"Hey, hey, slow down," Harlow said, as she helped the woman sit a little straighter. "I'm Harlow. That's Kayda. We aren't allied with vampires, elves, or Lachlan Shade. We're trying to get out of here, just like you. What's your name?"

It took the woman a few long seconds to decide whether Kayda and Harlow were friend or foe. Given the number of times she glanced over at the feral still pinned to the wall, Kayda figured the woman was mostly worried the sword couldn't keep the monster in place.

"Wren," she finally said, wincing. One cheek was bruised beneath her light-brown skin, her upper lip was swollen, one eye had purpled, and a trail of blue blood ran from below her hairline of short dark curls and down her temple. A sizable stain on the chest of her white shirt grew ever wider with each drop of blood. Her long green skirt was torn in a few places, and her bare feet were filthy.

While Wren's ears weren't pointed, Kayda was immediately reminded of a wood nymph.

Gently, Harlow asked, "Can you tell me how you ended up here, Wren?"

Wren visibly swallowed a few times. She spoke slowly, as if every word pained her. "I'm the resident earth witch. I'm in charge of the garden and this telepad station. Very few people in Elsher have access to the codes to operate the pads, and each one will only recognize a few people's blood or fingerprints to operate it. Somehow Lachlan Shade was told I was one of the few who knew how to operate this one. He had the other pads destroyed so no one could get in but made sure he had a safe way out." Her bright-green eyes slid toward the feral. "He left that thing in here with me to make sure I couldn't run off in case Lachlan needs to get back. He ordered it to kill me if I tried to damage the telepad in any way and to use violence if I saw a return request from Lachlan on the screen and I attempted to refuse him entry."

Kayda eyed the cuff chaining the woman to the pole. "Magic suppressant?"

"Worse," Wren said. "If I try to use magic, it reverses it back onto me. The cuts and bruises are from me calling Lachlan's bluff. Knocked myself out almost immediately."

Kayda chuckled. "Ballsy."

"Stupid," Wren muttered.

"Nah, definitely ballsy," Harlow said. "Any ideas on how we can get the cuff off you?"

"Lachlan said there are only two ways—either with brute strength or if the person who put the spell on the cuff—him—deactivates it."

Kayda gave her battle-ax a few swipes. "The chain is short and if you flinch, I might take off your hand, but it sounds like brute strength is our best option."

Wren's eyes were wide as she eyed the ax. "There's a catch."

Harlow sighed. "Of course there is."

"It's not just about breaking the chain," Wren said. "If the chain or cuff is compromised in any way, then the cuff will basically self-destruct. Best case scenario is it only blows my hand off. I also only have five seconds from the time it's compromised to get out of the cuff."

Harlow blew out a breath. "So painstakingly sawing the thing off won't work. And I'm pretty good with lock picks, but five seconds isn't a lot of time. And I don't have my tools …"

Wren lightly flailed her wrist, causing the ring circling it to slide along the pole a few inches. "There's no lock to pick anyway."

Kayda turned sharply at the sound of footfalls on the steps outside. Over her shoulder, she called, "It's clear."

Marisol, Joe, and Paola—all splattered with fresh blackish blood—cautiously stepped into the room. The feral still pinned to the wall issued a snarl of protest at the intrusion, but a warning buzz from the sword at its throat shut the monster up.

Kayda gave the new arrivals the Cliffs Notes version of Wren's tale. Her companions then launched into an animated discussion about how best to get Wren free.

Marisol said, "My main concern about freeing her before we start getting people to a new location is that I'm sure Lachlan has something in place that will alert him if the cuff on Wren breaks. He'll consider Elsher compromised. That might trigger this telepad station to be blown sky high like all the others."

Everyone cautiously scanned the room, as if they could spot a bomb tucked into a corner.

Paola scowled at Marisol. "So, what, you're saying we force her to send us to safety and then leave her here to rot?"

"Of course not," Marisol snapped. "I just mean—"

Kayda held up a hand to quiet them. "Mari's right. Normally I'd call the bluff. But between meeting Lachlan myself and Wren admitting her magic was used to kick her own ass, we have to assume Lachlan has fail-safes in place. Our best bet is to either get one of us out of here and to someone trustworthy who can come back and get Wren out of this, or—"

"Won't work," Wren said. "The only way to get someone into Elsher is if that person has clearance. The system won't recognize people without it. Everyone with clearance was either kidnapped by the Shades, working with the Shades, or dead."

Joe said, "That tracks. Despite working directly for the chancellor, I still only have low-level clearance."

Kayda's stomach churned. "Then the only option I see left is that all but one of us needs to get to safety, then that last person frees Wren. We just have to hope that's enough time to get us out of here before Lachlan can react and shut this one down."

Harlow was on her feet in an instant and in Kayda's face. Well, as close to Kayda's face as she could reach. Harlow jammed her fists onto her hips and glared up at Kayda. "That sounds suspiciously like you're planning to take one for the team."

"Wren said brute strength. I'm the best person for the job. And if that five seconds isn't enough time, it'll be better if there's fewer of you stuck in the blast zone. Besides, I can move really fucking fast when I'm motivated, and avoiding getting blown to shit is pretty motivating."

"Nope!" Harlow said, wagging a finger high in the air and pivoting away from Kayda. "Next option."

"I appreciate you all trying to include me in—" Wren started.

Harlow whirled on *her* now. "You don't get to take one for the team, either. Everyone stop with the self-sacrificing bullshit. We either all get out, or none of us do."

"Maybe Kay can call her bird boyfriend back here," Marisol said.

Kayda grimaced. She wasn't sure that enough of the avians would come back to get all of them out of here. The birds had only been in Elsher for a few minutes, and they'd all shown signs of sickness due to the poisoned air. As appreciative as Isa was that Kayda and her friends had brought the avians important information, Kayda figured the elders would err on the side of safety for their own people over playing chauffeur again.

"Ohh," Harlow said, standing stock still with her wide eyes focused on some point only she could see. Kayda often joked that it looked like an idea had just struck her like a bolt of lightning.

Kayda crossed her arms. "What weird shit have you come up with now?"

"Is there *anywhere* in town that gets decent enough reception to get a call out?" Harlow asked.

Joe tipped his head toward the door. "There's a spot nearby that gets almost perfect reception as long as the wind doesn't shift in the wrong direction. Follow me."

Everyone waited in awkward silence as Harlow and Joe left the station. The feral remained silent, but its gaze seemed to take in everything going on, as if it were assessing the precarious situation it was in.

"Any reason you haven't killed that thing yet?" Marisol finally asked, jerking her chin at the feral.

"I'm guessing the ferals outside attacked you because we tripped something in here," Kayda said. "Killing the feral guarding Wren might trigger something, too. Maybe that's giving Lachlan too much credit, but he's usually ten steps ahead, so I don't want to risk it."

Joe came back in long enough to squat beside Wren and exchange a few whispered words with her, and then he was out the door again.

By the time Harlow and Joe returned, Joe looked a little pale, and Harlow's smile was showing too many teeth.

Kayda jutted her chin at Harlow. "What in the hells did you do?"

"Help is on the way!" Harlow said vaguely, making it clear she wanted to keep the person's identity a secret for now—which meant at least one, if not several, people wouldn't approve of this guest.

Kayda trusted Harlow implicitly, but she also had her doubts about her friend's methods. It was no wonder Harlow and Welsh got along. Blowing out a slow, calming breath, she settled in to wait.

CHAPTER THIRTY-SEVEN

RENATA

R enata stood beside Dalton, their forearms pressed together. They were leaning into each other—holding each other up. There were at least forty other Elsher residents here. Most of them looked like they'd been roughed up before being shuttled here by Lachlan or one of his Shades. Renata hadn't seen Joan Calder anywhere. Did that mean the woman had been taken elsewhere?

Or, when it had become clear she hadn't known as much about portal creation as she'd claimed, had the Shades killed her?

The group was huddled in a clearing in a meadow. Overgrown grasses stretched in every direction, but the area they stood in now had been mowed or flattened. Renata didn't have the faintest clue where this meadow was. Lachlan had gotten everyone out via the last remaining telepad—which was operated by Wren, the hub's earth elemental. The telepad ride deposited them in the Branshire hub in Montana. She only knew that much because some of the others had been whispering about it.

From there, the group had been shuttled through hallways in what looked like a high-rise office building, directed down stairwells, and then bundled into SUVs with tinted windows waiting at the curb. A few employees of the office building had seen the lot of them—scuffed up, dirty, some crying—and hadn't offered so much as a concerned rise of an eyebrow. They merely peered out at the procession from the safety of doorways.

After driving out of the hub in a single file line, like a presidential motorcade, the SUVs headed into a rural area off a highway. Renata had been watching street signs and had every reason to believe they were still in Montana, but considering that she'd never been to the state before, it might as well be a foreign country.

When Renata and Dalton had piled out of the SUV, the hair on her arms had immediately lifted thanks to the electric crackle in the air. She knew that feeling all too well. After being forcibly shoved along by one of Lachlan's elfin minions, she'd found the source of the sensation: a portal—huge, swirling, and ... *stable.* She'd been caught between awe and horror. She'd shifted her gaze to a spot beside the portal to find Lachlan watching her with a small, knowing smile on his pretty face. He'd sensed her awe, as if they shared something unique and special.

He'd unnecessarily gestured to the portal, as if there hadn't already been a line forming as the Elsher residents were forced to step inside to be whisked off to Goddess knew where. The price for resisting had been paid early and swiftly.

Just before a woman had stepped into the portal, she'd panicked and fled. An elf had stopped her in her tracks. The elf's casted magic had caused the dry earth below the woman to give way suddenly—a sinkhole just for her. It swallowed the woman up, her screams abruptly cutting off as the dirt settled over her—a small mound the only evidence that anything had disturbed the ground.

No one had tried to escape after that.

Renata, with Dalton behind her, had stepped through the portal like all the others and ended up in this remote location. She had no idea if this was a hub or the mundane world or if they were still in the United States—hells, she didn't even know if she was still in the earthen realm.

Lachlan's abilities—and those of his followers—commanded portal magic that extended far beyond anything Renata could do. It was beyond anything she'd seen in Elsher, honestly.

So why the hells had she and Dalton been on that very short list? Because of the paper they'd written—a paper that hadn't been published yet, or even evaluated by the Symposium?

A snarl sounded behind her.

The unsettling noises from the prowling ferals still set her teeth on edge, but she didn't flinch every time she heard them anymore. The monsters were circling the group at large, snapping at people's heels if they got too close to the edge of the flattened circle. Beyond the ferals, two-foot-tall grasses—green and topped with small white flowers—swayed gently in the breeze. It felt more like spring weather than the summer climate she'd left behind in Elsher, but it wasn't as if that were enough of a clue to tell her where in the world she was.

In addition to the ferals behind the group preventing anyone from sprinting off into the vegetation, a smaller pack prowled around inside the clearing, slowly pushing the Elsher residents away from the dead center of the circle. That central area was populated by elves working on opening yet another portal. It was only in its beginning stages, but it was expanding with a speed that made Renata's heart flutter. Where had Lachlan and his people learned this? Was it knowledge gained while in exile, and he'd taught it to the others in record time?

As the elves worked, Lachlan began calling out names. The first batch—with the aid of ferals who herded people like a dog might herd sheep—formed a loose circle around the elves in the center of the clearing. Renata was too far away to hear the specific instructions the residents were given, but they soon began a series of spells or incantations. If a resident refused, Lachlan would attempt to convince them verbally. If they *still* refused, a feral was instructed to tear the person to pieces.

It only happened twice before everyone fell in line.

Another round of people was called up to form a second ring, this one behind the Elsher residents still working on their assigned spells. This circle was wider. The formation reminded her of a rune array, only instead of runes lining the nested rings, it was people.

She and Dalton were the only ones left who hadn't been called.

The second ring of people was tasked with casting arrays. Renata couldn't discern what most of them were for. Perhaps she could have, had she not been quaking so badly. What would happen when Lachlan realized that Renata and Dalton possessed an entry-level grasp of portal magic compared to him?

Dalton slipped his clammy hand into hers.

Three ferals loitered somewhere behind them. The monsters weren't doing anything particularly threatening, but every once in a while, she'd feel one right behind her, sniffing her pant legs or shoes.

"Can you tell what's happening?" Renata whispered up to Dalton.

Her friend's face was a mask, but his eyes darted about, meaning he was taking in everything he could, assessing the situation. He finally looked down at her and shook his head. "The arrays are for all kinds of things—safe passage, clarity of purpose, finding lost items. There're others I don't recognize at all. And then ..." He shook his head again. "Some of the incantations are in a language I've never heard before."

Somehow that made Renata feel better. She'd been so panicked, she'd thought her brain couldn't even process spoken *or* written language anymore.

"Do you—" she started.

"Renata Bernard and Dalton Edwards!"

Renata *did* flinch at that.

When they didn't move right away, a feral behind them snarled and headbutted Renata in her lower back. She yelped and stumbled forward. Dalton let her hand go, and the pair slipped between two women working on arrays and then under the clasped arms of the smaller ring of chanting Elsher sorcerers. The elves who ringed the portal were fully in a trance now, their heads thrown back as they chanted in unison. The portal was already four feet tall and nearly as many feet wide. Lachlan stood between the circle of elves and the smaller ring of sorcerers, waiting patiently for them to join him.

Newly arrived elves and several ferals stalked between the rings of sorcerers, making sure everyone complied with Lachlan's demands. Renata wondered what would happen if all the sorcerers turned against Lachlan at once. Or if one of them dropped their array at the perfect time to ruin the spell. Were there enough of them that they could overpower the Shades?

"You're not thinking of doing something stupid now, are you, Renata?"

Her gaze snapped to Lachlan.

"You have the meek, quiet countenance down pat," Lachlan said, "but I can't quite tell if it's an act or not. If you do anything ill-advised, know that it's Dalton who I'll send the ferals after first. You will watch as he's torn apart, and even if you know deep down in your soul that it wasn't your fault, his gruesome death will still haunt you. Same can be arranged for your families. I have contingencies piled on top of contingencies. Cooperate, and this will all go *much* smoother."

Renata loosed a shuddering breath.

"Now, Renata, explain in layman's terms the best way to distill a whimal chain."

Renata swallowed hard but said nothing. Being stressed always locked up her brain. How to distill a whimal chain? She couldn't even remember what a whimal chain *was*.

Lachlan sighed, then whistled twice.

Renata's heart rate doubled as black fog rolled along the ground. It wafted around the feet of the entranced elves before coalescing into a human-shaped form beside Lachlan. The shadows fell away, revealing the same vampire who had killed Megan. Renata's jaw clenched.

Lachlan said, "If you do not want Dalton to slip into the same trancelike state as your friend … what was her name? Miranda? Molly? Then I would suggest you start talking, Miss Bernard. The window for completing this is closing by the second, and if your hesitation or pathetic attempts at stalling me continue, a great number of people will pay the price."

"Don't do it," Dalton hissed. "We don't know what he's trying to do."

The vampire stepped forward. "No one was talking to you, boy."

Dalton sharply turned his head to glare at the man.

The vampire cast a spell and threw an array at Dalton before Renata could get a word out. Wasn't there a rule about never looking a vampire in the eye? An orb of swirling black flew toward Dalton, slamming into his face and swathing his entire head.

Dalton screamed, the sound all the more disorienting because Renata couldn't see his mouth. His entire head had disappeared into an opaque black cloud. The panic that seized her longtime friend had overtaken him so thoroughly and so quickly that tears welled in her eyes and bile crawled up her throat. He stumbled back and away from Renata. He wailed, covering his ears with his hands—hands that disappeared into the ball of black swirling around his head. "Don't! Renata, run! They're right behind you!" He started to run, but it was as if he was moving in slow motion. He broke into sobs, begging the vampire—Teo—not to kill her.

Renata, throat tight and pulse pounding in her ears, focused her tear-filled eyes on Lachlan. "I'll tell you if you leave him alone." Her voice wobbled violently, but she got the words out. A few tears slipped down her cheeks as Dalton continued to scream bloody murder. No one was anywhere near him. He was trapped in some horror only he could see, the vampire's shadow magic driving Dalton ever closer to the brink of insanity.

Lachlan held up a hand. The vampire muttered something about not being allowed to have any fun and then released his magic. The black cloud, as if made of thousands of black wasps, dispersed.

Dalton pitched face-first into the grass, unconscious.

Another tear slipped down Renata's cheek as her friend hit the ground with a sickening thud. She hoped he wasn't concussed now on top of everything else.

She started talking then, working through her portal theory. Lachlan's questions were intelligent and thoughtful, proving that he—unlike Joan Calder—actually understood her research on a fundamental level. One question in particular excited her so much that she'd pulled her secret notebook free before she realized she'd done it. Lachlan's eyes lit up like sun-dappled gemstones at the sight of it, but he neither demanded she hand it over nor snatched it away from her. He took up a spot beside her, merely peering over her shoulder as she pointed out key pieces of her theory.

A not insubstantial part of her was filled with self-loathing that talking to Lachlan ignited a deep sense of pride within her. Why was it that the first person besides Dalton who understood her work and how much it meant to her was a lunatic elf hell-bent on destroying life as she knew it in this realm? She was also disgusted with herself for being curious about the world he was trying so hard to make contact with on the other side of that portal.

Because this wasn't an intra-realm portal meant to offer a quick travel path between two locations in this realm. Nor was it as simple as reopening the bridge between this realm and the fae one. As much as she loathed Lachlan's methods, him finally opening a pathway to the fae realm would have been cause for celebration—even a reluctant one.

This was something else.

When he finally explained what he needed from her, and how her expertise was the final puzzle piece in getting this particular door open, she hesitated.

Dalton woke with a start, his back arching off the ground. The veins in his neck bulged. Swirling black tendrils wove around Dalton's back, his limbs, his neck. They twisted and coiled like rope, then tightened as if pulled by dozens of unseen hands.

Dalton gasped, eyes squeezed shut, limbs stiff and bent. His face went a horrible shade of puce.

"Okay!" Renata shouted. "Don't hurt him!"

Dalton's back slammed back to the ground, limbs slack. The shadows retreated, and the color returned to his face. It wasn't until she saw the steady rise and fall of his chest that she tore her gaze away to glare at Lachlan.

He was unfazed. He spouted no pithy declarations or snarky one-liners. He was a patient parent waiting for his misbehaving toddler to finish her temper tantrum.

"Begin," he said.

And she did.

Renata went into her own trancelike state when casting portal magic. The energy of the incantation took on a kind of physical form for her that was comforting in ways few things were—a warm blanket, a cat dozing in her lap, a long hug. The magic swirled around her in eddies. It pooled in her belly, traveled up her torso and out through her fingertips. No one could see her magic, not even her, but she felt it as if it were a part of her—some tangible thing that her body produced like oxygen and then exhaled into the world.

"Incredible," came Lachlan's voice, pulling Renata back to the surface.

Her arms lowered and her eyes fluttered open. At some point during her incantation, she'd dropped to her knees. She sat back on her haunches as she stared open-mouthed at the stable portal.

A portal that, for the first time, she could see into clearly. Instead of being a veritable black hole, another world lay beyond. She watched as an older woman stepped up to the portal as if it were a mundane doorway. Lachlan approached the portal, holding a hand out for the woman, looking for all the world like a footman offering assistance to a lady stepping down from a carriage.

"Lydia," he said in greeting, bowing his head as she, her hand in his, stepped from her world and into this one.

Lachlan helped out three people in total—two women and a man. They all appeared to be in their seventies at least, but given that they all were elves like Lachlan, guessing age was nearly impossible. Despite the trio being aged, their wrinkles were faint, and they carried themselves with the kind of poise that seemed to come naturally to fae.

The other woman was a bit weepy, reaching up to cup Lachlan's face for a moment before throwing her arms around him. Lachlan's arms remained by his sides.

The man squeezed one of Lachlan's shoulders and said, "You did good, son."

Son? Had Lachlan's parents been exiled, too?

The little family reunion didn't last long before Renata was put to work again. The newly freed elves listened to Lachlan's instructions like dutiful followers, clearly eager to assist Lachlan by any means necessary.

Renata kept her eyes open this time, marveling at how the world beyond the portal eventually winked out, overtaken by the more familiar swirling black, before a new scene revealed itself. The snapshot of the first realm—where Lachlan's parents had been—had shown the inside of a dwelling. This snapshot was of a landscape so desolate, the beige of the sandy ground almost seamlessly blended into the pale gray sky. Only the edge of a jagged boulder broke the bland, barren landscape.

So it was an extra shock when a creature suddenly filled the inter-realm doorway. It was a being that Renata immediately labeled as a "lizard person." It was covered in deep green scales, its eyes were bright yellow, and yet it moved mostly like a human.

Its scales, as dark as they were, were practically a neon sign when compared to the hue of its environment. Renata idly wondered if there were no predators the lizard people needed to hide from. Though perhaps these people *were* the apex predators.

A horrible roar sounded from within the portal—like a jet engine. The creature in the doorway flinched hard and immediately vanished.

Renata cocked her head, squinting. A slight shimmer in the inter-realm doorway confirmed that the creature had turned on some kind of camouflage, like a chameleon.

Lachlan spoke to the creature in a language Renata didn't know. It even sounded reptilian somehow. When the creature finally turned off its camouflage, so, too, did a veritable army behind it.

Renata's heart thundered in her chest. She half expected to hear screams of confusion and horror from her fellow Elsher residents, but one ring was locked into a portal-holding trance, while the others were holding their arrays for things like stability. Renata wondered again what would happen if all the sorcerers dropped their arrays. Would enough people willingly sacrificing themselves be enough to stop those reptilian beings from coming through?

Renata glanced over her shoulder from her spot on the ground, finding Dalton still passed out several feet away. A supervising elf abruptly squatted beside Renata.

"The beauty of this is that, now that the portal is open," the man whispered, as if they were schoolmates sharing a secret, "the rings of people from your little hub are merely a redundancy plan should the incredibly stable portal—thanks to you—falter. We've only ever accomplished this once—changing the destination of the portal in quick succession, I mean. The results then were quite disastrous. This area you're in now, with the cleared-out grass, was the blast zone. Nothing's been able to grow here since. Your research solved the problem. You should be very proud."

Renata clenched her teeth so hard her jaw ached.

"You can try to run," the elf said. "Lachlan would let you. Dalton, however, would be dead before you reached him. Please know that that's not an idle threat."

Renata's gaze whipped back to Dalton, finding him in a cage made of thorny vines. None touched him, but Renata knew the elf could close that cage around Dalton, puncturing him from all sides, without the elf moving from his crouched position beside her. She refocused on the elf, who had whirling green energy wafting about him like a personal fog bank.

With a mild air of disgust, as if he couldn't stomach how little fight she had in her, the elf said, "You could attempt to rally your troops now. Give a rousing speech about it being *them or us*. But honestly, if you were capable of growing a conscience, you would have by now. It's entirely too late."

As if on cue, the crackle in the air intensified. Renata watched in horror as reptilian creature after reptilian creature stepped out of the portal.

The Elsher residents finally began to panic then, dropping their arrays and fleeing for the tall grasses. When the ferals gave chase, Lachlan immediately called them off. In their haste, the first circle of sorcerers crashed into people in the second ring, snapping them from their trance.

They bolted, too.

The sorcerers scattered in all directions, like cockroaches fleeing from the light. Renata, however, didn't move. Where would she go? Plus, the elf was right: If she'd wanted to stop Lachlan's plan, she should have done it by now.

The elf who had been beside her had already wandered off to consult with Lachlan, so Renata scrambled on hands and knees to Dalton's side. The thorny cage was gone, but a few puncture marks marred his clothes and arms. She gently patted his face, quietly begging him to wake up. When he stirred briefly but remained asleep, she cast an array for water. It was a small, simple spell—the kind children mastered in grade school. It was all her taxed magic could muster up, though. She flung the array at Dalton's face, causing him to splutter awake. She cupped his face and forced him to look at her—it would show him she was okay while simultaneously ensuring that he'd see *her* before whatever was still climbing out of the portal.

His panicked breathing had only started to subside when a roar made them both whirl toward the portal. They scrambled to their feet and backed away, holding on to each other, as something *massive* stepped out of the portal—a portal that had doubled in size.

The ground beneath Renata's feet quaked as the thing made contact with the earth. Renata could only think "ankylosaurus" as she looked at the beast—an armor-plated reptile. A curved horn sprouted from either side of the beast's armored head—much like a ram—in addition to a pair of stone-like spiked protrusions that jutted from the underside of its wide jaw. A reptilian person sat atop the beast's head, holding on to the horns like handlebars. Four more people rode on the creature's back like the world's most messed-up parade float.

Renata's mouth went dry as she tore her gaze away from the beast long enough to glance at the portal. A line of the things patiently waited to come through. That patience morphed into something more harried as another terrifying roar sounded somewhere in the distance.

"We gotta get out of here," Dalton whispered in Renata's ear even though they were already slowly backing up.

In unison, they turned to bolt into the waist-high grass, only to come up short as Teo the vampire materialized in front of them.

"We're not quite done with you two, kids."

He flung his shadows at them.

Renata briefly felt like she was traveling through a portal again—weightless, body-less, and yet tumbling head over heels through endless space.

The abyss swallowed her entirely.

Some part of her hoped this was death—but she knew she wasn't that lucky.

CHAPTER THIRTY-EIGHT

HARLOW

When my guest of honor materialized, I braced myself. Joe had agreed it was as good an idea as any, though he'd looked like he wanted to throw up. I also noted that his hand hadn't left the handle of his spear since we'd rejoined the others in the now-cramped telepad station.

I didn't think Wren the earth witch thought this was the smartest plan, either, but she was also desperate for any solution that got her unchained from that pole and not blown to smithereens. The plan was entirely contingent on Wren's cooperation, because even with my guest's clearance via his boss, Wren was the only one who could approve his arrival.

Thankfully, she complied.

As Vaughn Rosen took a slow step out of the telepad and into the station, Marisol let out an impressive string of truly foul curses. I would have high-fived her had we been in different circumstances.

I hurried to place myself between Vaughn and the others, which was ludicrous, honestly, as I was the least equipped for a fight. Especially since my sword still had the feral pinned to the back wall. Even the feral seemed surprised by the arrival of the pure vampire. I couldn't tell if its snarls were of the "We're at max capacity for this room already, guys! This is a fire hazard" or the "Pure vampires are the filet mignon of people—let me at 'em!" variety.

I tuned the feral out.

I held my hands up. "Okay, before everyone freaks out, we've got three to five seconds to get Wren out of her cuffs once we start tampering with them in earnest. So we need speed even more than we need strength. I propose that—"

Wren stood before me, doubled over as she clutched her ruined hand to her chest. She cursed, pained breaths expelled in quick bursts.

A muted explosion sounded outside.

"Was that the gist of your plan?" Vaughn asked, unfazed.

I turned to the pole, to Wren, and back again. The cuff that had been keeping the witch in place was gone. Had Vaughn broken her hand to get it out of the cuff? "That … uhh … was the main thing."

Vaughn gestured vaguely toward Kayda. "The girthy one is the person who witnessed Shade's escape from exile, no?"

Kayda scowled. "The girthy one has a name."

"Yeah, it's *girthy maiden* to you," said a voice from the doorway. I didn't know the lady's name—she was mousy, had the faint remnants of a black eye, and seemed generally grouchy. She came up short once she'd pushed her way between Marisol and Joe. "Oh, fuck me. That's a vamp. Why are y'all shooting the shit with a vampire? And what exploded outside?"

The cramped room grew even more cramped as the rest of Kayda's group tried to pile into the small station. Alyssa crawled under legs to presumably get to Kayda but was wholly distracted by Vaughn.

The little girl stopped a foot away from the pure vampire, jammed her fists on her hips and stared up at him. "You the new stepdad from Tercla?"

Vaughn was clearly caught between being disgusted and amused. "Absolutely not. I do hail from Tercla, though." After a moment of staring at her, he took a cautious step back. "You're a pure … yet you smell like a hybrid. Were you born or made?"

Alyssa faltered—it was one of the few times I'd seen her rattled. "Born."

"Huh," Marisol said. "Interesting."

Alyssa fidgeted with the hem of her shirt. "My big sister at the group home was a born vamp, too. She told me not to tell anyone. The blood they made us drink turned her into a hybrid. I think it might have been poisoned blood or something, though, 'cause it made her so sick she died. It made me throw up."

Vaughn's gaze quickly scanned the room. "Where did you find her?" he asked the group at large.

"*She* has a name, too," Kayda said, then rehashed where she and her group had found Alyssa.

Vaughn, arms crossed and eyebrows smashed together, listened as he stared down at Alyssa. I had to hand it to the kid— she stood her ground. I wasn't sure if that was a vampire thing, a kid thing, or the result of a child needing to grow up too fast. Either way, while the trained and armed vampire hunters all but trembled in the presence of a pure, Alyssa maintained unflinching eye contact with him.

When Kayda finished talking, Vaughn's next question was aimed at Wren. "Any red flags yet?"

Wren's light-brown skin had gone ashen. Her ruined hand was clutched to her chest as she stood before the telepad control panel. The area around her knuckles was a sea of colors. She needed to get her hand tended to sooner rather than later. She tapped a few things onto the screen with her good hand. "Still okay," she ground out.

Vaughn turned to me then. "You said Camila got herself into some trouble?"

It was my turn to rehash events. Vaughn's expression remained impassive even after I'd finished my tale, but the rest of the group looked a bit shell-shocked.

Marisol whistled. "And here I was thinking riding on the back of a giant harpy eagle and eating cricket hash was exciting."

One of the newly arrived guys, who had a pair of glasses pushed up into his mop of curly hair, groaned and rubbed his stomach, begging Marisol to stop talking about insects.

"It seems safe to assume that the extra aid we requested in exchange for the attractant won't be coming," Vaughn said slowly. "Which means our options grow limited. The best idea I have in my arsenal is one Roch will despise."

I couldn't tell if he was thinking out loud or if he expected me to follow that last part. "Is Welsh okay?" I finally blurted, unable to hold it in any longer.

"He's fine. It's only been two days. He's certainly been well enough today to tell me to fuck off every time I deign to ask him how he's feeling."

I nodded, warmed by this news. "That tracks."

"Red flags aren't flapping yet, but they're certainly inching their way up the pole," Wren said, her breathing labored.

"All right," Vaughn said, turning to the witch. "Get the mundanes back to the Thero hub. They'll have to figure out where to go from there."

"Since when do we take—" the grouchy lady started, but Kayda cut her off.

"Shut up, Cathy. We're already running out of time, and we don't need to waste it listening to you bitch."

"Shots fired!" the guy in the glasses said, cackling.

Cathy made a mocking face at Kayda but shut her trap.

One by one, Cathy, GI Joe, Glasses, Vamp Hunter Joe, and Paola made their way into the telepad. I assumed that, since Wren kept sending people through, none of them were getting reduced to mist on the wind somewhere between here and Vancouver.

Marisol, though she was pale and her voice shook, stepped directly in front of Vaughn. "I assume you're taking Harlow and Kay somewhere else on some vampire mission. Make sure they come back to Luma in one piece."

Vaughn inclined his head.

She offered me, Kayda, and Alyssa a sad, cautious smile, then stepped into the telepad tube. Ten seconds later, she was gone.

"Are you taking us to *Tercla*?" Alyssa practically shrieked, hardly able to keep a lid on her excitement.

Kayda leaned toward me and stage whispered, "Was this second location thing part of your secret plan, too?"

I stage-whispered back, "I honestly didn't get that far in the secret plan. I was just hoping he would be compelled to help break my mom out of prison out of the goodness of his undead heart."

"My heart is quite alive, thank you," Vaughn said, walking away from Wren now that he'd imparted new instructions to her. She quickly tapped at the screen. "But we're not going to Luma—you know better than that, Harlow. If vampires were able to port into hubs, we'd have been doing so for decades. The only reason I could port into this one is because Roch is on the clearance list. This hub and Tercla have been in contact over the years at *my* behest because of my fascination with portals. Even still, this is the first time I've personally stepped foot in this place. His blood is what got me in, and he gave me a small vial of it solely because damn near everyone here is already dead."

He let us mull that over for a few moments before he added, "We're not going to Tercla, either, so your reunion with Welsh will have to wait."

"Aw, boo," Alyssa said, tightly folding her arms across her chest.

Vaughn gestured to the telepad. "Kayda, you first. Alyssa will follow next."

Kayda shot me a "You sure about this?" look.

I wasn't sure about anything but nodded anyway. Beyond vamps not being able to use telepads, I knew they couldn't stroll through the veils into Luma to bust my mom and Soren out of their holding cells, either. But I'd hoped that in addition to getting us out of here, Vaughn—and by extension Roch—could use whatever pull they had with our Collective to free her. It had been a long shot, but it was the only one I could think of.

Things were pretty bad when my only lifeline was a vampire I barely knew and who had no qualms about enthralling me to act against my own wishes. But Caspian and I had trusted him with Welsh, so I couldn't stop now. I chewed on my bottom lip as I stared at him.

Vaughn sighed and employed a sympathetic tone I mostly believed was genuine. "I don't know Sorcerer Avery personally, but as much as it sounds like he used you as a means to get intel on where the portal led, I'd also wager he knew you'd be safer in an unknown location than you would be in the Tower. Charging back into Luma will likely result in your swift death or being locked in a cell next to Camila's."

That didn't exactly assuage my guilt over indirectly abandoning my mom, Soren, Sera the Sickle, Tim, and Caspian.

Still, I figured he was right.

I also wasn't dumb enough to forget that Vaughn only ever agreed to help me when he needed something in return. As much as I believed Vaughn was right that Luma wasn't safe for me, I also knew he had his own agenda—an agenda that would piss off Roch by the sound of it, which didn't seem like the most prudent course of action, given the circumstances.

But I wasn't really in a position to negotiate. My most immediate fate lay in the hands of Vaughn and Wren.

The earth witch in question made a distressed noise. "A shutdown sequence just started on the screen. It's what we're supposed to initiate when a pad needs to go offline for repairs. Any telepads trying to connect to this one will be informed it'll be out of commission in five minutes. The closer a traveler gets to that shutdown time, the more likely they'll be lost in transit."

"Lost in transit" was inconvenient in reference to luggage. It was deadly when it was in reference to a person.

My sword issued a panicked buzz at Wren's declaration.

That momentary distraction gave the feral what it needed to break free from my sword's hold, and it came charging at us from around the telepad tube.

Despite Vaughn's otherworldly speed, the vampire froze—a brief but very real fear sparking in his eyes. The feral was on all fours, scrambling for purchase like a dog on slick floors.

"Stop!" Alyssa yelled, hand out.

The feral slammed to a halt as if it had just crashed into a glass wall. A breath later, its forehead was pressed to the floor between its two splayed necrotic hands. Vaughn was suddenly behind Alyssa, his vamp speed back online. My first thought was that he was using the tiny girl as a meat shield, but the look on his face was one of quiet fascination.

"Go outside, and don't come back here," Alyssa told the feral.

They weren't the most specific of instructions, but the feral took off like a shot anyway. I half expected Vaughn to and cut it down, but we all merely watched as the feral darted out the open gate in the hedge wall and disappeared from view.

Alyssa gave a full-body shudder. "That was weird!" She tipped her head back to gaze up at Vaughn. "Is that a pure vampire thing? Like, is that a skill that unlocks when I'm a teenager, but it happened super early cause I'm a prodidy or whatever? Oh, oh, is it because I have main character energy and the fate of the universe is in my hands?" She thrust her small fist in the air as if she expected it to be struck with lightning—a blessing from the gods.

Vaughn looked at me in dismay. "What on earth is it talking about? Is it broken?"

"Not to rush you, but we're down to four minutes," Wren said. Sweat coated her forehead and her lips had gone a little gray.

Kayda, after shooting me a "we'd better not get lost in transit" look, climbed into the telepad. Ten seconds later, she was gone.

"Wait! One second ..." I said and ran out onto the porch. "Rory?"

A piercing screech sounded from above me, and I clapped a hand over my chest. The massive falcon dropped from the roof like a miniature boulder, unfurling his wings at the last moment so he could land on the porch's railing. The wood creaked under his weight, and a few flecks of white paint fluttered to the ground. He cocked his head at me in question.

"Hi," I said lamely. "First, thanks for helping me earlier with the ferals."

"Caspian would have been cross with me had you met some terrible end," Rory said in my head.

It wasn't exactly "No problem, bestie! I like you even more than Welsh!" but I'd take it.

"I don't know if you're stuck here somehow because of whatever mission Welsh gave you, but I'm leaving Elsher," I said. "I don't know where I'm going, but I'm safe for now. Are you able to leave? I'd take you with me, but I know a telepad ride for animals usually means their insides end up on the outside. Maybe once you're out of Elsher you'll be able to talk to Cas again. He's stuck in the Collective's Tower."

Rory shrieked softly.

"Yeah, I don't love it, either. If you can't get through to Cas, go home and tell Julip that I'm with Kayda, and we're under the care of the pure vamps. Maybe Julip can tell Henri? Reception is iffy here, but we'll try texting the group chat after we get out of here."

"My mission was to ascertain what happened here in Elsher," Rory said. *"I'm still unclear. Caspian, I'd wager, would accept my leaving*

prematurely, as my new mission comes from you. He seems to ... like you."

"You don't have to sound so bummed about it."

He clicked his beak. "*Mundanes complicate matters too much. His last mundane companion nearly cost him everything.*"

"It was basically his villain origin story, though," I said. "And now you have a kindred spirit in ruining the Collective's day whenever you can."

Apparently falcons could smile.

"*May we meet again,*" Rory said, screeched, then took off.

That done, I hurried back into the station.

I climbed into the tube.

The telepad ride landed me in a new station in one piece. I'd hugged my sword to my chest like a stabby teddy bear and then instructed it to stay strapped to my side until we knew where we were and if it was safe for the thing to fly around.

Vaughn strolled out of the telepad next, and, to my relief, Wren stumbled out a few seconds later. I hadn't been sure if she'd be able to set the coordinates for own departure, especially with the countdown clock ticking ever closer to zero. I hadn't wanted to ask if she was joining us, in case I'd indirectly gotten her hand broken and then marooned her in a hub cut off from the world. Not to mention that at least one feral was running around in it.

The telepad station wasn't in a hub, the best I could tell. I'd heard rumors that there were telepads dotted all over the mundane world that could be used as a quick travel alternative while also being removed from the hub system themselves. The chance that the stations were abandoned was high. They were usually in remote locations, so keeping them maintained meant finding witches willing to take on jobs in the middle of nowhere.

From my vantage point, there wasn't much beyond the grimy windows besides weed-clogged fields and a cracked-asphalt parking lot that boasted a single car on blocks, the black plastic bag covering its back window flapping slightly in the breeze.

"Where to now?" I asked Vaughn, readjusting my hold on

Wren's waist. The telepad ride had zapped what little energy the poor witch had left.

Vaughn smiled in a way that I didn't like one bit. "We'll get her to a clinic, and then the rest of us are going to crash the Vampire Council."

CHAPTER THIRTY-NINE

HARLOW

It took the better part of two hours to reach our destination. Vaughn seemed annoyed at the speed we traveled, even though it included two more telepad rides and a rented car, but I supposed everything felt slow when he could move at practically the speed of light.

The Vampire Council's nest wasn't in a cliché city like Las Vegas or New Orleans—unfortunately—nor was it in a totally non-vampy place, like Des Moines or Salt Lake City. According to Vaughn, the location shifted every few months—not as a means to avoid detection, but because many of the elder vampires believed sunny climes helped their circulation.

I was seventy percent sure Vaughn was fucking with me.

The nest's current location was in North Carolina, in a

sprawling estate near Asheville. The humidity was so bad, the air felt like soup. Thick black clouds loomed ominously over the distant mountains as Kayda drove the SUV up the curving driveway that led to the mansion's front doors. A thunderstorm was brewing. The weather felt both volatile and oppressive, which seemed fitting.

I was a nervous wreck.

On top of everything else, texts to Felix and Caspian had remained undelivered for the past two hours, which made me fear they were locked in cells in the Tower the same as Mom and Soren.

No other cars were parked in the circular drive with a massive stone fountain in its center. This fountain, thankfully, was generic in design, and not topped by Roch's arrogant visage. I'd avoided asking about Roch while on this trip, because thinking about Roch made me think about Mom. And Rhiannon. And Caspian. And Welsh. Vaughn got testy when I started crying, so I'd spent most of our travel time trying to keep Alyssa entertained.

As Kayda stopped the car and threw it into park, though, I knew I couldn't avoid the topic of Roch any longer.

"Why is being here going to piss off your boss?" I asked.

Kayda turned to stare at the pure vamp in the passenger seat. Other than using his enthrall power on the cashier behind the Hertz car rental place, effectively getting us this SUV for free, Vaughn hadn't spoken a word in over an hour.

"The short answer is that he explicitly asked me not to," Vaughn said. "Roch is technically on the Council, but he doesn't agree with their policies, so he's gone rogue, so to speak. He meddles in their affairs in more underhanded ways. He plays political games. He's so subtle in his schemes that it's hard for anything to be tied back to him directly."

I wondered if this was connected to how old these vamps really were—their stories starting in Europe during times of plagues, royal courts, and high society. During a time where an artfully whispered secret, a carefully placed lie, or an alliance struck in a smoke-filled parlor could sully a person's reputation, destroy a person's life, start a war.

I supposed it all could have been the result of the vamps needing to craft drama because they existed with a level of comfort that removed daily struggle. I figured it was why the rich and famous often went off the deep end. Staring out at the Council's estate, with its spires, steeply pitched roofs, and ornate towers—like a French chateau transplanted here from another century—it certainly seemed like these people lived a charmed life.

When we all piled out of the vehicle, I said, "Are these vamps going to be as bad as Yannick? I really don't want to add 'vampire love slave' to my CV."

"You don't even *have* a CV," Kayda muttered.

I jabbed a finger at her. "Rude."

Vaughn crossed his arms and stared off into the middle distance, clearly deep in thought. He worked his jaw. "All I need you three to do is tell them your stories. These are old-school vampires, as you call them. They eschew most technology and they also appreciate grand gestures. Me bringing you here—and using mundane travel to do so—is a statement."

Kayda jutted her chin at him. "And going behind this Roch guy's back is a statement, too?"

Vaughn sighed. "Correct."

I didn't know the vamp well, but I could tell he was troubled. And not just about the bigger problem of Lachlan and his ferals. Vaughn was nervous about being here, specifically.

Without another word, he strode for the front door. Kayda and I looked at each other and shrugged, then headed after him. Alyssa scrambled to keep up.

My sword floated near my shoulder, discordant hum back in all its creepy glory.

"Do you want to wait in the car?" I hissed at it.

The humming stopped for three full seconds before the sword dropped to the smooth cement to tap its hilt twice.

"Thanks for sticking with me, even though you're scared," I said.

Instead of giving an overly defensive response, the sword's blade glowed blue. As the color faded, the off-kilter hum resumed.

Alyssa, conversely, was so excited she was practically bouncing as she held tight to Kayda's hand. At least someone was looking forward to this.

Before Vaughn reached the front door, it swung inward, revealing a butler. He was rail thin, short, and elegant, his suit exquisitely tailored. A liberal application of gel kept his fully gray hair styled in place. His red bow tie looked like a splash of blood at the base of his deathly pale throat. Though his crisp white gloves unearthed an unpleasant memory of Stan the hybrid, I knew this butler wasn't wearing the accessory to hide necrotic fingers. Still, the sight redoubled my apprehension about strolling into yet another nest of pure vampires.

"Mr. Rosen," the butler said with a slight British accent. He made a show of scanning the porch before settling his unblinking gaze back on Vaughn. "Mr. Roch has let his pet off his leash, I see."

Even I could see the way Vaughn's shoulders stiffened at that. This was going to be a whole-ass mess.

"And what are these?" the butler asked, finally deigning to look at the rest of us. "A human, a draken, and a pure vampire child—it's like the setup of an especially bad joke."

His accent somehow made the insults sound mildly charming, which I knew was largely an instinctual American reaction, powerless against the sound of the mother tongue.

He was still a grade-A dick-weasel.

I realized then that my sword was shielding itself behind me, shivering like a small child hiding behind his mother's skirts.

Vaughn regained his composure. "Lovely as always to see you, too, Wellingham. My companions and I are here with important information for the Council."

Wellingham sniffed. "It's considered rude to show up unannounced after your request for an audience has been denied. Repeatedly. You, for the umpteenth time, despite being Roch's obedient duckling, are not a member of the Council, Mr. Rosen. Without a Council escort, I cannot let you in." He angled his head to give me a quick once-over. "If you donate that one for tea, we can forget this indiscretion happened."

My sword issued a quick, violent buzz. Wellingham narrowed his eyes at me. I considered apologizing for accidental flatulence.

In a blink, an absolutely gorgeous man stood behind Wellingham. I eyed his high cheekbones, the light stubble along his jaw, and pretty hazel eyes. He rested a tanned forearm on the edge of the open door, emphasizing that he was a good foot taller than the butler. The only part of me that the vampire seemed interested in was the pulse thudding in my throat.

"Oh, do let him in, Rupert," the handsome arrival said.

Wellingham pursed his thin lips. I wasn't sure if he was more upset about the idea of letting us cross the threshold or the use of his first name.

"They finally roped you onto the Council, Enzo?" Vaughn asked.

Enzo tore his gaze away from my throat to offer Vaughn a dazzling smile full of perfectly white teeth, though they all came to a point. Every last one. Mom had told me that either evolution or mutation had altered some vampires' teeth. It was a stark reminder that, even if he looked human, Enzo was something else entirely.

"My sire was murdered a few months ago by a feral while he was on some Council business or other," Enzo said, not sounding the least bit upset about the death of his predecessor. "I knew I was next in line, but I thought I wouldn't have to do this for at least another century. Being a Council member is infinitely more tedious than I was led to believe. You being here is sure to liven this place up. If I have to look at one more ledger today, I may snap."

His gaze shifted to my throat again. He licked his lips. Maybe my sword and I should *both* wait in the car.

Wellingham delicately curled a lip in distaste. "As you wish, Mr. Costa. I am but a humble servant." He stepped back, pulling the door open farther as he went, and gestured us inside with an elegant sweep of his hand.

"I'll take them back, Wellingham," Enzo said. "You can go back to refilling the inkwells or whatever totally necessary tasks you need to complete to keep this estate running like a well-oiled machine."

As I shuffled inside, Wellingham muttered something about ferals murdering the wrong Costa. He was either too distracted by his apparent hatred of Enzo to notice my sword floating in after me, or he'd long since stopped caring.

The first thing that struck me about the interior of the place was how white it was—white-marble floors, white walls, white railing curving along a staircase made of white-marble steps. Down at the end of the long white entryway stood a pair of charcoal gray whippets. Alyssa gave a shriek of "Dogs!" and yanked her hand from Kayda's.

"No running, young lady!" Wellingham yelped. "This isn't a playground!"

Alyssa was off like a shot. The miniature greyhound-looking dogs were so startled that they crashed into each other in their haste to escape. They finally got angled the right way and scrabbled to get purchase on the sleek floors, their toenails clacking. The dogs and Alyssa disappeared around a corner and out of sight.

Wellingham unleashed a long-suffering sigh before closing the door behind us. He tromped up the staircase to the right of the entryway without another word.

Enzo, with his arm slung around Vaughn's shoulders, was already on the move. One hand gesticulated wildly in the air as he spoke, and the pair headed in the same direction as Alyssa and the dogs.

Kayda and I hadn't budged.

"I miss the days where you only got me into trouble in Luma …" Kayda muttered.

I swung my gaze up to her. "Seems like you're doing a pretty good job of getting into trouble all on your own. I mean, you adopted a baby vampire and got proposed to by a bird. That was all you."

"His name is Knuckles."

"That's upsetting," I said. "This high vampire Roch we've been talking about? My mom shagged him. He's apparently super in love with her, so I was hoping he'd use his vampy resources to get her out." My throat constricted so tightly, my knees went weak. "I just … left her there, Kay."

"That's bullshit, and you know it," Kayda said.

My sword tapped once on the marble floor. It was floating in front of us, now that the vampires were gone.

"That sorcerer asshat forced you through the portal," Kayda said. "There's no way you would have ditched your mom *or* Caspian on purpose." She cocked a hairless brow. "You only do that to me."

"*Ouch*, Kay!" I said, hand over my chest. "Are you *ever* going to let me off the hook for that?"

The sword tapped twice.

Kayda pointed at it. "What it said."

Deep down, I knew she forgave me—but she'd also give me shit about it for the rest of time.

"Anything I should know about dealing with pures?" Kayda asked.

Vaughn appeared in front of me, and I shrieked. I grabbed hold of my sword's hilt before it could embed itself in another ceiling. "Enough stalling."

By the time I blinked, he was gone again.

"*Ho-ly* shit," Kayda murmured.

I nodded. "I know."

Swallowing hard, I let my sword go and then started forward

on rubbery legs. I told her about magical malaria and how the survivors had gained heightened abilities. I warned her to avoid too much eye contact, though I didn't know if the vamps' enthrall powers would be less effective on a fae like Kayda.

Kayda led us through an enormous kitchen, down another white hallway, and to the doorway of a modern sitting room. She'd apparently followed the sound of Alyssa's squeals of delight as she chased the dogs. I assumed my friend also figured putting herself between me and the vamps was a good idea, seeing as they'd have no interest in draining *her* dry.

The back wall of the sitting room was made up of a series of windows composed of small panes. They were the kind of windows I would have expected to be filled with stained glass, but these were all clear and gleaming, revealing glimpses of the lush green grounds beyond. Plush sofas in beige, taupe, and tan were arranged in clusters around the room. Accent pillows, ferns in glazed ceramic pots, and stout lamps on elegant side tables offered bold splashes of color in yet another room with a mostly white or neutral color palette. I would have thought that meant the vampires were more reserved than their more modern counterparts. After taking in the gaggle of vampires in attendance, though, I knew I was wrong.

The vamps themselves were the focal pieces.

I'd thought Roch had been over the top with his cape, but this lot was dressed in everything from buckskin breeches to ruffled long-sleeved shirts, housecoats, puffy-sleeved gowns, and tight-fitting pantaloons. There were cravats and walking sticks and even a top hat. There was no real cohesion to the attire as a whole, so it was a bit like walking into a dinner party where the costume theme had been something vague, like "old-timey."

Alyssa, in her grubby jeans, Hello Kitty T-shirt, and worn tennis shoes, looked wildly out of place as she rolled around with the dogs on an ornate white rug patterned with navy fleur-de-lis. Given how often the dogs dropped into play stance before launching at the giggling Alyssa, they'd warmed up to her considerably. While none of the vampires lounging on the couches or clustered in small groups acted as if they wanted to toss the tiny vampire out on her ear, they were keeping a watchful eye on her all the same.

I scanned the room for Enzo or Vaughn. None of the assembled vampires were paying us much mind.

Suddenly, a deep ache filled my chest—something akin to grief, but so much worse. Worse than losing Dad; than thinking of Mom and Soren dying, abandoned, in Tower jail cells; than the idea of never seeing Kayda, Caspian, or my sword again; than the memory of Felix leaving me. It was all those things wrapped into one horrible emotion.

Then it doubled.

Tripled.

I clutched at my chest, hyperventilating. This was going to drown me.

It would *kill* me.

Kayda was in my face, shaking my shoulders, asking me what was wrong. My sword buzzed around us like an angry bee. Tears streamed down my cheeks, my mouth open in a silent sob. The throat-tightening tidal wave of grief was so overpowering, I couldn't even make a sound. My knees were giving out despite Kayda using all her considerable strength to keep me upright.

What seemed like a breath later, I was seated between two beautiful people—one man, one woman—on a cloud-soft couch. They were raven-haired, dark-eyed, and their warm brown skin was a shade similar to my own. I guessed Pacific Islander, but the longer I looked at them, the less sure I was that beings so breathtakingly beautiful could be from this realm.

I couldn't tell if they were twins or if they were one of those couples who'd started to look alike the longer they were together. They gazed at me like angels descended from heaven. Glancing at each in turn made that tidal wave of sorrow recede. They were here to save me, to shield me from the pain of loss. I knew I'd never feel anything like that again if they were with me. My protectors.

Just a taste, one of them said, but I wasn't sure if it was out loud or in my head.

I nodded dumbly, happy to give them anything they wanted. How silly for them to think they even needed to ask.

The sharp stabs of pain in my left wrist and the right side of my neck quickly gave way to a pleasure so deep, I moaned. I writhed under the pressure, wishing I could tear my veins open like a knife gutting a fish so they could have access to every inch of me.

Suddenly, I lurched forward, gasping for air like I was waking from a nightmare—like breaking the surface of a lake mere moments before drowning.

Kayda and my sword were in my face again. Someone—a man, I thought—was talking sternly. Not quite yelling but not far off.

"You're hardly one to make demands," a new male voice said. "You're not a member of the Council, and you were not invited. It's not their fault they believed you brought a snack as a peace offering."

The realization of what had happened to me snapped into sharp focus, my head clearing in an instant. I clapped a hand over my neck to stanch the bleeding, but it was immediately evident the puncture wounds had closed up already. I flipped over my left wrist, finding twin trails of blood, though the bite mark itself was gone.

I quietly asked Kayda, "Did Vaughn rescue me again?"

"Yeah," she said, voice hoarse from both worry and fury. "The whole thing happened in ten seconds flat. I couldn't have helped you even if I'd known what the hells was happening."

I smiled weakly at her. "Being human really fuckin' sucks sometimes."

A female voice asked, "Was that a vampire joke? How droll."

I peered around Kayda to glare at whoever was listening in on our whispered conversation, only to find dozens of eyes fixed on me. Eye contact with any one of them could result in me being bitten again. I hadn't even *looked* at the twins, though! What was the point of having rules if these bloodsucking freaks didn't adhere to them?

I dropped my gaze to the floor and shifted so I was standing in front of Kayda again, her bulk shielding me from the vampires' view.

"It's true that I'm not a member of the Council," Vaughn said. "But—"

"I'm glad we're in agreement about something," a man said, cutting him off.

Vaughn soldiered ahead anyway. "Surely you must know, Elder Allaband, that I wouldn't come here without good cause."

"I know nothing of the sort, Ancillae Rosen," the same guy said.

I hazarded another glance around Kayda, who was still pointedly staring out the door, clearly not wanting to even face the vampires if she didn't have to. Since most everyone was focused on a pretentious-as-fuck-looking guy standing beside a sofa, his slender hands stacked on top of a walking stick's pommel, I figured that was Elder Allaband. He wore shiny black shoes, tan tartan pants lined with bold black stripes, a fitted brown tweed jacket over a white button-up shirt, and a forest-green scarf wound loosely around his neck. His face was clean-shaven save for a dreadful mustache that curled up slightly at the corners. A black top hat sat upon his head. He looked like he'd just stepped out of a Victorian era painting.

"I don't presume to know the workings of your mind, nor that of your master," Elder Allaband added.

Given the way that Vaughn stiffened slightly and a few of the vampires tittered, I figured calling Roch "Vaughn's master" was akin to calling a grown man "boy." If I wasn't sure I'd be dead in a matter of seconds, I would have told them to pull their heads out of their asses because all this posturing was a waste of time.

But these vampires were old school, like Vaughn and Roch, and likely all had abilities that were even more heightened than the average vampire. I'd probably be worse than dead if I got sassy.

Kayda knew that, too, deep down, which was why she was keeping her back to them. Luckily they didn't seem to think she was being impudent.

Vaughn straightened his shoulders. "Alyssa, come here."

The young girl and the dogs had stopped playing a while ago, though they were all still seated on the rug, heads swiveling left and right as they followed the conversation like a ball being lobbed back and forth. I had no idea if Alyssa was aware of what was going on any more than the dogs were. She scrambled to her feet and hurried over to Vaughn.

"Tell them everything you told me," Vaughn instructed.

Alyssa turned to the group of waiting vampires and cowered a bit—every bit a child intimidated by adults. She bunched up the hem of her Hello Kitty shirt in her fists. She mumbled at first, so low I couldn't really hear her, but I knew the vampires could. When she finished her tale, ending with the tidbit that she was both a born vampire and thought "fae blood was icky," the assembled group muttered soft noises of interest.

"She's clearly been forced to consume fae blood, but she's, as far as I can tell, immune to its effects—at least so far as poisoning goes. Though I can smell it on her, she shows no signs of turning. And yet she can control ferals the way a hybrid can." Vaughn shot a pointed look at Elder Allaband. "I saw it with my own eyes."

Though the vampires didn't suddenly rush the girl, they all seemed to lean forward as one, suddenly finding the girl fascinating indeed.

"Roch," Vaughn said, confidence returning to his tone, "despite being the black sheep of the Council, has continued the work he vowed to complete. He has been working diligently in lieu of hosting balls or tournaments, instead of jet-setting around the world in search of exotic fabric. The attractant is complete." A few murmurs flitted through the room—some in awe, others presumably in reaction to the fabric comment. "I believe that Alyssa here could provide us with a solution to the feral problem that stretches far beyond what the attractant can do for us. The attractant is a defensive measure. If we were able to get to the bottom of her immunity to the poison, we could have an offensive tactic as well. We could turn the ferals against the hybrids— siccing their abominations on their owners. Not to mention that we could finally have an antidote to feral bites."

I glanced up at Kayda, knowing I'd see an expression of unchecked rage. She clenched her jaw and glared down at me. I shook my head.

We might be able to figure out a way *not* to turn Alyssa into a pincushion, doomed to a very long life as a vampiric guinea pig, but voicing how much we loathed the idea wasn't smart. Not one of them—not even Vaughn—had any real incentive to let us walk back out of here. Getting mouthy would help nothing. And I *really* didn't want to get snacked on again.

"And what, pray tell," Elder Allaband said, "are the other two doing here? I can't imagine what use we'd have with the likes of a ... *draken*."

Kayda's glower deepened.

I shot her a pointed look. "Keep it together."

My sword, which had been hiding behind me all this time, buzzed softly. I figured it was agreeing with me but didn't want to tap itself on the floor and possibly bring attention to itself.

"I fucking hate it here," Kayda hissed.

"Yeah, same," I whispered. "But we gotta trust the process or whatever."

Kayda gave me a *look*.

A female voice—which sounded very similar to the eaves- dropper from earlier—said, "This grows tiresome. The human *wasn't* delivered as a gift?"

Before I could react, Kayda was in the middle of the ornate rug, Vaughn's hands on her forearms. He'd decided to bodily move her when all we were doing was whispering furiously at each other.

A few of the vampires recoiled slightly, as if Kayda had just peed on the rug like one of the dogs.

Vaughn took up a position beside Kayda. "Tell them about witnessing Lachlan Shade's escape from exile."

The vampires seemed to lean forward as one again. I hoped that by the time it was my turn for show and tell, the lot of them would realize Vaughn really *had* come here for a reason.

The bloodsuckers listened intently as Kayda, in her no-nonsense way, told them first about the portal that had allowed Lachlan back into the earthen realm, then about what had transpired in Elsher.

Kayda said, "It might be worth noting that an Elsher resident claimed a feral spoke to her. It only said one word—'please'—but she said it sounded as if the feral was lucid enough that it was able to ask for death. Harlow and I heard another speak as well—it kept repeating 'Do not kill her' in reference to a witch it was guarding. They're either being turned differently, turned against their will, or mutating. Perhaps a combination of the three."

The vampires settled into thoughtful silence.

I, with great reluctance, spoke next, telling them about my harrowing experience in the Collective's Tower as well as recounting what Ethan—Chancellor Humphries's nephew—had told me about mutating ferals. "I'm sure you don't care to hear speculation from the likes of me, but Elder Costa himself said his predecessor was killed by a feral. It's like a majestic, healthy lion getting taken out by an emaciated hyena. If the hyenas are getting powerful enough to defeat the kings of the jungle, what hope is there for the rest of us?"

I might have sounded confident, but I said all of that to my shoelaces.

A slender finger with a long nail lacquered in red hooked gently under my chin and angled it up. I kept my gaze on my own nose, getting a headache from going cross-eyed. Keeping my eyes to myself was literally the only defense I possessed.

"Look at me, Harlow," the woman said, but *dammit* it was said in such a perfect impression of my mom's voice that an instinctive part of me reacted. The eye contact cemented me in place. My jaw ached from clenching my teeth so hard, and my legs felt like immovable tree trunks. My arms were glued to my sides. "This won't hurt."

I felt the woman in my mind, slithering around in my head like the smooth scaly belly of a snake coiling around my limbs. It wasn't an unpleasant sensation so much as an uncomfortable one. It was like watching your crush read your diary from when you were thirteen.

"Ah," the woman said finally and took a step back, removing her finger from my chin.

The moment she lost contact, her prodding magic slipped out of my head. I shuddered violently as control of my limbs reverted back to me. My sword buzzed angrily behind me.

The woman spun to face the assembled vampires. Her voluminous mint-green skirts swished about her ankles. Her waist was so thin, I wondered if she'd wedged herself into a corset. Her dark red hair was piled atop her head in a complicated style with a single tight corkscrew curl spilling over either shoulder. The ringlets rested against the high-necked bodice of her dress. "I can attest that she's telling the truth, for one. It also seems that she came into possession of the sword by happenstance, not thievery." The woman turned back toward me. "Are you honestly telling me that you gained an alliance with the sword simply by being … nice to it?"

I resisted the urge to say I hadn't *told* her shit.

"I'd …" I coughed and cleared my throat. "I'd say it was more that I respected it, so it respected me back."

My sword tapped on the floor once behind me.

"That means yes," I said, trying to smile at the woman, but it probably just looked like a grimace.

"And you gained knowledge of the sickle's history through touching it?" she asked.

I bristled. How had she gotten that much out of my head that fast? "Yes."

"But nothing about Likho's death?" the woman asked.

My brows smashed together. "No. Uhh … the sickle's memories were the first glimpse I'd gotten of Likho."

"Hmm," she said thoughtfully. "Likho was my uncle. His death has been a family mystery for years. He was a black sheep of the family—always lived off the beaten path, then lost his way when he got addicted to fae blood and turned into a hybrid. Nevertheless, he was my favorite uncle. I have one of his weapons. I had to purchase it for a ludicrous sum from an auction. Well, I didn't purchase it, a woman—"

"Cricket!" I said.

Several of the vampires eyed me as if I were a rabid monkey that had just escaped the zoo.

The redheaded vamp eyed me curiously. "Yes, her name was Cricket. How did you know?"

I told her about Haskins, assuming that if I wasn't forthright with whatever information she wanted, she'd just slither into my head to *take* it.

The woman nodded thoughtfully. "Perhaps you can pull memories from the hammer as well?"

She was asking, but I knew if I refused, either she or one of the other elder vampires would make me agree anyway.

"I'd be happy to try."

She nodded once and then practically glided back to her seat.

All attention shifted back to Vaughn.

He delicately cleared his throat. "If the Shades have advanced in portal creation far beyond anything the Collective can do, and he and his hybrids can control ferals, it's only a matter of time before they come after pures as well. We're currently no match for them. Their numbers far exceed ours. But if we pool our resources, if you work with Roch, if we track down the Shades' hidey-holes and flush his minions out like the rats they are, and if we band together with those who are trying to protect hubs and enclaves from being overrun and overthrown, we might have a chance."

Elder Allaband spoke first. "I wouldn't have pegged you as being so tenderhearted, Ancillae Rosen." He pursed his lips, making his mustache wiggle. "Give us a moment to discuss this."

A breath later, Vaughn, Kayda, Alyssa, my sword, and I were in the hallway outside the sitting room, the door to the sitting room closed.

"Goddess!" Kayda yelped, glancing around. "That never gets less freaky."

My stomach churned. At this point, I was developing anxiety about never knowing when I'd end up on another invisible roller coaster.

I glanced at Vaughn, who still looked pensive. "Did you know one of Likho's weapons was here?"

"I strongly suspected it," Vaughn said. "Elder Troya hauls that gaudy sentient sledgehammer out at parties sometimes, telling the story of how her uncle stole four of them out from under the noses of their mundane owners. I think she hoped that if she told the story enough times, someone would recognize the tale and reveal who had killed her uncle." His gaze roved over my face. "While I didn't bring you along as a proffered snack, your connection to the sword *was* my gift. Elder Troya owes Roch a favor, and me presenting you to the Council was a reminder of that."

"Without my sword, I would have been left behind," I said.

"Without your sword, I wouldn't have plucked you from Elsher at all."

I appreciated his honesty.

Sort of.

Kayda asked, "Do you really expect me to leave Alyssa here as a science experiment?"

"Of course not," Vaughn said, glancing down at the girl who

had her hand in Kayda's again. "I plan for her to be *Roch's* science experiment."

Kayda's jaw clenched.

"Roch is in Tercla, right?" Alyssa asked. "I can do science experiments if it means I get to go there." She tugged on Kayda's hand until she looked down. "*Please* can I go to Tercla?"

I frowned at the kid. She had no idea what she was asking for. But just because *I* didn't want to go back to Tercla—other than to see Welsh—didn't mean it wouldn't be the perfect place for the girl. I thought of young Audrey, Vaughn's daywalker assistant, and the schooling she'd gone through. Surely there were other born-vampire children in Tercla. Maybe Alyssa would thrive there, even if she *was* a vampiric guinea pig.

"While I do think she could be the key to our problem—and I will take her with me regardless of your protestations," Vaughn told Kayda, "I also wholeheartedly believe it's the best place for a girl like her to grow up."

Kayda stared at Alyssa for a long time before nodding tightly. Alyssa cheered, though softly.

Suddenly everyone *without* a human sense of hearing abruptly spun away from the door. A few seconds later, I heard the sound of pounding footsteps. A guy holding a laptop like a platter of hors d'oeuvres came tearing out of a room that led into the hallway. He came to an abrupt halt at the sight of us, almost losing hold of his laptop in the process.

My mouth dropped open. I hadn't seen his gorgeous face since my brief time at the Oregonian hub, back when he showed me his map that charted the clustered locations of fae disappearances, reports of Bliss, and portal magic fluctuations. His map had ultimately led Caspian and me to Lake Nacimiento and Ronan Doherty, who had helped us wake up Tim.

"*Samar?*"

His eyes grew to the size of dinner plates. Two more people came careening into the hallway after him, bumping into each other when they found Samar standing stock still. "Harlow? What are you doing here?"

I blinked. "I could ask you the same thing. When you said you picked up contract work for wealthy clients, I didn't realize your bosses were the freaking *Vampire Council*."

He winced and ran a hand through his thick black curls. "Guess we're both good at keeping secrets."

A beat of awkward silence ticked by.

Kayda asked, "Why were you running like your ass was on fire?"

Samar flinched and gave his head a shake. "Right. Shit. Uhh … the Shades just opened portals in two more small hubs, and …" He swallowed nervously and eyed Vaughn for a long moment before looking back at me. "An enclave. The pures fared even worse than the people in Mulgrew. Lachlan recorded a message that just turned up on the VHoA forum."

"Bring it here," Vaughn said.

We all huddled around Samar's laptop. Kayda had to pick up Alyssa so she could watch, too.

The still image of the video was just Lachlan Shade's face. The background was a textured gray. I pictured him sitting on an uncomfortable stool in a Walgreens photo center where people took terrible passport portraits. The photographer was probably bleeding out on the floor, out of view of the camera.

Samar clicked the play button superimposed on Lachlan's nose.

"Hello, hub residents. If we have not yet met, I am Lachlan Shade," he said, his voice calm and assured. He was strikingly handsome in that elfin way that was simultaneously mesmerizing and off-putting. "Three decades ago, the Collective banished me to another realm because they were threatened by me. When the hub system was first founded, the Collective promised that a top priority was to get the portals to the fae realm reopened. They started a branch of their government dedicated to that one task. Somewhere along the way, though, they grew drunk on their own power. Instead of finding a way home, they started stamping out individuals such as me who were doing the very work they'd promised to do themselves."

The camera's view panned backward as Lachlan stood. The camera followed him as he walked past the textured gray wall of a building and stepped into a cleared field that might have once been a paddock on a farm. It was largely overgrown with tall weeds now. A lopsided barn sagged beside a spindly tree in the far distance.

"Their lies were twofold," Lachlan told the camera. "First, they claimed that they were the only ones capable of veil magic; therefore, they naturally should be in power. Who better to lord over us than the only beings capable of crafting veils to keep our way of life hidden from the mundanes who would only exploit us?"

Two elves stepped into view and began an incantation. I had no idea what they were doing—witches cast magic differently from sorcerers, and elves cast differently still. I'd only seen elfin magic a few times.

I chewed on a thumbnail as I watched, heart thudding.

With a few more flourishes of their hands and shouted words in a language I didn't know, the elves thrust their arms upward in a V. Lachlan stepped aside.

My breath whooshed out as a tear in the overgrown field parted, like the flaps on a camouflaged circus tent opening wide. What stood beyond the invisible walls of the tent appeared to be the interior of a small home. A fire roared in the hearth behind a wooden table set for a meal.

The pair uttered another incomprehensible incantation, and the invisible flaps slid closed. The house disappeared, replaced by the overgrown paddock.

"It could just be an illusion, right?" I asked. "That's an elf thing ..."

No one answered me. After all, I'd seen another elf, back on the Winchells' property, drop a localized veil. The elf had used it to shield herself, Domino, and his troll minions from view until they were ready to attack. I already knew this was something they could do.

Lachlan stepped back into the frame. "Lie number two is that opening portals is nearly impossible. The Shades and I have opened four today alone." He cocked his head, as if listening to something. "Make that five."

The camera panned away from him to reveal what looked like the start of a ritual. A ring of elves stood with their hands clasped, deep in a chant. Behind them in a ring of their own were humanoid creatures, but they looked more reptilian than human. I wasn't sure if it was their mere existence that was most upsetting, or the fact that they were each casting rune arrays like a sorcerer.

Nested inside the ring of elves was a much smaller ring of three elves who all appeared to be older than Lachlan as well as two sorcerers. And young sorcerers at that—possibly younger than me. Recruiting young elves—young fae in general—made some kind of sense. They could be promised a return home. What could have made these young sorcerers willing to help Lachlan?

I remembered then that Wren had said Lachlan had taken Elsher residents with him. The idea that these two were being forced to help Lachlan because they were under duress was somehow easier to stomach. If these sorcerers weren't Team Shade, maybe they could fight back.

I didn't know much about portals, but already this one looked different. Bigger. Wider.

The only reason one needed to build a bigger doorway was to accommodate the size of whatever needed to walk through.

We all watched silently as the portal grew inch by inch. A time-lapse effect began. According to the timer in the corner of the video, twenty-five minutes of endless casting had occurred before the video slowed to normal speed.

And as it did, a snapshot of another world was revealed. It was a barren landscape practically stripped of color. Nothing much happened for several minutes. But then something winged and so massive it took up the entire horizon flew past.

Kayda clamped a hand over my forearm.

The beast was somehow miles and miles away, yet it could block out the sun. How big was the damn thing close-up?

Lachlan's stupid, beautiful face took up the screen again. "That is a yargrig. They do not attack if unprovoked. But its reign on this planet is why it's a wasteland now. The beast is a consumer of life. A destroyer of worlds. If our demands are not met, the yargrig *will* be provoked. My Shades and I prefer this realm, as we are familiar with it, but if we're not given what we want, we will find a new home. The options for us are limitless.

"You, however, won't fare as well. Not only do your illustrious leaders refuse to use their keys to unlock doors to other realms, their keys have grown rusty from disuse. They have failed you." He smiled, but it was a bit strained, as if his facial muscles were out of practice. "I give you all a choice. Join the Shades and aid us in wrenching the helm of this sinking ship from the hands of the Collective who are lost in the sea of their own egos, or be on the wrong side of history. If the yargrig enters this realm, there is nothing and no one who will be able to save you. You'll have a few decades to try, but by then the earthen realm will be as desolate as the one behind me. The reptilian people only had a few years left before their home was uninhabitable. I have rescued them. I can rescue you, too. But you must choose. Denounce the hub system by leaving it. The Shades will clear out the dissenters, and then the Restoration can begin. The hubs aren't going anywhere, but those who lead them are.

"Coordinates for Shade safehouses in the mundane world are on the screen. You have two weeks before the events of Mulgrew, Henatta, Lowell, Signet, and Urcor become commonplace. The sooner you clear out, the less blood will be shed. If your hub is destroyed, you'll have no one to blame but yourselves." He paused dramatically and glanced to his side. "Teo, do you have anything to add?"

A wispy black fog rolled along the ground behind Lachlan.

The camera panned back to reveal that the fog was taking shape as a person.

Vaughn loosed a tight breath. "Goddess dammit."

"That's the same asshole who uses shadow magic to manipulate Welsh, right?" I asked, my voice shaky as I glanced up at Vaughn. "Is Welsh safe there? Is Roch?"

I felt lightheaded as I realized Urcor was the enclave that had been hit, not Tercla. I was dizzy with relief one moment, terrified all over again the next.

The shadows fell away to reveal a striking man beside Lachlan. Black swam in the whites of his eyes. I recognized him, even though the only time I'd seen him was when he'd briefly inhabited Welsh's body via shadow magic.

Even as he materialized, his shadows pooled out behind him like an oil slick. Eighteen shapes oozed up out of the roiling shadows, like quickly growing shoots springing from the ground. Black-mist-shrouded people were revealed one by one—a shadowy army.

In an instant, I knew they were all infected with the same blood poison as Welsh, but these had all survived the transition.

Faun, shifters, draken, trolls, orcs.

"Kessler," Kayda said on an exhale. "*Shit*."

"This message is for the pures," Teo said, his voice smooth and unhurried. "You, like the Collective, turned your backs on your own people. You judged us and deemed us unworthy. Just as it's time for the Collective to lose their thrones, so, too, is it time for a shift in leadership among vampires. The so-called pures, without their Collective sycophants to reinforce the walls on their hideaways, will be tracked down and hunted like dogs. You will know what it's like to be without community, to be scattered on the wind, forced to eke out an existence in a world that deems you unfit. You have no place in the Restoration. Me and mine are coming for you. Even those who possess unnatural speed will tire eventually. That is when we will strike."

Teo went wispy again, floating away like rotting mist.

Lachlan raised an arm in the air and yelled, "Cease!"

Behind him, the reptilians dropped their arrays, the elves let go of one another's hands, and the innermost circle let their arms fall to their sides. The portal in the middle of their assembly flickered a few times, like an interrupted TV signal. The monstrous yargrig drifted past in the background again before the portal winked out.

The two young sorcerers immediately fell to their knees, panting. The older ones didn't seem to be faring much better.

The screen was filled with Lachlan's face once more. "You have two weeks to decide whether you're joining us in the Restoration, or if you're going to make the futile attempt to fight back.

"I would end with something trite here, like 'May the Goddess be with you,'" Lachlan said, offering a mocking laugh. He instantly grew serious. "But she abandoned you all long ago."

The screen went black.

Samar hit pause, freezing the screen on the first set of coordinates for the safehouses written in a bold white font.

The door to the sitting room opened, and we all whirled, finding the wide doorway comically filled with vampires in all their finery. Their expressions suggested they'd heard the video through the door and didn't like what they'd heard any more than I had.

Elder Allaband stood at the front of the pack, his ridiculous top hat sitting at a jaunty angle atop his head. In his usual pretentious tone, he succinctly said what we were all thinking. "Well ... shit."

Thank you for reading *Monstrous Allies*! If you enjoyed this story, please consider leaving a review. Reviews mean the world to authors. Reviews often mean more sales, and more sales means more freedom to write more books.

If you'd like to read a **free** short story about how Camila Fletcher and Lachlan Shade first met, you can find *Veiled Threats* at: https://melissajacksonbooks.com/the-charm-collector/veiled-threats

Next up in the gang's adventure is *Fallen Tower*. If you'd like to be notified when new books are released, you can join my newsletter at melissajacksonbooks.com.

If you're interested in a lighter story, try *A Mythical Case of Arson*, the first book in a fantasy cozy mystery series set in the same universe as the Charm Collector series!

Just when she thinks her day can't get any weirder, she finds a baby dragon …

Deandra Hendricks works her fingers to the bone at two jobs to keep her Los Angeles apartment. With a rapidly dwindling savings account, the prospects for her future are bleak. So when her cousin invites her to visit Axia—the hidden, magical hub their grandparents retired to—she agrees. Deandra doesn't possess a stitch of magic herself, but a long weekend vacation in a strange new town might be just what she needs.

Her first day in Axia is so bizarre, though, she wonders if her bleak life in Los Angeles hasn't been so bad after all. And, just when she thinks her day can't get any stranger, she finds a baby dragon trapped in a dumpster. At a loss, she takes a trip to the vet, hoping they can help find the little guy's owner.

The dragon, it turns out, only appears in its true form to her, while everyone else sees a dire wolf puppy. She and the vet discover that as long as the dragon wears his bespelled collar, his true identity is hidden. Someone went to great lengths to keep this supposed-to-be-extinct animal a secret.

Then the "dog" is accused of arson and is seized by authorities.

Determined to help him, Deandra searches for the real arsonist. She catches wind of a thriving black market that's populated by those who would stop at nothing to claim an animal this rare. She must work quickly to clear her dragon's name, because if he falls into the wrong hands, she could lose him forever.

Also available as an audiobook!

If you're looking for a ghost-filled paranormal tale, consider *The Forgotten Child*, a haunting mystery starring a reluctant medium.

ACKNOWLEDGMENTS

It feels good for this book in particular to be out in the world in part because of the cover. Back in 2020, I'd already been following Danielle Fine's Facebook page (Design by Definition) for a bit and loved her work. She posted a request for premade cover ideas, and I said something like "POC woman holding swords." I didn't have a story for it, but I liked the idea of trying to write an urban fantasy book one day.

Then she posted *that* cover, which was titled *Vengeance* at the time. I fell in love with it immediately. Danielle often posts a premade, then lets her followers know it will go on sale the following day at a set time, and it's first come, first served. I debated all day about buying a cover when I didn't have a story idea remotely formed yet. I asked friends if I should buy it. I asked my mom. I debated with myself some more.

For some reason, I can never start a book until I know the main character's name.

Then the name Harlow popped into my head.

That was that. I set an alarm (okay, several) to make sure I was at my computer at the right time. I knew other people had their sights set on the cover. I was so stressed that I wouldn't type "Mine!" in the comment box in time to claim Harlow.

But I won the auction. Someone's "Me!" comment came in just seconds after mine. They congratulated me on snagging her.

I'd won her! I was scared I wouldn't do her justice.

As her story formed, this particular cover got pushed back in the lineup. At first, it was book 3. Then the story expanded even more than I anticipated, and now it's the fourth book. It seems fitting, too, that this book is my favorite so far. It's been a long time coming. I purchased *Vengeance* back in October 2020—a day before my birthday, no less. (My friend Jennifer got me a gift card to Danielle's shop for my birthday—thanks, Jen!)

And to think this so far five-year journey all started with a premade prompt idea posted at random in a Facebook group.

Thank you to the readers who have been with me since the beginning. Thank you to the ones who saw how massive these books are and jumped in anyway.

Thanks, Mom, Margarita, John, and Emilie for beta reading this behemoth. Thank you to Cyndi, my beta reader turned editor, who has been reading these books from the start. At least I gave you more lead time on this one! And thanks to Garrett for being a typo hunter.

Thank you, obviously, to Danielle Fine for my covers, as this story probably wouldn't have existed had I not purchased that premade. Thank you, Tom Madej, for the maps of Luma and Elsher (Glad this second one is finally in a book for people to see!), Etheric Tales for the chapter header and scene break art, and Stephanie Hirschbrich for the VHoA logo.

Thank you to Victoria Villarreal, Mac Fowler, Chris Johnson, and Connor Brannigan for sticking with me on this long, full-cast audiobook journey, and to Phil Thron and Alexis Campbell for joining the gang on this quickly expanding series.

And, as always, thank you to Sam. It's almost a guarantee that *Fallen Tower* will wreck me. Get ready for lots of tears! You're the best.

ABOUT THE AUTHOR

Melissa has had a love of stories for as long as she can remember, but only started penning her own during her freshman year of college. She majored in Wildlife, Fish, and Conservation Biology at UC Davis. Yet, while she was neck-deep in organic chemistry and physics, she kept finding herself writing stories in the back of the classroom about fairies and trolls and magic. She finished her degree, but it never captured her heart the way writing did.

Now she owns her own dog walking business (that's sort of wildlife related, right?) by day … and afternoon and night … and writes whenever she gets a spare moment. She alternates mostly between fantasy and mystery (often with a paranormal twist). All her books have some element of "other" to them … witches, ghosts, UFOs. There's no better way to escape the real world than getting lost in a fictional one.